By

MW01490012

Table of Contents

CHAPTER 1

The helicopter soared across the pitch-black New York City sky, its rotors making a faint whipping as the lights from traffic and buildings populated the ground below.

"Alright, touchdown in three." The tactical squad leader barked. "We want them alive for questioning and easy clean up, stun rounds only. Take out the target, take the truck, and we'll go from there."

A motorcycle weaved through the New York City traffic, the rider wearing a black helmet with a black visor, an all-black leather jacket, and black cargo pants. He revved the motorcycle as he made a yellow light. The heads-up display in the helmet plotted his route for him. He skidded to a stop in front of a warehouse and took off his helmet, placing it on the motorcycle.

The helicopter landed, and the agents jumped off. One grabbed a large black duffel bag and hustled after the other agents. They moved through the back of the warehouse. Three men stood near a truck, smoking cigarettes while another scrolled through his social media. Others stood with guns, surveying the empty warehouse where harsh yellow lights watched from above. A stun bullet shot out of the dark, hitting the man on his phone in his neck. He convulsed, dropping his phone, which cracked before he hit the ground himself. The men smoking threw their cigarettes and reached for the guns slung over their shoulders. Stun bullets cut them down while tasers from behind took down the men who had their weapons ready.

"Get the keys," the team leader yelled.

Another agent tapped his ear, "Asset secure," he said.

"Providence Centurions," a voice said.

The agents turned to the voice, guns raised.

"Who the hell are you," one asked.

"Whoa, whoa, no need to yell. I'm a huge fan of your work.

Great job cleaning up these boys. I think I'll take it from her, and by the way, I love your matching outfits."

The man had black hair, brown eyes, and a well-built, muscular figure. His all-black outfit held compartments housing gear and a holster.

"Hands up, get on the ground, Now." The lead agent screamed. "Who do you think you are?"

"Have you ever heard the story of Perseus, the Greek hero? The man who slayed Medusa. He defeated her because of his cunning, and her pride. Every man to enter her presence turned to stone and she thought he would be no different. Until she was relieved of her head. I'm Perseus, and the Red Cyan is Medusa."

"Get on the ground now, base we have a…"

The man's cinnamon brown irises didn't flinch as he whipped a gun from his side at inhuman speed, shooting two bullets. He ducked under the gunfire of another man and uppercutted him with the gun. He threw his elbow back, hitting another agent in the face. He spun the man around him as another agent shot at him, hitting his teammate. The man in black shoved the agent off him, turned around, and shot both of them. He dropped the clip from his gun and reloaded it, killing the other agents in the warehouse. He holstered his gun and snatched the radio off a downed agent.

"All clear here, asset secured. We'll be on the move soon, over."

"Copy, good work," an agent on the other end said.

The man unzipped the duffel bag on the ground.

"Well, what are you doing here," he said.

Inside rested a large black metal cylinder with red energy flowing through clear sections of it. The man in black pulled out a device and scanned the cylinder. The screen on the device read 'Psychanium.' The man smiled, zipped the bag, and placed it in the back of the box truck. Four motorcycles pulled up behind him, and the men riding them dismounted.

"What do you want us to do with the bodies, sir," the man on his right asked.

"Nothing, I want Providence to find them," the man said as he closed the doors of the truck.

"Sir, are you sure that's advisable?"

"Did I ask you to question me," the man in black shouted.

"No sir, sorry sir."

"No, I shouldn't have yelled."

He pulled a white envelope from his breast pocket and placed it on a body beside the truck, the envelope had the words "Red Cyan" written on the front in cursive.

"What's next," another agent asked.

The man in black handed him the keys.

"The Psychics have taken too much from us. What is life if not the struggle against principalities, against wickedness in high places? You know the plan. 117 Moody Street."

"Yes, sir,"

The box truck turned on Moody Street in New York City as the gloomy morning sky lingered over the city. The truck made another turn into an alleyway beside a glass and metal spire. Inside, men and women in suits ran around, papers flying out of their hands, phones pressed to ears, and others typing as they walked while talking into earpieces.

The back of the box truck opened, and a woman in a smart black and white business suit grabbed the duffel bag. She looked inside, seeing the same metal cylinder as the man in black. She zipped the bag and walked towards the door. She swiped a keycard and entered the building from the alleyway, walking to the elevator and arriving at the 40th floor. She walked into an office and dropped the duffel bag in a corner before making her way back to the elevator and into the passenger seat of the box truck.

"This is Fay, bomb planted," the woman said into her earpiece as she pushed her lengthy, caramel brown hair out of her green-flecked hazel eyes. She sent an 'all agents on deck, meet a usual location' message through the tablet.

"Great work, get out of the blast radius," the man in black said as he paced on a distant rooftop.

People walked Moody Street, heads locked downwards and

looks of apathy on their faces as they stared into their phones or held high, showing off their luxury sunglasses as they took calls from their investment bank employments. Birds chirped in Central Park as the spire-like oaks glowed a brilliant green, ignoring the gray, depressing gloom of the overcast sky.

The man in black tapped a button on his phone screen, A crashing sound ripped through the city as the top of the building exploded. Another loud hum tore through the air as everyone stared at the building enveloped in a red bubble of energy while a red shockwave exploded from it, stretching across the sky, casting the glow of death as it washed over the city. Debris fell from the crumbling building, crushing bystanders as it collapsed.

The man in black ducked without thought as the bomb painted the sky red, and the shockwave pushed him back.

Through the rubble, blood and scar-covered people searched for their friends and relatives, engulfed in dust. Lifeless hands and legs stuck out from under large pieces of debris while pools and puddles of blood leaked out. First responders arrived on the scene, sirens and flashing red and blue lights filled the dust-choked sky while screams enveloped the air, echoing for miles.

Explosions rocked boats flying Providence flags in the New York harbor. The sound of alarms tore through the city as the ships began to dip below the waves.

The man in black dialed a number on his phone.

"This is Fletcher, get ready to sell our short positions of the stock of every corporation a Psychic family owns."

The person on the other end acknowledged the request, and Fletcher hung up. He pressed another button on his phone, and worldwide, billions of devices received a single text. "WE ARE THE CIRCLE." With an image of New York City on fire.

CHAPTER 2

Versia Ikakala sat in front of the dual TV screens underneath his Palo Alto house.

"Breaking News from New York City where a bomb has detonated on Moody Street," a voice on his TV said.

Versia's ebony brown eyes locked on to the two cable news channels covering the same story. "Terrorist Attack in New York " flashed over the screen of both channels. His phone buzzed as the notification from his news app came through. Videos from people around the world showed them in shock. Celebrities' social media accounts became littered with posts standing in solidarity with the victims and making hefty donations.

Politicians and World Leaders made statements condemning the cowards who perpetrated such a heinous attack. Versia buried his dark brown hands in his face as they showed footage of them pulling children out of the rubble. The news cameras panned showing crushed cars, cracks, and shudders of buildings around the primary target. Firefighters sprayed water onto the crumbling sections of the flaming building while police on the scene pulled people out of the rubble and an EMT wrapped a bandage around the blood-red arm of a survivor they'd found. A thick layer of gray dust coated everything in the vicinity as smoke choked the air. On the TV, Versia watched firefighters and other emergency personnel coughing as others put on gas masks. Versia shuddered as an icy sweat ran over his body. He took deep breaths as he composed himself, easing the thudding in his heart.

Versia's phone vibrated as hundreds of texts from world leaders, politicians, and celebrities gushed in. He turned off his phone and laid it face down. He leaned back in his chair, his hands covering his face. He ran them down his features before taking out his second private phone. His hands shook as he typed in the number. He raked his hand through his curly, short, midnight-black hair.

"Marissa, could I have a list of people potentially in the building?"

His hologram screen *dinged* as the list came through. He swiped at it, looking through the names and ages of the potential victims, at least three dozen children in the building. He buried his face in his hands again as tears flowed from his eyes, and a chilling slither ran up his spine. He looked up through teary eyes and turned to his satellite feeds. They spied over the Providence Headquarters as their naval fleet moved into open water as fighter jets, helicopters, and drones gathered on the runways. He turned his main phone on, and the hundreds of texts flooded in. He flipped it to silent and let them rain in. He dialed a number on his private phone as he composed himself, wiping away the tears. He sauntered upstairs and looked out the blinds as he put the phone to his ear.

A few dozen new vans had already gathered outside his gate. He looked at a bouquet of cyan-colored roses on a table nearby and picked up a flower.

"We have a situation," Versia said.

****

Inside Providence's base, Isazisi Irving's coffee-brown eyes locked onto his screens. His sienna brown hands folded in front of his mouth, the scent of metal from the black and red ring on his finger making its way up his nose with each breath. His left eye twitched as he watched

the dozen news channels showing in greater detail than the last the carnage the bomb had caused. Two red armor-clad Praetorian Guards

stood behind him as his generals and commanders coordinated their response at another table. His Navy moved into open waters while his air force and ground infantry stood by. He ran his hand through his jet-black, curly, short hair and muted the other new stations as one reporter spoke.

"Preliminary evidence suggests this attack is the work of an organization called The Circle. They claim to have stolen and used the Psychic organization Providence's weapons to commit this terrible crime," the reporter on site said.

The channel played new footage they'd obtained of a surviving piece of the bomb. The Psychanium scrap had the serial number 'DRRC1712224' and the words 'PROPERTY OF PROVIDENCE' carved beneath it in case any of the dozen other indicators appeared too subtle.

"Viewers may not know, but the Psychic Act stipulates any weapon belonging to Providence must contain the serial code DRRC. We can also see the signature of the Psychic known as The Red Cyan, the director of Providence, above the serial number, confirming this is a Psychanium weapon owned by Providence. This results in thousands of questions…"

He muted the broadcast as his eyes flicked over to firefighters pulling ash and blood-covered victims from the rubble, three of the bodies too small to be adults. Solid black splotches inhabited the concrete debris while fires raged. Isazisi leaned back in his seat, running his hands down his face. His head thumped while a glacial sweat ran down his back, and a ringing hit his ears.

Isazisi looked at his phone as the texts rang in, "POTUS", "Secretary of State", "President", and "Prime Minister" flooded his device. His phone levitated to his hand as he exercised his psychic powers, the texts blurring together on the screen. He turned off the ringer and set the phone face down as he leaned back in his chair.

"Well, this is going to be a long Tuesday," he said.

****

An Asian woman with flowing, ebony black hair sat up in her bed, rubbing her bleary eyes as she glanced at the TV displaying the news of the attack on New York. She cocked her head to the right as she read the words on the screen and let out an audible gasp. Her phone vibrated on her nightstand while a man with umber brown hair and white skin slept beside her.

She looked over at her clock. It read '10:00' while the location read 'Palo Alto, California.' She patted around under her bed, grabbing a black case. She opened it, revealing a sealed glass bottle of alcohol, the price tag still intact, and a rose-embossed crystal glass cup. She poured the alcohol into the glass and took a sip as tears welled in her eyes. She wiped them away as the man beside her woke up. He sat in the bed, rubbed his gold-flecked hazel eyes, and pushed a piece of hair out of his face. He stared at the glass in her hand.

"What?" She asked, looking around and shrugging her shoulders.

"Caitlyn, at ten in the morning?"

A blue bolt of electricity flashed across her chocolate brown eyes as she squinted at him.

"Why do all of you sound like my mother, especially you, Jake."

"Maybe because we care about you because I care about you?"

He looked at her faint red eyes.

"What happened?" Jake asked.

She pointed to the TV, and Jake read the headline "Hundreds dead in 'Circle' attack on New York City. Evidence points to Psychanium weaponry. How would they have those kinds of weapons?"

"It's called they stole them," Caitlyn said.

"We need Isazisi on this,"

"I'll assume he's already mobilizing,"

Jake looked at her phone, attempting to shake its way off the nightstand.

"Are you going to answer that?"

"Take a look at yours,"

Jake's phone vibrated on the floor. He picked it up and watched as hundreds of texts flooded in while dozens of calls rang.

Caitlyn took a last swig of her glass and put it down, before filling it again.

"Could you please not day drink?" Jake asked.

"What I do is none of your concern," she yelled.

Jake shifted his lips to the left and rubbed the back of his neck.

"I'm sorry," Caitlyn said.

"It's fine, um, yeah, we should mobilize too, this won't be the last attack," Jake said as he slid out of bed.

"Yeah, let's move," she said.

Caitlyn slid out of bed and saw a bouquet of midnight blue roses on a table in the room. She walked over and ran her fingers over the petals. She said nothing, walked into the bathroom, and stared at herself in the mirror. Her pupils flashed blue as lightning bolts crested them, and the mirror shattered, dropping pieces onto the marble sink below. She stared at her face in the mirror, split down the middle by the cracked pieces. Jake rushed into the bathroom.

"Are you ok?" He asked.

"Yeah, just," tears formed in her eyes, "what have we done?"

"You didn't do anything."

She reached for her glass.

"I might sound like your mother, but maybe you shouldn't," he suggested.

"I know I shouldn't," she said as she pushed the glass off the counter, it shattered.

Jake leaned on her, wrapping his toned arms around her, and rubbed her stomach.

"I'm not pregnant if it's the baby you're worried about," she said.

"Would you like to be?" He asked.

She chuckled, baring her ivory teeth.

"Your powers, my powers, we could have little storm babies," Jake said.

He made a finger-sized tornado and clouds in his palm and let it onto the counter. Caitlyn touched the clouds, and lightning shot from them.

"Now my mom would love that, little Psychic babies, for her to mold into assassins," Caitlyn said.

"We can raise them our way, no outside interference."

"There's an idea," she said as she spun, pecked him on his lips, and pushed him out of the bathroom.

"You're cute, but this house has thirteen bathrooms. I think you can find your own," she said, her teeth still showing as she closed the door.

Jake grinned and left the bedroom.

*****

"Thank you," a woman with long, dark hair and olive brown skin said, flashing a pearl-white smile as her blonde-haired flight attendant handed her a milk-white mug with a brown liquid.

She took a sip as a man with rustic brown hair, earthy hazel eyes, and a frown, wearing a tan suit, walked into her section of the jet.

"Ma'am, you should turn on the TV," he said as he played with his fingers.

She swiped her hand, turning on a holographic TV. Her hand covered her mouth as her smile fell. She patted the seat beside her without taking her eyes off the screen, feeling for her phone, and dialed a number.

"What do you mean Isazisi is indisposed?" She asked.

She put the phone against her chest.

"Have the pilot reroute to New York, I want eyes on," she whispered.

The man in the tan suit gave her a thumbs up.

"Tell him it's Reese, and I'm watching a Psychanium bomb go off in New York City at one in the afternoon on a weekday."

She paused as the person on the other end spoke.

"What do you mean he's handling it? Circle agents infiltrated Providence? Ok, uh, mobilize our forces across the eastern seaboard. I'm rerouting to New York now. Seal off the site, nobody in or out. This will not be the last attack." Reese said. "Where are the Praetorians on this? They're in reserve? And the Renarri? Also, in reserve? Why? This attack is global. Send word to our agents everywhere. I want a lid on this, now."

She hung up, stood, and paced around the cabin before throwing her phone into a tray of drinks and yelling something explicit. She picked it up and shook off the liquid.

"How long till we're in New York?" She asked her agent as she rubbed her forehead.

"One hour, Quick Response Forces are already moving on Circle cells whose locations we've known. The Circle hasn't been a problem till now. Why such a bold move?" He asked.

She popped the lid off a crystal bottle of transparent liquid and filled her glass before taking a long swig. She looked right, where a bouquet of red roses sat on a table. She picked up a rose and stared at it.

"It's a message showing the world they can touch a Psychic."

"And what will our response be?"

Reese glanced at him. "In kind."

*****

The Indian woman's scope panned across the landscape. Her extensive, jet-black hair fluttered in the soft wind while sunbeams pierced the palm tree cover and glowed off her almond-brown skin.

Her target exited his high-rise apartment and walked towards a row of black SUVs. He looked side to side as his security stayed attached to his hip. Her earpiece beeped as a message came through.

"I'm working," she said.

"It's important, Jasmine," the man on the other end said.

"Everything is important. Nothing is special," Jasmine responded.

"A bomb was detonated in New York City."

"Tragic, but there are attacks on third-world countries every day, and no one cares. Sounds a bit below our pay grade?"

"Evidence says it's a weapon stolen from Providence."

Jasmine's breathing halted as her earthen brown eyes squinted.

"A Psychanium bomb exploded in New York City?"

"Yes, an estimated 700 plus dead,"

"What," Jasmine said as she put her target in the crosshairs.

"Every Psychic is mobilizing. This is the worst terror attack on American soil in decades. The White House wants answers, the CIA wants answers, the FBI, NSA, politicians, everybody is losing it right now. They want to know how the deadliest weapons since nukes made their way into the hands of terrorists."

"Sounds like a question for Isazisi, not me."

"You're a consultant for Providence. They'll want answers from you, too."

"Give me eight hours."

"Whatever you say."

Jasmine slid the bullet into the chamber and pulled the trigger, splattering her target. She slinked into the shadows as frantic yelling and screaming from the man's security followed her action.

*****

Isazisi turned away from the TVs and looked over to the left corner of his desk, where a blank white envelope rested.

"What is this," he asked his head of security, who stood in the office.

"I don't know, sir."

Isazisi opened the envelope to cursive handwriting.

"Think upon the sins of your ancestors."

Isazisi threw the envelope and letter onto the ground. Red lasers shot from his eyes, turning the paper to ash. His eyes still glowing red as he looked up.

"They delivered a handwritten note to my office?" Isazisi yelled. "How?"

His head of security tapped his ear.

"We don't know. My people are telling me the footage is gone."

"Gone?" Isazisi asked as his eyes settled. "How many security failures can we fit in one day? How did they even get in here?"

"We believe The Circle may have turned agents or perhaps inserted them."

"They left a note in my office," Isazisi said. "A handwritten note delivered to your office. That's personal, a touch a Psychic would bring."

Isazisi composed himself and double-tapped his chest, building his Psychic Suit without the helmet. An all-black armor with red lines of Psychic energy flowing through it, and a flowing black cape with a red line running down it ending in a circle. At the center of the palms and soles were red glass pieces for the suit's energy dispersion. He left his office, flanked by his red armored Praetorian.

"What else is new," he asked as he walked down the hall where Providence agents ran past him to the staging areas.

"Seven agents were killed in New York City, and of course, the stolen weapon," his head of security said. "They also attacked the fourth fleet which was in Brooklyn Navy Yard at the time. We don't know the extent of the damage or the cost to human lives yet, but our people are on site. Reporters and politicians are asking what the bomb was even doing in New York. Do we have a response?"

"Tell them the reasons are classified. What can we do for the agents' families?"

"They'll be taken care of by Providence per your past precedents.

Agents found this addressed to you at the scene of the crime. It's sterile, not even a speck of dust, let alone prints."

His head of security handed him a plastic bag containing an envelope. The envelope had 'Red Cyan' written on it in red cursive ink. He took the envelope out of the bag and opened it.

"How many will die for your traditions?"

"What does it mean, sir," his head of security asked.

"I don't know. What else?"

"A brokerage account, we can't trace shorted stocks of every corporation owned by your family and other Psychics. They made billions. We suspected it's a Circle related account."

"What are my family's stocks down?"

"Thirty-seven percent."

Isazisi shifted his lips to the right as the letter and envelope turned to ash in his hand and blew away. He gave a hand signal to his Praetorians and they stood at the door as he entered his holographic command center. He stood at the center and looked at the hologram projector around him. A bouquet of red roses sat on a table in the corner of the room. He stretched his hands towards them, and one floated to him.

"Anything else?"

"Strategic Central Command is mobilizing. Terror groups and criminal organizations have released statements praising the Circle's attack."

"Tell SCC I want drone strikes on these groups, let them know any supporter of the Circle is an enemy of us."

"I'll have them relay it to Africa Regional Command and Asia Regional Command."

General Grount entered the office, flanked by two troops under his command.

"Sir, our forces are mobilizing, and intelligence is already working on gaining access to Circle servers. I suggest we perform a multipronged attack, and we may cripple their forces before they can launch another attack." Grount said.

"Thank you, general," Isazisi said as he stared at the man, his psychokinesis peering into Grounts mind.

Grount left his command center and made his way to the military staging area of the base. Isazisi set the flower down and followed him out minutes later. Grount stood giving orders to a group of agents under his command. Isazisi walked towards him, flanked by four of his Praetorians.

"You're not good at hiding your thoughts, General," Isazisi said.

Grount turned around, and the agents behind him pulled guns, pointing them at Isazisi. From around the staging area, Providence agents pointed guns at Grount and his agents.

"Who else defiled our family?" Isazisi asked.

"Why don't you find out," Grount called back, arms spread.

Five of the Providence agents pointing guns at Grount turned their weapons onto others beside them, causing loyal agents to turn their guns onto them. Looks of shock rippled through the group.

The Praetorians activated their blades, the trademark sound ringing through the staging area. The air tensed as Circle agents looked from side to side while beads of sweat formed on their foreheads. Isazisi signed to them, and they eased.

Isazisi stood in silence before speaking. "You've wounded us. I give you props for that, but I have a proposition. The fifty of you hunt me on Prismatic Island. The first side to yield is the winner. If you win, you're free. If I win, well, you'll already be dead." Isazisi announced.

His generals, who watched from a balcony, shared looks. Isazisi looked at his twitching hand and halted it.

"And if we refuse?" Grount asked.

The Praetorians flanking Isazisi activated their weapons.

"You could fight the Praetorians if you like."

"The island sounds fair to me," Grount said.

The eyebrows of Isazisi's generals rose as horizontal wrinkles appeared on their foreheads as they each hid the widening of their eyes.

"Hail the Circle," Grount's troops yelled.

"I would've picked the Praetorians," Isazisi said as he smiled.

CHAPTER 3

Isazisi stood in the bay of a helicopter as the doors opened to the jungle terrain below. His black cape whipped in the roaring wind as his suit scanned the green island.

"Circle agents will know the terrain," his suit's AI said. "They've already landed and begun to set their defenses. Barricades, tanks, and missiles based on what they took from the base."

"Noted," Isazisi said.

"Sir, are you sure you're ready for this? Your heart rate is spiking, and a dozen other medical indicators of stress and loss of rationale are occurring." The suit's A.I. said.

"I'm perfectly rational."

Isazisi's helmet formed over his head. A black construct with two red lines of energy flowing where his eyes would be. The suit's camera eyes activated and his heads-up display jolted to life. He jumped out of the helicopter and crashed into the ground, landing on one knee and a fist, cracks forming around his landing zone.

Isazisi stood and walked as the suit scanned the terrain around him. After a few minutes, he found a shallow river. Three Circle agents sprung from behind a fallen palm tree, each holding pistols. They pulled the triggers and shot reddish-white lasers, flinging his suit into a tree and snapping the ancient plant in half.

"Ow," he said.

The suit's red head-up display flashed yellow error symbols.

"What hit me?" He asked the suit.

"Psyhcanium weapon stolen from the armory."

"Great, they have their hands on even more of our metal."

One of the agents held the trigger down, shooting a sustained laser. Isazisi pushed himself upwards, but the energy beam pushed him down. A hologram display showed the suit's structural integrity falling. Isazisi opened the back of the suit and fell out. He hit the ground, grabbed a gun the suit built for him, and shot the man on his left in the foot. He screamed in pain and fell sideways as he held at his foot. Isazisi shot him twice in the chest as he fell. The other men looked over at their downed partner. Isazisi didn't hesitate.

He rolled out and blasted the first man with a psychic shockwave from his hand. The man flew backwards, hitting his head on a rock. Isazisi swung the gun over and shot the other man twice in the chest. Two more men popped out from behind a tree, brandishing Gatling guns with gaping holes instead of different barrels. The inside of the barrels glowed reddish white. He sighed as his suit reformed around him.

A blast of energy shot out, pummeling him into a wall of rock behind him, leaving cracks in it as the beam stopped. They shot another beam, which exploded on him, bouncing him off the rock wall. He twisted himself into a better position and skidded, using the suit's hands and feet jets to stop his sliding.

He stood from his stance as they shot another blast at him. He shielded himself with his Psychanium weave cape, charring the outside. He used his psychokinesis and grabbed a large trunk, throwing it at the men, and crushing them underneath. He walked towards the Gatling gun, which rolled upright and shot off like a rocket. He flew after it.

"Is he following it?" Grount asked.

"Yes, sir."

"Self-destruct it."

After only a mile, the gun stopped and hovered upright. A massive explosion fueled by Psychanium tore through the sky, painting it in red and sending Isazisi in a downward spiral. He hyperventilated as his hand and foot jets sputtered while the suit displayed a yellow reboot timer. He smashed into the ground with a dull *thud*.

"Send a squadron to the site of the explosion. Commander Reig. If he's alive, finish him." General Grount said.

"Yes, sir," Reig said. "Anything we should know going in?"

"The suit is made of Psychanium. Take the big guns."

"Yes, sir. What can you tell me about Psychanium?"

"It's an alien metal millennia-old and stronger than any other substance. From a meteor in the sky that landed in Africa, if you can believe that. Do not underestimate it."

Reig and sixteen others stepped into all-black SUVs and drove to the site of the explosion.

Isazisi awoke in a dark part of the jungle, the trees blotting out the sunlight letting a single beam of light pierce through where he'd fallen. He saw fog everywhere through the suit's camera eyes.

"Sir, it's a miracle your suit survived. Once again, are you sure you're mentally fit for this?" The suit asked.

"I'm fine."

"Your vitals say otherwise. Your heart rate is three hundred bpm. If you weren't a Psychic, you'd be dead."

"Stop monitoring my vitals."

"You gave your mother control over health-related systems.

"Right."

The fog and darkness cast an eerie gloom over the whole location. The contorted trees looked like screaming faces while the damp humidity clung to the vegetation, its presence choking them. In the distance, SUV engines roared while their tires worked their way over rocks, fallen trees, and the other jungle terrain.

Isazisi sulked into the thick canopy as the SUVs stopped and men emerged. Psychanium claws projecting red-hot psychic energy extended from Isazisi's gauntlets. He spied two men and sliced both of them to shreds before they could register his motion. The other men turned around to red and black corpses.

"Sir, Red Cyan's taken down two soldiers," Commander Reig told the General.

"Stay alert, don't be a cautionary tale," Grount said.

Two red energy ropes came out of the suit's wrists and snared two men by their feet, ripping them into the underbrush.

Isazisi threw an SUV with his psychokinesis, crushing four men. He shot the gas tank with a palm laser from the suit and it exploded into an orange fireball, lighting up the jungle and leaving nothing but the blackened frame of the car.

One man shot into the trees, but his bullets found nothing. The eyes of the agents darted from side to side as the wind whipped by while Isazisi moved through the trees at speed. They created a small circle around the last SUV, and another agent manned the roof-mounted machine gun. Isazisi walked out in the open. They shot at him and the bullets crumpled upon impact with the suit. Isazisi created a weapon in his hand, a jet-black katana with a red line running up it, splitting in two on its way to the tips. Isazisi's suit's AI displayed "Red Cyan Sword" on his HUD.

"Guys, can we not?" Isazisi asked as the bullets bounced off his armor.

They stopped firing.

"Thank you." He said.

He dashed at the men at inhuman speed, cutting three of them down. The other men dropped their guns and ran. Isazisi's suit locked onto them as he ignored the bullets pounding his suit from the SUV-mounted machine gun. Three small missiles shot out from his shoulders, killing the men. The shoulder-mounted missiles targeted the man with the machine gun and shot him.

Isazisi turned to the fleeing commander and landed in front of him. He threw the man against a tree. He moved for the gun at his side as he wriggled into a sitting position. Isazisi snatched his arm and squeezed it, breaking it. The commander grimaced in pain but held his tongue.

"You Psychics are some feral creatures," the commander rasped.

Isazisi pinned him against the same tree.

"I would like the location of the base camp, please," Isazisi said.

"I'm already a dead man, but not on the inside like you. How did it feel, watching a weapon you created used to end the people you were supposed to protect?" The commander asked, laughing but wheezing as the cuts stung. "Men, women, and children killed in New York by a weapon you made, and that's only the beginning,"

Isazisi said nothing.

"What? Reminds you of your childhood trauma, a more personal bombing?"

Isazisi held his steel exterior.

"You can cry if you like. We understand you haven't done it in years. When you're a Psychic, the world can't see you cry, right? Or are you still working on killing the stigma?" The commander asked, still chuckling.

"The base," Isazisi said.

"For ten thousand years Psychics have fed nothing but violence into the cosmic vending machine, and now their bitter drink has arrived. You, and this world, will choke on the cold sludge of your ancestor's actions."

"The base."

"I'm a dead man, and here lies my dying gift."

The man's skin cracked as red energy bottled inside him.

Isazisi backed away, priming his suit's jets as the AI showed scans of an experimental bomb embedded in the agent's chest.

"Say hello to the devil for me," the commander said.

The bomb exploded, and Isazisi made a cross in front of his chest, creating a red energy shield. He slingshotted back as his shield shattered from the blast, lighting the sky red as the shockwave bent trees and hurled rocks for miles while the water around the island rippled into torrential waves.

Isazisi put down his arms as the island settled. The suit's structural integrity read eighty-five percent. He looked at the car-sized black crater in front of him with charred bits of bone jutting out of the ground at various angles.

A searing pain ran up his side. He looked down at his upper abdomen, where two large pieces of Psychanium shrapnel cut through his suit and entered his body. He dropped to one knee as the adrenaline wore off and the throbbing began.

"Both pieces are inches from your liver and kidney," the suit's AI said.

"Yeah, I think I can feel that," he said as he grimaced under his helmet."

He held his hand over the wounds and ripped out the shrapnel with his psychokinesis, groaning from the pain. The suit's nanites pulled back, and he blasted the scars with a white substance from the suit's lower palm.

"That should hold the wound while your rapid healing takes effect," the suit's AI said.

He flew and landed on the peak of the extinct volcano on the island. The two thousand-foot structure covered in greenery provided a birds-eye view of the island. Below, the trees swayed in the wind, their leaves blown to and fro as the sun glistened off the rocks and wood. He tapped his suit's wrist, connecting to a Providence satellite, and scanning the island.

"There." The suit's AI said.

The suit found an unusual cluster of trees twenty miles from the volcano. The suit's AI showed him a before and after of the exact location.

"They've moved the vegetation," the AI said.

He soared toward the area and scanned for heat signatures. He found them along with the resting heat signatures of the Circle's weapons. Three anti-aircraft missile launchers, and five tanks on the ground, with another six Chinook helicopters on stand-by.

He curled his cape around him, creating a sharp point, and dived into the trees. He cut through like a knife and landed with one knee and fist on the ground with his head down. He stood as the tanks turned their barrels and fired. He dodged a shell from the tank on his right and shot red lasers from his eyes at it, causing it to explode.

He placed one hand on the tank closest to him and fired a laser. It exploded like a firework as the tank shells inside it combusted. The other three tanks shot, one after another bouncing shells off the armor. One tank rushed him, he threw it on top of another tank. Using his psychokinesis, he crushed them together and attached a bomb to the baseball-sized sphere of tanks. He pitched it at the final tank's barrel. The ball smashed into the last tank's barrel as it fired a shell. The whole tank exploded in a magnificent fireball as bits of hot, twisted metal rained down from the sky.

The anti-aircraft missiles leveled off, firing at him. He took to the air, wrapping his cape around himself, and the missiles exploded against the Psychanium cloth. He locked onto the anti-aircraft missile launchers and fired dozens of shoulder-mounted mini-missiles. They hit everywhere, distracting the targeting system of the launcher as three well-placed missiles from his suit destroyed it. More twisted, charred bits of metal rained down as the last of the Circle's weapons burned.

Isazisi landed and walked towards the helicopters. Circle agents walked backward while firing at Isazisi, the bullets bouncing off the suit. The General's helicopter took off, leaving his troops behind, the other five followed.

Isazisi shot one's rotors and brought it down. It exploded in a massive fireball as it crashed. He threw an undetonated anti-aircraft missile at one more, causing it to explode in another spectacular fireball. He took to the air and smashed through one helicopter, metal pieces of the rotor and body crashed onto the island. He flew at another and smashed in through the side, it exploded as Isazisi tore out the other side.

He turned his focus on the last two. He slammed one into the ocean and under the water's surface, electricity moved on the helicopter, followed by the orange fireball as it exploded, sending bubbles to the surface. Isazisi grabbed the last aircraft from the front and looked the traitor in the eye. He pushed off the helicopter, created a black and red orb in his hand, and threw it at the aircraft. It ripped through and absorbed it like a black hole, leaving nothing in its wake before dissipating in a black shockwave. Isazisi landed and his helmet retracted.

"Scan the island, see if..." he began before nausea took over his body.

He placed his hand on a tree, stabilizing his body. He put his back on the tree and slid down as sweat rolled across his body and his head spun.

The suit opened, letting in more air as the A.I. rattled off health metrics in his ear, but he couldn't hear, like he was underwater. Vertigo took over as a sharp pain stabbed his chest. He inhaled and exhaled at a sprint as more spinning set in. Numbness and tingling ravaged his hands and feet. He raised his hand to his face. It trembled. He clutched his hand. His breathing intensified as more frigid sweat rolled over his body.

"What happened?" He asked the suit as the effects dissipated, and he touched his face for any signs of further symptoms.

"Symptoms suggest a panic attack."

"What? I don't have panic attacks anymore,"

"It would seem you do. The mental toll exerted on your body over the last twelve hours depleted your body's defenses. I would suggest you resume taking your antidepre..."

"I'm fine," Isazisi said, cutting off the A.I. as the suit built around him while he stood. "This is my first one. It's from the fight."

"It's your first one in weeks,"

"Do not notify anyone of the panic attack,"

"Sir, your mother said to, and it could be symptomatic of your bipo...".

"That's an order."

"Yes, sir."

Plan a route to base." Isazisi finished.

CHAPTER 4

"Mr. Silas, are you leaving for the day?" The receptionist asked.

"Yes indeed, I gotta pick up flowers for my daughter, her birthday was yesterday." The older man replied. He had graying hair and thin round glasses, the soft wrinkles in his face projecting as he smiled.

He stepped on the elevator and pressed the button for the ground floor. The elevator dinged as it opened. Outside the glass doors of the high rise, a mob of protestors pressed against a line of police. Signs read 'Psychic Money > Our Lives.' Others said. 'Down With Superpowered Oligarchs.' Silas stepped out of the building and into a swarm of protestors and reporters.

"What do you say regarding the recent attack in New York City?" One yelled over the crowd.

"As the world's leading researchers and activists for Psychic rights, what is your stance on this tragedy?" Another shouted.

The lead protestor climbed on a makeshift platform and grabbed a megaphone.

"How can Duncan Silas be an activist for Psychic rights? Why do the wealthiest, most protected oligarch classes need activists? He is a shill of a lawyer and a black hole for Psychic money. He should be in prison with every Psychic." The protestor yelled into his megaphone.

Police approached and dragged him off the makeshift stand before kicking out its legs. Silas ignored the chants and stepped into a black SUV waiting for him. A splotch of pie hit the window as he closed the door. The police identified the thrower and brought her to the ground, cuffing her.

The SUV pulled up to Silas' apartment. He stepped out into the dim garage and the SUV drove off.

"You know, the secret agent man of shadows effect would

work a lot better if you didn't drive around in a six hundred thousand dollar car painted red," Silas said.

Isazisi stepped out of the shadows.

"And Versia, it's fine to use someone's front door when you want to talk."

Versia stepped out from behind a concrete pillar.

"It's great to see you boys, you're looking strong."

"Great to see you too, Silas," Versia said.

"You don't look like you've aged a day," Isazisi said.

"You're funny," Silas said. "I'll assume this has to do with New York, it's rare two Psychics visit me."

"Now that's unfair, all of us attended your granddaughter's eighth birthday party," Versia said.

"Fair enough. Have either of you been to New York yet?"

"Resse is on the ground now, we have agents all over the scene," Isazisi said.

"Not yet, I'll pay a visit soon," Versia said.

"Legally all of you are clear due to the Psychic Act, but let's say you've pissed off your fair share of people," Silas said. "And Isazisi, your island stunt played well for public opinion. Do you still want me to draft a statement, or is your division of Providence lawyers already on that?"

"I think they can handle it."

"So what are the next moves," Silas asked.

"We think the Circle will follow up New York with attacks on more major cities, the plan right now is to go after their leadership and stop whatever attacks we can," Versia said.

"I took the liberty of compiling whatever I could find on short notice, I got my hands on some good stuff," Silas said.

"That quickly," Isazisi asked.

"There's a reason I've been on retainer since you were embryos. Ahh, your fathers and I, we really tore it up in our youths, we were no joke back then."

"I've heard the stories," Versia said.

"The mission in Azerbaijan has to be a fake story," Isazisi said.

"I assure you, that was one hundred percent real. Speaking of which, tell those boys to come out and see me, it's been far too long."

"Will definitely relay the message," Versia said.

Isazisi nodded.

"Do you need anything from us," Versia asked.

"I'm sure we'll be fine."

"You're prominent, and connected to us, that makes you a target," Isazisi said.

"The CIA didn't send me behind the Berlin Wall because they thought I was an easy target."

"That was forty years ago," Versia said.

"I'll be fine, thank you for the offer. I appreciate you boys coming to see me, even under these circumstances."

"Of course," both of them said.

They hugged him.

Both of them got in their cars and Silas stepped on the elevator.

In an all-black SUV with dark-tinted windows sat Fay with headphones on and a dish pointed at the conversation. She dialed a number on her phone.

"Fletcher, Duncan Silas just met with the Red Cyan and Cyan. He's compiled a dossier on us, what do you want to do about it," she asked.

"I'll handle him, move the plan into phase two," Fletcher said.

Silas arrived at the penthouse floor and opened the door to his apartment. He put down the flowers he'd bought as a young girl rushed and jumped into his arms as he stepped inside.

"Oh, you're getting too old for me." He said as he lifted her. His daughter walked out of the kitchen.

"Rachel, please don't kill Grandpa," she said as she leaned against the wall.

Rachel hopped out of her grandfather's arms and ran into the kitchen.

"We're baking a cake, she's pretty excited," his daughter said.

"How are you, Amy?" Silas asked.

"Scared for her. For you. If they're targeting Psychics and

people related to them, you could be in danger." Amy said.

"I'm a lawyer, who would target me,"

"People hate lawyers, and nobody in that building had a connection to a Psychic. You are the most outspoken supporter of Psychics, and people hate you for it."

"People will hate things they don't understand or are different," Silas said. "I am simply an ambassador between humans and Psychics."

"No, you are the human face of the Psychics," Amy said. "And you don't have an army or access to the strongest metal in the world. You have a granddaughter they can target and a family they can hurt."

"If you think we need protection, I can ask."

"Mom, the cake," Rachel yelled

"Thanks for the flowers, Dad."

Silas sat in front of the TV as the evening news droned on in the background. He sifted through his mail and found a black and gold invitation addressed to him, a church sermon to pray for victims of the New York attack. He read the time on the invitation, 8:30 PM, and looked at the clock, 7:30 PM.

"Amy, I'm going out," Silas said.

"Ok, be safe."

He reached the apartment complex garage and raced to the sermon. He stayed after sitting in the silent church, his hands clasped around a gold cross. He stood and left the church. Fletcher came out of the shadows and stabbed Silas in the stomach. His eyes expanded as his hands grabbed at the knife in his stomach. Fletcher slammed Silas against the black stone wall and twisted the knife. Silas groaned as he slid down the wall. Fletcher left the knife in him and ran.

Police erected yellow caution tape around the church in the morning while other officers placed a white cloth over Silas' body. A black SUV pulled up. Versia stepped out of the back, and an officer lifted the tape. He walked towards the detective. They pulled the cloth off the body.

"Oh no, Amy," Versia said as crime scene photographers took

pictures.

Versia put on a pair of white gloves and pulled the knife from Silas' stomach. He tapped on the knife with the knuckle of his pointer finger. It rang.

"It's a Psychanium knife," Versia said. "They're sending a message."

Versia placed the knife in a plastic bag the CSI opened for him.

"We also found this, it was addressed to you," the detective said.

Versia put on gloves and the detective handed him a white envelope with "Cyan" written on it in cursive. He opened it.

"Ten Thousand Terrors, Ten Thousand Years, Ten Million Lives. How many will suffer for your heritage?"

"What does it mean," the detective asked.

"I don't know," Versia said as he placed the envelope in a plastic bag and put it in his pocket.

Reporters had gathered around as the detective exited the scene.

"Preliminary evidence suggests the knife used on Duncan Silas is made of Psychanium. We are not ruling anything out, but we believe the Circle is involved and sending a message that anyone who is an ally of the Psychics is an enemy of us," the detective said. "No further questions, as the investigation is ongoing."

The detective walked towards a police tent. The reporters watched Versia hand the bag with the knife to a Providence agent.

"Versia, Versia, Versia." The reporters yelled.

Versia walked under the tape to the waiting SUV.

Another sedan pulled up, and Amy rushed out of the car. Two female police officers held her back as she reached the tape.

"That's my dad," she yelled. "That's my dad."

The detective signaled the two officers to let her in. She raced past the tape and to her father's body. She covered her mouth and turned away, tears rolling down her face. A police officer guided her out, but she collapsed to her knees.

"Get away from me," she yelled.

She sat against the wall, tears streaming down her face. The officers placed the white cloth back on the body.

Versia put his phone to his ear and Isazisi picked up.

"What did you find at the office," Versia asked.

"It's been ransacked," Isazisi said as he stood in the middle of a room with papers scattered, filing cabinets thrown over and computers ripped out of the wall. His agents combed through whatever they could. "My agents are looking for whatever they can, but the Circle was thorough."

"Did you see what happened to Duncan, they estimate he died three hours after talking to us," Versia said.

"We should've put security on him."

"Amy is here, should I say something?"

"No, let her grieve, in front of the media isn't a good place to do that."

"Got it. Let me know whatever you find in the office," Versia said.

"Got it."

Isazisi hung up and put the phone in his pocket. He looked around the room. His irises turned a cloudy red as his eyes saw in multiple spectrums. He saw something under a pile of papers. He walked towards it and put on a pair of latex gloves. He reached into the mound of papers and pulled out a hard drive. He rapped it with his knuckle and it rang with Psychainum's trademark sound. He put it in a plastic bag and stood. He snapped his fingers high in the air.

"I want every inch of this building searched," Isazisi yelled. "Commit as many people to it as you need. Start from that side," he pointed to his right and swept his arm to the left, "and search every inch, literally. There is nothing in here that we do not touch. I don't care how long it takes, bring in the drones if you have to."

"Yes sir," the lead agent said. "You heard the man, start over there."

****

Verisa sat on the side of his bed in his house. He rubbed the bags under his eyes as he looked outside at the constant camera flashes, reporters, and the growing crowd of protestors. He stood and walked downstairs. The TV turned on as he walked within sight. A news channel where a family member of a New York victim gave an interview about the attack. Versia waved his hand, turning off the TV as he looked away. The crowd chanting outside had grown louder. He double-tapped his wrist, activating Psychanium sound dampeners in his house's walls and silencing the ever-growing crowd.

He turned the TV to an alternate news channel. The headline read of Red Cyan's massacre of Circle agents on his Island.

"This is nothing but a publicity stunt, a show. It is a Psychic who is directly responsible for this tragedy trying to save face," a reporter said.

Versia swiped his hand, turning off the TV.

He walked over to his elevator, which led down to his underground lab. Versia sat before the theater-sized screens and pulled up his satellite feeds. Covert communications with U.S. allies flashed on his screen, and messages came in as he typed. Versia couldn't resist the urge and turned on a news channel.

"Last night, prominent lawyer and avid Psychic rights activist Duncan Silas was found dead outside a local church. Authorities suspect the Circle as the murder weapon is confirmed to be a Psychicanium knife." The reporter said.

The reporter continued as Versia muted the broadcast and pressed the contact Vashti with two pink hearts next to it in his phone. The phone buzzed on her nightstand. She picked up the phone as she stopped staring at the ceiling.

"How are you feeling?" Versia asked.

She sat in bed, pushed her inky black hair from her face, and rubbed her chestnut brown eyes as she came back to reality. Sunlight hit her honey-molten light brown skin as she looked through the blinds at the protestors and reporters in front of the house.

"I don't know." She said. "How are you feeling? I know the

attack struck a chord. Personal, on a different level. They killed Silas. I know he was good friends with your father. He was like family to us."

"They did that to hurt us. The Psychanium knife was unnecessary," Versia said. "We should've put a security detail on him around the clock. We should've known they would come after him."

"It's not your fault," Vashti said.

"Yeah, people seem to be saying that,"

He hung up, and his phone buzzed with a digital invitation to a celebration of Duncan Silas's life.

Under the twinkling night lights, he drove in a luxury sports car to the venue. Police had thrown a security net around the building while reporters clamored for comment from behind metal gates. He stepped out of the car and walked inside the building. A large poster of Silas's face rested on an easel near the entrance while a woman stood behind a table selling copies of his last book. A Chinese woman with flowing black hair, wearing a silk midnight blue dress walked up beside Versia and took his arm.

"Vashti couldn't make it?" The woman asked.

"Unfortunately not," Versia said.

"That's a shame."

The duo walked towards Amy, surrounded by people consoling her. She looked up.

"Caitlyn? Interesting seeing you here. Thought you would be out indulging." She said to the woman in blue.

Caitlyn squinted at her.

"Duncan meant the world to my entire family," Caitlyn said.

"Not enough to put a security detail on him," Amy remarked.

Caitlyn held her face.

"I'm sorry for your loss." She said.

"No, you're not, and neither are you, Versia. Both of you are Psychics who prance around the world in a lap of luxury and safety you didn't work a day to earn, yet I had to tell my daughter her grandfather, the best person she could've had in her life was killed, even though he's on retainer for the most powerful people in the world, that's because of you," Amy yelled.

"Amy, please," Versia began.

"Don't. His blood is on your hands, and the blood of everyone from New York. And we already know you won't face any consequences for it. I guess that's my father's fault. He worked tirelessly defending all of you, yet you didn't see fit to reciprocate the favor." Amy said as tears rolled down her face, she wiped them away.

"I will not be here if they are," Amy said.

"We are sorry for your loss," Caitlyn said.

"Leave," Amy said. "Now."

They turned and left the event.

"Where to now?" He asked.

"I have a file for you," Caitlyn said.

She tapped on an address in her phone and sent it to his car. They drove to the high-rise building and took an elevator to the penthouse. Caitlyn scanned her hand, and the door clicked open. They stepped into the house, and the lights turned on. They stepped into the house, and the lights turned on. Versia glanced at a table where half a dozen bottles of pills lay spilled.

"Caitlyn, what is this?"

"I'm miserable, and I took a few pills, nothing serious."

"You can't keep doing this. You'll OD."

"No, I won't, and they're prescription. I didn't bring you here to judge my life choices."

"Caitlyn, you'll get yourself killed."

"Oh, like I haven't already tried." She said.

She opened up her fridge and took out two ice balls. She grabbed a glass from the cupboard and poured an expensive-looking alcohol from her counter. She kicked off her heels and leaned against the island.

"I would offer you, but I know you don't drink."

"Caitlyn, it's getting worse. We can find you help," Versia said.

"You want to talk about getting me help? Don't you have anything to be worried about, or should I say anxious?"

"That wasn't funny, Caitlyn," Versia said.

"It wasn't meant to be, anyway. I didn't bring you here to judge my life choices."

"When your life choices reflect poorly on Psychics we..."

"Exactly, everything is about our image, isn't it? I would break the tabloids if I walked into an AA meeting, wouldn't I? If a picture of those pills ever leaked, we would never hear the end of it. That's what killed Duncan, isn't it? We needed to protect the image we spent billions cultivating, right."

"I don't know how Duncan or our image relates to the fact you're becoming an even worse alcoholic." Versia spat.

"You sound like my mom, except she had control over me for eighteen years."

"Caitlyn, I care about you, what you're doing is..."

"What I'm doing is coping; if you dislike how I do it, you can leave. Let's not act like you're not on the pills, too." She said.

She tossed him a USB.

"This is what I wanted to give you anyway."

"Caitlyn, New York wasn't your fault. Silas wasn't your fault."

"Then whose fault is it? Who's fault is it Rachel will grow up without her grandad? Who's fault is it that we killed 700 people in New York? Who's fault is it that the weapons we made are in the hands of terrorists?"

"Not yours."

"You can leave now."

Versia left the penthouse. Caitlyn stared at her half-empty glass and threw it at the wall, shattering it. Tears rolled down her face as she walked to the outdoor balcony. She looked down over the edge and imagined herself falling. She rocked against the railing, daring it to snap, she wiped her eyes and walked back into her house. She poured another glass before dumping a bottle of pills into the drink. She held it in her hand, and blue lightning bolts flared off her fingertips, stirring the pills into the brown drink. She sat in the darkness and took a sip.

****

Vashti held up a light pink disk to her face. It had darker pink lines of Psychic Energy flowing through it.

"It's beautiful," Versia said. "Like you."

Vashti couldn't help but blush.

"There's a pilot program when you first put on the helmet, which details the suit features," Versia said.

"Noted," Vashti said.

Versia walked to the lab beneath his house, searched "symptoms of depression" and read through the list. He closed the tab and opened his palm before him as he spun in his chair. A cyan light burst above his palm before settling down—a core crystal.

"The Pink and Ocean Blue Core Crystals are still in storage. What would you like to do with them?" His AI asked.

He closed his fist and the crystal disappeared in his hand. The robotic arms working in a glass case beside him settled into their chamber, and he looked over his shiny silver metal Psychic Suit bolstered by the cyan lines running throughout it. It's cyan glass palms glowing as well. The suit's energy radiated onto him.

"Keep them. We might need them sooner than we thought."

Vashti put her pink helmet on and sat.

"Hello, Vashti, and welcome to the Pink Spider Suit. Please say your name for voice confirmation and a quick rundown of its capabilities."

"Vashti," she said.

"Thank you. As the name suggests, the Pink Spider Suit's abilities take after the many spiders present in today's world. Abilities include sticking to any surface, webs, and your signature weapon, the Twin Spider Fang Daggers. These are the sharpest Psychanium blades ever forged and produce unique venom "PyroPosion".

"Okay, how do you shoot webs?" She said to herself as she stuck out her arm and angled her hand downward.

A holographic strand of pink webbing shot out and stuck to a hologram tree.

"Ok, what's next?"

Her suit's HUD changed as it activated Venom Mode. The HUD added a green hue to its standard pink.

"In venom mode, energy arrows are set to stun or kill."

She set it to stun, and the computer system targeted seven holographic cylinders. The seven targets exploded into orange cubes as her arrows hit them. She created two holographic daggers in her hand and flexed her fingers around them. She threw the daggers hitting two targets before blasting another two with her palm lasers.

"I think I've got the hang of it."

"Simulation over." The female computer voice said.

The holograms turned off.

"Congratulations. Welcome to the Pink Spider Suit."

****

Isazisi stood in the bay of a Providence VTOL jet flying deep into the jungle, flanked on both sides by additional jets. Below them rested an ancient city where the Circle had set up a base of operations. He looked down and clutched his right hand, stopping its shaking. Dozens of his agents, Providence Centurions clad in black body armor, had specialized, futuristic weapons in hand they checked and loaded. They put on their all-black helmets with glowing red eyes. Isazisi's suit formed around him, followed by a katana in his hand. The Circle agents on the ground looked up and scrambled for their weapons and their files.

"Don't give them a second to delete, shred, run, or breathe," Isazisi said.

Three of the seven jets descended and Isazisi and his Centurions jumped from the bay onto the greenish-yellow grass and vines covering the city's once golden-yellow stone roads.

His troops fired, cutting down Circle agents. The agents moved deeper into the Circle's encampment, tapping each other on the shoulders to signal movements and using hand signals to direct each other. They shot at more agents as other Centurions ran inside their tents and plugged in drives, shuttling Circle files to Providence's servers. Other agents collected paper files and other materials. Isazisi cut down two Circle agents with his katana. He turned at blinding speeds and reflected multiple bullets with his sword, cutting one clean in half. He boosted forward, cutting down the other two shooting at him.

More bullets hit his back, bouncing off the Psychanium armor. He blasted the three agents with red lasers fired from his eyes. More of Isazisi's troops landed, taking down the Circle's men as they worked into the camp.

Inside the city rested a treasure trove of history. The old, faded buildings still gleamed gold in the sunlight as luscious green vines covered them.

Missiles placed on top of crumbling buildings fired at Providence as they took cover behind the buildings and tents. The Circle composed itself and fired back.

"Fire on their positions," Isazisi ordered.

His jets above fired on the Circle and their point defenses. Bullets shot from the jets, cutting down more of the Circle's troops. Other jets turned their fire on the missile launchers and destroyed them. Explosions rocked the city as artillery combusted.

The remaining Circle agents threw everything at Providence as they fought toward the Circle's tents at the base of the golden-yellow temple in the city's center. One popped out with a rocket launcher and fired it at a group of Isazisi's troops. He boosted over and created a nanotech shield on the arm of his suit. The RPG exploded on contact, saving the troops. Isazisi's helmet retracted. His eyes glowed red as lasers shot from them, cutting down the Circle agent who fired the rocket.

"You good?" Isazisi asked an agent.

"Yeah, thanks," they said.

Isazisi boosted towards a group of Circle agents on his left and one threw a Psychanium flash bang. It exploded in a white light, blinding Isazisi. His ears rang as his blurry vision cleared in time for him to watch a Circle agent sneak behind a Centurion. Isazisi couldn't move. The Circle agent shot the Centurion in the back of the neck. Isazisi watched his body hit the ground, and red lasers fired from Isazisi's eyes, cutting down the Circle agent. Isazisi rushed over. He pulled the agent's helmet off. His eyes glazed over, and a pool of red formed underneath him.

Isazisi cursed as other Centurions collected the body. Isazisi stood and returned to the fight.

Centurions surrounded the Circle agents. Four popped the cyanide capsules embedded in their teeth, killing themselves, but Providence captured the others before they could do the same. Centurions threw them on their knees as the remainder of the jets landed. A Providence agent set a camera on a tripod as other Providence agents placed dead agents in body bags, Isazisi looked away, a grimace on his face.

"They're Psychic marks," the suit's AI told him as he looked at hieroglyphs carved into the temple.

He walked to the temple's top, where a Psychanium box with a handprint scanner rested. He examined the box. It had a Providence logo on its side. He removed his gauntlet and put his hand on the scanner. It read it and turned red as he wasn't a match.

"You can't hack it," the suit's AI said, "Psychanium tech isn't vulnerable to your powers."

He brought the case down the steps.

"Who is your leader?" Isazisi asked a captured agent.

They said nothing. Isazisi held his hand in front of the man's face, reading his mind with his Psychic powers. He sifted through the man's memories and he screamed, fighting Isazisi's powers, but passed out.

"Him," Isazisi said as he pointed.

They grabbed the man he nodded towards.

"You won't get anything from me." The man said as he struggled in the two agents' grip.

They dragged him to the box and placed his hand on the scanner. It clicked open, revealing a hard drive. Isazisi took it out and handed it and the box to two agents.

"Give this to our technicians. I want everything from that

drive on our servers," Isazisi said.

"Yes, sir."

He turned to the fourteen remaining Circle agents.

"You can defect. Give us information, and we will grant you immunity." Isazisi said.

Their leader spat at Isazisi's feet. He looked down and crouched.

"I've made fields run red with the blood of my enemies, my ancestors have killed for disrespect. They would expect me to do the same." Isazisi said.

The man rotated a small knife in his palm.

"We'll never yield."

The man lashed out with the knife, stabbing at Isazisi's neck. The knife stopped, a red aura of Isazisi's psychokinesis around it and the man's hand. He strained as the blade remained still. He dropped the knife at Isazisi's feet as his face contorted in pain.

"Yield is no longer an option," Isazisi said.

"Isn't this a bit personal for you? The great Red Cyan couldn't protect the one thing he car..." The man said before an agent to Isazisi's right punched him across the face.

Isazisi's chest burned. His katana formed in his hand as two of his troops dragged the man to the edge of a hole. His other troops stood the remaining thirteen up and marched them to pre-dug holes. His troops had begun digging similar holes around the compound. They kicked the Circle agents to their knees at the edge of the large rectangular hole.

"Kill them all," Isazisi said.

His troops raised their guns to the heads of the remaining Circle agents and fired. The bodies dropped into the pre-dug holes as their leader watched. He held his face.

"An ability we don't talk about is sensing emotions," Isazisi said.

"You're not ready for what's coming," their leader said. "This world will burn,"

Isazisi raised his sword and cut off the man's head. His body fell into the same hole.

"You'll feel my pain now," Isazisi whispered.

He looked up.

"Photo it, file it, and clean it up," Isazisi said.

"Yes, sir."

Isazisi walked to his jet and boarded it. He arrived at his base after the jungle expedition.

"The clean-up crew is on the way. The site will be buried as per your orders." His agent said. "We're handling the bodies, and agents will comb through Circle's items for anything of value."

"Thank you for the update."

He walked off the jet as two soldiers carried the case behind him. He approached a vault and raised his hand over a sensor. Red wisps of energy flowed from his hand to the vault, causing the enormous circular Psychanium door to unlock and swing open. He took the case from them, and walked to the back of the vault, placing the crate on a rack. Isazisi pressed on the screen outside the vault, and the security system turned on as the vault closed. He walked to the control center of the base. One commander stood at the command center, a tablet in hand.

"Sir, Agent Murphy is KIA," The commander said. "Shot in the neck."

"I know. Didn't his wife have a baby last month?" Isazisi asked.

"Yes, sir,"

Isazisi said something explicit.

Thunder rumbled in the distance as lightning flashed across the overcast sky. A row of black SUVs pulled up to a quaint white and blue house. Isazisi left the middle SUV, flanked by Praetorians and Providence Centurions. He knocked on the door three times. A red-haired woman with soft brown eyes and pale white skin opened the door. She looked around and staggered before leaning against the door.

"No," she said. "No."

"I cannot express how sorry we are," Isazisi said.

The woman slid down the door, crying. She screamed as she covered her face. Isazisi knelt beside her.

"Don't say a word to me," she yelled.

"Ms. Murphy, If you need anything, ask," Isazisi said.

"Leave," she screamed.

A Centurion handed him a folded black and red flag. He knelt and placed it beside her.

"His service will not be forgotten," Isazisi said.

"Leave," she yelled. "Leave me."

"I'm sorry," Isazisi said as he stood and walked back to the cars.

CHAPTER 5

Isazisi put on his smart glasses.

"M.E.G.A.N, are you there," Isazisi said.

"Megan, A.I. interface is going live," she said. "Yes, boss. Happy to be here."

He walked out to the car awaiting him and sat in the back.

"Megan, what's the probability the Cir..."

Isazisi looked out of the car's windshield, seeing frozen traffic on the bridge. In the sky, a large black flaming object crashed through the atmosphere. Isazisi opened the window and leaned out.

"Megan," Isazisi said. "Why is a Jaeger robot out of orbit?"

"I don't know. According to the system, it's still in space." She said.

The robot crashed into the water beside the bridge, the sharp end slicing into the riverbed. The shockwave tore through the water, flooding the bridge and washing off cars and people as it shook like an earthquake struck.

The satellite's top opened and the rhombus-shaped vessel transformed into a massive robot. It had a dark red optical sensor and stood one hundred feet tall. Out of its wrists slid two blades cloaked in glowing red energy. The robot smashed a part of the bridge, flinging more cars and people into the water.

Isazisi placed a finger on a small pad and sank into the seat as his suit built around him. First, the hands, followed by his torso and legs. He took off the smart glasses as his helmet formed. The display glowed red as Megan booted up in the suit conscious.

He took off into the sky and hovered around the robot as it marched toward the city.

"Megan, show me its weak points."

"There are none," She said.

"Wait, wait. What?" He asked.

"You designed it to have no weaknesses," Megan replied.

"Shi..."

The robot slammed him into the bridge before he could finish. He pulled himself out of a hole and took to the sky again, dodging another strike by the robot.

"Do we know why it's attacking?"

"System recorded a breach."

"By who?"

"We're searching. It came from the inside. There is no way this can be an outside entity."

"How do I take it down?"

"All weapons are online," She said.

He smashed into the robot's chest and bounced off.

"What is that, Megan?" He yelled over the robot slashing a building.

"It's equipped with Psychanium-powered shields."

"How do I take it down?"

"You can't do it alone without causing massive damage to the surrounding area."

The robot slashed at him again, catching him in the torso. The red energy blade sliced through the suit's nanties, burning as it tore through Isazisi's skin. He yelled as his entire right side stung and prickled, a searing pain shooting through his nerves, and burning skin poisoning his nose. The suit crashed onto the bridge's remains. Isazisi pulled himself to his knees as he fingered the rough gash in his side. He looked down at the eight-inch long red and black tear in his side, still steaming from the robot's blade. He stood up, still clutching his side. Red lines coated the wound as his body healed it while the suit's nanites rebuilt the damaged armor.

"Megan, I need options." Isazisi rasped.

"You can't win alone without causing massive carnage," Megan said as a phone icon popped up in his HUD.

Versia's phone rang.

"Hello," Versia said.

"Versia, the Circle hijacked a Jeager and is attacking a city. I can't destroy it myself."

"You can't take it yourself?"

"Not without leveling half the city in the process."

"On my way, I'll bring a friend."

Versia's jet took off at Mach 10 from his private hangar and flew toward the city, arriving in minutes.

"Vashti, you're up."

She nodded and fell backward from the jet as the robot took two gas tankers and threw them at Isazisi. They exploded, sending a cloud of fiery smoke hurling into the sky. Vashti spiraled down through the flames and landed in the smoke.

"Okay, where is the robot?" She asked.

The computer in her smart contact lens responded, plotting a path through the smoke. She found the towering robot and flung two webs up it, propelling herself to its head. She jumped down, pulling the robot off balance. She threw a web bomb at a nearby wall. It shot a web across the river, tripping the staggering robot into the water.

The Jaeger surged out of the water and redeployed its swords, slamming one on Vashti as she created a bubble shield. The sword smashed her through the bridge and into the water below. More explosions rocked the bridge as the robot refocused and slashed at the jet. Versia fired the jet's weapons, knocking the robot back. The robot regained its composure and swung again, destroying the jet in one swift motion. It exploded in a spectacular fireball. Versia double-tapped his chest, building his Psychic suit around him as he plummeted. The suit flared to life and fired its thrusters before he slammed into the water, propelling him up with a cyan-colored trail behind him. The robot slashed at Versia again, burying the suit under its blade and slamming him into the bridge. He rolled out from under the blade and blasted a succession of lasers from his palm at it, the robot's shield reflected the attack.

Versia's HUD scanned the robot.

"You'll need to draw its power away from the shield," Versia said to Isazisi.

"Got it."

Versia flew at the robot, smashing into its shield. It staggered and focused on Isazisi, who landed on the remains of the bridge. The robot's sword glowed red as it swung at Isazisi. He created a shield, absorbing the hit. The robot exerted more pressure and cracks formed in the shield.

Versia's HUD scanned the robot's power distribution and plotted his route. He flew at the robot at full speed and smashed through the shields, tearing a gaping hole in the robot as he came out the other side. The robot fell backward and sank into the shallow water. Versia landed.

"We need to talk," Isazisi said.

CHAPTER 6

They watched a broadcast of the attack going viral with top-down shots of the robot in the water on dozens of new stations from Isazisi's plane. Video of Providence troops touching down and giving aid to people played while VTOL jets lifted the damaged robot out of the water.

"Here's what we know. After infiltrating parts of Providence, the Circle stole and is using our weapons in attacks across the globe. The attack in New York was a Providence weapon. The bomb in Dallas we covered up, a Providence weapon. The robot attack here, our weapons, and by now, they're going after your weapons, too."

"I... don't have weapons," Versia said.

Isazisi looked at him.

"So this missile-equipped spy satellite? The missile sites deep in the jungles and deserts?"

"Okay, fine, a few hundred weapons."

He looked at him again.

"Okay, a few thousand, but I never use them."

"Isazisi, Versia, what is that?" Vashti asked.

They flew into a massive storm system. Lightning flashed across clouds as the wind and rain whipped around at hundreds of miles per hour.

"Megan, analysis?" Isazisi asked.

"An unprecedented storm." She replied.

"Versia, don't you have a storm-creating satellite?"

"Yeah, it's encrypted."

"Same with my robot."

A psychanium-generated lightning bolt hit the plane, knocking out the lights and sending it reeling toward the ocean.

Alarms blared around the aircraft as it plummeted into the sea and exploded on contact. Fiery metal pieces rained everywhere as three objects blasted out of the water.

"I have a lead," Isazisi radioed as he flew into the atmosphere, "can you handle this,"

"We got it," Versia said.

"Megan, pinpoint that signal. I need an exact location," Isazisi said as he flew in the general direction.

"A volcano off the south coast of India, predictions say it is close to erupting."

"Plot a course."

Minutes later, he landed on an island in the Indian Ocean. He looked at the pristine white sands and luscious green plant life within the island before looking up at the volcano standing hundreds of feet in the air.

"Megan, scan for life signs."

"There's a twenty-man team up there."

Megan showed him the infrared of twenty people, eighteen of them holding assault rifles and the other two in front of computer screens. He took off and landed in the volcano. The Circle agents opened fire, and the bullets bounced off him.

"Seriously, guys, can we talk about this?" He asked.

They said nothing.

"Guess not." He said.

He moved his hand to the right, and three people flew into the wall. Two swords came out of his wrists. He flew at them. He sliced through two, stabbed one other, and shot the other thirteen with his shoulder missiles, leaving the two scientists. They grabbed two nearby pistols and shot at him. He aimed at both of them, and they dropped their guns and put their hands up.

"Leave," he said.

They rushed out to a waiting helicopter.

"Megan, send the drones after it."

"Yes, boss." The panel on a Providence satellite opened in space, and three pods came out. They broke through the atmosphere and came apart in the sky, revealing three drones.

"Cloak the drones and set them to follow," Isazisi said.

The drones obeyed Megan.

"Alright, what am I looking at," Isazisi said as he turned to the computer screen.

"It's a two-fold operation. Geologists researched lava flow patterns in the earth's mantle while programmers used a coding algorithm designed to try to brute force access to the Providence mainframe with a pre-plugged-in drive. Extremely energy-intensive."

"Access like that can only come from the inside." He said.

"Your agents have compiled a list of potential Circle suspects, and I can go through the ones who work in our tech department."

"Do that, and have the drones report where the helicopter lands." He said.

****

Out of the storm came a fist made of wind. It smashed into Versia, knocking him against the water. He hit and skipped like a stone. He fired his thrusters, regaining balance, and flew at the fist. Out of the water shot a vortex of liquid. It threw the suit upwards while another lightning bolt came and slammed him into the waves. The winds surged, causing the water to swirl and form into a large hurricane, spinning counterclockwise, pulling them in.

"You awake, Meadow," Versia asked.

"Always, sir." She said.

"Upgrade the weapons system with firmware 17-B," Versia said.

Meadow downloaded the upgrade via his satellites. Three rods dropped from the back of his suit, lengthened in the air, and exploded, damaging four of the drones in the storm and allowing him to fly out.

The storm pulled in Vashti who fought against the force. Versia scanned the inside, finding dozens of small plus-shaped drones receiving signals from his rogue satellite, moving in formation and causing temperature changes inside the storm to create the wind.

"Vashti, let the hurricane take you. On the inside, switch to explosive webbing and target the drones," he said.

She let herself go and fell into the storm's center, shooting each drone with her pink explosive webbing, drone after drone erupted in flames. A fist of water discharged from the water and grabbed her. She pushed her jets to the max, but the water pulled her down and squeezed. It broke her right-hand jet. On her holographic display, her arm glowed red, followed by both her leg jets breaking. Her legs on the holographic display showed more red.

"I'm going down." She said.

****

The Circle's helicopter landed at a building in the nearby desert. The drones hovered and analyzed the target building, streaming the footage to Isazisi as a holographic image. A metal building complete with anti-air and ground artillery, he landed a few feet from the building entrance. The guards there didn't hesitate to sound the alarms. More guards ran out the front gates. He blasted through them and flew into the building to a caravan already leaving, one large all-black eighteen-wheeler with heavy armoring and three black SUVs in front and three in back. He flew after them.

He flew beside the SUV pair in the back and created four orbs in his palm. He threw two orbs into each vehicle. The orbs floated and spun around each other in a decaying orbit. They smashed together, creating an explosion, and the cars flipped up and rolled off the cliffside. The caravan sped up. He launched a mini-missile at the last SUV in the back. It exploded in a spectacular fireball before it rolled off the side of the cliff, still coated in flames.

The SUVs switched to a "T" formation, with one car in front of the truck and two beside it. One SUV dropped off, and a man inside smashed the back window. Machine-gun fire raked through it. The bullets did nothing to Isazisi's armor. They switched to a grenade launcher, they fired one, and it exploded on contact, smashing Isazisi into the road.

"Providence grenade launcher," Megan said as Isazisi pulled himself out of the hole in the ground.

He took off again and shot a laser at the car. It exploded, crashing into the rock face. The other SUV dropped off. They smashed the back window and pushed a thin-looking cannon barrel out. He threw one orb into the car, and it exploded, blowing it to pieces. He flew ahead and landed in front of the last SUV. He moved his hand to the side, and the SUV tumbled down the nearby cliffside. The truck swerved around him. The top of the trailer opened and out came a soldier. He held a black assault rifle with Providence markings on the side and shot red beams of energy at Isazisi, who dodged them in the sky. Isazisi landed on the trailer, and two swords emerged from his wrists. The soldier dropped back into the truck as Isazisi sliced at his head, catching a few locks of hair. Isazisi threw a two-inch beaker-shaped energy bomb in front of the truck, and it exploded, causing the driver to lose control and swerve into the desert rock. He smashed a hole through and dropped into the trailer. The soldiers fired at him, and the bullets bounced back and hit them. Isazisi looked around at the carnage in the back of the truck and found a single piece of paper with black text on it stuck to the wall.

The whole truck exploded in a brilliant fireball, lighting the desert in an orange hue as the heat crystallized the sand around it. Isazisi rose from the ashes of the explosion.

"Megan?"

"A two-megaton explosion." She replied.

"Any evidence left?"

"No."

"What else?"

"I wasn't able to read what the paper said, but your UN hearing is in two hours,"

Isazisi cursed and lifted off, returning to base.

The water pulled Vashti in. Underneath the waves, she descended deeper into the blue, farther from the Hurricane's influence. She shot back up and hit the small drones with her pink webbing. Explosions rocked the storm and the hurricane dispersed.

She shot out of the dissipating hurricane, and her wrist buzzed. She looked down at it.

"We have to get back. Isazisi's having a hearing in front of the UN council." She said.

"When?" Versia asked.

"Two hours."

Two hours later a thousand miles away Isazisi took a deep breath and walked in.

CHAPTER 7

Isazisi walked in with an expensive red and black suit on. He sat before the committee and placed both hands on the desk before him.

The head of the committee spoke first, "You know why we're here, correct? Terrorists have seized your weapons, which you and other Psychics assured us could never fall into the wrong hands, allowing them to perform acts of terror around the globe without any warning or means of tracking them down, resulting in thousands of casualties."

"Yes, and I, along with other Psychics, have tracked and taken down the cells my people have found. I believe the body count is pushing into triple digits, don't act like I'm doing nothing." Isazisi said.

A series of whispers and looks spread through the crowd, surprised by his tone.

"You have the tone of a man who knows he belongs in a cell but his daddy bought him out."

"Do you have a real question, or is this just performative?" Isazisi asked.

"You created the problem, and it's your place to fix it. You watch the news, I'm assuming. The New York attack. Seven hundred and fifty people died from a weapon you created and assured would be a 'peace-keeping mechanism.'" The committee leader shouted.

"The events of New York were tragic, but if we don't stop them, that will be a scratch on the surface of their violence. Allow me and my people to fix it. We are working around the clock to track down cell after cell, and strikes are being carried out worldwide on known cells." Isazisi continued.

"You and other Psychics have not even sniffed the potential of facing the consequences for what you've caused. Many would like evidence you are doing anything at all." The committee leader asked.

"Of course," Isazisi said. He double-tapped his wrist, and a hologram display came to life. "This is a mission carried out in the Andorra mountains. Here are the bodies left by the drone attack." The video showed bodies hauled away in black bags by Red's agents. "Another was carried out in the south of Yemen. Here's the crater from the missile strike, a ground invasion of a fake town deep in the forest of Maine. Here is footage for the helmet cameras." The video showed Providence agents holding advanced weapons taking out armed terrorists, and for the last bit, the events in the jungle. Displays showed pictures and videos of Isazisi's fight with the Circle in the ancient city.

"It may sound redundant, but do you have more information on the group carrying out these attacks?"

"It's a group called The Circle. We have limited knowledge of them, except for their most publicized goal. Subjugate the world and cause the death of every Psychic. It is cliche, but with my technology, realistic. Even so, we are pushing them back." Isazisi said.

"Why do they want to take over the world?" A man on the left of him asked.

"Their motivation stems from a deep-seated hatred of Psychics, a schism within the world thousands of years ago, and again decades ago. Psychics punished the Circle, and we, as their future generations, are to atone for the sins of our fathers. They think Psychics are the problem, but in reality, they're deranged zealots chasing power by any means necessary. They view us as everything wrong with the modern world and see poetic justice in correcting it using our metal against us."

"And how long do you think before this goal is achievable?" Another asked him.

"Our estimates say seven to ten days," Isazisi said. "In my opinion. Even less with the proper application of my technology, but like I said. We are pushing them back."

"How did they amass enough resources to take on Providence

without any major intelligence agency finding out?" A member sitting on the far right asked.

"This wasn't a spur-of-the-moment decision; they've planned this for decades. According to our intel, they've amassed billions in funding through counterfeit goods, drug trafficking, human trafficking, and myriad other illicit operations, including contract killing, war profiteering, and acting as mercenary forces. Their illegal enterprises are intertwined with several legal businesses, stock market investments, venture capitalist investments, and cryptocurrency funds. For example, a brokerage account shorted the stocks of every company owned by a Psychic family hours after the attack, netting themselves billions. As for their numbers, they recruit high-level members as paid mercenaries or fanatics and impressionable, usually young individuals from dark web forums and other websites as expendable grunts. As for how they avoided detection, we believe they're intertwined with multiple governments across the planet, including our own."

A series of noises rippled through the crowd at the shocking information.

The committee leader rubbed his head. "Seven days before they could steamroll the world and enough connections to get away with it." He said.

"We're dealing with it as fast as we can," Isazisi said. "Our resources are considerable."

A group of men in black burst into the courtroom and shot their guns into the air. Everyone dropped to the floor, screaming. The woman in charge walked in as they fired off more shots into the ceiling. Isazisi stood and buttoned down his suit. They aimed their guns at him.

"Get on the ground, now."

He walked forward. One man shot at him, a circular nanotech shield formed on his arm, blocking the bullets.

"Put your hands up now."

He put his hands up in fake surrender. He slammed the shield into the ground, and red crystals sprouted up, moving toward the Circle agents throwing them against the back wall. The woman in charge reached for her pistol. Her hand stopped inches from the holster, and a red aura surrounded it as Isazisi held her hand in place with his psychic powers.

She looked down, confused.

He threw the shield, which bounced off, slamming her into the back wall. More people clad in black charged in. The man at the head of them knelt beside her and took a pulse.

"What have you done?" he asked.

Isazisi double-tapped his chest, and his suit deployed. They shot at him, and the bullets crumpled on impact. Two swords slid out of his wrist, and the men ran out, shooting at him.

He flew after them as the men loaded into large pick-up trucks, each with miniguns welded to the bed. In each pick-up, one person took up a position at the minigun and sprayed him with bullets. The other men fired at him with their rifles. They took off speeding down the streets. The trucks were equipped with steel shovels in front of them to smash any cars out of the way. Isazisi flew above them and shot two of the trucks with a laser. They exploded and veered off the road into the trees.

The trucks charging down the road screeched to a halt and took up defensive positions.

More trucks roared out from every direction, encircling Isazisi. Out of each truck shot a chain. He struggled, but the chains held fast. Megan scanned the chains, Psychanium alloy.

"We got him, " a man radioed to the other end. "I haven't yet introduced myself. My name is Nicolas Fletcher, and I've wanted to meet you for a long time. New York, tragic indeed, a mess. One of my better ideas if I do say so."

"You're sick," Isazisi said as he patched into his satellite and ordered a laser strike on his location.

"Just a visionary and there must be suffering for our vision."

"We picked you up on CCTV and satellite. You killed my agents in New York, stole our bomb, and killed 700 people," Isazisi said.

"A fraction of the number of people killed by you and your

ancestors. It wasn't hard. You got cocky, though you were untouchable. Your wealth and power go to you. You thought because you have glowing eyes, no one would dare challenge your rule," Fletcher responded. "Have you heard the Greek myth of Prometheus? He defied the gods of Olympus and gave fire to mankind. For his theft, he was to be punished eternally. He was tied to a rock and every day an eagle would eat his liver. It would grow back overnight and the eagle would be back again, every single day. You are our Prometheus, you have given us fire in the form of Psychanium, and you, along with this world, will be punished for it eternally. Although I supposed the bird in your case would be a peacock."

"First I'm Medusa, now I'm Prometheus. You're Persus, and now I assume Zeus?"

"You know your mythology."

"Our ancestors were the basis for those stories. Who do you think was throwing lightning from the sky."

"You're not a god."

"You'll pay for my dead agents,"

"I think you should be more preoccupied with the here and now."

"You already have the bomb, what's next?" Isazisi asked.

"I'm happy you asked because I wanted to take this time to explain our entire plan in detail," Fletcher said.

A man behind Isazisi cocked a gun.

"Look up," Isazisi said. "I'm closer to Zeus than you."

A red light expanded as it raced to the planet. Fletcher ran to his truck and took off as the laser crashed down to earth, vaporizing the vehicles around Isazisi's suit. He shrugged off what remained of the charred and broken chain. The last truck drove through the forest over the rugged terrain.

"We have to get to the plane." A man in the passenger seat said.

Rocks and branches crackled under the truck as it traversed the terrain. They came to a clearing, and Fletcher tapped on his wrist, the hologram projecting the thick brush and fallen trees turned off, exposing a runway and a small air traffic control building. The projector had a Providence logo on it. The truck skidded to a stop, and four men jumped out.

Fletcher turned to one man and held his neck as he pulled him close.

"You know what to do," Fletcher said. "No matter what, we will not forget you, brother."

Fletcher hugged the man.

"I love you like only a brother could, Andrew. Come home to us."

The man nodded.

Three of them ran to the plane and took off from the runway, and the last man ran into the air traffic control building. Inside stood a sixteen-foot-tall mechanized battle suit. He climbed in and powered it on. He walked out of the building and trudged into the forest. Isazisi watched the plane as it flew south. He looked down, and in front of him stood a gladiator-like battle suit.

On the one hand, it had a giant all-black sword with silver stripes going down it, while on the other arm, a large shield and, rather than a hand, a mace with spikes. He recognized Psychanium and other bits of his technology on the Circle's suit. On Isazisi's left forearm formed a red energy shield, and hexagons formed in his right hand, creating the Red Cyan Sword.

Isazisi charged at the suit. The suit swung the mace at him, and he bounced it off his shield. He slashed at the Gladiator suit which blocked it with his shield and threw Isazisi back. The Gladiator charged him and brought down his sword on Red. He stopped it with his. The suit pushed down on him, and the rocks underneath Isazisi cracked and folded upwards as he resisted. Isazisi pushed the Gladiator's sword back up as a red energy pulse exploded between them. Isazisi sidestepped the suit's mace and grabbed it. He threw it back into the suit's face. It crumpled part of the Mech's face, causing it to stagger. It regained its balance and swung at Isazisi.

Their swords continued clashing as they fought. The Gladiator rushed forward and pinned Isazisi to the ground. It swung its Psychanium mace at him, smashing into the side of his head. Pieces of his armor flew off. Isazisi flew out from the Gladiator's grasp. It swung at him, but Isazisi caught the sword and drove it into the Mech's head. It staggered and stood still. Isazisi tore his sword through the Gladiator's torso and ripped it out.

The suit dropped to its knees and opened. The pilot fell out, and the man pulled himself up against the leg of the suit.

"Looks like that's it." The man said as he clutched at his bleeding stomach. He let out a hoarse chuckle.

"Start talking," Isazisi said.

"This world will never love your kind. Why fight us."

"Not an answer."

The man snorted and coughed as he spat up blood. He reached into his pocket and injected himself with a clear liquid.

Isazisi said something explicit.

Meadow read his vitals. His heart had flatlined, and he'd stopped breathing.

"Never mind," Isazisi said to himself.

He took off after the plane.

"Megan track the plane," Isazisi said.

"Got it," Megan said. "Ten miles out from the Atlantic coast."

He caught up to the plane and fired off two missiles from his shoulders at it. One hit the engine, and the other hit the gas tank. The plane exploded in a spectacular fireball, and the charred remains splashed into the water.

"Target destroyed," Megan said. "Sending drones now."

Three men broke the still surface of the water a few minutes later. They swam to a nearby speedboat, painted a perfect match for the water. A man on board threw a ladder at them, and they climbed up.

"You think we fooled him?" One man asked.

"No, the drones will be out here any minute, and those are what we're going to fool," Fletcher said.

They grabbed CPR dummies of themselves, complete with

their facial features, plastic internal organs, and a dozen other props. They used a blowtorch, burned part of them black, and tossed them into the water. The dummies sank along with the plane wreckage. Minutes later, three drones flew down. They scanned the surface for any sign of bodies and dived beneath the waves. The drones spied three charred bodies with no heartbeat and weak heat signatures. The drone flew out of the water and back to a Providence base.

"We did it." The man beside him said.

"For now," Fletcher said. "Keep a low profile for a while. If any of us survived, he'd know we all did. Well, we got targets on our backs now, boys," Fletcher said with an ear-to-ear grin. His two comrades shared a look with uncertain eyes.

****

"Anything new on the Circle?" Isazisi asked Megan.

"They're still at large, but chatter picked up on them talking about a strike at the Secretary of State's house during his annual World Forward Forum. The usual company alone is more than enough of an enticing target for the Circle."

"Was this passed on to the police?"

"Yes, police, Secret Service, FBI, CIA, DSS, etcetera. They're throwing a joint net around the house and scaling up security. There's a shoot-on-sight three-mile perimeter around the house."

"That won't stop them."

"Well, the Secretary of State will be ecstatic to see the President's largest donor in attendance," Megan said.

An invitation appeared on the HUD.

"Thank you, Megan." He said.

"My pleasure," She replied

****

Isazisi pulled up to the gate of the property in his jet-black sports car. He showed the guards his invitation while others searched the outside of the vehicle for explosives. They waved him through, and Isazisi drove in another mile. He parked his car and stepped out. Six guards stood at the door brandishing automatic machine guns, while others stood with bomb-sniffing dogs and other means of detecting unauthorized weapons.

Isazisi walked into the event to diplomats and world leaders everywhere socializing with each other and discussing what new projects could forward worldwide economics. Outside, behind the house, three black vans from the catering company drove into the complex. They showed their invitations and identification to the guards and continued in. They entered the house through the kitchen in the back, shot everyone with suppressed pistols, and took up positions around the house serving food. Isazisi tapped his ear.

"Megan, it's been an hour." He whispered.

"The chatter could have been incorrect." She replied as the Secretary of State walked in. Everyone stood and clapped as he walked down the soft velvet-colored stairs. He talked to and shook hands with everyone in attendance. The servers pulled guns from under their trays and shot half the guards in the room with suppressed pistols. The rest pulled out the automatic weapons slung over their shoulders and took cover as machine-gun fire from Circle agents on the balconies pinned them down. Everyone screamed and dropped for cover. Security burst into the room to be cut down by the Circle's agents' machine guns. They pointed guns at the government officials as they scanned for their target. Isazisi stood in the middle and adjusted his gold and red crystal cufflinks.

"Get on the ground, now," an agent yelled, pointing a gun at him.

Isazisi whipped his hand, shooting a psychic shockwave, and throwing several of them into the wall. They fired at him. He slid behind a metal table and flipped it on its side. Bullet holes riddled the metal as they continued the onslaught. They stopped shooting at him and grabbed the Secretary of State along with a few other leaders and led them out at gunpoint, throwing them into the back of the black vans. Isazisi jumped over the table and ran out the door. He hopped into his car, pushed the start, and shot off. One van dropped back, and the dual doors swung open to four men in the back with submachine guns. They shot at him. He dropped off to avoid fire.

"Megan, send the drones." He said.

"I can't connect to the satellites," she said.

"Fix it. I'll do this on the ground."

He put his hand on a custom-installed screen on the center console. Two red stripes going through the middle formed on the car's exterior. He stepped on the gas, surging forward, and caught up to the last van. It shot at him, but the bullets bounced off the car. He accelerated and slammed into their side. The van spun out of control and crashed off a bridge. The fireball from the explosion rose into the night. Isazisi pressed down harder on the pedal and the vans drove off the road and landed on a bullet train using specialized tracks.

"How the..." He began. "How did they sneak a bullet train into this country and build its specialized track without anybody asking questions?"

"Unknown at this current time," Megan said.

Isazisi continued forward, keeping pace with the train. He made a turn to jump on the train but crashed into another train. His car slammed off of it, hit the ground, and rolled. Isazisi curled in the seat till the car stopped. He kicked the door of the totaled car open and touched the gash at the top of his head, recoiling his hand as it stung. The sonic boom could be seen in the darkness as the red suit entered the airspace. He connected with the suit and took off after the train. The track ended in a ramp into the ocean. Isazisi aimed, but the front three cars merged while the back three did the same and jumped off the ramp. Isazisi flew closer to the other vehicles. The three cars in the back exploded. Isazisi took off and escaped the explosions. The other fused cars landed on a small container ship, skidding to a stop with sparks flying. He flew after it. A long-barreled laser weapon on the bridge turned around and blasted him with a blue laser. It exploded on contact, and Isazisi spiraled into the ocean, splashing down with a trail of smoke following him.

****

Fletcher walked down the dark streets of Austin, Texas. Careful to avoid the gaze of the dozens of cameras in the city. He turned onto a road and looked up at the cathedral. With its sweeping arches and towering spires, the imposing structure lit up in golden lights stood in silence. Fletcher walked into the cathedral and sat on a bench. The priest stood at the pulpit reading the scriptures.

"I didn't know Psychics were Gods. Why would they need a cathedral," Fletcher called.

The priest looked up. "The High Psychic's Cathedral is a house of worship for the one true God. The Psychics simply built it. It is not a shrine to them."

"Yet they prance around like gods, attempt to give and take both life and freedom like gods."

"If that is how you feel, run for office. You won't take their power from these halls." The priest said.

Fletcher stood and picked up a nearby scripture.

"And what does this book say about power? What does it say about false gods? That is what Psychics are, false gods, and they deserve to be punished for their disrespect of natural law." Fletcher said.

"You're not religious are you?"

"Not particularly,"

"If that is how you feel about Psychics, you will not make change from these hallways."

"I will make change, but I'm here to offer you these for now."

He handed the priest a plane ticket and a prepaid card.

"I heard Cancun is beautiful this time of year. I wouldn't want to be in Isazisi for the next few days." Fletcher said.

"Is there something I should tell the world?"

"Not if you want anyone alive in your extended family to stay breathing. Unfortunate, you have no one for us to target."

"I understand." The priest said.

Fletcher walked outside to a waiting SUV and stepped in the back seat. His phone rang, and he answered.

"We've recovered his body from our people within Providence," a woman said over the phone.

Fletcher's face remained unchanged.

"His condition?"

"He injected himself with the toxin, but not before multiple stab wounds."

"Have we informed his family? They didn't know who he worked for." Fletcher said.

"Andrew was like your little brother. They wanted you to be the first to make any decision," the woman said.

"They're nothing but murders. They'll know the pain they've caused one day when it's returned to them tenfold," Fletcher said. "His sacrifice will not be in vain. It's like Hercules and his twelve trials. Andrew is one of mine."

"Hail the Circle," the woman on the phone said.

Fletcher hung up and punched the back seat before him, yelling and screaming. He laid back in his chair and covered his face with his hands.

"Where to sir?" His driver asked.

"Back to base, we have lots to plan for," Fletcher said.

Fletcher walked into a room surrounded by screens while in a circular area below sat people typing away at computers.

"Where are we with the endgame Doctor?" Fletcher asked.

Fay sat in a corner typing into her phone, she looked up at his voice.

"We believe we've cracked the technology, Providence's security measures are no pushover when it comes to their tech." The Doctor said. "Still, it will take a few days to calibrate it to our needs, plate tectonics and mantle movement are not easy sciences."

"What do you mean?" Fay said.

"Well, if the waves aren't calibrated and directed properly, they'll cause eruptions in places we can't predict or don't want them to. We cannot rush this. This isn't simply setting off a bomb in a building, this is world-altering stakes."

"You said a few days. Our attack will keep the Psychic's focus where we want it. We appreciate your work, Doctor, and hope to see it in the field." Fletcher said.

"It will be beautiful," the Doctor replied.

****

The helicopter landed on a yacht off the coast of Brazil. Both Versia and Vashti stepped off.

"Welcome aboard. I will be your diving instructor. You said you wanted to dive into the Yauallian ruins." The instructor said.

"Well, that's why we're here," Versia said.

"Get to know my employees while we set up for the dive. After all, your life is in their hands." The man said.

Vashti spoke to them in perfect Spanish.

"You speak Spanish?" The man asked.

"I'm a quarter Puerto Rican and 3 quarters black, my mother taught me," Vashti said.

"Interesting mix," the man said.

He left to set up for the dive and came out a few minutes later.

"You never said how you came upon wanting to visit these ruins?" He asked.

"Light reading," Versia said.

The men on the yacht pulled guns from their jackets.

"No one has visited those ruins in centuries. What's your business there."

"Exploration," Versia said.

"To find what?"

Vashti flung out her hands, and two knives came out of each, hitting the men. They fell, clutching their bleeding necks. She pushed the others off using her psychokinesis, dropping them into the water.

"Take us there, and you'll live," Vashti said.

They changed into their diving gear and sat on the yacht's railing. They fell backward into the water and swam into the blackness before entering an underwater cave. A large animal skulked behind them as they trod water in front of the cave.

"I hope you brought your weapons. The one thing preserving this site is its presence of sharks." The instructor said.

Hexagons formed in Versia's hand, creating his katana. The great white shark charged at him, hitting him head-on and knocking him into a rock wall. It turned towards Vashti and rammed her head-on, sending her reeling into the cave. The guide pulled out an underwater modified machine gun and shot at the great white. The bullets hit the shark's thick skin, and it swam to safety.

They continued swimming into the cave and the current picked up, pulling them in a circle. They spun faster and faster as the current dragged them down. Stone structures shot out and clamped around their feet, ancient weight traps. Versia's ears popped as he looked around the underwater structure. He stretched out his hand as the weights pulled them down. He shot a Psychic shockwave from his hand, destroying part of the structure. The current slowed as the structure crumbled, and what he did triggered an underwater earthquake. The ground shook, and cracks formed in the walls around them. The entire structure collapsed, dropping large chunks of rocks on the divers. Versia and Vashti dodged the stones with their powers, but rocks fell, entrapping their instructor. Seconds later, drops of blood flowed upwards. A new structure revealed itself after the wall collapsed, sucking them in and hitting them with a dose of green. Exotic birds and wild animals roamed through the city's greenery-covered ruins as the duo pulled off their masks.

"Are we going to acknowledge that?" Vashti asked.

"He was a Circle sleeper. He already gave them our location," Versia said.

"So we let him die."

"What difference could we have made?" Versia said.

"I thought you, of all people, valued human life," Vashti said.

Versia double-tapped his wrist, showing a hologram of a transmission going through.

"I don't know how long till they'll be here, but we have to find the book," Versia said.

They walked up the steps of the yellowing temple. The steps had luminescent arrows pointing travelers to where to go. The duo came to a large stone cap at the top of the temple. The cap had inscriptions in an ancient language.

Meadow scanned the cap and indicated it weighed a few thousand pounds. Versia grabbed it with his hands and lifted it with ease. The top of the temple shattered, dropping them into the interior. It still had a faded yellow color, similar to the outside, yet glowed.

"Well this is clean for a thousand years of solitude," Vashti said.

In each corner rested a gold rectangle, along with gold lines stretching from each rectangle converging onto one point at the center of the temple, a cinnamon-colored book with rough corners and yellowing pages. The cover had scratches and a Circle symbol. Versia grabbed the book, and a door slid open. They walked outside, and Versia held the book up in the sunlight. A bullet shot through the book, turning it into a flutter of pages, and both of them leaped behind a large boulder in front of the temple as Circle agents rained gunfire on them from their all-black machine guns while snipers perched in trees aimed with laser sights and scopes. Versia looked at the few pages still in his hand and tossed them. Vashti threw three knives, hitting three targets. Versia threw two knives, hitting two targets. The remaining agents continued shooting at them. One whizzed past Versia, the heat radiating onto him as it soared millimeters from his skin.

From behind, sharp icicles pierced Circle agents on the ground as the snipers in the trees became encased in ice as an all-white Psychic suit with ice blue lines on it hovered in mid-air and landed. The helmet retracted, revealing an Indian man. Versia walked over, did their handshake, and hugged him with one arm.

"Good to see you, Sanjiv," Versia said.

"Good to see you," Sanjiv said.

Vashti hugged him.

"Good to see you. I know the Jasmine situation was hard on both of you," Vashti said.

"Yeah, it was a thing," Sanjiv said.

"So what are you doing here?" Versia asked.

"Project Red, he's hitting a Circle base in the Middle East. Supposedly, they've designed Psychanium-aided nuclear weapons. The White House is mad because they paid US scientists to help with the designs. They want this plugged a week ago. Thought you'd like to know."

"Thanks for the heads up," Versia said.

"Should we drop in and help him out?" Sanjiv asked.

"Of course," Versia said.

****

They arrived in the country after Project Red. He had already removed the front gate guards and confronted more security. Their bullets bounced off his all-red armor. He stretched out his hand, and Psychic shockwaves flew out, knocking the guards back into the walls. He continued forward, approaching the complex.

"Where do you think you're going," A voice yelled.

Project Red turned around and looked towards him.

"Issac is it," The man asked.

Project Red's helmet retracted, revealing a man with short brown hair, white skin, and brown monolid eyes.

Two metal gladiator suits rose from the ground, each black and silver—one with a sword and shield and the other with a hammer and shield. The men climbed into both suits. They both stepped towards Issac. Red hexagons formed in Issac's hand and created a flame-red Korean geom sword with a brilliant red aura glowing around it.

The first suit swung its sword at him, but he blocked with his own. The second suit slammed its hammer into his back, throwing him through a nearby wall. Issac groaned inside the suit as he pulled himself out of the debris. The sword gladiator suit boosted forward and sliced at him. He rolled out of the way. Six mini missiles formed on his back and shot at the suits, exploding around them. Issac boosted forward and punched the hammer suit in the face. The hammer suit swung on him again, smashing him into the ground. The suit returned its hammer and prepared to bring it down on Issac. The suit struggled and turned around to its hammer, encased in ice. He turned to Sanjiv, who double-tapped his chest, forming a white suit with ice-blue lines on his body, The Project White Psychic Suit. Issac rolled to his feet and pulled his red cape behind him.

The sword suit had pulled itself up and looked at the two suits. It flew at Sanjiv. Time slowed around him, and a white sword formed in his hand. Sanjiv's sword met the other suits. The gladiator struggled, but Sanjiv held his ground. A rocket-powered mallet formed from nanites on Sanjiv's right hand and uppercutted the sword suit. It staggered before regaining its balance. Issac blocked the gladiator hammer strike with a nanotech shield formed in his arm and kicked the suit. He blasted it with a shot from his hand laser, and it slammed into a wall, leaving behind cracks. Sanjiv blocked another sword strike and swung his arm, sending a barrage of razor-sharp icicles toward the sword suit. It blocked four, but the others scratched at the suits, carving shallow gashes through the metal. The two gladiators circled Sanjiv and Issac.

"Get down," Issac said.

Sanjiv ducked. Issac spun around, firing star-temperature lasers at the two suits that blocked them with their Psychanium shields. Sanjiv from below shot two ice beams at the suits, and they both staggered.

Issac shot an orb of red energy into the sky. It exploded in the air, causing small energy meteors to fall. They crashed into the two suits surrounding Issac and Sanjiv and leveled everything in their path. When the dust settled, the meteors had decimated everything, and the two suits lay there, charred. Only their Psyhcanium weapons had survived. Versia and Vashti landed.

"Those were Psychanium-made and powered suits," Versia said.

"We're both of you watching the whole time?" Issac asked.

"You seemed to have chemistry," Versia said.

He walked over to the charred suit on his right and touched it.

"Providence will clean this up later and recover the Psychanium," Versia said.

"What next?" Issac asked.

Their wrists buzzed at the same time.

"I guess that's for us," Versia said.

"Yeah," Sanjiv said.

Issac shot off into the sky and disappeared in a sonic boom. Sanjiv shot off next, leaving Versia and Vashti.

CHAPTER 8

"The quick bunny hopped over to the carrots and nibbled to his heart's content," Jasmine read to the group of children at the library.

"With a big smile, he hopped to his other friends and excitedly led them to the carrots he had found. They hopped over and ate till they fell asleep. The End."

Jasmine closed the book and handed it to her assistant. The children stood and ran off into other parts of the library while parents came up and thanked her for reading to the kids. She picked up her black business jacket and put it over her black knee-length dress.

"Ms. Shahvaya, they've canceled your 1:00 library reading. They're saying parents aren't comfortable having a Psychic read to their kids after what happened in New York." Her assistant said.

"That's unfortunate," Jasmine said, her lips contorting. "Did we send flowers to Amy Silas? Tragic what happened."

"Yes, I sent a bouquet of black roses as you instructed."

"Thank you, Madi," Jasmine said as they made their way through the library.

A young girl came up to Jasmine, who knelt beside her.

"My mommy said you're going to save us from the bad people," the girl said. Jasmine had to lean in to hear.

"Don't you worry yourself. You'll be fine," Jasmine said with a white smile.

She cupped her hands and created a glassy black ball with wisps of smoke inside it. She gave it to the girl.

"If you're ever scared, look in there, and you'll see yourself as I do," Jasmine said.

The girl looked inside, and her eyes expanded. She hugged Jasmine and returned to her mom, who typed on her phone.

"Sanjiv's called you multiple times. I keep telling him when you're ready, you'll reach out," Madi said as they walked out of the library and to a waiting car.

A group of protestors had gathered outside of the library. The lead protestor held a megaphone.

"Right there is Jasmine Shahvaya. Jasmine is a consultant for Providence and, per my inside sources, is responsible for the cruelest weapons in their arsenal, a weapon designed to melt your insides. What's worse is she attempts to wash her and her family's image by reading books to children. Her family has ruled India for thousands of years, not as kings, but from the shadows, as dealers of the most valuable metal on the earth, and she is heir to this dynasty, yet what has she brought to us, nothing but death." The man screamed as he walked towards her. Jasmine's security stepped in front of the man.

"I hope you rot in hell," the protestor said. "You're not saviors, you're not guardians, you are typos, the universe's incorrect equation, you are not humans, you are monsters."

Jasmine's security shoved him and ushered her and Madi into an all-black SUV. They drove to Jasmine's high rise in the city and took an elevator to the penthouse floor. Minutes later, three raps tapped the door and she opened it to Sanjiv holding a bouquet of white and blue roses. She hugged him and let him in.

"I heard a protester got in your face today," He said.

"Nothing we don't deserve," Jasmine said.

"Deserve is a strong word."

"A bomb in New York killed 700 people. A bomb only we are supposed to have, a bomb we promised everybody would never stray from our hands."

"It wasn't your fault," Sanjiv said.

"So I've heard," Jasmine said, folding her arms. "So, are you around, or does Isazisi have a mission for me?"

"I wanted to see you," Sanjiv said as he handed her the roses.

She inhaled the roses, turned around, and walked towards her kitchen. She placed the roses on the counter in the center of her kitchen.

"We're not a thing, that ship sailed a while ago," Jasmine said.

"What do you mean that ship sailed, you're the one captaining it," Sanjiv responded.

"Oh, so it's my fault, not you, and Isazisi, and Versia and the rest of you, all your secrets, your little boy's club where you pranced around the world acting like spies, destroying any goodwill we had left, spending money you didn't earn, killing people who didn't need to die, hiding all of it from me, and Reese, and all the others."

"What we did was follow orders from the top, they didn't want you involved, because they didn't know how comfortable you'd be with the things we did."

"I'm not comfortable with the things you did, especially after what was my last mission for years, and you all decided it was ok to go around bombing people and torturing them?"

"Everything we did, was to ensure what we have today, we were young, and we thought what we were doing was right, and it was."

"And you're still trying to defend it. You were killing people who you could've arrested, you were using our weapons to target people the top brass of Providence didn't like. Isazisi wasn't even the director at this point, all of you just blindly followed orders."

"We didn't want to tell you after what happened on your mission, you already started to pull away..."

"That was after I found a file in our room, of you and the others standing over a pile of bodies, what was I supposed to do? You knew how I felt about things at that time. Then you lied to me about it, saying it was fake when it wasn't."

"What does this even have to do with our relationship?"

"You were not under orders to not tell me, all of you decided you weren't going to tell the women in your lives and then when I did find out, you decided to be a liar about it."

"Well, you have no problem killing now."

"I reserve that for people who deserve it, not like you and your boys club who do it because you think it's fun."

"I don't even know what you want me to say, the fact we fell apart cannot only be because of the task force."

"I don't want to get into it."

"Then you never want to get into it."

"What were we, a fling?" Jasmine asked.

"I'm not sure. We both wanted more, and you know that." Sanjiv said.

"You know how unstable both of us were at the time. Nothing good would've ever come from that," Jasmine said.

"We can't know that," Sanjiv said.

"I'll assume Isazisi has info for me," Jasmine said.

"Yeah, your protestor might not be any protestor. Madi's smart contact took a picture, and he pulled all the info Providence could get."

He handed her a folder, and she read through it.

At night, the protestor awoke to clammy, frigid, shadowy hands caressing him as he slept, along with the whispers of dismembered voices. He shot up to Jasmine standing in an all-black Psychic Suit at the foot of his bed, her helmet off. He lunged towards a bedside table for his gun.

"I wouldn't," Jasmine said.

She let the bullets from his weapon fall from her palm and hit the wooden floor in a series of clinks.

"Nice apartment for a professional protestor."

"I work hard on the side, too," the protestor said as he pulled his red blanket closer to his body.

"We pulled your bank records and hacked your texts. We know what they offered you to infiltrate protests and instigate with a Psychic. Your first purchase shouldn't have been the most expensive apartment you could find."

"What does it matter to you?"

"Many people would be more than happy to have Providence kick in your door and drag you out in cuffs, bringing shame to you, your family, and everything you've ever represented, but I'm giving you a chance. Who paid you?"

"I can't, they'll kill me."

Jasmine's skin turned pale, and her eyes turned black. She

lunged forward like a shadow and whispered in his ear. Black streaks moved across his face, spreading from his ear. His eyes turned silky black, and he screamed. He rolled around in the bed, attempting to escape whatever he saw. Jasmine flicked her hand, and his eyes returned to normal. The protestor panted as beads of sweat formed on his body.

"Ok, ok. The name's James Gritz. He contacted me and offered a ton of money to instigate with Psychics."

"Where can I find him?"

"When I talked to him on the phone I could hear loud music in the background. I googled him, and he owns a club called 'Ice Island,' I'm sure you can find out wherever that is."

"Your help is much appreciated," Jasmine said before disappearing into a wisp of black smoke.

Sanjiv sat in Jasmine's apartment. He ran his fingers through Japamala beads as he waited for Jasmine. She appeared in a wisp of black smoke.

"The person who contacted him is based in the club Ice Island. I had Providence pull a file on him. James Gritz. He pushes drugs, girls, and weapons through his club while running a small casino there for money laundering. Prosecutors couldn't nail him on anything, so he walked. We don't have the same issue." Jasmine said.

"It's been a while since we've been out together," Sanjiv said.

"We can talk after the mission," she said, rolling her eyes.

"Of course."

Jasmine knocked on the large metal door to the club. It slid open with a shrieking grind. A muscular bouncer with black hair and brown eyes in an all-black tuxedo looked her up and down in her black, backless, knee-high sequin dress.

"Do you have an invitation?" He said, with a sneer on his face and a large scar on his nose.

"Do you know who I am?" She asked.

The bouncer did a double take on her.

"Yeah, yeah, I saw you on the news, that bomb in New York. What the hell are you doing here?"

"I'm here to see your boss, James Gritz."

The sneer on his face contorted.

"Ain't nobody named James Gritz here. Last I heard, he's in Europe on business, but I'm the bouncer. What would I know?"

"I'm here to see James Gritz."

The bouncer motioned to another large man.

"Said she wants to see Mr. Gritz," the first bouncer said.

"Ain't nobody here named Gritz. You should get lost before any trouble comes of this. You look like a nice girl," The second bouncer said.

Sanjiv walked up behind her.

"Having trouble getting in?" He asked.

"This your lady?" The second bouncer asked.

"Yeah," Sanjiv replied.

"I suggest both of you find another place to party. Wouldn't want any blood getting everywhere." The same bouncer said.

"Who's?" Sanjiv asked.

The first bouncer pulled out a gun, and Jasmine reacted, throwing her knee into his wrist. He grunted in pain while Sanjiv punched the second bouncer in the face. They raced into the club, where they encountered more security. They both ducked as shots rang out. Jasmine rushed forward, ripping the gun from the man's hand and raking him across the face with it. She slid behind a wall as bullets riddled the location where she'd been. She retaliated, shooting the bouncer. Sanjiv slipped under gunfire and disarmed a bouncer. He shot another two running towards him. He ducked under the swing of a bouncer and body-slammed the man into a wall. Two icicles formed in his hands, and he stabbed them into the man, pinning him to the wall. He screamed in pain as he grabbed at the two icicles in his shoulders.

"Hey, hey, hey," A man yelled. "You're scaring the patrons. You wanted to see Gritz. Here I am."

Jasmine dropped the clip from the gun and threw it to the side.

"Let's talk in my office."

Grtiz led them to his office, and his bouncer closed the door behind them.

"What's with the song and dance out there? If you needed me, I'm sure the two of you could've handled it a different way."

"Your security said you weren't here," Sanjiv said.

"Well, now I am, what's the fuss?"

"Your Circle connections," Jasmine said.

Gritz looked at his bouncer and nodded. The bouncer left.

"I'm not a member of that cult. Occasionally, they come around and ask for a gun or two, pay top dollar. Other than that, I have nothing to do with their attacks. As you know, I don't deal in Psychanium for obvious reasons," He said as he motioned at the two Psychics sitting across from him.

A brown-haired woman with a tray came to the door outside Gritz's office. The bouncer stopped her.

"He's not taking any visitors."

"He'll want to see me."

The woman slit the bouncer's throat, he fell against the wall and slid down. The woman opened the door.

"Theo, I said not to..." Gritz began. "Fay?"

Jasmine looked up at the mention of the name. The woman pulled a gun from underneath the tray and shot Gritz. He slumped over.

Jasmine reacted as Fay raced out of the office, and Sanjiv followed. Club music pulsated as the woman weaved her way through the dancing patrons. Jasmine followed her through the crowd while Sanjiv followed from the catwalk above. A punch hit Jasmine from the crowd. She looked around at a sea of people dancing, a leg swept her off her feet. She stood and looked around.

"I can't find her," Jasmine radioed.

"Hold on, I see her," Sanjiv said. "She left the crowd, and she's moving towards a hallway in the back. Sanjiv hopped over the railing and followed her in. Jasmine caught up to him. Half a dozen shots rang out, hitting Sanjiv. He fell with a grunt. Club patrons screamed and flooded out the exits as gunshots rang.

Jasmine knelt beside Sanjiv who bled from six different holes in his abdomen.

"Stay with me, stay with me," she said as she slapped his face to keep him conscious. His eyes glasses over as she tapped her wrist, activating her emergency beacon. Her smart contact scanned for his heart rate while a Providence medical jet landed on her position and put Sanjiv on a stretcher. They asked her questions, their voices faint and distant to her. She had to lean against the wall to stabilize herself. She stumbled, following the stretcher to the medical jet, and two Centurions helped her up.

They flew to a hospital while Jasmine held his limp hand the whole way.

"If you love me, you won't leave me," she whispered into his ear.

They brought him to a Providence hospital and wheeled him off the jet. Jasmine stayed back. Her black dress had blood on it, and she looked down at her shaking hands. They had splotches of red on them. She leaned back against her seat, motionless.

The doctor came out to her a few hours later.

"He's stable. Took six Psychanium rifle rounds. Four hit his stomach, two hit his chest, they missed his heart by inches," the doctor said.

"Thank you," Jasmine said.

She walked into Sanjiv's room.

"How are you feeling?" She asked.

"It's not the first time I've been shot," he joked.

"Yeah," she said. "Gritz will live. We'll send people over to question him once he's recovered enough from his injuries."

"What you said to me on the jet," Sanjiv said. "What does that mean for us?"

"Sanjiv, I can't be hurt by losing anyone else."

"You won't lose me."

"I almost did," she said.

She'd left his hospital room and walked into a large office.

"Her name is Fay, the woman who shot him," she said.

"We have one name on file. Fay Harlow, she's a high-ranking

Circle agent, we've wanted her in custody for a while." An agent said.

"Find her," Jasmine said. "I'll handle the rest."

****

Caitlyn squatted, perched on a gorgeous Hong Kong skyscraper, the crescent moon illuminating her Chinese features. The silver sliver cast a cold, gentle light over the city while billions of stars danced across the sky above her. Her jet-black hair fluttered in the night's wind as she looked over a nearby skyscraper, a flat glass and metal spire stretching above the skyline.

The flashing red and blue lights of Hong Kong police surrounding the building pulsated below her while the abductors made their demands. She jumped off her perch, and the jets on the back of her midnight blue Psychic Suit puffed out compressed air, allowing her to latch onto the tenth floor undetected. The dark blue lines of energy running through her suit pulsated as she stuck to a glass pane and pulled a midnight blue arrow out of her quiver. Bolts of lightning streaked up and down the weapon. She stuck it onto the glass, and three arms extended from it, cutting a hole with lightning-hot tips. She pulled it from the pane and kicked in the piece it had cut. The glass shattered as it hit the floor, alerting two guards to her presence. She threw the arrow she had in her hand at one man, hitting him in the chest. She engaged in hand-to-hand combat with the other guard. They traded blows until she had him on one knee. She slipped behind him, snapped his neck, and let the body drop onto the linoleum floor with a wet thud.

She moved on without a sound, traversing up seven more floors with no encounters. On floor seventeen, she encountered four men. They each pulled out six-inch knives as they fanned out to flank her from four sides. In her hands, hexagons formed in the shape of a bow, creating The Lightning Bow and small blades extended from both tips. The men struck first, stabbing at Caitlyn. She blocked their blades as she walked backward, fending them off. One man rolled behind her and drove his knife into her back. The knife shattered into a million pieces while the man staggered as his hand still vibrated from the knife's destruction. In one swift motion, she pulled an arrow and shot him in the chest. She slit the other three's throats, killing them without a second thought. She moved up the building without a sound, taking out additional guards with the Lighting Bow. She came to the 40th floor, snuck into the rutters, and watched from above. The man in charge walked around his blood-covered hostages with a baton.

"Duck, duck, goose," he said as he settled on one.

He drew back the baton and swung forward. Caitlyn threw a device at the wall behind him, generating electromagnetic waves, pulling their guns and the baton to the back wall. She shot three of the defenseless triad members with arrows to the chest and dropped down, hitting four more of them with her bow. A blade came out from the bottom of her bow, and she jabbed it into the ground. Electricity rippled through the floor. It electrocuted the last standing triad members, who fell, clutching their chests.

"What the...?" The leader of the triad cell said, backing away from her as she walked towards him.

She cut the government officials loose, and drew two arrows, shooting the triad leader in the chest. The freed government officials turned around to thank her. She led them to the entrance of the building, where they exited to great fanfare from hundreds of worried civilians on the ground, Caitlyn disappeared onto the roof without a trace. She jumped onto another building and made her way to a waiting car Versia sat in.

"Circle agents caused the hostage situation. While everyone focused on that, they hit a Providence Hong Kong armory." Versia said.

"What'd they take?"

"Everything."

Caitlyn cursed.

****

Isazisi dragged himself back to the beach. He opened the suit while lying flat on his back, taking a deep breath of fresh air.

"Sir, the suit is airtight and can filter oxygen for days. Please stop overreacting."

"Fine, where am I?"

"Off the coast of Florida."

"What, how?"

"The underwater current dragged you."

"How long was...?"

"Nine hours."

"Where's our nearest base?"

"They're already on their way."

A row of SUVs pulled up to the beach, and Isazisi stepped in. They drove him back to base and he walked on a jet back to home base. He watched satellites around known Circle bases tracking their troop movements and weapons shipments. The feed cut.

"Megan, what happened?"

"Missiles struck three of our satellites." She replied.

"Fire on their known bases in zero population areas," Isazisi said as his eyes darted around the screen.

Across the world, missile silos opened, satellite lasers charged up, and fighter jets took off from Providence aircraft carriers. The missiles took off into space and crashed back down to Earth, hitting their targets. The satellites fired, incinerating Circle bases in the deserts and the rainforests, and his fighter jets dropped bombs on Circle-controlled Islands throughout the oceans.

"All hits confirmed. We're dispatching troops to confirm kills," Megan said.

"Retask the satellites onto finding new bases," Isazisi said.

"Yes, sir," Meadow said.

Isazisi walked into the courtroom once again. His curly, onyx black hair combed, forming a perfect hairline, and his starry dark brown eyes sparkled in the camera's flashes as his tuxedo complimented the entire look. Cameras flashed around him, and reporters talked amongst themselves before the hearing began.

"So, you're telling us you were in the house when they took the Secretary of State and didn't do anything." The committee leader said.

"If I attacked, they would have killed the guests. They rigged a bomb under the house to explode if a small machine embedded in their skin didn't detect their pulse until after a certain time. The Secretary of State would be dead if I attacked along with everyone else in the house."

"Couldn't you contain the air around the explosion?" The committee leader asked.

"They had multiple bombs, and I didn't know which one would go off," Isazisi replied.

"But still, you could have done…something?" The committee leader asked.

"If I could've done anything, I would have tried," Isazisi said.

"Frankly speaking, there is a vocal minority who wants to see you court-martialed for everything you've caused." The sub-committee leader said. "But, I still believe in the good you can do. I was great friends with Duncan Silas. A man who dedicated his life to more than himself. If he believed in you, I have no reason not to."

"Thank you. The threats won't ever stop, and they won't hold back, neither will we."

"Unfortunately, I must continue with the questions. I apologize if my tone comes off as condescending. How did they escape you that easily?"

"They built bullet train tracks through a city without anyone bringing it up. A company called 'ForTrack.' built the infrastructure. They won a government bid to build new high-speed lines and paid off government inspectors to ignore and falsely report their progress. The company has no employees, and its executives are off the grid. I was then shot out of the sky by a Providence weapon when I gave chase."

"That's disappointing." The committee leader said,

contorting his lips.

"Hypothetically, what would happen if the Circle used your weapons on the wider world, worse than attacking buildings?" The leader asked.

"Chances are it would end up killing a sizable portion of the population," Isazisi said. "They'd want to kill Psychics because a large enough attack disrupting and overwhelming emergency services while leaving them with a monopoly on Psychanium technology is more than likely their endgames."

"That's hard to hear, but Duncan said he would put his trust in a Psychic. He said to me before his death that you are the most motivated Psychic when it comes to taking down the Circle. When I pressed him for details, he said it wasn't his place to share. Whatever it is, I will not ask you to open yourself up on camera, but I want everyone to know. I have my trust in you."

"Thank you," Isazisi said.

****

Vashti walked down the street late at night in a low-cut dress with high heels. The crescent moon shone above as a man sat on a bench where she walked past.

"Hey baby, let me buy you a drink," he shouted.

"I don't drink," she said.

"One time." He said. "Come on, you're pretty."

He stood and followed her. Vashti picked up her pace, she stumbled in her high heels. Another man walked towards her from in front, and she darted into a nearby walkway where three other men came out from behind boxes, crates, and a garbage can.

"This one's a beauty. She'll sell quickly." A man said.

"What," Vashti said.

A man rushed her from behind and chloroformed her.

A black van pulled up, and they dragged her in and zip-tied her. On top of a nearby building, Isazisi followed her with a sniper rifle.

"The tracker in her dress is active," Isazisi relayed to Versia.

He slid down a wooden plank to the next building and stayed with the van. It drove eight miles and stopped at an all-black warehouse with a gray roof, the doors ripped off their hinges and wooden planks placed to conceal the inside. The warehouse roof had large holes from years of neglect, and Isazisi took up a perch and aimed inside. The men dragged her out of the van and sat her on the floor with three dozen other girls. Most had makeup running down their faces and marks on their skin from where their abductors had hit them.

"Contact our buyers, tell them the bidding starts at 20 thousand each." One man said.

"You can let us go, or you can face a Psychic," Vashti said.

The men in the room turned to her, their faces red with anger but with eyebrows perked up in surprise. The other girls in the warehouse looked at her with puppy eyes and hands pleading, afraid they'd be beaten again for Vashti's actions. A man walked up to Vashti and slapped her across the face. The sound rang as he followed through. Vashti recoiled, her skin red from the strike. The other girls recoiled for her and shrunk themselves down, avoiding the eye of their captors.

"Shut your mouth. You're lucky you're worth more with your tongue intact. No Psychic is coming to save you." One man said.

She lifted her untied wrists. Everyone in the room stopped breathing for half a second and raised their guns. They looked around, eyes darting from side to side and heads of swivels as they searched for who neglected to tie her.

"You said you restrained her." One man shouted.

"She was." Another replied.

"Shut up, tie her again."

He walked forward with the rope in hand to tie her again. A sniper shot rang out and hit the man in the back of his chest. Everyone ducked and the women screamed. Vashti made her move. She swept the man closest to her off his feet, bringing him down to her level. She swung on top of him and punched him in the face, knocking him out. She rolled off him in one motion and onto her feet. She threw two pink shurikens, hitting two men in their necks. Isazisi sniped another man in the back who made a run for it. He jumped down onto the roof and dropped into the warehouse. He pushed the sniper barrel in, switched the gun to rapid-fire, and shot at the traffickers.

Vashti blocked one man's punch and hit him in the face. She dodged a secondary strike and elbowed the man in the neck, causing him to double over. She kneed him in the face and skirted the knife swipe of another man. He swung again, catching her in the cheek. She reeled from the cut but blocked another strike, and kneed him in the elbow, causing him to drop the knife. She hit him with a strike to the neck and a knee to the stomach. She threw him down face first, slamming him against the concrete floor of the warehouse. Versia landed in the building as Isazisi took cover while the traffickers returned fire. Versia ran out and kneed an attacker, throwing the man into a set of crates. He ducked as another trafficker clubbed him with their gun. He elbowed the man in the stomach and swept him off his feet. He blocked another man who swung at him and kicked him back. He rolled, grabbed a loose gun off the floor, and shot three of the traffickers. He threw the weapon, hitting another trafficker in the head. The last man shot at Isazisi, who slipped under the gunfire and disarmed the man. He fired off one final round, missing Isazisi by a millimeter. A burning radiated onto his skin as the bullet whizzed by his face. A woman screamed in pain as it entered her stomach. Isazisi knocked out the last man and ran to the side of the bleeding woman.

"She's lost a lot of blood," Megan screamed in his ear as he ripped a shirt off a trafficker and pressed his hands on the wound.

"What can I do," he asked Megan.

"She's bleeding internally. The bullet frayed into shrapnel on its way in. Pulling out the individual shards with your powers would cause more bleeding while using your powers to cauterize the wound would result in an explosion as it's an incendiary round."

"That's our weapon," Isazisi said, his voice trailing.

"Unfortunately so," Megan replied.

"Scramble a medical jet to my location, priority zero," Isazisi said.

Within minutes, they loaded the woman into the jet and flew to the nearest hospital. Other agents took statements from the other thirty-five women and arrested the Circle agents still alive. An agent came up to Isazisi, his hands still coated in blood and shaking.

"Sir, we have the man who shot her. He's the Circle task force leader. His name is Ethan Palmer." the Providence agent said.

"Have him placed in an interrogation room on sublevel seventeen," Isazisi said as he forced his hands to stop.

"Yes, sir."

Isazisi entered the hospital and took an elevator to the floor of the woman. The doctor stood there waiting for him. Isazisi read his face. His eyebrows contorted in a tight shape, his lips, while sealed, could be seen practicing the words he would say, his hand tapped against the clipboard while he steeled his already failing face. The doctor took a deep breath before he spoke.

"She died fifteen minutes after arrival. We couldn't remove the shrapnel from the bullet, and she'd already lost too much blood for surgery. Whatever weapon hit her ensured the kill. We couldn't do anything." The doctor said.

"Thank you," Isazisi said as he looked away.

The doctor left to attend to his other patients, and Isazisi sat in a waiting room chair. He interlocked his fingers in front of his mouth and released a deep breath as he blinked his eyes rapidly. His right foot shifted with discomfort as he sat. He took his hands from his mouth and looked at them as they shook.

"Another Providence weapon, huh," he said.

He walked to the room and looked at the body through the window as he played with the black and red Psychanium ring around his index finger. Only her neck and face remained uncovered by the white sheet as her pale and lifeless body lay motionless. A Providence agent walked up behind him.

"We're contacting next of kin," The agent said.

"Offer to pay for the funeral anonymously," Isazisi said without turning away from the window.

"Yes, sir." The agent said. "The group's leader is in custody awaiting interrogation."

"Thank you," Isazisi said as he looked at her body for the last time. He turned around and left.

****

The man woke up in a dark room, both arms handcuffed to a chair and still groggy from the knockout drugs. He licked around his dry mouth and lips. The lights flashed on, and he grimaced at the change in brightness. The same girl his people kidnapped sat across from him on the other side of a metal desk.

"Hey beautiful, whatcha gonna do to me." He said as he laughed until she slammed his head into the desk.

He recoiled hard, his nose bleeding.

"If this is an interrogation, I'm not saying a thing." The man said.

"Where is The Chairman's based?" She asked.

"The Chairman? The last agent that got too close got mailed back in a box. What do you think he'll do to you."

"Nothing as terrible as what he'll do to you," Vashti said.

She stood as Isazisi entered the room.

"Where's my lawyer? Don't I get due process?" The man asked.

"Mr. Ethan Palmer," Isazisi said without a hint of emotion. "Her name was Savannah."

"I asked for a lawyer," the man said.

"We don't have to do that," Isazisi said as he placed a photo on the metal table. "She was nineteen, her birthday was last week, she was a pre-med student on her way to becoming a pediatrician, and you killed her. That's one murder charge, along with another thirty- seven counts of human trafficking. Tack on your ties to a terrorist group, and you'll leave prison in a coffin." Isazisi said.

"Lawyer." The man said.

"We don't have to do that," Isazisi said. "It's not like the Circle would spend a dime on you. They've never liked your methods of trafficking. They see them as crude, dangerous, and risky. They prefer to use fake modeling agencies to target women in countries that won't care, places like Africa, South Asia, Latin America, and Eastern Europe. They'll let you rot, and because of what you did to her, I'll make your life hell wherever I send you."

The man panted at a sprinter's pace. "You can't do that, it's illegal." He said.

"I operate in a gray world, where nothing is clear, a world where my actions around the world secure the freedoms of millions in exchange for the vilest acts Providence can commit. When it comes to the Circle, it's nice to have a black-and-white enemy. Nobody will care what I do to you, talk." Isazisi said.

"There, you said it. You said what everyone knows, but none dare to speak." The man said, chuckling. "What makes you different from us? A piece of paper giving you the right to trample over whomever you please? How many flags bearing your family's symbol fly outside Providence's base? How many millions did you and the other Psychics spend buying Capitol Hill last year?

Governments blindly give you power under the guise of security, yet we took your weapons for years without detection. You have access to billions of dollars, yet millions starve. You hold the keys to unlimited clean energy, yet the world still pumps fossil fuels into the air. You could end every war on the planet with the snap of your fingers, yet your weapons are the most coveted items in war zones. Who are you to speak of black and white?"

"Don't take the moral high ground," Isazisi said.

"Don't act like you don't love it. The violence, the death, the suffering you cause to those you perceive as your enemies, you revel in it. You kill, maim, and torture, yet are placed on the cover of magazines as a hero. What we've done is show the world what you are: nothing but hypocrites, liars, zealots. Your army, how large is it? Five million strong, six million, eight, ten? Does it matter? The world will let you prance around with an army of millions, loyal only to you and your own, yet shriek when we do the same?" The man said.

"I'm not a terrorist," Isazisi said. "My disposition to do violence is reserved for those who deserve it."

"To your people, you're not a terrorist, yet how do you determine who deserves your brand of death? How many countries have you and your ancestors destabilized chasing your objectives? In how many of those countries was that the objective? How many governments have you overthrown to force your will? How many war crimes have you committed chasing what you call peace? How many elections have you rigged, chasing a leader who would be loyal to your cause? How many people have you alone killed? Most of those extrajudicial, of course. How many people do you lock in your prisons, depriving them of due process and ignoring the need to justify their incarceration?

How many versions of Guantanamo Bay do you and your 'covert ops' division run, torturing people until they give you what you want? Your family, along with the Psychics, are the greatest cause of human suffering on this planet. Your tradition is to cause the human race suffering until they kneel before you in fealty. Your metal could solve wars, hunger, anything, yet you hide it away under the guise of sacrality and tradition. The world knows it, I know it, even you know it. Your heritage, your legacy, and your tradition are nothing but murder, destruction, and indifference to suffering. If I'm a terrorist, you and your family are the best the world has ever seen."

Isazisi didn't answer.

"You see the thing with labels. They complicate everything because each is a two-way street." The man said.

"You don't believe any of that, do you?" Isazisi asked.

"You didn't answer my questions." The man said.

"You didn't answer mine," Isazisi said.

"Refuse to answer my questions. The world will know one day, as for you. We will take this world by any means and right the wrongs your people have propagated for centuries. If that means killing a few million people, I'll do it because whatever sacrifice will be the saving grace of millions more. But what I love even more is the blood is on your hands, the same way it's on mine. This world will shatter under the weight of your actions." The man said with a smile on his face.

"You're sick," Isazisi said.

"Aren't we all a bit sadistic in the head?" The man asked.

"I've entertained you long enough. You said you'd answer both of my questions, start talking," Isazisi said.

"He wouldn't talk, I had to pull it from his mind. A high-level Circle leader is moving by convoy with high explosives. I can hit it.

"Got you, we'll be on standby if you need anything," Versia said.

****

Isazisi perched on a cliff overlooking a dusty mountain road where below an eighteen-wheeler flanked by six SUVs rolled up the road. Isazisi slid down the cliffside and kicked an SUV off the cliff.

"What was that?" A man asked.

Isazisi threw orbs through the windshields of the two others in the front. Their orbits decayed and they smashed together like two neutron stars, exploding and killing everyone inside. Both cars swerved out of control and flipped on their sides. The truck stopped in front of Red. The other three SUVs came to a stop beside it. Seven men jumped out of each, brandishing machine guns.

"Step off the road," one of the men said.

Isazisi raised his hand and blasted the megaphone from the other man's hand.

"Move, or we will shoot."

"That's the Red Cyan." A man to his right whispered in his ear.

His spine froze. "Fire," He yelled.

They shot, and the bullets bounced off his armor. His shoulder missiles ascended, and he took them out with one strike. The truck driver drove forward, attempting to ram him. The truck hit and crumpled in a "V" shape around him. He walked around back to open the door, but it swung open, surprising him. A woman lashed out, hitting him. She kicked him into the overturned truck and threw an electromagnet at him. It stuck to his chest and pulled him towards the nearest metal object, sticking him to it. By the time he had pulled himself off, she disappeared.

"Where'd she go?" He asked.

Megan scanned the area. "She's gone," Megan said.

"Did you scan her face?"

"Yes," she said, showing him an image of her and her known associates. A name caught his eye.

Isazisi sighed. "Megan," Isazisi said.

"Yes."

"Call Ivan Kakorski."

He flew up and towards a Providence base.

From underneath the truck, the woman uncloaked. She held a Providence device near her chest hiding her from detection. She brought out her phone and pressed a contact.

"He's going after Kakorski. Get to him first," she said.

CHAPTER 9

Isazisi's jet landed in Caracas, Venezuela. He already had a dozen troops on the ground. People moved in and out of the airport like usual, but Isazisi wasn't taking any chances. He stepped off the jet, and his agent rushed him to a five-car convoy of bulletproof cars.

Two all-black Psychanium SUVs in front with armed troops in both, a red SUV with dark tinted Psychanium-infused windows and tires in the middle, and two more black Psychanium SUVs behind him. The convoy took off at the same time, driving towards the wealthier part of the city.

The vehicles entered an upscale part of the city. Their cars fit right in with the series of luxury vehicles adorning each house, golden gates, white stone driveways, and ivory walls. The adornment of each house blinded him. They drove to the end of the three-mile-long neighborhood with its clean asphalt roads while the rest of the country crumbled. The cars pulled into the most prominent house on the street. The gate opened in preparation for them where they saw a series of luxury cars parked out front. Isazisi's troops jumped out of the vehicles and set up a perimeter while Isazisi stepped out of the middle car and walked through a line of his agents. A man stood waiting there with his security force behind him.

"Ivan, how are you?" Isazisi said with a cordial smile.

Ivan approached him and pulled out a gold pistol, holding it to Isazisi's forehead.

"You shouldn't have come. This country isn't your type."

"You're the one holding a gun to my head," Isazisi said as his Centurions spread out, encircling them, their guns cocking.

He pulled the trigger. The bullet stopped millimeters from Red's forehead, still spinning. It dropped to the floor with a metallic clink.

"Still powerful as ever," Ivan said while chuckling.

"Sir, you shouldn't have done that," Ivan's head of security said. He raised his hands and pulled the trigger again, killing his head of security. The body dropped to the ground with a wet *thud*. Isazisi looked at the body and said nothing.

"Come, we must discuss why you're here," Ivan said.

Isazisi signaled to his security force to wait.

He walked into Ivan's house. High-priced furniture adorned each corner, along with gold on everything. A group of Ivan's women sat around on the chairs near the pool. He kissed a woman on the cheek as he walked to a table covered by an umbrella. They sat across from each other while the server gave Ivan a beer.

"You want one?"

"I don't drink."

"You Psychics don't know how to have fun," Ivan said.

"We have plenty of fun," Isazisi said.

"So, what are you doing in my country?" Ivan asked.

"The Circle."

Ivan shifted in his seat at the mention of the name. His fist curled into a ball as he scratched at his thigh and rolled his shoulder against the chair.

"I know you sold half your drug empire to them, it's the source of their funding in this region, and I need to know their main base of operations. Where are they making the drugs?"

"I can't tell you that."

Isazisi raised his hand, and two of Ivan's guards' necks snapped in unison, and they fell into the pool.

"I know where you shop for mercenaries. Nobody will miss them."

"I can't tell you that," Ivan said again.

Isazisi made a fist and the windows on Ivan's house shattered, raining glass.

"Would you like me to start torturing people? You've seen my favorite methods."

Ivan stayed quiet.

"You don't own it anymore, and they don't own you," Isazisi said.

"I can't. Get out of my house." Ivan said.

Two of his guards walked forward, and their necks snapped after a single step. Isazisi made a fist, and Ivan's irises turned red. Around him, the landscape changed. He and Isazisi, while his house had become engulfed in flames, with only a few wooden stilts holding the rest of it up. Flames engulfed the pool, and it had turned from a clear blue color to an oil-filled black pool.

Bullet-ridden bodies or skeletons replaced where his guards and women stood. Above him, red smoke filled the sky. He raced to the front of the house where the gate had melted into a puddle of gold. His car exploded, and the shockwave and heat threw him back as a hot piece of shrapnel flew at him. He fell back in the chair and stumbled off it as he struggled to gain composure. His pool returned to normal, the house hadn't burned down, and the sky was clear blue. His cars in one piece, his other women and guards alive. Two of the women walked over to console him.

"What the hell." He yelled.

"I showed you I can take everything and everyone you love, everything you've built, and burn it to the ground."

"But, how did I see it? I felt those cars explode, the heat of the flames. I coughed because of the smoke, the bodies, the pool on fire. I smelled the oil..."

"I took over your brain's cerebrum. It's a complex psychic trick. Few of us can do it. So, are we going to do business?"

Ivan stayed quiet. Isazisi raised his hand, and two of Ivan's guards slammed into the wall behind him.

"That's four dead. Are we ready to talk?"

Ivan's guard handed him a pen and paper, and he wrote the address of an abandoned warehouse.

"You're on the right side of history," Isazisi said.

"Funny, considering how much effort your ancestors put into rewriting it," Ivan said.

Isazisi walked back to the front of the house as Ivan's face still twitched. He signaled to his guard, who leaned in.

"Gather our forces and prepare for an attack."

The guards walked to their communications center. His servant came to collect his beer bottle. Ivan threw the bottle to the ground and let off shots.

Isazisi stepped into the car, and they drove back to their base within the country. On the way, the first car in their convoy exploded, and the Psychanium tanked the hit, protecting everyone inside. A flaming car rolled into the intersection, blocking their way. Isazisi signaled to his people to stay in their cars as dozens of bullets bounced off the cars.

"Is this Ivan?" An agent asked.

"No," Isazisi replied.

Bullets hit the vehicles and bounced off.

"Megan, release compartment B18-46."

Back at Isazisi's base, a smooth-edged rectangle took off like a rocket. It rotated and flew towards Venezuela. As it neared its target, pieces of the rectangle broke off to form a streamlined shape. It spread its wings and sped up. It reached Venezuela and dropped small bombs on the cartel members. They scattered as pieces of asphalt flew into the air. The mini-jet followed them, shooting down the cartel members as it tracked them back to their leader. The mini-jet flew around in a circle above the building, scanning for the material. It relayed back intel showing an active drug operation with dozens of people working it inside.

"At least we know he didn't lie to us." His agents said.

"Yeah," said Isazisi.

****

Hours later, Isazisi perched on a building overlooking the drug operation. The drone identified a weak point on the roof he could drop in through. Isazisi tapped the front right of his neck, forming a red mask over his mouth and nose as his katana and a pistol formed in his hands. He jumped from the building and crashed into the roof. Cartel members at white foldable tables with beakers and cylinders looked up as wood, glass, and metal scattered everywhere from Isazisi's entrance as he shot in every direction. Glass broke and powder and chemicals sprayed everywhere. Cartel guards shot at him and he flipped over a metal desk, taking cover behind it.

"Megan, how many are there?"

"Twelve." She said.

He put down the sword and two black and red orbs formed in his hands. He threw them behind him. They clattered to the floor. The shooters looked down at them. They rose and spun in a decaying orbit, crashing together creating an explosion. Isazisi grabbed the sword, popped out from behind the desk, and shot again. Cartel members on a catwalk shot at him, the bullets grazed his skin. Beside him, several black SUVs crashed in through the walls, and a group of men jumped out and shot at him. He moved another desk with his **psychokinesis** to shield him from the bullets.

"Everybody stop shooting. Bring the hostage." Ivan said.

Isazisi stood behind the desks, crossing his gun hand over his katana hand.

"Anybody moves, and I snap your neck," Isazisi said.

Ivan held a gun to a woman in a headlock who worked at his house. She wore a skimpy flowing dress, with tears on her face.

"If you don't surrender, I will put a bullet through her head," Ivan said.

"And?" Isazisi asked.

"Don't play hard. Enough people know what happened at that hospital. The Circle has people everywhere. This gun is loaded with the same bullet, and I wonder what it does to a head?" Ivan said.

"I get over loss quickly," Isazisi said.

"I'll make this one equally personal," Ivan said.

"Do I know her?" Isazisi asked as his suit deployed.

"No, but did you know the seven hundred people in that building? Did you know the girl they killed?" Ivan asked.

"A decade of knowing me and you still have no idea who I am," Isazisi said. " I know who's your favorite at home, and I will slit her throat while she sleeps beside you if you don't put your weapons down and tell me what I want to know."

"And why would I do that?"

"Latvia, you know what I'm capable of."

Ivan's face fell at the mention of the country.

"You win. What do you want to know?"

Ivan shoved the woman over to Red, and he moved her behind him.

"Where is El Montar? That is what he calls himself."

"He's not here," Ivan said.

"Tell me where he is, or maybe I'll fry your favorite one in her sleep. How does waking up to the scent of burning skin sound," Isazisi shouted as he pointed his gun at Ivan.

"I'm right here." A man said with a Spanish accent.

A man stood on the remaining catwalk in camo. He wore a red bandana tied to his bicep and a Latin American revolution hat. He had a bandolier of grenades and shotgun shells around his chest in an "X" shape. He had two magazines on his chest and an AK47 in his hand.

"What, are we starting a revolution?" Isazisi asked.

"Funny."

"I have one question, and you can go on with your work. Where is she?"

"I cannot tell you that for free."

"I'll fry Ivan, kill the rest of them, and beat it out of you myself. Or name your price. You know I'm good for the money."

"Similar to you, I care nothing for Ivan, and my men are replaceable, but we all have something we want from each other. You want answers from me, Ivan wants his whores safe, yet we cannot agree."

"I just dropped in through the roof and started shooting, what do you think I'm going to do now that I'm on the ground? I will smoke everybody in here, test me."

"You will get no such information from me..."

Isazisi pulled the trigger, killing the man.

Everyone in the room's jaws dropped.

"He was talking too much, I did us a favor. Somebody in here better tell me where she is, or I will start blowing heads off."

"Fortified mansion, east Columbia," a man who perked up from behind a desk said.

"You're lucky Ivan, count your days you fat prick," Isazisi said.

"I'm not even fat..."

"Shut your mouth before I put a bullet between your teeth. Did I say you could speak? No? Then make your top lip, and bottom lip, best friends, and stop using your words, or I will stop using mine." Isazisi said while he flashed the gun.

Red's people entered the building and led the woman Ivan threatened to a waiting vehicle. Isazisi flew upwards, crashing through the roof of the building again. He flew towards The Republic of Columbia.

"I hope all his people burn in their sick afterlife," Ivan said as he walked to a waiting SUV.

Isazisi hovered on the edge of the mansion's no-fly zone. Megan showed anti-air missiles on the pedestals around the gate and the mansion's roof.

"They're expecting me, Megan, what's the situation?"

"Anti-air missiles. At least fifty men on the ground. Two tanks, a military-grade attack helicopter ready to take off at any moment, dozens of short-range missiles with a five-mile range."

"These aren't Providence. Who's getting them these weapons?" He asked.

"I'll run a backtrace," she said.

Isazisi tapped on his wrist, and the entire suit turned invisible as he landed inside their no-fly zone. He took out the two guards at the front gates. The suit's hand opened up, revealing his. He pressed a finger to the keypad. Red lines spread onto the keys as his powers hacked it, causing the gate to swing open. Isazisi uncloaked and walked in.

One guard shouted on coms. "We have a front gate breach, the Red Cyan Psychic Suit. Get that Apache in the air and the tanks locked on him."

They didn't even shoot at him, knowing their efforts would be futile. The Apache took to the air. It fired missiles at him. They hit and exploded on impact, the suit didn't have a scratch. The helicopter shot at him, and the bullets crumpled like toothpicks against his armor.

"Is this the best you've got," Isazisi yelled.

The roof of the house opened and out rose an all-silver weapon with a long barrel. It fired, and the shot knocked Isazisi back, sprawling him over the cobblestone driveway.

"Megan, what is that?"

"Electromagnetic railgun. Minimal damage done to suit."

Isazisi shot the helicopter out of the sky. One laser to the back rotor, and it spiraled into the pavement, lighting up the night sky like a firework. The railgun shot again. He sidestepped the projectile. It shot again and clattered off the suit, dropping to the floor. Jaws dropped as they stared at him and shot. Isazisi blasted them with his palm lasers. The tanks turned to lock onto his position. They fired. The shells bounced off the armor and fizzled out. He shot both tanks with wrist missiles, and they exploded in a brilliant orange fireball. Agents of The Circle ran into the forest near the mansion.

"Megan, where's the target?"

"Subterranean level of the building."

Megan showed him an X-ray of an elevator going a few dozen feet into the ground. He flew over to the doors and blasted them open. He landed. The mansion's interior had deep, rich velvet red carpets, with the stairs covered in white carpet and gold banisters—a rectangular crystal chandelier above him and classic paintings adorning the walls. Isazisi floated over to the elevator. He reached for the button.

"Touch it, and I shoot him."

A holographic screen projected, live video from the room underground. Isazisi's target held a gun to a hostage's head, with four other men in the room holding assault rifles to more of their heads.

"We have fifty boys and fifty girls down here. An American charity building schools for villages. You should rethink your action."

"My stance is thought," Isazisi said.

Isazisi crashed in through the floor, and everyone took their guns off the hostages as they looked up for a second. Isazisi threw out knives of energy and hit each of the soldiers in the side of the neck, leaving her.

"Everybody out," Isazisi said.

Everyone ran for the elevator and stairs. The woman held a gun to the last hostage's head.

"Hi, we haven't met before. I'm Jessica, and I'll spray his brains over this room if you take a single step."

"With what gun?"

She looked at the pistol in her hand. The barrel had crumpled, sealing it shut. She loosened her grip on the hostage, and he ran free.

"I don't think we need to be on a first-name basis," Isazisi said."

"Well, I guess I already threw it." She replied.

She threw a knife, and he caught it inches from his mask.

"I've heard you're more than your suit. Is that what you are, a shell?"

The suit front opened, and Isazisi stepped out.

She smiled and charged him with a knife. He caught her hand before she could finish her swing, twisted her in the air, and shoved her back. She jump-kicked him and he grabbed the heel of her boot in the air and suspended her with his psychokinesis. He let her go, and she dropped to the floor. She swiped at him with a knife and he dodged her swings, not breaking a sweat. He caught her hand on her swing, pushed off, and swung around her, grabbing her with his legs and throwing her to the ground. He landed on his hands and sprung onto his feet. She threw another knife. He dodged it, but she grabbed his arm, propelled herself, wrapped her legs around his neck, and slammed him into the ground. He sprung onto his feet again. She fought him hand to hand, pushing him back with her techniques. They fought into the front garden of the mansion. She threw a kick, he caught her boot in the air, spun her, and dropped her.

Fluorescent spotlights from Providence helicopters lit her up like festival lights as dozens of guns trained on her. She looked around and put her hands up. Isazisi punched her in the face with a right hook, dropping her unconscious.

****

Isazisi entered the room, and the woman whom Ivan had threatened finished giving her statement. He sat across from her.

"Are you feeling ok, Camila?" He asked.

"I'm fine," she said.

"Anything I can do for you?" He asked.

"What's the cost of your generosity?" She replied.

"Working for Ivan is a quid pro quo world. I don't function like that," Isazisi said.

"But you do have to. The stories Ivan used to tell us stories of you and him in the past, what you would do to people while chasing what you wanted, the orders you would give your troops, the way you would tear people to shreds if they didn't give you what you wanted. He did it to scare us, to tell us if we ever turned against him, he would do worse. He told us a story of your mission in Latvia, where you chased an arms dealer supplying Psychanium weapons to terrorists. A contact in the town let the information of your mission slip and Ivan said he watched you drown the man and pull him out twenty-six times, even when he gave you the dealer's location after the first three times. He said you shot him and left the body in the town square with a knife in his throat. He said you both chased the dealer through the forests of Latvia before he could enter Russia. He had thirty men scouring the forest, looking to kill you and Ivan, but you turned it into a game, mercilessly killing them. People found staked to trees, others bleeding out over the forest floor, others with their heads cut clean off. Others burnt to a crisp, and others dead in ways I don't want even to say. He said you found the arms dealer. Ivan said you tore his mind to shreds, handed him a knife, and he slit his own throat to make the nightmares stop." Camila said.

"I've never done anything to a person who didn't deserve it," Isazisi said.

"Maybe, but I feared you until today. I knew you wouldn't hurt any of the other girls, but still, we feared you because what Ivan said sounded like stories of evil." She said.

"How long have you worked for Ivan?" Isazisi asked.

"This is my third year. My family had nothing; we couldn't leave Venezuela and barely put food on the table, but we survived. When Ivan came, I took the only opportunity to help them I could, but I never let him defile me like he did the others. He touched me a few times, but never did I let him do to me what he did to the other girls. The other girls would cry to the rest of us, telling us what Ivan made them do for him. He's a monster. So many times I wanted to kill him, end him in his sleep, but I never did." Tears flowed from her eyes. "He hurt them, and he's still breathing. He deserves your form of justice. He should never have the chance to hurt another woman again."

"He'll get what's coming to him. Is there anything I can do at all?" Isazisi asked.

"My family will no longer be safe in this country. Can you help them?" She asked.

"Of course," Isazisi said.

"The only thing I can tell you is that Ivan and the Circle have projects in the Middle East. Supposedly, a Circle head should be traveling in the UAE in the coming days, and they have a base buried in the sand. That's what I know." She said.

"Thank you, but what I'm doing isn't quid pro quo," Isazisi said.

"Anything that takes Ivan down has my support," Camila said as she wiped away a tear.

"I promise you. Nobody will ever hurt you or your own again. We are Psychics. We Protect." Isazisi said.

****

Ivan's troops moved through the jungle, approaching a small house made of whatever resources could be scrounged from the surrounding area of a tiny village on the outskirts of Caracas. They'd parked their SUVs a few thousand feet away and moved on foot toward the house. They looked at the hut with infrared binoculars and confirmed five heat signatures.

"Targets identified," one man radioed.

They moved through the village and set up outside the house when the wind rushed from behind another home.

"What's that?" Ivan's agent asked.

"I don't know, I didn't see anything." Another replied.

The wind whooshed by again as the agents looked up. Three figures stood on the roof of the stone church constructed in the center of the village. The outlines of blazing red energy snaked down the katanas each of them held, casting a red glow upon the town.

"What are those?" One agent asked.

The figures disappeared in an instant, and a blade cut down Ivan's man from behind. He fell without a sound. A red glowing rope wrapped around the leg of another and dragged him into the darkness, where a glowing red blade awaited as arrows from the darkness cut down two more men. The head agent looked around, panting heavily, eyes darting from side to side as beads of sweat rolled down his face. A sharp pain coursed through his chest as he looked down at a blade impaled through him. The figure ripped the blade out, and Ivan's man dropped to his knees. Four figures stood in front of him.

"Who, who are you?" He asked.

"We are the Renarri. The Red Cyan sends his regards." A female voice said.

She raised her sword and cut off his head.

****

"Thank you for this," Camila said as her family stepped out of a red SUV on the tarmac.

A plane awaited them on the runway.

"You don't have to thank me. Everyone deserves a chance at a better life." Isazisi said.

Camila's family embraced her and spoke in rapid Spanish,

telling her everything she'd missed working for Ivan. Camila turned to hug Isazisi.

"The world will tell us you're nothing but a killer. They haven't seen the real you." She said.

She let him go and raced onto the plane with her family. It taxied down the runway and took off. Isazisi touched his warm, burning chest. His hands weren't shaking, and his mind stopped racing. He looked at the ring on his finger and turned to step on a second jet waiting for him.

****

Jessica awoke in a white, hexagonal-shaped prison. She walked to the front glass and slammed her fists on it

"Sorry about the punch. I could've found a cleaner way to knock you unconscious." He said as he stepped out of the darkness.

"Spare the apology. I've heard the stories. Your torture won't work. I won't say a thing." Jessica said.

"That's not my job."

He turned around to walk out. Jessica slammed her fists against the glass, triggering the alarm.

"I will kill you," Jessica yelled.

"Beings who eat planets have said the same, I'm still here."

"What?"

"Take that as literally as possible," Isazisi said as he left the room.

CHAPTER 10

Versia sat in his underground HQ, working at his hologram table. A hologram of the suit's arm rose and he slid his hand into it.

"Meadow, run Version Three Thruster test," Versia said.

"Running."

Three hologram targets appeared over the table, and he shot them.

"Version Three Thrusters are reading five times as much power as the previous model," Meadow said.

He sat in his rolling chair, his momentum pushing it towards his desk.

"They have one of the most powerful men in the world, the most powerful bombs in the world, to what end? All they need is the most powerful tech in the world." He said, talking to himself and Meadow. The idea clicked.

"Meadow, what is the most powerful tech in the world?"

"I'd say the new AXL Psychanium-powered computer chip, a joint project between Tokyo and Silicon Valley," she replied.

"Elaborate."

"A series of Silicon Valley tech giants and Japanese firms are working on a computer chip. The details are tight-lipped, but rumors say it's quantum-level technology using Psychanium,"

Versia double-tapped his chest, building the suit.

"Continue work on Project Constellation," he said. "I guess I'm going to Japan.'

Versia landed in Japan and met with his Japanese contacts.

"Koji, what do you have for me?"

"Word around the office is anyone with insider knowledge will be at this underground casino. That doesn't mean they'll give it up easily. We can't go in there, but you happen to not operate under the same rules as us," Koji said.

"Appreciate the help," Versia said as he handed Koji a fresh stack of cash.

Versia walked to a local fish market under the stars in his most expensive suit. He found a vendor in a distant corner of the market. He said the code phrase to a woman working on the fish. She looked up and opened a blue plastic tarp, exposing a silver metal door. He walked through to four men in suits with clear plastic earpieces running down their suits and up to their ears.

"Aren't you a bit young to be here?" One man asked. Versia grabbed his hand and twisted it behind his back. He yelped in pain.

"Please don't ask me that," Versia said as he dropped him to the floor and walked through the metal detector.

The other guard let him into a world of hand-tailored suits, silk ties in power colors, and diamond dresses dazzling in the light and flowing with opulence as they draped upon the ground. Luxury watches adorned wrists, studded with glittering diamonds and scintillating emeralds, others subtle but invaluable to the right eye. Playing cards and poker chips in dozens of colors worth unfathomable amounts covered the green tables. He took an entire champagne bottle off a server's platters as he walked towards the back room. He opened the door, and everyone turned around.

"Who are you?" The man at the head of the room asked.

"Either A. You're going to tell me what I want to know. Or B. I'm what you would call an ice-cold bottle of champagne problems." Versia said as he flashed the bottle in his hands.

His men pulled out their guns.

"Aren't you a bit young to be in a place like this?" A man asked.

Versia looked at him. "I wouldn't want to be the next person who says that."

The women in the room laughed.

"Aren't you a bit young to be here?" The same man said again.

Versia waved his hand, throwing the man against a mannequin. Everyone else in the room ran out. A man who stayed seated nodded and his men moved towards Versia. One ran forward and swung at him with his gun. Versia ducked and punched him in the stomach, followed by elbowing him in the arm, and he dropped the gun. The other three ran to fight him. He ducked, allowing one to kick the other in the face. He slammed the champagne bottle against a man and ducked under another punch. He punched the same man twice in the stomach as one swung the gun at him. He sidestepped and grabbed the man's arm, cracking his hand back, and elbowed him in the throat. Versia hit him with the bottle, causing him to fall into a group of mannequins. Another one threw a punch from behind. He sidestepped and grabbed the man's arm, and elbowed him in the stomach. He ripped the gun from his grasp and hit him in the head with it. The third one stood back up and swung at him. Versia evaded every strike. He grabbed his arm and drove his knee into the man's elbow, it cracked, loud and clear as he screamed in pain. Versia hit him with the bottle before kicking him into the wall. The last one pulled a gun. He held it at Versia.

"Alright, kid, get out of here, and I won't have to pull this trigger."

Versia kicked his gun out of his hand. It bounced against the wall and clattered to the ground. Versia hit him across the face with the champagne bottle. The man staggered and dropped to the floor.

"You'd think this would have broken," Versia said.

He dropped the bottle, and it shattered.

"Okay, man, we don't, we don't have to do this. I'll tell you whatever you want to know."

"Where is the hand-off of the prototype?"

"What prototype?"

Versia kicked him out the window, and before he fell, Versia wrapped a silk scarf around his neck.

"Where's it happening?"

"Fine, fine, it's happening here. Right now. Please, don't drop me," the man pleaded.

Versia tied the scarp to a metal pole coming out of the building.

"You better be right," Versia said.

"Wait, don't leave me here," The man squealed.

Versia buttoned his suit back up and walked out of the room. Gunshots sounded from around the room as a group of men in all-black suits barged in and shot at him. He dove for cover behind a money cart as everyone ran out while cash and poker chips rained around the room from stray shots. The courier lay on the floor in a pool of blood, and they'd taken the suitcase from him. They shuffled out the doors backward, still shooting, and ran away. Versia ran out. The entrance guards put out a hand, stopping him, but he dealt with them as the rest of the men hopped into SUVs and took off speeding.

"Meadow, send the car."

A dark blue sports car uncloaked from behind a blue tarp. Its headlights flashed to life as the engine roared with dominance. It pulled up beside him. He opened the door and stepped on the gas, shooting off.

"How many Meadow?" He asked,

"Six vehicles." She said.

He pressed on the gas. The back SUVs two dropped off and shattered their back windshields. Men with machine guns popped out. They shot at him and the bullets bounced off the car's Psychanium body. They switched to rocket launchers, and those, too, exploded against the vehicle's frame, leaving it without a single scratch. He pressed a button on the steering wheel, and two missiles shot out from the bottom half of the headlights. The SUV on the right exploded, catapulting into the air. He drove by as it rolled behind him in a flaming twist of metal and rubber. He pressed a button on the infotainment screen, shooting two lasers from his headlights. They hit the back wheels of the SUV, spinning it out of control and into the bushes. As Versia drove past, a metal ball popped out his taillight, rolled underneath the crashed SUV, and exploded, lighting up the Tokyo sky in a wild burst of orange. The road split off, and two cars drove each way.

"They're trying to lose me."

"The road merges again in another two miles," Meadow said.

Versia made a hard right, the wheels kicking up smoke as he drifted the vehicle while the two cars shot at him. He pressed a button on the infotainment screen, and seconds later, the two SUVs became smoking piles of rubber and metal. He slammed his foot on the gas pedal, the speedometer climbed, and the wing on the back rose as his speed increased. He shot out onto a bridge, it sparkled with blues, yellows, and reds from the neon-lit Japanese symbols on it and rainbow LEDs running up the suspension straps. He accelerated at the two SUVs still in front. They pulled out another rocket launcher, and they fired. Versia jerked the steering wheel right. The car jumped as it drove horizontally onto the suspension straps of the bridge. Eyes once on the road flicked to his car as he drove up the straps and launched off them. His vehicle flipped as he flew through the air, placing him above the SUV. The sunroof opened, and he shot a psychic shockwave from his hand. It caused the 4runner to buckle under itself and explode. The car flipped back over and landed on its wheels, continuing forward and driving off the bridge.

He drove up beside the last SUV and slammed into it. The car swerved out of control and into a group of potted plants. Versia skidded to a stop and exited the car, building the arm of his suit, and his katar blade slid out. He cut the door off the SUV and brought out the suitcase. He opened it to find nothing inside. He grabbed the driver of the car.

"Where is it?"

The driver pointed up. Versia watched a commercial airliner do a low fly-over as it gained altitude. He dropped the driver.

"Meadow, where's that plane going?" He asked.

She did a quick search of the flight records. "London, England." She said.

****

Twelve hours later, Versia watched a drone outside the airport in London. A man with a silver suitcase walked out and to a nearby car.

"It's that one, boss," Meadow said.

Versia set the drone to follow, and it trailed the car for miles as it drove into the English countryside and to an abandoned nuclear plant with multiple idle and rusting steam vents. Versia walked outside to the Providence airfield. The roar of the Psychanium fighter jet deafened him. The plane gleamed with a shiny silver color with cyan lines running through it. Minutes later, he entered the plant's airspace.

"Unidentified aircraft, exit this airspace, or be shot down." The air traffic controller said.

He said nothing back. Two fighter jets from the compound pulled up beside him.

"Exit this airspace, or be shot down." One of the jet's pilots said. "I repeat, exit this airspace now or be shot down."

Versia boosted forward.

"Engage target," A man on the ground yelled into coms.

The jets boosted forward, shooting at him. He barrel-rolled, dodging their fire, and opened his flaps, throwing his backward while the jets chasing him veered out of the way.

"What the..." One of the pilots yelled.

Versia shot off two missiles, hitting both targets.

"I want more jets in the air. Now." The base commander barked.

Six more fighter jets took off from the runway in the complex. Bullets flew everywhere while rockets exploded as they missed their targets. A few bullets struck Versia's jet and bounced off without leaving a scratch.

"Base, this thing isn't going down." One of the pilots said after he hit it with an air-to-air missile.

"Get me a visual on it." The base commander said.

A camera on the bottom of the jet trailing him turned on and zoomed in on his aircraft. On the ground, they watched his jet on the screens. The base commander rubbed his forehead.

"It's a Psychianium jet, you idiots. Conventional weapons won't pierce it." The commander barked.

"How do we fight it," the pilot yelled, barrel rolling as Versia took a shot at him.

"You don't." The commander replied.

Versia launched two more air-to-air missiles, and they both found their targets lighting up the sky with more explosions.

"We can't beat this thing," A pilot yelled.

The bottom of the cockpit opened, and Versia fell out, diving towards one of the steam vents as the battle in the sky raged. His suit deployed as he neared the ground, and he used the hand jets to stop, landing on one knee and one fist. The suit folded back into his chest piece. Above him, his jet went supersonic and flew out of the complex's airspace.

"Target has left our airspace, return to base and prepare for possible intrusion," A man said.

Versia tapped his chest, turning his suit's cloaking into an outfit matching other soldiers at the complex. He snuck into the complex's heart, blending in with the other troops. They had troops in black and scientists in white lab coats working on Circle projects, with vehicles parked nearby. The base commander walked in with a posse of troops.

"Alright, boys, we have a double agent in our midst." The man said.

Murmurs rippled across the crowd of soldiers and scientists.

"We're checking everyone's ID cards."

He tapped his wrist, and everyone's ID card lit up green except Versia. Everyone turned to stare at him. The commander walked up to him and put a suppressed pistol to his forehead.

"Give me one reason I shouldn't kill you right now."

"Because it would be a waste of bullets," Versia said.

The commander laughed.

"He thinks he's bulletproof."

Everyone cracked into laughter.

"I dare you, pull that trigger."

The commander put the gun back in his holster.

"I like this one, kill him." He said.

The troops readied their weapons. A nano-shield built on Versia's arm, and he slammed it into the ground as the agents shot. The suit's cloaking turned off.

"He's a Psychic. Get the case out of here," a man yelled.

A man ran and grabbed the case. Versia shot him in the back with a laser, and he fell. Another man grabbed the case and jumped into one of the SUVs parked in the complex. A few more people raced in, and they sped away. More people jumped into the SUVs to mount massive guns. They circled him, shooting. One rammed into a metal wall with the SUV. He pulled himself out of the wall with a quiet groan as a katar blade came out of his wrist. He sliced the car clean down the middle.

"Meadow, where's the case?"

"Half a mile from exiting the complex."

"Stop it."

"Yes, boss."

Outside the complex, his car turned on with a loud rumble. The headlights flashed to life as the screens inside the vehicle activated, cementing the A.I.'s control. It shot off like a rocket and blew past security at the complex gate. It drove over a small hill, lifting before it crashed back down. Meadow came up to the SUV, and it slammed into its back wheel, throwing the vehicle onto its side as it rolled down the dark brown dirt road of the complex. A man exited the capsized car and threw the case to another SUV. Several SUVs drove around in circles, masking which one held the case.

Inside the main building, a wrecking ball from a crane slammed into Versia, sending him into a metal wall leaving a human-sized dent. He stood as the wrecking ball came back around. He stopped it with one hand and shoved it back, causing it to wrap around the boom and pulling the crane down, blocking the path of reinforcements. The base commander stood across from him and a ring rose around him, and built him a steel suit, painted black and silver, with hydraulics on its arms and legs.

"Now it's a fair fight," he said.

Rockets fired on the legs of the commander's suit, propelling him forward. He body-slammed Versia and punched him in quick succession. Versia flew backward again, this time stopping himself with his hand jets. The commander boosted ahead and pummeled Versia with punch after punch from his hydraulic-powered fists. The suit shrugged off every strike. The commander picked him up, threw him across the room, and boosted forward again, pinning one of Versia's hands down with his foot that extended out in a plus shape. Out of one of the commanders hands shot quick-dry cement, pinning Versia's other hand. He hammered his helmet repeatedly, the Psychic suit taking every blow.

"Boss, please stop messing around and focus on the task?" Meadow asked. His car slammed into two more SUVs, sending them rolling.

"Fine."

He brought up his hand, ripping through the cement. He did the same with his other hand, causing the commander's suit to flip. He punched the suit in midair, shattering its chest plate into pieces as it flew across the room. Versia took off, punching a hole through the roof. He hovered for a few seconds, scanning the area. He located the car and flew down towards it. He landed and shot out the wheels of two more SUVs, careening them into each other. The last SUV merged with three more, and they gunned towards the exit. His 720s drifted by him. He slid in as it drove, grabbed the wheel, and shot off in their direction. Four missiles shot from the car's engine cover, finding their targets. Versia drove by and grabbed the case.

"Release the drones and block off the exits. He doesn't leave here alive." A Circle agent yelled.

At the front gates, black and yellow steel barriers rose, blocking the exit. A swarm of drones took off from the top of the building and flew towards his car. Versia looked in his rearview mirror.

"Meadow, what is that?"

"Experimental Providence Vector drones." She said.

They shot at him and he turned the car, sliding on the dirt to avoid their fire, driving towards the complex.

"I can't lead those back to the city, Meadow. Find a way to shut them down."

"I can't. They're on a closed system."

"How do I disable them?"

"Destroy the computer."

She brought up a hologram map on the car's HUD. Versia tore a hole through one of the walls of the complex. His tires screeched, kicking up smoke as he gained traction on the floor. The drones followed, five or six exploding while trying to squeeze through, or others ripping fiery holes through the ceiling and walls as they chased him. He drove through the complex, crashing through cars, tents, and tables as he tail-fished, but the drones stayed on target.

"Where's their setup?" He asked.

"Turn left up ahead," Meadow said.

He made a hard left, skidding on the floor. The drones followed, ripping through their computer system as they chased him. They jerked in the air and dropped like rocks. He spun the car hard and drove out.

"Plan a route..." Versia began.

He braked hard. In front of him stood a battalion of armed soldiers.

"Step out of the car," one of them shouted.

Versia's hands tightened on the steering wheel as he revved the engine.

"Step. Out. Of. The. Car." The same man yelled. "Now."

Versia held firm.

Versia pressed a button on the steering wheel. Bombs the car had dropped around the complex erupted into balls of fire. Aided by the guns and gas spilled everywhere, the inferno grew in strength, enveloping everything in its path. Versia gunned it out of the base and ripped through metal barriers as the complex burst into flames behind him. Twisted burning bits of metal rained down along with ashes from the fire. Versia stopped and opened the case to the AXL Psychanium-powered computer chip.

"Call Providence. Tell them we have new material for their vault." Versia said.

CHAPTER 11

A woman sat in a Vegas Casino at the blackjack table. She flipped over her cards, a perfect twenty-one, her fifth in a row. The others at the table groaned and slumped back in their chairs. Others threw their cards on the table and stood, shoving their seats in as they left the table. She pushed her ebony black hair out of her face and looked up with her starry brown eyes as three men approached the table.

"You don't look twenty-one. We're going to need ID." They said.

The two burly and muscular men shifted in their all-black suits, white shirts, and black ties. They had clear earpieces running down their necks and a telltale bulge in each of their right suit pockets indicating a firearm. They led her to a backroom in the casino and sat her at a table with two chairs. Another middle-aged man sat across from her. He put a pistol on the table and asked her one question.

"What are you doing here..." The man looked at her ID. "Mai."

"Gambling," Mai said as she examined her pink-painted nails.

"What are you doing here, Mai?" He asked.

Her face remained unchanged.

"I happen to have well-connected friends in the underworld." He said as he slid a file onto the table. "According to this, you're one of the highest-ranking members in Providence. We've never had such an esteemed guest in our establishment. There's so much we'd like to ask you. You can tell me now or in a few minutes, minus your fingernails."

"No point in lying, but if I'm part of Providence, don't you think Isazisi would retaliate? He would hunt you down and twist your mind to play your worst fear on constant repeat until it stops your heart out of terror, at which point he will bring you back and do it again and again and again until he hands you a knife, and you carve out your own heart to make it stop, the price for a finger. Anything else, and he will hurt you in ways the rumors of have scared me enough I've asked him to leave me out of it." She said.

The man stood and swallowed. "Well, it's not torture. The Circle wants you dead. Kill her."

The three men pulled pistols from their suit pockets. She flipped up the table as they shot at her. The bullets hit the table, sending splinters flying in every direction. Her ear beeped, and she pressed it.

"Now isn't the best time," she said.

"You're bulletproof. Every time is a good time." The person on the other end said as bullets whizzed over her head.

"Semi-bulletproof, my shield has limits."

She pulled a fan from her dress and threw it. One of the men yelled as the razor-sharp edge sliced them.

"Orders from the top." The voice in her coms said.

Three more men with SMGS entered the room from another door off to the side and riddled the flimsy table with more bullet holes. She pulled another fan from her dress and threw it, hitting one of the men in the chest. Three more entered the room with assault rifles. A distinctive sound cut through the air as soon as they came in. She stood from behind the table. The tuxedo-clad men lay dead on the floor with blood on their once-white shirts. In the doorway stood three of Isazisi's guards. The Red Praetorian. Each wore red, plated Psychanium armor and carried Psychanium dual-sided blades. She pressed her ear.

"He sent the Praetorian?"

"I did say from the top."

Mai cursed under her breath.

The Praetorian led her out of the casino, to the astonishment of the guests.

"Must be important if Isazisi sent you," Mai said.

The Praetorian said nothing.

In perfect increments of four feet stood red-clad Praetorians leading up to an all-black SUV. Two came out after them, with the man she had sat with.

"What are you gonna do with him?" Mai asked.

The Praetorian once again said nothing.

She stepped into the SUV and looked away for a second. By the time she looked back, the Praetorians had vanished.

She walked through the Providence base's silver and clear sliding doors where Isazisi stood over a glass case. Inside rested a Psychic suit, a shade of light pink with hints of pale green and black.

"You called?" She asked.

He put a tablet on the table beside him. A hologram rose from it. She watched what played on it.

"You brought me in for a Circle mission." She said.

"I know how personal it is to you," Isazisi said.

"It's personal to all of us," Mai said.

A green and pink suit arose out of the glass case while nearby, a small rock-sized piece of Psychanium glowed as lasers bombarded it. It burned red and deformed, freeing a light pink crystal with green highlights. It floated into her hand, her eyes glowed pink while lines appeared in her skin as she closed her fist around it.

"This is the Pink Fēngshàn suit and its weapon," Isazisi said.

A Praetorian walked into the room with a red case. He opened it and inside rested two Psychanium Chinese fans in the same color scheme as her suit.

"These will cut through anything."

She walked around the suit.

In another glass case, she saw pieces of Psychanium forming into a red Psychic Suit.

When she entered, he led her to a garage-looking area. The lights snapped on and inside sat a sports car painted in colors to match her suit. Mai ran her fingers over it.

"It's beautiful." She said.

"Even better, the body, chassis, drivetrain, and every other metal part are full Psychanium. The glass and tires are Psychanium-infused, rendering it near invincible. It's worth millions." Isazisi said.

"Thank you." She said, her voice a few octaves higher than usual.

"We're sending you to the UAE. The Chairman's second in command, codenamed 'The Counselor, ' is moving in an armored convoy towards a black site in the desert, out past the city."

It showed a hologram with a bus in the center, flanked in front by four sedans and four SUVs, and in back by another four sedans and four SUVs.

"From our recon, we can tell the cars are bulletproof, while his bus is more akin to a bunker. Are you ready for this?"

"They gotta find better names," she quipped.

Isazisi stared at her.

She rolled her eyes.

"I'm ready." She said.

The car raced towards the convoy, its engine roaring through the empty desert.

"We've got a vehicle on our tail, came out of nowhere," a man in the trailing car radioed to the bus.

"It's Providence," The Counselor said. "Deal with it."

The back windows of two SUVs opened, and miniguns poked out, showing Mai in a rain of lead. The bullets bounced off the car like paper bags thrown in the wind. She accelerated.

"It's a Psychanium car, you idiots. The bullets won't pierce it." The Counselor yelled into his radio.

Out of the top of the two back SUVs came two rocket launchers. They both fired shots at the car. She swerved to avoid the first while the second grinded against the car's side door and staggered into the desert.

"Aim for the road or the bottom of the car. If we can force it offroad, it won't fare too well in the sand." The Counselor relayed.

She pressed a button on the center console and, out of the car's headlights, shot two missiles. They flew under the SUVs and blew up. The vehicles popped into the air and crashed down, rolling in the dunes of the surrounding desert. She sped up, and two other SUVs dropped off the bus to form a barricade. They launched a salvo of everything they had at the car. The barrage bounced off as she plowed through the SUVs, capsizing and rolling them into the desert. She pressed another button, and two discs detached from the bottom center of the car. They hovered and flew under the two sedans, attaching themselves and exploding in brilliant fireballs, crashing the vehicles into the other two sedans. She drove by and threw four black and pink balls out of the windows. They landed near the cars and hovered, spinning in a decaying orbit until they crashed together, causing a massive explosion and a column of sand to rise in the background. Two SUVs and two sedans dropped off, protecting the bus's rear. She stretched out her hand and made a fist. The two SUVs rose and crashed into each other in the air, falling onto the desert sand.

The sunroofs of the two sedans opened, and out poked laser weapons. They shot at her car, and she swerved out of the way as the shots left craters in the road. The subsequent shot glanced off the vehicle, sending her skidding into the desert sand. The car rolled several times and rested on its wheels a few feet from the road, undamaged, but the wheels struggled to gain traction on the grainy solid. She stepped out, her suit's arm built, and she shot one of the sedans, hurling it into the air. The bus and the one last sedan sped off. She drove back onto the road as the car gained the needed traction. She pulled up to one of the incapacitated sedans and stepped out, putting her finger to her ear.

"Target lost, but I've got people who might have information." She said.

"I've contacted Interpol in the UAE and our base there. Take one of their members to this location. I have a second asset on-site to assist you," Isazisi said as he watched a satellite feed.

She dragged one of the unconscious men from the car and threw him into the passenger seat. She drove into Dubai and the Interpol station. She stepped out with the man she'd taken from the car floating behind her as she walked in. She threw him into an interrogation room and walked to the other side of the glass partition, where one other person stood. She had light brownish-white skin with long, flowing brown hair and was dressed in a patchwork of slimmer Praetorian armor pieces, with a flowing, black silk outfit underneath. At her side rested a red-hilted Psychanium katana in a red sheath. A hologram of Isazisi appeared.

"Mai, you'll work with Reese on this one. We have eight hours before the investigation transfers to Interpol. Find The Prophet and get out of their way." Isazisi said.

"I'll need less than three," Resse said.

Mai sat in one of the chairs as another man walked in and sat beside her. He had a tablet in his hands, watching the cameras. Reese walked into the interrogation room. The man sat there smiling.

"You know why I'm here." She said.

"With that black silk, I hope I know why."

She recoiled and grabbed him by the neck, throwing him against a wall.

"You misogynistic, disrespectful. Do you know who I am?" She said.

The audio faded out as she threw him into more walls and slammed him on the table.

"Is that legal," the man sitting beside her asked.

"For her? Yes." Mai said.

Reese walked out of the room.

"We have a location," Reese said.

They looked in. The tile walls had shattered in the places she had slammed him against, the table broke clean down the middle, and blood on the walls. Reese walked into a conference room, where high-level members discussed their next move. She walked to the screen at the head of the room and pulled up a location.

"They're held up here, underneath this parking garage. They have a secret room installed. CCTV picked up the bus parked there. I recommend we hit it now," Reese said.

"And how did you come by this information," a light-skinned, clean-shaven, Arab man wearing an all-black suit with a black shirt and tie asked.

"Check on your prisoner. I can be persuasive."

"So you mean you beat him?"

"I got what we need, Fariq. Move your officers into position."

He said nothing as he picked up his cellphone.

"We have a location. Move our officers to encircle it. This could be our biggest raid yet," Fariq said.

Within minutes, military-grade police transport trucks drove off from the station; they had the parking garage cornered on one side. Officers in all-black bulletproof gear and assault rifles took positions inside and around the garage as Fariq, Reese, and Mai watched from the top floor of another section of the garage.

"Send him in now." Fariq radioed. "We need a positive voice ID from his wire."

The captured Circle member walked towards the elevator and pressed a button on the concrete. The elevator opened for him and closed after he stepped in. He pushed the down button and walked out as it reached his floor. The Counselor laid under a raised vehicle, tuning the white painted, low-slung, skeletal, single-seater car.

"So they let you go? No strings attached?" The Counselor asked.

The other man nodded.

"Great, get in the van, we're leaving now." The Counselor said as he tossed him a black duffle bag."Put this on."

"Where are we going," he asked.

"Don't ask questions, go."

"I think I have a right to know. I'm part of this team..."

"Part of this team," he spun around and pointed a pistol at him, "you sold out your team. You don't think I can see a wire through a jacket?" He asked.

"Chill out, Joe, Joe," he shouted.

"Voice matches, move in," Fariq barked into his comms.

"Wait, pull your officers back," Reese said. "Something's off."

"Mercenaries handed their positions by genetics will not order me around."

"Handed?" She sighed as she couldn't move Fariq's position on the matter.

She continued to watch as the officers moved in.

The all-white car exploded from the ground in the opposite direction as a modified van exploded from another hole. Officers chased it. As it passed each pillar, it triggered remote explosives, causing the garage above them to crumble. The vehicles sped off untouched. The headlights on Mai's car came to life as it sped out from the garage. Mai's smartwatch pinged, and she jumped from the top of the parking garage. She entered the car, and the whole system sprung to life. She shifted the car into drive and took off after the skeleton car as the police scrambled to start their vehicles. Reese jumped from the garage while Fariq took the stairs.

"Where are you going?" He asked as her red sports car pulled up. She opened the door.

"To do your job. Now, find a car. The van is getting away," Reese said.

Mai weaved through the evening traffic of Dubai. She pressed on her holographic center console display. From the back of her car launched a drone. It flew toward the skeleton car and took potshots from a mini machine gun mounted to its bottom, and they bounced off. The drone scanned the Skeleton car as Mai pressed the 'Autopilot' button on the holographic display. The AI took the wheel, and a holographic display of the skeleton car appeared.

"Graphene shell over a carbon fiber frame, over a Psychanium alloy mix, two thousand horsepower, weighs fifteen hundred pounds, top speed estimated to be three hundred mph." She relayed to Resse as she pressed another button and retook the wheel.

The road widened, and traffic lightened while local police joined the chase. The Counselor looked in his mirror at the police cars. He hit the paddle shifter three times, causing three metal balls to release from the back of the vehicle. As each of the police drove over them, explosions ripped underneath the cars, flinging them into the sky. The police cars crashed, rolling to a stop on their sides and roofs. The Counselor entered a tunnel, and Mai followed. He sped up, and she pressed a button on her steering wheel. Two harpoons shot out from her front splitter and hooked onto the back of The Counselor's car. She hit the brakes, and her wheels skidded to a stop as the cable pulled taut. His car shook as it accelerated, and his wheels kicked up smoke while her Psychanium weave wheels stayed latched onto the ground. He poked his hand out from the door and shot a red energy weapon the car's windshield absorbed, causing the harpoon to fray. He let off the accelerator, and his car shot backward, crashing into her. He accelerated again. This time, she let off the accelerator and shot forward with him. She let the fraying cables go and chased him. He took off into the desert, and her car skidded to a stop before entering the sand.

"Tracker planted," she said into her com.

Reese chased the van into the city. She opened the door and jumped from her car onto the top of the truck. It drove into a tunnel and slammed into the wall. She wobbled and pulled her katana out, stabbing it into the roof. They exited the tunnel. She hopped to the side of the van and pulled her sword back against the roof's metal. The van tilted and fell over. She pulled her sword out and rolled onto the ground. The van landed on its side and ground to a stop on the asphalt, she stood and walked toward it, she walked around to the front, the back door exploded off, and out came a man, he had a pistol pointed at her.

"Stop," He shouted. She flicked her hand back, and his hand turned the gun towards him. His finger pulled the trigger. She pulled the driver out and reached under the dashboard to rip out a small black hexagonal box. A crowd had gathered around the capsized van, news reporters filed out of vans as two Providence VTOL transport jets landed, and agents apprehended the occupants of the van, cleaned up the body, and towed the van into the air by one of the jets, landing back at the Interpol building.

Resse walked in, and Mai sat with Fariq.

"So you got nothing. You tore up the city streets in exchange for nothing," Fariq said.

"I didn't tear up the streets, and I didn't get nothing," Resse said.

She placed the black hexagon box onto the table and touched it. Red energy lines spread across it. She pulled out a USB and connected it to the computer in the room. It brought up a map showing a location in the desert 40 miles outside the city.

"They can't be there, it's sand," Fariq said.

"The base would have to be underground," Reese said.

"How would they build there with no foundation and nobody noticing?"

"The same way they built bullet train tracks through urban areas," Reese said.

"Prepare your team." Fariq said, "I'll run overwatch from here."

Reese and Mai walked outside to three waiting VTOL Jets. They walked to the middle one, and the jets took off and flew into the desert. When they landed, Reese, Mai, and a platoon of troops came out, and they walked forward a few hundred feet.

"It's here," Reese said.

The wind blew sand toward them, keeping the door caked in a layer of golden-yellow dust. Mai's fans folded out. She moved her arms in a hand pattern and pointed her fans in the opposite direction. The wind reversed and blew into the ground, clearing the sand away and exposing a large metal trap door. She ripped the door off its hinges and threw it into the nearby dunes, revealing a set of concrete stairs. Reese waved her hand, her troops moved into the building, guns ready, and the two Psychics followed. They descended a few flights of stairs and came to another solid metal door. Reese stomped on the ground. Psychic waves pulsed out from her foot, showing her everything: every person in the room with her, everyone underground in the complex, every camera and sound sensor in the building. She opened her eyes and ripped the door off its hinges, setting it down nearby. They ventured deeper into the complex and came to door three.

"They'll hear this one if I..." Reese began.

The door flew off its hinges, sending scorching shrapnel flying everywhere. On the other side stood a new suit, built like an all-metal rhino, but standing on its hind legs, it had a car-sized sledgehammer in one hand and an even larger gladiator ax in the other.

"You're not the only ones who can build suits," it said through a speaker.

The Rhino suit swung its hammer, and from inside the hilt came a chain. The head of the hammer hit Mai head-on. She braced herself as she slammed into a wall. The hammer retracted as she pulled herself out of the rubble. She stood, her eyes glowing a light pink. Lasers shot out of them, and the Rhino suit put up its arm to defend itself. She jumped at him from fifteen feet across the room, aiming her fist at the suit. It swung its hammer, and her fist collided with the hammer mid-air, causing both to skid backward. Resse's katana formed in her hand as she rushed at the Rhino suit. Its ax and her katana collided. They held at a stalemate, the rhino's white glowing eyes staring into hers.

The rhino pushed her off, and she skidded back using her sword as a brake. The rhino lunged forward and swung its hammer. The duo jumped out of the way as it formed a deep crater in the solid concrete floor.

"Scan the ax, Megan," Resse said.

The contact lens in her eyes flared to life, and a holographic side screen appeared at the top right corner.

"The ax is sold steel with diamond edges and trace amounts of Psychanium," Megan said.

"Trace amounts?"

"There's a five-centimeter Psychanium layer over the diamonds on the blade."

"Will it cut us?"

"Yes," Megan said.

Reese jumped out of the way of another hammer swing. Two black and red orbs formed in her left hand, and she threw one at the Rhino suit. It rolled underneath and exploded, pummeling the suit into a wall. She threw the other orb, which exploded in a red wave of energy, hitting the suit again. The Rhino stood as bolts of lightning crackled on Reese's sword. She swung it at the suit, shooting the bolt from her sword, driving the suit into another wall. The Rhino stood, its ax beginning to glow a warm red color. The Rhino smashed the ax into the ground, and a wave of energy washed over the room, slamming the Psychics into the wall behind them. Mai touched the back of her head.

"Ow," she whispered.

She stood and flew at the rhino suit, latching onto its head. Her eyes glowed pink as her lasers burrowed into the eyes of the rhino suit. The suit flailed, trying to throw her off. It dropped the hammer, grabbed her with its human-sized hand, and threw her across the room. She bounced on the floor a few times and skidded to her feet. If the red bruises and cuts weren't enough, the steam in her eyes, the flatness of her lips, and the tension in her eyebrows told the story.

Her suit built around her, she extended her arm, and from her wrist rose a missile launcher, she fired. The Rhino suit took the full force of a Psychicanium nanotech missile. It stood reeling from the hit as a katar blade formed from her wrist. She flew at the Rhino and sliced at its leg, leaving a deep gash in its hamstring. It swung its ax. She caught it and shoved it aside as her hand turned into a full-blown sword. She swung at the suit, meeting the hammer. The Rhino suit kicked her back, and she skidded to a stop a few feet away. From its chest shot a beam of energy. Mai formed a shield with the suit, scattering the beam as she skidded back a few feet. She sidestepped the beam and flew at the Rhino, kicking the suit in the head. It dropped the hammer and touched its face, finding a deep, long gash on the side of its head.

The suit retaliated against Reese. It slammed her clean through the concrete wall hard enough for sand to leak. The Rhino suit's eyes turned a dark yellow, indicating a mode change as it wrapped its metallic fingers around Reese. Missile launchers formed on Mai's shoulder, firing at the Rhino suit, which put up its arm to shield itself. The flames engulfed it, causing it to drop Reese, who rolled to safety. The Rhino swung its axe, attempting to clear away the flames. It dropped both its weapons and shot two chains from its hands. They both grabbed onto Resse. The Rhino suit electrified them and shocked her. Mai rushed to help her.

"Get down," Resse yelled.

The blue current of electricity stemming from the Rhino suit flashed between red and white before the red took over. Dark black clouds formed over them in the desert. Colored lightning flickered in the sky before a bolt of red lightning crashed down on Resse. The current traveled through the metal chains and fried the Rhino suit, its paint turning from a dark gray to a deep black as it burned to a crisp. Its glass eyes cracked and exploded as the suit fell over with a metallic *thud*. Mai came out as Resse dropped to her knees. Mai ran over to her.

"Told you I had it," she whispered and collapsed in Mai's arms.

CHAPTER 12

Versia entered New York City airspace and set down in a closed-off area of the city. A place no one wanted to be, but at the same time, everyone wanted to be—the aftermath of the Circle's attack. A thick gray layer of dust still covered most of the landscape. Yellow caution tape at the area's edge and gray stone barriers painted in an alternating reflective orange pattern kept civilians out. Providence troops guarded the area against any potential daredevils or aspiring reporters. The suit retracted into its chest piece. Versia saw Allen helping with the clean-up. He lifted large chunks of rock and metal onto a truck with his psychokinesis. Versia approached him.

"How's it going?" He asked.

"As well as the aftermath of a terrorist attack," Allen said.

Versia looked at the barrier where a large group of protestors had amassed.

"Leave our city. Leave our city." They chanted as they stood with signs holding crude drawings of the Psychic suits with large red "x's" painted over them and signs saying 'Psychic Money > Our Lives.'

Versia helped lift a large chunk of the building with his powers and moved it to a truck. One of the workers yelled to his supervisor. Versia bounded over to him and saw a man killed inside the building. They'd landed on the large metal screws used in the concrete. He turned away as his enhanced hearing picked up a faint sound, Allen turned towards it, too. Versia lifted another large slab of the building, finding a man alive. Versia rushed over to him.

"W-water." The man said.

"Get him water," Versia yelled.

Both the man's legs had screws going through them, and one of his arms was crushed by a slab of concrete. A layer of dust coated his pale body. Above them hovered a drone taking pictures and video.

"Get that drone out of here," Versia said.

The Providence troops identified the person piloting it and grabbed him. Versia came over.

"Move the drone, or I'll shoot it down," Versia said.

"It's pretty expensive," the reporter said with a smirk.

"Bill me," Versia said.

The reporter obliged and brought the drone to his hand.

"The pictures and video got shared the second I took them. Now reporters will ask a survivor exactly what it felt like for a military-grade bomb to go off beside his office." The reporter said.

Versia let him go, pushing him back into the crowd, which had grown with the new sharing of pictures from the site. They'd begun chanting dozens of slogans activists had shared across the internet. Vashti landed at the site.

"You're one of their favorites. Can you calm them down?" He asked.

"I'll do what I can." She said.

Versia left the site through one of the secret entrances, and he walked around the streets of New York till he came to a building. Without a crunch to his footsteps, he entered the foyer and took a hallway to the right. He passed a sign reading "Post New York Attack Group Therapy." The Psychics had paid for it for anyone affected by the attack. Versia sat in a chair in the back corner near the door.

A man stood to speak.

"My eight-year-old son, he's, he's, the biggest fan of the Psychics. He has every toy, every pajama, and every piece of merchandise they've ever sold. Cyan is his favorite."

Versia smiled.

"He lost his mother and his sister in the attack." The man said.

Versia's demeanor changed, leaving his once lightened face dark and dejected as the man cried.

"It was my daughter's first day interning at the law firm her mother worked at." Tears streamed down the man's face. "Her first day. She was only sixteen," he wailed. "Sixteen. Now I have to tell him the people he worships, he idolizes, are responsible for their deaths." The man sat and buried his face in his hands.

Another woman stood to talk.

"My brother is a druggie, he's on his way to recovery now, but it was bad. He knocked up a fellow user and had a seventeen-year-old daughter he decided to never be around for. Everything that could go wrong did. She got mixed up with the wrong crowd. Drugs, gangs, extortion, a boy she once associated with even went down for murder. Still, she got arrested and had four pounds of four different illicit drugs. She should have done a few decades in prison, but due to her age and the brutal upbringing she had, a friend of ours in the police let her go as long as we promised to take care of her. Yesterday would have marked one year since we welcomed her into our home. She cleaned up her act, got a job with our friend, and worked well for seven months until." The woman sobbed. "Until she got torn to shreds by the Circle. They said in the autopsy report for the type of damage she sustained, she'd have had to be within twenty feet of the bomb to be unrecognizable. Everything was on track for her to be the perfect redemption story. She would have given TED talks." The woman chuckled. "Now she's gone, and I can only hope she's in a better place." The woman said.

Versia looked down at the ground. Another man stood. He introduced himself like the woman.

"I-I lost my son in the attack. He was the best and brightest kid, a straight-A student, the nicest person you could ever meet with the biggest smile." Tears flowed from the man's eyes. "He graduated college three months ago with a law degree. It was a dream for him to work on Moody Street. Everything was on track for his life to be perfect. He got a full ride, a 12-week pregnant wife, and their wedding was already planned for next week. Then, the wrong place, the wrong time. He should have been home, helping put the final touches on the wedding, but he was a completionist and hated to leave anything undone, he rushed to the office and said he'd be a few hours. Then, we got the call about the attack." He wiped tears off his face again but couldn't hold it back anymore, nor did he want to. "They said he was a few floors under it, so rather than vaporized, he was crushed, flat, they said, a red paste they had to scrape off the concrete. My son, the baby's father, her future husband, gone." The man said.

Versia stood and left the room. He leaned against the wall outside as he clutched his chest, his vision became blurry as he stumbled. He composed himself as his powers sustained him.

"Meadow, create a fund, transfer seven five million into it, and contact the other Psychics. Tell them to match it. I want everyone affected to be cared for for the rest of their lives," he said.

"Done," Meadow replied. "Where to?" She asked.

"When's the next vigil?" Versia asked.

"Eight o'clock tonight." She answered. "Will you be in attendance?"

"Yeah."

A row of SUVs pulled up outside the building. Versia got in the back, where Allen sat on the other side.

"You had the same idea?" Allen asked.

"Yeah," Versia replied.

The SUVs drove down to the site of the first attack. Allen and Versia waited in one of the tents set up during the clean-up effort till the clock struck eight. They exited the tent to the cool breeze and piercing darkness of New York City. A crowd of people, more extensive than anything they'd ever seen had gathered around the site. Each person held a single white candle with a faint orange flame glowing on each. Each person placed their candle at a designated spot and stepped back as others did the same.

Both Versia and Allen, flanked by Providence's troops, approached the crowd. Versia held a cyan-colored candle, and Allen had an orange one. The crowd parted as the two Psychics approached; people glared at them, and others remained emotionless. They both placed their colored candles down among the sea of white.

"Go to hell. Both of you." A man from the crowd said.

The two Psychics turned around to one man standing there. He held up a picture of a man in a tuxedo.

"You don't fight for us, you don't fight for good, you fight for yourselves, for your glory. Who avenges us when this happens? Who snaps their fingers and makes everything go away when you mess up? Ask yourselves that." The man said.

He turned around to leave, and the duo stood there, wordless.

****

Versia landed on the balcony of his New York City residence. He walked inside as his suit retracted into its chest housing unit. He walked to the bathroom and turned on the water. He plunged his hands into the stream and brought the water to his face. He looked up in the mirror. The image moved, forming a second Versia in the mirror.

"What the...?" Versia began.

"Who do you think you can save?" Mirror Versia asked. "Vashti? She will die in your arms."

The mirror morphed to show a bleeding Vashti in her suit, Versia holding her lifeless body in his arms, a sword driven through her stomach.

"Caitlyn? If she doesn't kill herself first?"

The mirror morphed to show Caitlyn pale and lifeless with faint red slits in her wrist, lying in a hospital bed. The EKG had flatlined.

"Jasmine? All it takes is one bullet."

The mirror showed a lifeless, bleeding Jasmine with a red circle on her forehead, her weapon lying beside her on the concrete, the flashes of news cameras taking pictures of her body.

"Sanjiv? He will die of grief without Jasmine."

The mirror showed Sanjiv standing on the edge of a snowy mountain. He let himself fall off the edge.

"Issac? He's not a god, as much as his time among the stars

deludes him to believe."

The mirror showed him on his knees, firing raging around him and a sword through his chest. He spat up blood before his head bowed.

"Reese? Her death will push Isazisi over the edge, and what he will do, will destroy everything.

The mirror showed Isazisi at a funeral, a lifeless Reese in a coffin. They closed it and placed a Providence flag on it before lowering it into the ground.

"Isazisi? Because of her death, he will take this world before allowing it to descend into what he has deluded himself into thinking is darkness."

The mirror showed Isazisi sitting on a black throne, his eyes glowing red, and two rows of Praetorians on either side of the walkway to his throne. On government buildings worldwide hung the flag of Providence as legions of Centurions marched through the streets.

"Can you even save the world? Can you even save yourself? How long before the cold blade of justice exacts its toll on you? How many thousands will die before you admit you've failed? The righteous and upright Psychic is a failure. He couldn't even protect his best frien..."

Versia punched the mirror, shattering it. Versia jolted himself awake as his wrist buzzed.

"Meadow, did you track my sleep?" Versia asked.

"You were in REM. Based on your heart rate, I would assume it wasn't a pleasant dream."

"Yeah, what's the situation?"

"Hostage situation, you better get down there, or it could be grim, and very public."

"On my way," he said.

His wrist buzzed again.

"Time for your dose," Meadow said.

Versia groaned. "Do I have to?"

"If you want not to have a nervous breakdown when trying to defuse a bomb, yes,"

He grabbed a bottle of pills off the desk, the bottle said 'Anti-Anxiety' with a green throwing-up emoji drawn after the words. He popped two pills in his mouth and swallowed them.

"Next dose," she said.

He picked up a metal case from under the desk and opened it. Inside rested three metal epi-pens with a cyan-colored liquid inside them. He took one out and laid out his arm. He injected it into his upper forearm.

"That should hold you for 72 hours," Meadow said.

"Yeah," Versia said.

CHAPTER 13

Isazisi arrived home and entered his house where a dark-skinned black woman with long, black, flowing box braids sat on a chair with a drink in her hand

"How'd you get in here?" Isazisi asked.

"I run the other secret US intelligence division. It wasn't hard." The woman said.

"Really, Hailey?" Isazisi asked.

"Yes, but I'm Reese's cousin. She gave me the code," Hailey said.

"I still don't get how you're cousins," Isazisi said.

"Our family history is complicated; what you need to know is she's half black, I'm full, and we have family members mixed with a dozen other things. You can do the math later. How is Reese? Is she okay?"

"Doctors said she'll be fine. I came to get her roses," Isazisi said.

"Oh, the garden Resse and I planted? Is it still here? " Hailey said as she walked to the back of the mansion where the garden was—every color of rose, blue lilies, gardenias, orchids, and more. Isazisi picked a handful of dark roses and wrapped their stems.

"Fifteen years ago seems so long," she said.

"So what do you need?" Isazisi asked.

"I report to two people on this planet. The director and the president. The Secretary of State is missing, and the general public doesn't know the other exists. Both are breathing down my neck, and it's ice cold." Hailey said.

"Tell them we're trying not to overcompensate and make it worse," Isazisi said.

"I don't see how you could make this any worse," Hailey said. "Anyways, the CIA is sending in an asset. She's meeting Versia, and she's Psychic. I wanted to let you know," Hailey said.

"Thanks," Isazisi said.

"Get payback. They took too much from us," Hailey said.

"More than you know," Isazisi said.

****

Mai sat outside Reese's hospital room inside Providence's base, her hands clasped in front of her as she stared at the floor in silence. She shuddered as beads of sweat rolled down her back. Isazisi sat beside her.

"I guess now is as perfect of a time to tell you as ever," Mai said. "Two years ago, in Afghanistan, Helmand Province, the mission for Providence. You read the report but I never told my side. As you know, we got ambushed on our way home when I asked to check a location out, off books, a place we never should've gone. They pinned us down from every direction. Armored vehicles in a circle protected us until they threw a grenade into the circle. I could throw the first one back, but they threw a dozen. They showered us with shrapnel. Some of us survived, but they shot a rocket at one of the Humvees, opening up a path and they moved in. I was unconscious at this point because shrapnel had hit me, but the story is the sky turned black, and the wind picked up tearing the Taliban members to shreds with hurricane-force winds. They said I was out for two days. I wrote a personal apology to the families of everyone who died on the mission and swore to myself I'd never allow anyone close to me to be hurt again, but I did." Mai said. She let out a deep breath as tears rolled down her face.

"I let the Circle hurt people close to me, for years I didn't let it go, for years I toured the earth seeking revenge, I realized no matter how many people I took down, I could never change the past, so I focused on my future. Protecting what I have now means you, Reese, and so many others. Reese will be fine, but letting go is the only way to find peace." Isazisi said.

"Thank you," Mai whispered as Isazisi embraced her.

He stood and walked into Reese's hospital room. He put the roses in a vase and touched Reese's hand as he spoke in an ancient Psychic language. He let her go and turned, and left the room.

****

Resse snapped awake. Her eyes were blurry, and her vision was dark on the outskirts. She forced herself to focus her sight, clearing it up. She turned from side to side, and she lay on a white hospital pad in an all-black room. Her vitals disappeared from a screen in the bed as she raised her head. Two Praetorian Guards stood at the door. She looked down at her arms, which both had IVs. She looked at a small table beside the bed with a few roses in a vase. She smiled at Isazisi's affectionate display.

"How long have I been out?" She asked the guards. They said nothing.

"Never mind, I forgot you only speak to Isazisi. Megan," she said. "How long have I been out?"

"Twelve hours," Megan replied.

"Twelve hours," She screamed as she pulled the IVs from her arms and swung her legs to sit in the center of the bed.

She stood and stumbled before regaining her balance. She walked over to a closet, closed the curtain, and put on her clothes. Her red armor pieces floated to different parts of her body. She walked out the doors and down the hall into a bustling foyer. Nerdy scientists running around with folders bulging with papers dashed past men in full tactical gear heading towards the hangar. She left the medical ward and entered the rest of "The Iris". The Providence command center. She walked towards the elevator, got in, and pressed the button for Red's office.

"Please speak for voice-activated clearance." The computer said.

"Resse," she said.

"Accepted." The computer said.

Right before the elevator closed, a female scientist got in. She pressed a button for the science division's floor. For a few seconds, they stood silent until the woman looked over, and her eyes grew wide.

"Oh, my God," the girl yelped. "You're Resse, the Red Peacock. I-I am such a huge fan of yours. I'm Alexandra Pierce. I work in R&D, you know, studying Psychanium."

"I love that," Resse said. "It's so fascinating, and there's so much we don't know. Come by my office sometime, and we can discuss your research.

"Oh, thank you. That would be amazing."

The woman got off the elevator, it ascended a few more floors, and arrived at Red's office. It scanned her face and the doors opened.

"I should put my sword through your heart," Reese said.

The twelve Praetorians reacted, ready to take Reese down. Isazisi raised his hand, and they settled.

"You should've woken me up on the jet."

"Even with your rapid healing. That much of your lightning is dangerous. Twelve hours is a safe recovery time. The world didn't end in that time."

"I don't care." She said. "I had the right to be awake."

"I got you a gift."

"Stop deflecting."

A capsule rose from the floor. Inside stood an all-red Psychic suit.

"Wow," she said.

"The Red Peacock Psychic Suit," Isazisi said.

The glass opened, and she touched the suit while another much thinner capsule rose, and a red core crystal floated inside.

"We found it by superheating one of the core ingots with Psychanium-powered lasers."

She held out her hand. The crystal floated to her, resting above her hand. She closed her fist as the red light leaked from it. It disappeared as she connected with the crystal.

"Thank you," she said. "Where to next?"

"I'll have a helicopter prepped and the suit loaded. You're going to Dubai," Isazisi said.

He pressed a button on his desk; minutes later, she stood on the helipad above the building. She got into an autopilot helicopter and took off. Isazisi appeared in a hologram in front of her.

"There's a quick refresher program on the suit. Maybe take a look,"

"Noted," she said. "Ok, let's see how this works." The suit's helmet formed.

"Welcome, Resse," Megan said. "As you know, this is the Red Peacock Psychic Suit. What else would you like to learn?"

"Weapons." She replied.

"You have over five hundred seventy-six weapon combinations."

She looked at her hands. Circular icons with small illustrations and text beside them appeared on the heads-up display, detailing her options.

"Including your 'Peacock Feathers'."

"Peacock Feathers?" Resse asked.

"Yes." Eight floating appendages in the shape of pentagons detached from the back of the hologram suit in front of her. "These are your 'Peacock Feathers'. Full Psychanium independently powered sentries with cloaking, homing, cameras, and holding enough power each to level eighty square miles of land."

"What else?"

"Targeted lightning strikes, lightning grenades, lightning mines, lightning webs, wrist and shoulder missile mounts, wrist swords, and your palm lasers."

"Well, let's see it in action."

CHAPTER 14

The clock in Resse's hotel room read 7:30. She got out of the shower and put on a sleeved red sequin dress, two gold Psychanium bracelets, and two gold Psychanium chandelier earrings, each with a ruby in them and peacock feather design. She put on a gold necklace with a ruby in the middle and a peacock feather design beneath it. She left the room to a car waiting for her on the ground floor and got in. Isazisi appeared in a hologram.

"Thank you for your last mission." He said.

"You're welcome," she replied.

"You know your objective at this party."

"Find proof he's financing the Circle, don't kill him, and blend in. Easy." Reese said.

"I love you." He said as he signed off.

She smiled at the sentiment.

She arrived at a palace-like building. Luxury cars worth more than houses dotted the parking lot while the building gleamed like a gem in the night. She exited the vehicle and walked towards the entrance, flashing her invitation. One of the door guards stopped her.

"You look a bit young to be here?" He asked as his eyes caressed her.

"Don't start with me," she shrieked.

The door guard stepped out of the way. "My apologies."

She entered the palace to find gold everywhere. Diamond studded mirrors, jewelry, and artworks on display, gems the size of her head on crystal pedestals behind bulletproof glass. She walked over to the bar section and asked for a drink. The bartender nodded. A small group of three boys and four girls walked over to her.

"Hey." One girl said in a way too high-pitched. They looked to be in their early twenties. She coughed, and her voice returned to normal.

"I love those bracelets, and those earrings are beautiful. What are they made of? Gold?"

"Psychanium."

The group's jaws dropped. Everyone in earshot turned their heads to sneak a glimpse at the jewelry. Even the bartender peered over.

"Wow, that's impressive."

"Thank you," Resse said. "As for the earrings. The center gem of each is a ruby, and the peacock feathers are red and clear diamonds.

"Amazing, but how did you get your hands on Psychanium for jewelry? Even governments only have a few pounds, and those are usually diplomatic gifts." The same girl said.

"My family knows people."

"Come, you should meet my uncle. He's the one hosting this party."

She followed them deeper into the house.

"Uncle, you have to see this." He turned around.

"What is it?" He said.

One of the girls whispered into his ear, which perked while his eyebrows rose.

"May I?" He asked.

He ran his finger over the bracelet.

"You'll have to tell me how you got these for a trivial purpose. You're aware they're worth millions."

She nodded.

"Don't forget the earrings." She said.

The crowd around her chuckled.

"Swing by my room later, ask any of my security, they'll bring you," he said in her ear.

She nodded as he left.

"Wow, by the way, I'm Carson," the girl said.

Every head turned to spy a glance at the dress as they walked by.

"Oh, and the dress is Psychanium too." She said to Carson.

Everyone in earshot turned in shock.

"I'm going to the bathroom," Resse said to Carson.

She walked to a security guard near the stairs and said the word Carson's uncle had given her.

"Right this way," the guard said.

They walked up the stairs toward a pair of gold-encrusted doors with diamonds for handles. Two security guards opened the doors as she approached. She walked in as he appeared from inside the walk-in closet.

"Hey, you didn't catch my name. It's James, and you? "The Girl in the Psychanim Dress'."

"Resse," she said.

Her eyes flicked over to the laptop lying open on his desk. James took off his tie and unbuttoned his shirt.

"I don't think we should," she said.

"Why not? It's not like anyone's around."

"We met two minutes ago?"

"Does it matter?"

She tapped one of her bracelets, starting a hack of the laptop in the room.

"OK, she said, but first, how I got these Psychanium bracelets."

A bolt of red lightning shot from her hand, and James crashed into his bed's wooden headboard. She turned towards the door. His security team barged into the room, guns drawn. They shot, and the bullets bounced off her dress. She blocked one of the guard's guns as he swung at her with it and threw it into the face of the other guard, swept the first guard off his feet, and punched him in the face as he used the dresser to slow his fall. She throat-chopped the other guard and slammed his face on the same dresser. She sprinted out of the room as her wrist buzzed with the words 'download complete.'

"Hey," The other guards yelled as they drew their guns and chased her.

She darted up the stairs and opened a door at the top, dashing out onto the roof. Three guards followed her.

"Calm down, and we can end this peacefully."

She backed onto the edge. On guard shot at her feet, she staggered.

"That's a warning." The guard said.

They shot again. She blocked it with the bracelet and stumbled backward, falling off the roof. A loud crash and glass shattered as she landed on one of the security cars.

"Resse?" Carson called out. She stumbled out of the flattened car unharmed and pulled glass shards out of her hair, before double-tapping her sleeve. A red supercar uncloaked and drove to her, the door opened, and she got in.

"Resse, wait."

Carson got in the car before she drove away.

"What are you doing?" Resse said.

In the palace, James's guard woke him.

"She's escaping, red sports car. We already have teams chasing her.

"Tell them," he paused, panting and sweating. "Catch her, or I'll kill each of you myself."

"Yes, sir," the guard said.

Six modified SUVs drove out from the side of the house, followed by three MRAPS and a helicopter.

"The files she stole could put us behind bars for life. Do not lose her." James yelled into comms as he descended a set of hidden stairs.

Resse weaved in and out of late-night traffic doing two hundred mph.

"Resse, what's going on."

"So you know how I said I got these bracelets because I 'know people' well. I work for Providence. I'm also a Psychic."

Carson said nothing as her jaw dropped. A rocket launcher shot rang out from behind them. Reese swerved to avoid it as it exploded beside them. Machine gun fire raked the back of the car from James' people.

"It's a Psychanium car. Aim for below it. Try to flip it." James said, watching the feed from the helicopter's cameras on a guard's tablet.

On a second tablet, a blacked-out figure appeared.

"You lost it?" The figure rasped in a tone far too calm for James' taste.

"That information will put you in a Providence prison for the rest of your life." The figure said in the same tone. "We will not spend a dime defending incompetence. Retrieve it, or it's your head."

"I know, I know," James yelled, as his hands shook. "What do you want me to do?"

A false wall opened near him, and he recoiled at its existence.

"Don't look so surprised. Everything you have is because of us. Version two of the Rhino suit is ready. Take it, kill the girl, and recover the information. This represents a significant investment. Do not fail us." The shadow figure said.

"I won't," James said.

The Rhino suit's eyes glowed white as it came to life.

The MRAPs caught up to her vehicle. They closed in on both sides, and the car jostled as the two massive vehicles body-slammed it. The gunner swung the turret down to face the car. A barrage of shells rained on the car.

Resse hit the brakes, the mirrors of her car caught in the wheel wells, dragging the MRAPs back, and the two vehicles spun with Reese. She braked, sending the car skidding sideways. The driver of the third MRAP crashed head-on into the driver's side of the car, and the front end of the MRPA crumpled as it met the Psychanium door. The truck sailed over the car, crashing back down, rolling to a stop, and exploding.

The second MRAP drove towards them. Resse shifted into drive, drove straight at the MRAP, and drifted, grazing it. She opened the door mid-drift and jumped out as the right arm of her suit built, forming a katar blade. She stabbed the blade on the hood of the MRAP. The truck keeled forward as she crushed in the front of it, the windshield shattered, spraying the occupants with shards of glass, and the car flipped over her, landing on the roof and grinding to a stop a few feet away. A missile launcher formed on the wrist of her suit, and she fired. The MRAP exploded, sending a wave of heat washing over the surrounding area.

The third MRAP drove at her, and a dual-sided energy blade formed on her hand. She sliced at the MRAP as it drove at her —the vehicle split in half as the Psychanium blade decimated it. The two sides rolled forward and collapsed, exploding. Her car pulled up beside her. She got in to find Carson, shaking.

"What. Was. That."

"Relax. I do this every day," Reese said as she closed the door.

A hammer smashed into the car, throwing it down the road like a bowling ball, crashing into the rough asphalt and side barriers before landing upright. Intact along with Resse, but Carson bled from where she'd slammed her head.

"Carson," Reese yelled. "Carson."

She took her pulse, weak.

Carson groaned. "I... I think I broke a few bones."

"You'll be fine. Hang on for me."

Her smart contact scanned Carson's weak vitals.

"She needs to be stabilized. She has less than ten minutes," Megan said.

Reese whispered something explicit.

"Resse..." Carson said as she slipped out of consciousness.

Reese got out of the car, and her dress molted around her into a black silk suit with red plates of armor on it—a red katana formed in her hand. The Rhino suit smashed its hammer into the ground, wobbling the asphalt as the ax in its other hand rested over its shoulder. She jumped at the suit and brought her sword down, meeting the ax. The Rhino suit swung its hammer at her legs, sweeping off her feet. The Rhino brought down its ax on her chest, but she rolled out of the way. Her Psychic suit formed around her. Its hand turned into a dual energy blade. She swung at the suit, catching it in the jaw and sending it crashing into the road, wires and sparks flying. The suit touched the wound and ripped off its mouthpiece—a new one formed from the layer underneath it. The Rhino suit swung its hammer, smashing Reese into the pillar of a nearby bridge. She pulled herself out and flew at the Rhino suit. Her hand turned into a long, one-sided red energy blade. Her sword and the ax collided, and the resounding shockwave tore up part of the road. The Rhino suit pushed her off. Thrusters appeared on the back of the suit's feet, and it took off. She flew after it. Missile launchers built on her shoulders, they fired, each exploding near the suit, knocking it off balance in the sky. She grabbed the suit and threw it into the ocean. It crashed down, forming a ripple. A katar formed on her wrist as she flew in after it. She punched the suit out of the water. It hit the asphalt, rolling to a stop on its back. Resse flew out of the water and landed with one foot on its chest. She stabbed the katar into it.

"I'm one millimeter above your chest..." She began.

The Rhino swung its hammer, throwing her to the side and ripping off pieces of itself as the katar went with her. The Rhino suit flew off again, and a katana formed in Reese's hand. She dodged the Rhino suit and jumped onto it, stabbing through its power source. The suit lost power in the air and dropped like a rock, grinding to a stop in the middle of traffic. She ripped her sword out and turned the armor over. She crushed the face mask and ripped it off. James had a bloody nose. She grabbed the neck of the armor and ripped off the rest of it, putting her katana to his neck.

"Give me one reason not to." She said.

"I don't beg," James said, grimacing. "Make your choice."

She glared at him as she continued holding the blade to his neck. She pulled the knife away, and two Providence jet spotlights lit James up. Agents dropped from the jets on ropes. They clamped specialized cuffs on James's wrist. She double-tapped her wrist, starting her car. It drove over. She opened the door and lifted Carson onto a stretcher.

"Take her to our Dubai base. Full med evaluation. She doesn't have long."

"Yes, ma'am."

Resse drove back to her hotel room as she awaited news on Carson. She picked up her phone and dialed a number.

****

The red SUV arrived at the standoff site. Versia got out of the driver's side door to a dozen black and red SUVs parked in front of the mall. They had red lights flashing on their grills, mirrors, and windshields. Dozens of Providence agents had guns on the hoods of the SUVs and in their hands, primed and aimed at two suspects in the mall. Other agents had sniper positions or had set up in the building. Dozens of news vans had set up outside the mall each live reporting on the developing situation.

"What's the situation?" Versia asked.

"Two suicide bombers, one male, late twenties, the second one, female, also late twenties, both have Providence bombs fashioned into suicide vests, four hundred civilians inside." The agent said. "Evidence suggests they posed as a couple to alleviate any suspicion of a lone wolf, they shot one agent in the shoulder, he'll be ok."

"Ok, ok," he took a deep breath. "I'm going in," Versia said.

He walked towards the entrance, every news camera panned onto him moving towards the building, the whole world watched in near silence as he entered the mall and approached the two bombers. They turned to him, flashing their fingers taped to the triggers. He passed in front of the line of tense Providence troops inside the mall and put his hands up as he got closer.

"Stay back," The man yelled.

"Ok, ok, what do you want, what do you need?" Versia asked.

"I... I... I don't know, I don't want to die." The man said.

"Let me disarm the bomb, my powers can hack it," Versia said. "All over in half a second, but you have to let the people go first."

"No. No. The people stay." The man screamed.

"What about you?" He asked the girl.

"We... need... to... stay..." She said, fumbling over her words.

A stack of cups on the food court counter fell over. The two bombers raised their hands and the people in the mall screamed, the Providence agents cocked their guns.

"What... was... that?" The man asked.

"That wasn't us," Versia said.

"Don't lie to me. I will kill all of us." He yelled, choking on the words as tears rolled down his face.

"You don't want to do that, you have a life, a future, people who care about you," Versia said.

"Stop it. Stop it. Don't talk to me like that, don't talk like that." He yelled, coughing on his tears.

"Ok, you want me down to earth. Here. You shot at a Providence agent, that's life in prison with no parole if they don't shoot you first and throw the body in a landfill. But I can stop that if you give us information on the Circle, this goes away, you'll be under the protection of Providence, and no one will ever harm you, or your own again." Versia said.

The girl stood and ran to Versia, she hugged him, and he could sense the fear radiating off of her. He touched the bomb, cyan lines spread from his hand, disarming it, he handed her off to Providence agents.

"Let everyone go, and I can help you, anything you need," Versia said.

"No, no. They said Psychics are the bad ones, the Circle is saving the world, saving the world from you." The man said.

"The Circle lied to you, let everyone go, and we'll get you whatever you want," Versia said.

"No, I don't know, I... I...." The man began. "Look at the death and destruction across the world fueled by your weapons, they said to look at the countries you've destabilized and people you've hurt."

"That wasn't us, that is the Circle lying to you. Let us help you," Versia said.

"How do I know that?"

"If that bomb goes off, I die too, and I'm still here to try and save these people, does that sound like the bad guy," Versia asked.

"Ok, ok, ok." The man said, still panting. Versia signaled to the people, they raced out of the building.

"Now, what do you want?" Versia asked.

"It doesn't matter, after this, you'll lock me in a cage, torture me for answers I won't have, tear me limb from limb till you have what you want, the second I hesitated to let off this bomb, I died. Might as well set it off now" The man said.

"That won't happen, not if you give us intelligence on the Circle and future attacks," Versia said. "All you have to do is tell me what you need."

"It doesn't matter." He said.

The man pulled a gun from his pocket and placed it against the side of his head.

"It doesn't matter." He said again.

"We can help you, what do you need?" Versia asked.

"It doesn't matter." He said again. His finger quivered on the trigger.

"You don't want to do this, we can help you, what do you need?"

"I-I-I don't know, I don't don't know anymore, It doesn't even matter." He pulled the trigger. Versia turned away as the people outside screamed. He looked back at the motionless man on the floor.

Versia said something explicit under his breath.

The Providence agents stepped forward as he approached, guns still primed. Versia touched the bomb strapped to the man's chest, cyan-colored lines spread from his hand, hacking the technology in the weapon and defusing the bomb. Versia walked out as the Providence agents exited with a body bag. Every new station recorded in total silence. Hundreds of cameras clicked as agents held the line while reporters pushed forward to ask him for a comment. Versia got into the back of one of the Providence SUVs, one with tinted windows and soundproofing. He ran his hand over his face and neck. He grabbed his phone and made a call.

CHAPTER 15

Thousands of cards and memorabilia had been made out to the victims of New York. Every night hundreds gathered to place seven hundred fifty candles, one for each victim. A brown-skinned Indian girl sat across the street, watching the cards and homemade artwork swaying in the wind. She grabbed her chest as she looked at one of the murals painted near the attack site, vomit came up her throat and she forced it down. She stumbled, but her powers saved her. She looked at a newspaper stand. The headline said. 'Rumor: Psychic's to pay for New York City Memorial'.

Jasmine pushed her jet-black hair out of her face and under her hood as she watched the site. Her wrist buzzed and she looked down at her smartwatch. Isazisi sent her a message. She stood and walked towards the excavation site, still hawked by reporters. She took off the hood and black sunglasses and every reporter rushed to her for a comment.

"Do you think Psychics are to blame?" One asked.

"Did you design any of the weapons used in the attacks?" Another asked.

"Did you..." Another asked.

Every question was more provoking and personal than the last, but she said nothing as Providence agents left their posts to shield her from the sea of reporters. They lifted the yellow caution tape and let her in. She walked to a VTOL jet on standby waiting for her and it flew towards a Providence base.

Jasmine sat in Isazisi's office, she played with a wisp of Shadow Energy in her hand as she waited for him. He walked in and handed her a file. She opened it and read through it.

"Fay Harlow?" She asked. "You found her?"

"She's in Rabat, Morocco, setting up connections with Western politicians away from home," Isazisi said, " I know how personal this is to you. She's also enhanced, one of the first test subjects for the Circle infusing humans with Psychanium technology, she won't go down easy."

"They did it?" Jasmine asked.

"And it worked," Isazisi said.

"Then I want to kill her," Jasmine said. "She shot Sanjiv."

"Capture. She has valuable information," Isazisi. said. "You'll be given Shadow Squadron."

"I want to kill her," Jasmine said.

"She's too valuable alive."

"She's too slippery alive, it'll take one misstep and she'll disappear off our radars forever, even if I capture her, how long till she breaks out," Jasmine said.

"The order is capture, once we have what we need from her you can ask the UN if they want to throw out the Geneva Convention for you," Isazisi said.

"Fine," Jasmine said.

"You'll be given Shadow Squadron."

"How fitting for the Shadow Psychic Suit," Jasmine said.

A group of sixteen women from multiple races wearing specialized black body armor with a unique symbol on the shoulder came in. One of them stepped forward, a dark-skinned black woman with braided black hair.

"This is Mariah, she leads Shadow Squadron," Isazisi said, introducing her. "They came from Reese's special program. We have your gun as well."

"No, Fay is special, she shot Sanjiv, she deserves a unique bullet," Jasmine said.

Isazisi gave Jasmine full access to a lab along with enough Psychanium to craft a new weapon. She waved her hands, taking control of the robot arms in the lab. One of the arms picked up a large trunk of Psychanium. The lasers cut at the material, forming a long, round sniper barrel, the front an inch wider than the rest of the weapon along with semi-circles cut into it and a flip-up sight. Two other robot arms painted it black. The lasers cut and welded together multiple pieces into a sleek, futuristic, black sniper with intricate designs over it. The clip-fed into the gun diagonally near the trigger rather than upright.

"This electromagnetic railgun version of your sniper is powered by Psychanium waves, which as you know act magnetic under the right circumstances," the computer relayed to her. "The weapon will push a projectile five times the speed of sound."

The arms guided the gun over to a window and placed it. Jasmine took the gun in her hands, she aimed it, feeling out the weight. She placed the weapon in an all-black case and handed it to one of Red's agents waiting outside who took it to a waiting jet. Jasmine followed him out to the tarmac and walked on the jet.

Jasmine took a deep breath as the scope of her weapon panned across the skyline of Rabat, Morocco. She knelt on top of a building with one knee on the ground and the other as a table for her elbow. The gentle yellow and pink sunset cast a picturesque hue on the location. On the beach, the water lapped against the golden brown sand as the last of the tourists stumbled home and a cool ocean breeze swept over the land. Jasmine's pupil dilated with the temperature drop and zoomed in on her target.

The rest of Shadow Squadron had perched on different buildings, each with their weapons aimed at the same complex. Her target appeared in the window. Jasmine watched her through the scope and put her in the crosshairs. Fay looked over at a glint on the roof of a building. She left the crosshairs of the sniper and walked down the steps. Six women exited the building before her.

"We've been made," Jasmine said. "Take them out on the ground."

"How do you know?" One of the members of Shadow Squadron asked.

"Move," Jasmine said, as pushed the barrel of the sniper in, converting it to a rifle, and slid down to ground level, slinging the weapon over her back.

She moved through the corridors separating buildings as a drone watched from its invisible perch. She moved towards the building and hid by the corner as Fay's first squad walked by. A sniper shot rang out, hitting one of them in the center of the forehead, startling the others. Jasmine struck. She kneed one of the women into a wall and punched her across the face. She dodged the punch of another and hit her in the stomach. She punched the same woman in the face and elbowed another behind her. She kicked the same woman in the stomach, sending her into a wall. She threw a knife at the last woman, hitting her in the chest. She moved towards the building with Fay who burst out the back door and made her way to a line of SUVs behind the building.

"They're moving." The drone pilot said.

Jasmine picked up the pace and ran into the building. Above her, Shadow Squadron moved from rooftop to rooftop on Jasmine's position. The line of SUVs moved as Jasmine reached the back of the building. Jasmine bounded to the top of another building and chased the SUVs on foot. She stopped and pulled out her gun, the barrel extended and the scope rose. Time slowed around her as she aimed at her target, she pulled the trigger hitting the gas tank of one of the SUVs, it exploded, catapulting upwards and landing on its roof. She shot two more yielding the same result. The last two SUVs took cover under an arch. The occupants stepped out and ran into another building. Jasmine and multiple members of Shadow Squadron followed them up to a large apartment with gargantuan glass windows and white ceramic tiles. Jasmine created a black ball of shadows in her hands and rolled it into the apartment. It exploded into a cloud of thick, black smoke. Jasmine waved her hand, changing the eyes of the Shadow Squadron members. They entered the apartment, the red lasers from their guns swinging through the smoke. Shots from Fay's guards rang out, riddling a wall near Jasmine with bullet holes. Jasmine returned fire. A yell rang out, indicating her bullet found a target. The two sides exchanged more bullet fire as they moved through the smoke, each looking for a target. More fire rang out as the smoke cleared. Jasmine shot two of Fay's guards and moved through the apartment, swinging her gun. She tracked down Fay who stood near a row of large windows.

"Does the Red Cyan always send a woman to do his job?" Fay asked.

Jasmine shot at Fay who ducked, as the bullets missed by inches. Fay slid behind a wall as Jasmine emptied the clip in her direction. Fay sprang out from behind the wall, kneeing Jasmine who blocked the strike. Fay threw a punch, but Jasmine blocked it and threw a kick to the head, the strike grazed Fay. She pulled a knife from her pocket and sliced at Jasmine who dodged. Fay did a downward strike with the knife, Jasmine blocked her wrist and kicked her back. Fay ran forward again, slicing at Jasmine, she flipped the knife, catching it as she stabbed at Jasmine who blocked the knife and kneed Fay in the stomach. She threw Fay into the cabinets in the kitchen, smashed them, and then landed on the floor with a pained grunt. She stood up. Both women panted from the fight. Fay threw a kick at Jasmine who dodged the strike, Fay sliced at her neck, missing by inches. She stabbed the knife horizontally, bringing it back again and catching Jasmine in the cheek, leaving a shallow red gash. Jasmine touched her face, ignoring the injury as her powers closed the wound. Jasmine threw a kick at Fay who dodged, she landed a punch to Fay's face and kneed her in the stomach, she threw her across the room and onto the floor. Fay stood again breathing heavier than the last time. Jasmine made two fists. She punched Fay and kneed her back, she threw the woman against the wall and kicked her again. Fay spit out blood and retaliated.

She hit Jasmine with a series of attacks, each one more violent than the last till the two women, both bruised and bloody, eyes flicked to a pistol on the floor. They both lunged for the gun, Jasmine snatched it and shot at Fay, shattering a window in the process. Fay jumped out and landed on a thick metal pole. It fell, propelling her to the other side of the alley. Jasmine jumped too, also grabbing onto the pole, one of

Shadow Squadron's agents jumped as well, grabbing onto the pole. Jasmine grabbed Fay's foot. She pulled a Psychaium knife coated in a black liquid from her jacket and threw it at Jasmine, she missed. She threw another, grazing Jasmine and cutting a shallow gash in her side. Jasmine grimaced. She threw another, it missed Jasmine and hit the Shadow Squadron agent in the shoulder. She let go and fell, Jasmine looked back as the woman sailed through the air and landed in a shallow puddle of greenish water. Jasmine yanked on Fay's foot, tripping her onto a pile of wooden crates. Jasmine raced towards the Shadow Squadron agent. Jasmine's heads-up display read the name Sarah. Jasmine knelt by her, lost for words, her contact lens scanned Sarah, she'd broken her lower leg in the fall and blood flowed from her open wound. Jasmine reached for Sarah, her hands trembling.

"Help," Jasmine screamed, her head pounding as her eyes darted from side to side as sweat overtook her hands.

Other members of Shadow Squadron rushed to Sarah's side. Jasmine pulled her hands back, still shaking. One of them touched their earpiece

"Send Medevac, one injured," She yelled.

Within thirty seconds a jet had landed in the alley and a full med team moved her to the nearest Providence base. Jasmine sat on the ground, frozen, unable to say anything, two Shadow Squadron agents helped her onto the jet. Her vision was opaque, yet clear at the same time. Her head throbbed as the ringing in her ear grew louder, her legs couldn't find her footing and her breathing became rapid and erratic. She sat, slumped over, leaning against the back of her seat, hands still shaking.

Providence agents arrested Fay and loaded her onto another jet. Jasmine held Sarah's limp hand throughout the entire flight as the med team worked on her while they approached the base. They landed and wheeled her off towards the medical ward. Jasmine stayed on the jet, silent, motionless, her hands still shaking and her breathing in her ear, the screams of Sarah still echoing in her head.

After a few minutes, she stood and limped off the jet,

clutching her side. Black lines had spread from the site of the cut as the gash turned black. Sanjiv walked out to the tarmac.

A silent moment passed between them before he said, "Do you want me to take care of that?"

"Sure," Jasmine said.

She followed him to the medical bay. Jasmine sat on the examination table and removed her ripped shirt. She had a black sports bra underneath. Sanjiv guided his hand towards the six-inch gash in the side of her stomach. He hovered above it to start the healing process. Jasmine sighed and placed his hand on her skin.

"You've touched more of me before," She said, rolling her eyes.

The gash burned as Sanjiv's powers froze out the poison, allowing her body to heal the wound.

"Is she going to survive?" Jasmine asked.

"We don't know," Sanjiv said.

"That's two people almost killed because of me," Jasmine said.

"Neither of those is your fault," Sanjiv said.

"Sure."

"They are not your fault, why is your toxic trait taking credit for everything."

"It's just who I am. I still think about us," Jasmine said.

"What tore us apart?" Sanjiv asked.

"We tore each other apart," Jasmine said. "I went to a dark place during our final months together. That's why I was the way I was on the jet." She took a deep breath. "Your task force was part of it, but a lot was going on in my life. I was eighteen, she was twenty-two. I led a kill squad for our clan, we were on a mission, in a hostile nation, and my right hand, Avi, she. It was supposed to be covert, but they pinned us under fire, and she was shot twice. The first bullet missed her heart, she would've survived, and the second tore it in half. She died right there. I don't remember much of what happened after, but they said I turned into a monster of shadows, with glowing red eyes. They said I massacred everyone and then was out for hours. That's when it came back to me, reality hit. Every day for a month, that image was in my head. Avi going down to those two shots. We never even caught who did it." Jasmine cried. "She was my brother's fiance, it broke him, he cried every day for months; everyone said it wasn't my fault, I wasn't to blame, but I still did. Every day, I thought about what I should have done differently, what we should've changed, but nothing would bring her back. Now, seeing another one of mine go down, brought me back to that, a feeling I thought I got over. That's what happened, I pulled away, causing you to pull away, and everything fell apart and from there, I don't even know. Then you got shot and that brought back everything because I didn't know if I'd lose you too."

"Why didn't you say this when it happened, who knows what we would've been?" Sanjiv asked.

"You asked everyone but me about it," Jasmine said.

"I guess I did," Sanjiv said. "You seemed like you didn't want to talk about it, and then you were already mad about the task force, so I wanted to give you some space."

"I was cold during that time, so I understand that. We can agree mistakes were made?"

"Yeah."

Sanjiv's wrist buzzed.

"What's the news?"

"She'll live," Sanjiv said.

Jasmine's shoulders loosened as she exhaled. Sanjiv leaned in towards Jasmine, and she leaned towards him, their lips inches away from each other before they both pulled back, it wasn't the right time.

****

Versia sat on a black curved couch in the glass-lined workshop below his house, watching the flat-screen TV turned to a news station. He projected different constellations in his hand as he watched. The headline scrolled by read "Circle suspected of handing off stolen Providence weapons to Jihadi terrorists." The screen turned to shaky camera footage; people screamed in Arabic as large explosions rocked the ground behind a hill, hitting the village beside the one of the person filming. More shaky camera footage showed another village. Terrorists clad in brown and camo shot into crowds and threw grenades into houses. One had a Providence bomb in his hand. He threw it into the village as the pickup trucks drove off, it exploded in a red shockwave, leveling the village and killing hundreds in seconds. The station flipped back to the female reporter.

"The eighty-mile hike to the last safe place in the entire region can only be described as a pathway through hell, a modern-day Trail of Tears taken only by the most desperate. Simple farmers, mothers with children, fathers, single husbands, people living simple lives, driven from their homes and displaced by warring factions. Forced to raid deserted villages and even carcasses for the most basic of necessities. Uprooted by a never-ending war, bolstered and emboldened by the addition of Psychanium weapons to the front. Villages that would've taken hours to massacre can be leveled in seconds. Clear on display, the effects of the Psychic's mistake and the vileness of the Circle have further escalated the violence and torn apart the lives of these innocent people throughout the Middle East." The reporter said. "This woman is still looking for her family. She says terrorists heading north took them, previous victims of kidnappings in this region have been sold into slavery, or worse. Is there anyone who can even help her?" The reporter asked.

Versia rubbed his heart with the lower palm of his hand, he wheezed as he pulled his hand back, clenching his fist. The news feed switched from the videos in the Middle East to the events of the mall Versia saved.

"Earlier today at a mall, one of the Psychics disarmed a possible Circle-based suicide bomber, saving the lives of hundreds. Unfortunately, one of the bombers decided to take his own life before the Cyan Psychic could help him." The reporter said.

"What's wrong?" Vashti asked.

She sat on the chair, one leg up and her back on one of the armrests. "Nothing." He said. "Your hand is shaking," She said.

He grabbed his right hand to stop the motion. The TV flipped to more footage from the Middle East. Around them, multiple glass panes shattered as Versia's energy radiated.

"You don't have to be like this," she said

"I have to, I don't need anyone questioning whether or not my finger should hover over the most powerful trigger in the world because I show emotions." He said.

"Then what's wrong?" She asked as she slid close to him. "You can tell me." She said as she leaned on his shoulder.

"I can't look at this, and do nothing," Versia said, referencing the news broadcast. "Look at what happened at the mall, we thought he was in his late twenties, but he was seventeen and strapped a suicide bomb to his body, then, he shot himself in the head, imagine what he'd have had to go through to think his life isn't worth anything more. For me to have all the power in the world and not do anything." He said.

"It's not your fault," Vashti said.

"Yes, it is," Versia said.

He pointed to the TV displaying shaky video of a Psychanium weapon going off over the ridge of a mountain, leveling another village in one strike. This time the camera fixated on the bodies left behind from the carnage. Men, women, parentless children who'd hidden, waiting for rescue.

"You don't understand. I designed that weapon for Isazisi." He said as he pointed to the screen showing the aftermath of a bomb. "I designed that weapon for Providence to be a maximum casualty offensive ordinance. I designed it to take out reinforced bunkers and level mountain ranges to destroy terrorist bases hidden inside of them. Now, a weapon I built murdered two hundred innocent people," Versia said.

"The Circle chose what to do with the weapons. You didn't press the trigger. You know why we built those, you know what they're for and why they exist. If the Circle takes them and twists their purpose all we can do is stop them before they hurt more people." Vashti said.

"Still... I...I...I have to go." He said as he stood. He walked towards a glass cylinder containing his suit. He touched it with his pointer finger and the suit's nanites latched onto his body, building around him, coating him in his armor. The helmet formed, and the HUD flashed to life. The roof opened, and he flew out.

****

The terrorists invaded another village. They yelled to each other in Arabic. One of them fired into a crowd of unarmed villagers as another kicked the door open of a house packed with cowering people and threw a Providence grenade. Another terrorist kicked open the door to another house and sprayed rifle fire inside. They dragged the women to tarp-covered trucks and sat the men down, giving them a choice between joining, or dying. The men who refused received the backs of guns to their heads.

"Kill them all," a man said in Arabic.

Silver balls with flashing cyan lights dropped from the sky all around the terrorists. One man reached for one.

"Don't touch it," another man yelled to him in Arabic.

He pulled back his hand as the balls exploded into cyan-colored smoke. A metal suit dropped from the sky with a metallic *thud*. The terrorists turned towards the sound as they waded around, unable to see in the smoke. Verisa punched the terrorist closest to him through a wall twenty feet away, throwing him out of the smoke. The others fired in the general direction and the bullets bounced off Versia's armor. He blasted one out of the smoke with a laser and blasted another two with dual lasers. He kicked a nearby truck into another four of the terrorists, crushing them. He shot a small circular weapon from his wrist. It latched onto the truck and exploded.

The terrorists yelled at each other as they fired into the smoke. Additional terrorists shot from behind him. He held out a hand projecting a shield in front of himself. He flew out of the smoke, punching one of the terrorists. A katar blade extended from his left arm, and he sliced one of the terrorists, the same hand turned into a rocket-powered mallet as he swung it back, it rocketed forward punching another terrorist. He flew at another one, slicing at him with a dual-bladed sword. He kicked another one into a wall, leaving cracks as the man hit. From behind another terrorist shot at him with a rocket launcher, the rocket exploded against his armor. He turned around charging his lasers and shot the terrorists with lasers from both palms, the man rag-dolled and slammed into the wall behind him, lying motionless. Meadow sent him an alert.

"Reinforcements approaching." She said.

She displayed aerial footage of the approaching four-car convoy of open-bed trucks in his HUD.

"Do I have any drones in the area?" He asked.

"You have one two miles out." She said.

"Take out the convoy." He said.

The drone banked around in the sky, and the camera swiveled, scanning as it locked on its targets. Two rockets dropped from the wings of the drone. They shot forward and hit, destroying the entire convoy.

"Targets destroyed," Meadow said.

From behind him, one of the terrorists hit him in the side of the head with an empty weapons crate, it broke against his armor. He turned to the man who inched backwards and blasted him with a sonic pulse from his wrist, throwing him back. The terrorist regional leader crawled to a truck nearby. Versia shot a circle from his wrist, disabling the truck. He pulled the terrorist leader to him and the man shook as cyan-colored lightning flowed through his body. Verisa dropped him.

"What do we have in the vicinity?" Versia asked.

"Stolen missiles, eight miles west." She said.

He flew west. His suit zoomed in on the missiles and he blasted them with dual lasers, the missiles exploded, taking dozens of terrorists with them. He flew south towards more weapons. An anti-aircraft missile took off from the ground, knocking Versia out of the sky. He impacted the ground and pulled himself up from a crater as the terrorists shot at him from range. His helmet retracted and a cyan laser shot from his eyes. The missile rack exploded, taking the guards with it. He took off again.

"Convoy, north, civilians identified."

He flew north and landed in front of the convoy with a deafening sound. Triangular mini-missiles formed on his back, and they launched, destroying three of the five trucks guarding the abducted civilians. Terrorists jumped out of the other two and fired at him. He blasted both the trucks off their wheels and lasered the rest of the terrorists. He opened the tarp over the truck, and the civilians inside screamed and cried. They whispered to each other.

"A Psychic," one of them said in Arabic.

He helped them out of the truck. A young boy ran to hug him, Versia knelt on one knee and extended an open palm as his suit's nanites pulled back, revealing his flesh, the boy put his hand on Versia's. Hundreds of feet away, a single reporter's camera clicked, taking the soon-to-be iconic shot.

Versia arrived back at his house. The suit retracted into its chest piece and he waved his hand, turning the TV on again. Every news channel, every magazine cover, and every newspaper showed the picture of Versia and the boy, their hands touching along with shaky footage of him fighting the terrorist in the area.

Vashti sat on the chair, she sprang up and kissed him.

"Don't ever let anything take your heart. Please. Don't." She said.

CHAPTER 16

The door, flanked by two Providence agents slid open as Jasmine approached, she entered the room. The metal cover over a glass box rose, revealing the person inside. Fay Harlow.

"Hasn't even been twenty-four hours and they've waterboarded me five times," Fay said.

"You chose to be a terrorist," Jasmine said as she stepped closer to the glass.

"Did I? Or did I choose to be a guide? To fight for a cause bigger than myself?" Fay said.

"What's the end goal, money, power, what?"

"We don't deal in simple things like money, we deal in the future of humanity, and to secure that future, you and your evil must be purged from this earth."

"What does that even mean?"

"Of course you would think about money, all the dollars in the world, and still not enough to buy your soul back," Fay said.

"My soul? My soul has been gone for years, you took it when The Circle killed my cousin. Then it died with the last bomb I ever set off."

"Interesting you speak of bombs."

"You've killed over five thousand people. For what?" Jasmine asked.

"As if your hands are clean," Fay said. "How many people have you killed? How many fathers, mothers, brothers, sisters, aunts, and uncles have you taken? Why is it any different when we do it?"

"I have standards," Jasmine said. "I will never assassinate anyone in front of their child. I will never assassinate a child. I will never use bombs because I can't control who they hit. I will never assassinate a person who doesn't deserve it."

"And who decides who deserves it? Who made you the judge,

jury, and executioner? A panel of people who work for your interests?" Fay asked.

"I once killed a terrorist who planned to poison the water supply of a city with two million people. If he succeeded, over three hundred thousand people would've died. They called me because no one else could do it. I saved three hundred thousand people and didn't receive a single thank you, because it's my mission. I wasn't given these powers to glorify myself. I was given them to help people." Jasmine said.

"That's the problem with you Psychics. You see yourselves as divine beings sent from above to save our fragile world. You represent everything wrong with modern-day society. The worship of superficial perfection, the glorification of people handed their positions rather than earning them, and the value of dollar amounts over human lives. What we are exposing is you, and the world for what it is. A corrupt and lawless chessboard, where the weak and shadowy hands of those in power move everyone else around like pawns. Collateral damage here and there is fine, right? But you, you are so much worse. Is what we're doing wrong? That doesn't matter, what does is that our result is for the betterment of humanity. You could end hunger, wars, and poverty, cure anything ailing humanity within months with what you have, yet you hide it away under the guise of sacrality and tradition. You represent everything wrong with society, and we are going to tear it down. It doesn't matter how many people we kill, because the next generation will only know a world of the Circle. A world where Psychics never existed. If what it costs is a few meaningless lives, we're the ones willing to pay that." Faye said.

"You think if we couldn't end hunger, poverty, and war we wouldn't? Unlike you, we weigh the lives we take."

"If you value life more than the greater goals of your people, you will fall to us, every single time," Fay said. "Nobody is too important in the Circle, that's what separates us."

"Valuing innocent life is not a weakness. To end a war, how many soldiers, politicians, leaders, and civilians would we have to kill before the fighting stops, how many before we would say it's too much? And no, no Psychic was handed this." Jasmine said.

"Oh, is that so? Your family controls every major industry in India and has existed since the inception of Psychics. You. Jasmine Shahvaya. Crown Princess and one of the seven heirs to the Shahvaya Dynasty, a family worth what? An estimated five trillion dollars. Everything you have was given to you on a silver platter." Fay said.

Jasmine smiled and rolled up her sleeves. She rubbed her forearm removing the makeup to reveal a long scar leading up her arm.

"No, it wasn't. I got this when I was 15, a red hot Psychanium knife ran the length of my arm by a target I handled, till today the scar remains, my powers weren't developed enough to heal it at the time, and the bone is still weaker than the rest of mine. I trained fourteen hours a day, six days a week to become what I am today. I was left in the middle of a jungle in India at the age of twelve with a rifle, pistol, and knife. I survived for two weeks alone and completed my objective. I trained so much every day that I'd go to sleep with sprained ankles, bloody knuckles, and fractures, every night, and wake up at five AM to start my training again. I wasn't raised like a queen, I was treated like a soldier. Nearly every Psychic was. This new world you want will never exist. Over my cold dead body." Jasmine said.

"Interesting choice of words," Fay said. "Yes still, you stand for, defend, and continue to profit and live off the gains of an institution responsible for so much pain and suffering it's incalculable. What happened in Targistan, the genocides across the continents, anywhere Psychanium was found, death at the hands of your ancestors would follow. The sacrality of your metal was worth more than the sanctity of life, yet 'over your cold dead body'. Then as the victors do, you rewrote history. Your ancestors were so disappointed in their actions that they even hid them from their future generations.

"What happened in Targistan?"

"That's for you to research."

"Some of what past Psychics did was horrible, but I had nothing to do with it. Will I make amends for their actions any way I can, yes, but you're no saint. So where's the next attack?" Jasmine asked.

"So why did you stop using bombs on your missions?" Fay asked.

"What?" Jasmine replied.

"You say you never would use a bomb because you can't control who they hit, exactly when did you stop using bombs?"

"That doesn't matter."

"Oh yes, it does. Who do you think you hit as collateral?" Fay said. She scoffed. "Years ago, when your family sent you on a mission for Providence. The Red Cyan, newly appointed head of Providence, wanted to send a message to the world, right? Let them know he was here to continue in the steps of his forefathers. Psychanium arms dealer, right? But he asked you to kill him with a specific weapon, a Psychanium bomb, designed for maximum shrapnel. The apartment complex he lived in is where I lived, a memo was reportedly given to clear the building, but it never reached my family. While every other family evacuated, I sat there, eating dinner for the last time with my family. You didn't even check for stragglers, you bombed it. I still remember the ground caving in beneath us, my mother, father, and brother falling through as the flames rose. They didn't even get to scream.

When they dug up the rubble they found four charred bodies instead of the one they should've, and you know what they did, they told you, and covered it up. You set off a bomb killing everyone I loved and allowed them to cover it up, while I was forced to fend for myself on the streets. Till today I have Psychanium shrapnel still lodged in my body, too dangerous to remove. And you, you carried on with life as if nothing happened, returned to your palace, and continued to kill with impunity. The Circle gave me a home and a purpose, and I will spend my last dying breath to make sure you suffer for what you did to me." Fay said.

"That was you?" Jasmine asked. "You think what happened that night didn't break me? Do you think I walked away from that unhurt? That was my last mission for years. We looked for the victim, but never found you. We wanted to help, even try to make up for what we did." Jasmine said.

"I walked away without a family. Nothing will make up for what you did," Fay yelled. "The only thing I wish is I killed your boyfriend in front of you, maybe then you'd feel a fraction of my pain."

"We didn't mean to do that to you."

"It doesn't matter, you did. And everything was taken from me, so if you know what's good for you, you would kill me where I stand because I will make you and the rest of the world suffer." Fay said.

"So you would have others suffer the same pain as you?"

"It's turning the world against Psychics, they'll feel my pain now."

"Where's the next attack?" Jasmine asked.

"You know, Fletcher told me a story once, it describes you perfectly. He loves Greek mythology and he told me about Pandora. She opened a box that led to all the evil and suffering in the world. You and your Psychics are Pandora, the box that unleashed evil upon the world, and we as The Circle are here to correct that. I hope the world is just, and you pay for your sins."

"If I'm Pandora, what are you?"

"I like to think of myself as Athena. A goddess of heroic endeavor. Standing up to you."

Jasmine snorted. "Where's the next attack?"

"If waterboarding didn't work, what more can you do?" Fay asked.

"Nothing, we've hurt you enough," Jasmine said.

Jasmine turned and left the cell.

****

Lesik hit Ava across the face. "I will ask one more time before it's a bullet in your head."

She spit out blood.

"Where is the drive on the tanks..." he caught himself, "materials, we are moving."

"I'm not sure."

He hit her again and picked up a power drill.

"Let's hope a hole in your cheek will let out answers." He clicked the drill spinning the bit.

"Well, I think I have everything I need. The handcuffs on her wrist fell off. The other two men in the room pulled out guns in surprise.

"Please, let's skip this."

A purple aura appeared around the guns followed by a few moments of silence.

"Well shoot her," Lesik said. "We can't," one of the thugs said, straining.

Purple six-pointed stars hovered above both her hands. Two more rings showing hieroglyphs appeared on her wrists, along with another larger ring with definitive line patterns on her upper arm. The thugs in the room turned their guns towards each other.

"What's going on?"

They shot each other.

"Lucky for you, I have a meeting to attend."

She threw one of the stars above her hand at his chest.

"Don't worry, Providence is on the way, this should hold you for now."

Another star appeared on the floor, she jumped through.

****

Agent Gomez walked down the darkened street, she shivered as she passed under a dim street lamp. The wind pierced her jacket and numbed her ears as she turned into an alley and climbed an old fire escape to on top of an abandoned building. She crawled in through the broken skylight and dropped to the catwalk, she slinked to the ground floor cloaked in the shadows and watched the arms deal go down.

"Now these, these are the best we can do."

The arms dealer bought out a capsule containing Psychanium.

"Impossible," the buyer said.

"No, we lost fourteen guys stealing this from the Circle."

He slid it out onto the table. He picked up a metal baseball bat and handed it to their strongest guy, he slammed it on the Psychanium as hard as he could, breaking the bat in half.

"What's your price..." They continued talking.

Gomez slipped through the shadows and to a crate around twenty feet from them, she clicked it and it slid open. Inside rested neat rows of egg-shaped weapons, they had a metal top and bottom, and a clear section in the middle, with a blue liquid-looking substance.

"Hey," A man snapped.

She whipped around and pulled out her gun.

"FBI, nobody move," She yelled.

They shot at her and she took cover, returning fire. The doors to the building burst open, and a figure entered, fast as lightning, cloaked in night. They sliced through the calves of one of the arms dealers, who fell to the ground. They shot at the figure, who deflected the bullets with a midnight blue katana. They sliced through another arms dealer, they tripped one and drove the sword into his chest, kicked another into a wall, and shot a needle from the base of the hilt into the same man's chest. She launched a midnight blue throwing knife at another one of the dealers, it hit his neck, dead center. She threw another one, burying it in another dealer's chest. The blue hood over her head came off in the fight, whipping her jet-black hair around and revealing a girl with a metal, midnight blue mask covering her nose and mouth. Her caramel-colored light brown eyes lit up with bolts of lightning as she stabbed the last dealer in the chest and picked up the Psychanium capsule. A man hit her in the back of the head with a bat, she doubled over and stood up, uppercutting the man who fell to the floor.

Agent Gomez stepped out. "FBI, identify yourself."

Caitlyn pressed on the bottom right jaw of her face mask. "Caitlyn Shen."

She walked over to the crate Gomez had inspected and opened it, picking up one of the eggs. She pressed her ear.

"They have them Versia, hundreds of them."

"Hundreds of what?" Gomez asked.

"Agent Mia Gomez, I didn't take you for a field agent though, I thought you would be more R&D," Caitlyn said.

"I'm Testing a new weapon in the field, but wait, wait. How do you..?"

"I read your file."

"Oh," she said with a tone to her voice indicating how she viewed the question she had asked.

"These are Psychanium energy bombs," Caitlyn said.

She tossed one towards Mia, who caught it. "Careful, I'm not bulletproof," Mia said.

"It's a Psychanium weapon, it would kill me too," Caitlyn said.

"How?"

"Psychics are more durable than regular humans to a degree against most conventional weapons, yes, but Psychanium, to us, is like steel to humans."

She took her katana and made a shallow cut into her forearm, causing it to bleed. She pulled the sword away and the wound healed.

"So if this exploded right now..."

"We and the entire city would be vaporized," Caitlyn said.

Mia's face fell.

"Don't worry, Psychanium is the most stable element in the universe, it would have to be hand detonated, not jostled around a bit," Caitlyn said.

Mia dropped it into the foam housing and snatched her hand back.

"We have to track down the rest of these if even one levels a small building..."

"The amount of firepower in this room would level the

surrounding twenty miles," Caitlyn interjected. "As I said, vaporize the whole city.

A team of FBI agents entered the building, secured the crates for transport, and swept the building for any evidence or items of interest.

"They'll be moved to the Psychic Deep Storage Vault at The Iris in Texas," Mia said.

"I know, but I think you should meet the team."

"What team?"

They entered the lobby of a high-rise building, and Caitlyn guided her to a private elevator.

"Caitlyn Shen." She said, voice confirming for the elevator's security protocol.

The elevator scanned her body and rose.

"Versia owns the top seventeen floors, they're for R&D, we're going to floor one twenty-seven."

As they rose to floor one hundred ten the elevator doors turned clear. People in white lab coats hustled around, researching Psychanium and its properties, weapons, and a dozen other tests. They arrived on floor one twenty-seven to a spacious glass and metal home. Expensive art hung on the walls along with vases made of Psychanium crystals on pedestals. A girl sat on one of the chairs, she had what looked like a ball of spider silk in her hand. Versia leaned on the balcony, looking out over the city. He looked out over the city lights without saying a word before turning around. "We're waiting for one more. A six-sided star surrounded by a circle with hieroglyphs in it appeared in the room. Ava came through.

"Did she come through a…"

"Each of us has a unique connection to a mystical element," Caitlyn explained. "Mine is Lighting, hers is Spider abilities. His is Psychic energy, and hers is Magic."

"Magic? As in Abra Cadabra?"

"Sort of. Ava?"

She moved her right hand over her left hand. In it appeared a white bunny. It hopped out of her hand and toward Mia. She picked it up. She petted it. Ava threw a purple dagger from her hand. It hit the bunny, causing it to disappear and turn into translucent, glass-like purple butterflies, which flew around the room until they faded into a cloud of purple dust.

"What was that thing in your hand?" Mia asked.

"It's called a Sphinx." Another appeared in her hand. "It's a way of keeping magical Psychic energy in check by releasing a small amount of it at a time." She said.

Caitlyn handed Versia both a glass cylinder of raw Psychanium and one of the Psychanium energy bombs recovered from the Circle.

"This means the Circle is ready for a different kind of war. They don't want to stop at taking our weapons, they want to make them." Versia said.

Versia opened the capsule and put a shard of Psychanium on the table. He held the shard floating in between his thumb and pointer finger and pushed towards Mia. It entered her body. Versia's eyes glowed cyan, her eyes glowed Yellow. She landed in a luscious mid-day jungle.

"Where are we?"

"Inside your mind."

"What?"

"Well, technically it's a manifestation of your consciousness projected by your Psychic powers."

"What? I thought that's genetic if I didn't come from one of those lines..."

"You have the genes. Because of the Circle, we've ramped up our efforts to continue discovering those of us with latent Psychic genes we can activate, some people have them, but are so dormant we can't tap into them, or we can only tap into them partially, but one hundred percent of your blood is Psychic, you just never had the environment to cultivate your powers. You are the Solaris Psychic." He said.

She came back to herself, a yellow energy poured from her body and dissipated. The Solaris Yellow Suit.

A yellow energy appeared in Mia's hands. It faded.

"I feel like. I can't even describe it." She said. "It's like I feel every atom at the top of my fingers"

"Your powers are sun-related, once properly cultivated you'll have access to the energy of an entire sun. You also have your Psychic shielding. It's an invisible protective layer on your skin making you more durable, you're not bulletproof, but you can take more than one or two before going down, but it will hurt. Swords will cut through it but will take extra force to penetrate as deep, and Psychanium will end you like that," she said with a snap. "Your healing is also sped up, but any damage done by Psychanium weapons will take longer. There's also one more thing Caitlyn would like to explain."

"Have you heard the stories and legends of Psychics so powerful they could level cities with a look, wipe countries off the face of the earth with a swipe of their hand, Psychics who could move faster than lightning, Psychics invincible to every weapon fired their way?" Caitlyn asked Mia.

"Yeah, but I thought those Psychics were long dead,"

"They are, but we as their descendants can still access it. The name for it in our language is complicated, but it translates to the Psychic State, our eyes glow, lines form on our bodies, and we tap into every ounce of Psychic energy around us."

"Then why aren't we always in the Psychic State?" Mia asked.

"Initially, the first Psychics used it as they pleased, but over time it morphed into a defense mechanism that while we can access, we have limited control over our actions outside of protecting ourselves, accidental misfires of the ability have leveled cities unintentionally," Caitlyn said.

"Psychics level cities intentionally?" Mia asked.

"Not in thousands of years," Versia said.

"Can we be killed?"

"If struck with a weapon made of an alien metal, yes, you will be killed," Versia said.

"The easiest way to sum it up is it turns us into near gods, but only well-trained Psychics can access it, when they do, there's no telling who or what they will destroy, therefore its use is outright avoided unless the absolute worse comes to worse. Even a life-or-death situation won't trigger it without extraneous circumstances. Psychics have killed each other accidentally in the state with no memory of what they did so it is a topic many Psychics like to avoid due to a Psychic king who accidentally killed his queen, and almost ended the world in a fit of rage. It is not a power to be trifled with."

"That is, wow,"

"Only well-trained Psychics can access it, so don't think you'll accidentally tap into it without years of training," Ava said.

"What would you define as a good time?" Mia asked.

"If you need to stop a black hole or a planet-killing asteroid, that's a good time," Versia said.

Two silver cases rested on an all-glass table near Versia. He picked up one, walked over to Mia, and opened it. Inside rested a velvet canvas with three objects inside. A six-sided solar yellow hexagonal triangle Psychanium Nanite housing unit, and two solar yellow bracelets.

"These use our generation two Psychanium technology."

She put on the two bracelets and attached the chest piece to herself. He picked up the other case. Inside rested two silver and yellow Ring Blades made of Psychanium. They had an outer ring with a handle on one side and an inner ring; the two rings were connected by a wide intricate set of spokes with yellow psychic energy flowing over them.

"These are the Solaris Ring Blades. Forged from the core of Eta Carinae out of pure Psychanium, they will cut through anything, make no sound, and always return to your hands. She touched them and they faded into yellow hexagons.

"When do we begin?" She asked.

"Your Core Crystal," Versia replied, as he waved his hand over a holographic table.

"Here," he said.

"The Temple of the Sun. Your Core Crystal appeared here. There's the base camp of a German science paramilitary faction nearby, they probably have it."

"What do I do?" He tossed her a set of keys. "Go find it, if the Circle gets their hands on that, it would be a worst-case scenario."

"I'll get it." She said as she drank the rest of her glass.

****

"Herr Neur," a man yelled. "The temple. It's glowing."

A man exited his tent. At the top of the temple glowed a blinding yellow.

"Go, retrieve it, this is what we've waited for."

His team put on hazmat suits with special visors and made their way up the temple.

"Don't touch it, we don't know what it could do."

A shaking pair of hands took the Core Crystal with a pair of tongs, it dimmed as the tongs closed around it.

"Good, bring it down, that thing has more destructive power than a nuke," Neur said.

His agent placed it into suspension in a machine.

"For years, I have waited for this moment, to have one of these crystals before me. Go. Bring the spear." He said.

They brought a two-pronged spear made of a dark gray brushed titanium. The blades extended from a rectangular stage to a curved shape, up into a point, and back down in a straight line, curving out to make space for the crystal.

Neur put on a metal glove and picked up the crystal. His hand shook before he forced it still. He dropped it into a space between the blades. The entire spear shook, rose, and fell back onto the table. Yellow lines appeared throughout the metal before fading.

"Did it work sir?" One of his people asked.

"It's beautiful. Begin scans and call the Circle. Tell them we have their billion-dollar weapon ready."

Skeletal robotic arms emitting scanning beams moved above the spear while the glowing white table it rested on took scans from the bottom.

"Test the crystal, I want to see if we can crack it, see

what secrets it houses. one billion watts, concentrate it, three-millimeter beam," Neur said.

"Yes sir." A scientist said.

A small device held by a robotic arm moved over the spear.

"Begin," Neur ordered.

One of the scientists typed on his keyboard. A thin red beam of light shot from the device in the robotic arm's hand, hitting the crystal head-on. Nothing happened.

"Increase power."

"But Herr Neur..."

"Do it," he barked

The scientist turned a dial, and the beam grew hotter and hotter, until the crystal reacted, releasing the energy it stored from the laser back into it. A bolt of yellow energy erupted from the crystal and into the robotic arms above it, disintegrating them on contact. The lights turned back on.

"Fascinating. Why did it not destroy the spear as well?" He asked himself.

"Herr Neur, you must come see this."

He walked over to a computer screen.

"The crystal, it's changing the metal into Psychanium."

"Impossible. It's only been in contact for a few hours."

"Fifty-six percent of the titanium has already changed to Psychanium." The scientist said, pointing to the scans.

"It must be warping the metal to fit its needs. Interesting, we must test this. Hit it with the armor-piercing rounds. If it is Titanium, it will shatter after a few shots, if it is Psychanium, the bullets will crumple upon contact." Neur said.

A robotic arm lifted the spear while a compartment opened in the roof sliding out a minigun.

"Fire," Neur said.

The minigun released a barrage of bullets on the spear, they crumpled like paper. Neur took off his spectacles.

"Beautiful." He whispered.

"It has reached one hundred Psychanium sir, the attack must have sped it up."

"Gentlemen consider yourselves blessed to be a part of this new history"

Everyone clapped and Neur picked up the spear. He paused, frozen for a second, as the power coursed through his veins.

"It's beautiful, I understand now," he paused. "It's not only the power to destroy, but the power to create.

He walked out of the tent. The science team followed him. He stretched out the spear towards a clearing in the forest behind the encampment. Out of the ground sprouted new trees, growing to maturity within seconds.

"It's beautiful." He thought for a second and created another object. The spear rejected it, releasing yellow energy and throwing Neur back.

"Nein, Nein, Nein," he yelled.

"What's wrong Sir?"

"I attempted to create a Psychic Suit. The spear rejected it.

"Why?" The scientist asked

"Perhaps it only creates organic life. Nevertheless, we will find out, continue running tests," Neur said as he placed the spear back on the table.

Mia's jet entered the airspace above the jungle, its cloaking hid it from people below as she landed two miles out from the German's camp. She tapped her left bracelet, bringing up a detailed 3D hologram map of the seventeen hundred square foot complex, containing seven tents. One in the middle for science and research, and the other six as living quarters. The map also displayed the temple they had camped near. She decided she'd sneak around and attack from the high ground via the temple. Using the map, she zoomed in on the center tent, the holographic display showed the spear, and at the center rested her solar yellow core crystal. *They've already begun weaponizing it.* She thought. She double-tapped her bracelet causing the hologram to retract. The bracelets plus her chest piece turned her invisible. Moving faster than anything they could perceive she had already snuck on top of the temple. She hid behind one of the pillars as her smart contact zoomed into the camp, and her earpiece picked up their conversations.

"This is the most boring post..."

"We got the spear, let's..."

"Herr Neur, each crystal is connected to an aspect of the Psychic powers..." She continued listening.

"You can't build a suit with it, it's like it's programmed to not allow it."

"Then I'll need you to reprogram it, that is what your exorbitant salary is for, correct? Neur replied

"Sir, I can't. This is an ancient Psychic Language, I can't even comprehend what the crystal is communicating to us, it..."

Before he said the rest of it, the tile she stood on caved, she slapped her hand over her mouth to contain a yelp and hit the ground a hundred feet down. Before she could fly back up, the hole closed itself.

"What the..." She said as she looked around and flinched at the skeletons.

They didn't look decayed but looked preserved, arranged with respect, with their hands crossed in "X's" in front of their chests. The floor had intricate carvings matching her suit, even the bodies had been arranged to preserve the pattern. She had an urge to touch the floor and pressed her entire palm to the circle she stood in. The lines carved in the floor glowed yellow as Psychic energy flowed through them, and her eyes glowed yellow.

Outside, the Circle helicopter had landed and out stepped one of the Circle's leaders.

"I'm hoping this was worth our investment, and for your sake, is as you promised."

"And more Mr. Max," Neur said, beaming.

They looked towards the temple as yellow lines coated the exterior of it.

"The temple's activated," Max said.

"Only a direct descendant can do that. Set up a perimeter. I want a bullet in whoever activated it." Neur said as his people brought out the spear.

Max looked at it. "It changed the metal to Psychanium? He asked as he ran his fingertips over the blade. "Beautiful."

"Name your price," Max said.

Inside the temple, she walked over to a wall with a large image of a woman painted on it. She had brown skin and yellow armor, along with multiple suns painted above her. Mia ran her fingers over them as they glowed yellow. A voice spoke in her head clear as day.

"Welcome, Mia. Descendant of the Sun. You may now claim what is yours. You are a direct descendant of Solaris, what they in the ancient world called the sun goddess, but as you know, was gifted abilities by her Psychic powers. Her beauty and intellect were unmatched for centuries. Using this, she unified her people and became one of the first female leaders on this earth, a trailblazer for her descendants, a line of strong female Psychics. Her final gifts to her descendants rest here. This temple is your power, it is your birthright. Claim it, and burn those who would dare oppose you in Solaris' unquenchable flames. You are Mia Ra Gomez. Demi-Goddess of the Sun. You are the Solaris Yellow Psychic.

Outside the temple, a blinding light shot from its peak, and out of it rose Mia. Her eyes glowed yellow as lines appeared on her skin, She landed. Max signaled to his troops, and they raised their guns and fired. The bullets melted as they approached her.

"Burn," Mia said.

Yellow lasers shot from her eyes causing explosions to rock the ground, scattering the Circle's agents.

"Use the spear," Max said.

Neur pointed the spear at Mia, and a yellow beam from the crystal shot at her, throwing her backward.

"You have my gift." She said as she stood.

She stretched out her hand, and the gem flew to her hand. A beam of yellow energy erupted from her as the lines in her skin flared. She waved her hand, scattering Max's troops as their guns melted in their hands.

"Who are you?" Max asked.

"The Demi-Goddess of the Sun. Solaris." Mia said.

Her ring blades formed in her hands, and she threw them, they flew around like a pair of frisbees, hitting the remainder of Max's troop before the blades returned to her hands. Neur said something explicit in German as he pulled out a pistol. She turned around. He shot. She threw one of her ring blades. It sliced clean through the bullet, throwing sparks before it cut clean through his gun. She threw the other blade into the center of the camp, it buried itself in the ground as her other blade came back to her. She threw it at her blade in the ground, and they crashed, throwing a shockwave across the camp, ravaging everything.

"I'll kill you," Neur said.

She looked around the camp. Troops sprawled, tents overturned, and decimated computers and servers. She double-tapped her wrist, contacting Providence.

"They'll be there to pick up the garbage soon," Mia said.

Neur said nothing as her suit built around her, and she took off.

CHAPTER 17

Reese pulled into the garage, stepped out of the car, and opened the door to the mansion. She entered the living room. Shattered vases lay strewn across the room, the walls had three large dents in them, indicative of a punch, and others had long gashes in them like an animal had rampaged through. Lamps lay shattered and glass lay strewn everywhere. She dropped her bag on the table and looked for Isazisi, she found him sitting against the wall. She could sense how hard he held back tears, burying his face in his knees, as his katana lay beside him.

"What happened?" She asked.

"Burst, the energy exploded from me, it shattered everything." He said.

"And the walls?" She continued.

"I wasn't feeling like myself."

"Are you ok?" She asked.

Her hand glowed with red wisps as she waved it above his head, scanning his psyche. A mind lock protected it.

"Do you need to talk?" She asked, sounding like the therapist he had.

"I don't know." He said. "We don't talk about it, but every kill is a toll, every hostage dead is a toll, no matter how much I feel I'm protecting the world or carrying out the greater good, it still hurts every time."

"She squeezed in beside him.

"Is this about the Circle?" She asked.

"A bomb, with my signature written on it, killed seven hundred fifty people, it can't be more personal. Thousands of innocent deaths on my hands, my responsibility, thousands who won't have a family member tonight, that's on me." He said.

"That's why we keep fighting." She said.

"I don't like to tell people how personal this fight against the Circle is, what they took from me, but I can't let them take anymore. I have to protect the one thing in my life that's always in danger, the one thing I can't live without. You." He said.

"But the threats are real, and I don't know if I can protect everything. My suits, Providence they're...they're also a part of me, but you, you're the most important part. If you died because of the Circle, that'd be six I couldn't protect. I would never be the same, I don't think I could ever live in a world without you. Everything would crumble around me. I'd keep trying to kill myself to be with you, knowing every time it wouldn't work. It would be endless suffering." He said.

"Don't even get me started on the government officials breathing down my neck, people are scared, but we used to give them hope. Now they look up in horror as buildings collapse from weapons we made."

He buried his head further in his knees.

"I'm a shell." He whispered, still straining to hold back tears.

"I can't show weakness, or emotion, or remorse for terrible people. We are beacons of peace, and no one can believe in gods who aren't perfect."

"We'll take one problem at a time." She said to him in a soothing voice as she leaned her head on his shoulder.

"Why do you think it's called Providence, we're supposed to save people, to protect them."

"This isn't the end." She whispered.

"We have all the power in the world, everything we could ever need, and we still failed. More weapons than entire armies, more finances than entire countries, more manpower than we could ever need, a monopoly on the strongest metal in the universe, and superpowers, we have superpowers, and we failed when the whole world counted on us. Now our weapons have killed thousands of innocent civilians while we hide out in million-dollar mansions, protected from accountability by laws our ancestors spent billions lobbying for." Isazisi said.

"You can't blame yourself, it's every one of us. We dropped it, not you." Reese said.

"I don't know." He said. "They'll ask us why we do what we do. Why do we put our lives on the line to protect people who will never care about us." Isazisi said.

"Why do you do it then?" Reese asked.

"After seeing what the Circle did to the people I cared about most, It told me I wasn't given these powers to let it happen to anyone else. I can make jokes in front of sub-committees, and courts, and let people think we have everything under control, but the truth is I've never been this out of control in my life, and I hate it because I killed everyone in those buildings. I did, whether or not I pressed the trigger. It's my fault, but I can never let them see I've lost control, I can never let them see anything besides a steel exterior because if they do, panic ensues and everything is worse than before." He said.

"We can't change the past, we can stop the next attack, save the next victims, that's it," Reese said. "I know, and that's what hurts most." He said. He rested his head on Reese, as tears left his eyes.

....

The woman cracked open the paint cans on the ground. She tied her black hair back with an ocean blue hair tie. Her chocolate brown eyes twinkled in the Florida sunlight while her ocean blue painted nails gleamed in them. She rubbed a bit of blue paint off her light brown skin before she made her way to the top of the building and attached a harness around herself. She clipped it to a hook on the building's roof and pushed off the edge. She rappeled midway down and raised her hands, pillars of liquid paint rose and she directed the colors creating a mural on the wall. People who recognized her gathered around, recording on their phones. A red and white news van pulled up and out stepped a reporter and her cameraman.

"What is she doing?" A girl whispered

"Isn't that Lily Taulauniu," another said.

"Isn't she a Psychic?"

"Well, the paint isn't moving by itself."

The news channel had set up and the cameraman panned onto the reporter.

"We are here reporting live from Aureli Street in Miami where the Psychic Lily Taulauniu seems to be painting a mural, we're not sure what it is but we believe it is a tribute to victims of the Circle attacks. As we know there was a building explosion in downtown Miami which killed 540 people. Authorities ruled it a severe gas leak, but due to multiple attacks across the globe, many people have suspicions it may have been a Circle attack. Access to the attack site has been strictly regulated, even to families of the victims." The reporter said. A dark blue sports car pulled up to the site as a group of protestors jumped out of white vans with their trademark signs. They chanted as Lily continued painting. Versia stepped out of the car, and the protestors' chanting increased to screaming as Versia walked up to Lily's painting and examined the swooshes and swoops in vibrant reds, green, and a dozen shades of blue. As Versia looked at it he could almost make out a person crying. Lily rappelled down the wall and detached the harness.

"It's a bit different from your other paintings," Versia said.

Lily looked up and down the street covered in the dozens of murals she'd painted over the years.

"It represents pain, not a new concept to us," Lily said.

The reporter came closer to the painting and the cameraman panned onto it.

"We have a mission for you," Versia said.

"Great, where am I going?"

Lily's wrist buzzed, she looked at it and her face fell.

"Hold that though, meet me at the house," Lily said.

An ocean blue suit formed around her body and she took off.

Lily landed at a large mansion complex on the outskirts of Miami. She burst into the house and made her way up the stairs, she threw open the doors to her grandmother's room where her mother and aunts stood around a woman standing beside her bed.

"Mom, you need to rest," Lily's mother said.

"The only thing I need are car keys and freedom, but you would like to keep me locked in this house," her grandmother responded. She looked over towards Lily.

"Lily, what are you doing here?"

"I got an alert that something was happening to you."

"The only thing happening to me is false imprisonment," Lily's grandmother said. "You know what, everybody but Lily out."

"Mom..." Lily's mother began.

"I'm still the matriarch of the family, all of you, out, you can come back when I'm finished."

Lily's mom and her aunts left the room.

"My powers are dwindling, I can feel my time is coming," Lily's grandmother said.

She pulled water from a cup beside her bed and held it in a sphere above her hand.

"You know, we've done terrible things in our history, my generation. For thousands of years the Psychics that came before us laid the groundwork for the power we freely abuse today. Genocides, massacres, screw-ups in history we covered up, now your generation has lost our sacred metal to the hands of our greatest enemy. What we did to the Circle, they are punishing you for our actions. My generation thought we crushed them. We killed everyone we could find, they didn't spare anyone, and it seems we missed. Lily, you need to be different from me, from us. What we did caused the tragedy today. When you defeat the Circle, do it another way." Lily's grandmother said.

"We'll be different," Lily said.

Her wrist buzzed.

"I'll assume that's a mission. I remember in my prime when I was the Ocean Psychic Suit. Carry on my legacy Lily, defeat the Circle, but be different from us."

Lily opened the door to her house where Versia sat in her living room reading a magazine. He placed a silver cube on the table and tapped the top. A hologram display came to life.

"This is the Niang Spire, their new billion-dollar hotel in Sydney, Australia. Chatter has told us the Circle within the next twelve hours will attempt to set off a bomb at the opening day ceremony. An estimated five thousand people will be attending. If they take down the building it will be the deadliest Circle attack so far.

"I'll handle it," Lily said.

The CEO of the Niang Corporation cut the ribbon, rapturous applause followed as they took people on guided tours of the building. Lily walked around the ceremony and walked into the building, her smart contact scanned for Psychanium signatures. Outside the building hid hundreds of Providence Centurions cloaked in the shadows on the lookout. One of the tour guides with a black duffle bag walked on a service elevator. Lily's smart contact scanned his bag as the elevator closed. Her contact continued the scan as the elevator shot up the building. 'Match' her smart lense read.

"We have a match," Lily said, "evacuate the building."

Providence's agents evacuated civilians in the building as Lily pulled the fire alarm, and multiple Niang employees pulled guns from their tuxedos and shot at the guests. Lily raised a wall of water from a nearby fountain in the lobby, she pulled the water into a spherical cross around her and threw darts of water at the Circle agents. Providence Centurions entered the building and shot at Circle agents, covering fleeing guests. Lily bounded up the stairs past guests racing down the stairs. Her contact tagged the location of the bomb. She kicked open the door to the floor of the Circle agent. He had dropped the bomb and stood in the elevator which closed. Lily ran to the duffel bag and ripped it open, the timer had thirty seconds on it. Lily looked around and her smart contact detected a heat signature. She dashed over to a maid cart where a child curled behind it. Lily said something explicit under her breath. She picked up the child and ran down the steps, the bomb exploded and Lily shielded the child, the whole top of the building collapsed into the bottom of it, Lily blacked out as the building collapsed on her.

Lily came to with her ears ringing and the kid in front of her, she lay on her side with hundreds of thousands of pounds on her right shoulder. The building shifted above her as she looked past the kid at the Providence bomb six feet from her face. The serial number DRRC92517 painted on it. She said something explicit under her breath.

"Are we going to die?" The child asked.

"No, we're not, don't you worry, they'll get us out of here," Lily said.

The building shifted again, jostling the live bomb.

Versia's suit touched down inside the sealed-off site of the building collapse

"Twelve hours since the collapse. Two trapped. One kid, ten years old, and Miss Taulauniu," a Centurion said.

"What's taking so long, can't we gravity crane the debris?" Versia asked.

"We've detected a potentially live munition in the rubble, we have no way to tell if the Circle tampered with it."

Versia said something explicit.

"Gravity crane it, we can't sit here and wait for it to go off or for the building to crush them, I can feel her slipping."

The Providence agents moved a large silver crane over the rubble. Dozens of news cameras panned onto it.

"We've been told to evacuate the area due to a potentially live munition in the rubble, they are attempting to gravity crane the Psychic Lily Taulauniu and one other person trapped under the building." A reporter said.

Versia nodded to the technician who started the gravity crane. The crane lifted hundreds of tons of concrete and steel.

Lily turned to the sound, the child closed his eyes as the light from outside penetrated. The bomb rolled off the rubble and stopped inches from the kid. Lily grabbed the kid in her free arm and leaped out of the debris. She slid down the rubble to the ground, her entire right arm covered in blood. She put the kid down and collapsed.

Lily woke up in a hospital bed, her entire arm wrapped in

white. Versia sat in the chair beside the bed.

"We found out the bomb wasn't live, Circle tempered with it," Versia said.

"Interesting," Lily said.

Isazisi walked in.

"Glad you're alive," Isazisi said.

"Great to see you too," Lily said. "I talked to my grandmother before the mission. She told me to look into our history, a deep dive, I suggest both of you do the same."

"What did you learn?" Versia asked.

"Maybe we weren't always the good guys," Lily said.

****

Isazisi stepped into his office.

"Security level nine," he said.

Metal sheets slid down over the windows behind his desk as the air vents shut and a metal sheet rose, covering the door.

"Megan, access Circle files, pre-1970,"

She stayed silent for a few seconds and responded "Access denied,"

"On whose authority?"

"The Psychic Council." She responded.

"The Psychic Council hasn't existed in hundreds of years, director override."

"Director override failed."

"On whose authority?"

"The Psychic Council."

Isazisi sighed as he rubbed his head with his thumb and pointer finger.

"Run decryption."

"Decryption failed," Megan said.

"Show me the code," Isazisi said.

Megan brought up a holographic interface of the code.

"It's constantly rewriting itself, it would take a team of MIT students 15 years to crack this."

"Can you crack it?"

"Per my calculations, it would take me six years straight, and I'm an AI."

"Well, I'm a Psychic."

Isazisi typed at his desk, working on the code, it blocked him but he circumvented it as the two played a game of chess, after a few minutes Isazisi cracked it.

"Access Granted," Megan said. "What would you like to know?"

"Start with everything post World War Two," Isazisi said.

"The Psychics have destroyed the Circle many times in history. The most recent after the war and the advent of nuclear weaponry, the Circle sought to obtain and copy the design of a nuclear weapon to form an independent state. World powers not wanting another independent nuclear state looked for ways to covertly crush the Circle's push for freedom. The Circle seeing this turned to Psychanium weapons thinking the Psychics would support their quest for freedom. They peacefully stole a cache of Psychanium weapons and made plans to carve out their state." Megan said.

"And what did we do?"

"The response of the Psychics was far more violent than it needed to be. They felt the sacrality of their metal was trifled with, and they massacred everyone they could find as punishment. Not the first time in Psychic history. Their planes rained fire from above while Psychics killed everything that moved. The Circle's leader at the time Alexander Fletcher the First was murdered in cold blood by your great-grandfather after surrendering."

"Fletcher?"

"Yes, Circle leader Fletcher is a direct descendant of the one killed, his great-grandson to be exact. Few survived the hunt and ran to hide in the shadows. The Psychics later covered up the massacre, ashamed of their actions. That is the modern history of the Psychics and the Circle." Megan said.

"What can you get me on Fletcher today?"

"Compiling...Boss, you're not going to believe this. He worked for us."

"What do you mean?"

"Fletcher was more than likely estranged from the Circle at his time because he led a medical division for us, Project Ajax, which was a way to use Psychanium technology to create and heal cells in a way never seen before. He must've known about their agents in our ranks and said nothing. Shortly after you took over as Director of Providence he attempted to steal and sell the research, fearing your more militaristic vision would lead to funding cuts. Internal affairs found out about his data breach and shut down the whole project after a larger investigation found out funding was misappropriated across the division, they cited fruit of the poisonous tree as a wider justification. Your legal department litigated him into the ground and took everything he owned."

"That's interesting."

"There's more. Remember that Andrew man, who killed himself. His sister was in a relationship with FLecher, but she was sick, and the research he was doing could've saved her. I think he blames you, because the final order for the shutdown was approved by you."

"I remember that."

"Espionage kept tabs on him for a little bit, but he dropped off the radar after he joined a Mexican drug cartel."

"So all of this is because of the research project we shut down?"

"From the evidence we gathered, marriage was on the table, he really loved her, and she died just weeks after the project was shut down. In his depositions, he said he was just days away from the cure and needed just a little more time, but you'd already shut it down at that point and litigation had begun."

"Wow, we created him," Isazisi said.

****

The helicopter landed on the helipad within the Providence prison. Versia stepped out of the vehicle and inside the gray slab of a complex before walking to an interrogation room. Behind the glass stood The Chairman.

"Mike Mangham, ten years in special forces, another five with the CIA, retirement, and now the Circle, what did they offer you? " Versia said.

"They offered me freedom, and now the great Cyan himself has seen fit to visit me in my lowly cell." The Chairman said.

"I've been busy," Versia said. "You know, dealing with terrorists."

"You call us terrorists, yet we're visionaries, teachers if you will. We imagine a better world, and to build that, the old one must crumble." The Chairman said.

"And the people you kill, what about them?" Versia asked.

"What's the term we use, collateral damage is it?"

"I don't use that term."

"Even so, when you kill thousands, the world cheers, when I do it, I'm a terrorist. How many countries burn effigies of you and other Psychics?"

We don't kill without extreme justification."

"Really? Hmm. The Red Cyan is a murderer, the best the world has ever seen, thousands of confirmed kills worldwide yet he is not a scourge on the planet?" The Chairman asked.

"Everything Isazisi does is justified by a legal panel," Versia said.

"Of people who work for him? That's not even the worst part, you have acknowledged your culture of pain and suffering. If I'm a terrorist, what are you?" The Chairman asked again.

"We don't kill innocents," Versia said.

"Who decides who's innocent? Everyone's guilty of something, it's a matter of degree." The Chairman said.

"Then I guess we're all just the killers," Versia said.

"You, The Red Cyan, and five other Psychics top a government list comprised of the most dangerous individuals, ranging from mercenaries, government agents, war criminals, terrorist leaders, assassins, rogue agents, and anyone sadistic enough to kill indiscriminately, yet once again, I'm the terrorist?" The Chairman asked.

"You're a terrorist because you kill people who've done nothing to deserve it," Versia said.

"Everyone is guilty of something." The Chairman said.

"You set off a bomb in New York City," Versia said.

"And Providence hasn't set off bombs in the largest cities in third-world countries? As I said, to build our new world we will build on the ashes of the old one. In our new world, you will not even be a memory. Your culture of death and destruction will be erased, and they will only know of the Circle." The Chairman said.

"You're insane," Versia said.

"Like you said. We're all just the killers." The Chairman said.

"We aren't like you."

"You Psychics are the New Deities. Sent from above to save us in our carnal and infernal state. With your thrones and palaces and armies. If you can cut at the neck of a deity. The people will no longer believe. We have cut at your throats and try as you will, the bleeding will not stop. We've shown the world you are not infallible. You are not the Psychics of old who could level countries with a look. You simply masquerade as them, throwing around the legacy and wealth built by men much greater than you. You are a shadow, a caricature, a disgrace to your heritage. An institution responsible for more death, destruction, and suffering, than any entity in the history of this planet."

"Is that what you've been told?"

"Fletcher loves his mythology, and do you know what he described you as? A gilded Ares. A god of war, a god of death. You masquerade as the good one, a man who despises violence yet is forced to commit it, but deep down you are a man who loves his war. Who loves the chase, loves the feeling of his sword cutting down all who oppose him and his people. You are Ares, and you kill for fun as he does. Hide it as much as you like, you are no different than your ancestors, no different than those murderers."

"I'm done here," Versia said.

"If you're curious, look up the Night of Ten Thousand Terrors in your hall of records. I'm sure whatever you find will be most eye-opening"

Versia didn't even turn around.

"An empire built on bones will crumble as the souls of the dead reach up for vengeance."

Versia didn't answer as he left the cell.

****

Versia arrived at his Los Angeles home, the protests outside his Palo Alto residence had gotten far too unmanageable. He hung the keys to his Aston Martin on the wall as he took the elevator down to the residence's underground lab. A woman sat at his computer, typing away. She has flawless, glowing, chestnut brown skin, her hair done up as radiant black Fulani braids with light blue and light brown woven into the braids, and her baby hairs styled into an intricate pattern of curls and wisps on her forehead. The white screen reflected off her dark brown eyes.

"Don't worry, it's my account, not yours." The woman said.

"Should I ask what you're doing?" Versia asked.

"I'm a CIA consultant, I'm consulting." She said.

"I still have no idea what you do, Yemani," Versia said.

Yemani plugged a USB into the computer's port.

"It means I'm an agent with special privileges."

"You are heir to the Omi Dynasty and a Psychic, why not Providence?" Versia asked.

"Y'all don't need me, CIA does," Yemani said.

Versia accepted the answer.

"I guess I'll ask it, what are you doing?" Versia asked.

"Sending files to the CIA, we have the most secure servers in the world, your computer is one of a few that links with ours,"

Yemani said.

"Where are they sending you?" Versia asked.

"Barcelona," Yemani said.

"I had a productive conversation with the Chairman," Versia said.

"You know he's insane right?" She said.

"He'll get what's coming to him," Versia said.

"They all will," Yemani said as she pulled the USB from the computer.

CHAPTER 18

The light blue Jaguar F-Type drove down the streets of Barcelona like the jungle predator its badge indicated it was. She turned down each street, the soft, yet aggressive purr of the cat's engine and the allure of its unique color turning heads everywhere it went. She turned into a building and parked her car. She entered the building where the CIA had set up an off-books base to track the Circle.

"What do we have?" Yemani asked.

"A Barcelona cell. We think after the failed attacks, several cells are beginning to go rogue. They don't want to take credit for the attacks anymore, it's too much heat. We think their central command still wants to spread the message, but smaller pockets don't. Intel suggests the Barcelona cell of the Circle will try to set off a bomb here." The agent said, touching a well-populated and visited area of the city. "And blame it on radical Catalan separatists."

"What are the potential casualties?" She asked.

"They could kill up to two thousand,"

Yemani said something explicit under her breath.

"Do we know where they are?"

The agent typed on the keyboard for a few seconds, accessing both CIA and Providence satellites.

"Providence gave us a potential location they extracted from a top Circle member. Right. Here."

A lifeless gray slab on the outskirts of the city showed up on the screen. The screen turned to a different spectrum, revealing an intricate web of tunnels beneath the building.

"Intel suggests less than ten hours before the attack."

"Then we better get moving," Yemani said.

Two dozen agents clad in black tactical gear along with Yemani lined up outside the building. Two agents moved forward in silence, planting charges on the door hinges. They exploded in silence, melting the hinges followed by two agents removing the door and laying it on the ground. They moved in, swinging the barrels of their guns toward every nook and cranny. One of the agents made a hand sign indicating "all clear" as they moved towards a set of dual doors in the back. Two agents opened the doors revealing a wide staircase into the unknown. One agent took a step but Yemani held her hand in front of him. She caused the water molecules in the air to turn to mist, revealing a web of lasers.

She touched the wall, lines of energy extended from her hands, canvassing the wall and hacking the laser implants. The agents moved forward, down the stairs, and through another set of doors at the bottom and into a large underground web. A shot rang out, grazing one of the agents. They fired back, moving through the tunnels as Circle agents fired at them. They caught one CIA agent in the arm. He fell with a pained grunt as the bullet lodged itself in his shoulder. His team members dragged him to safety as they shot back at an invisible target. Another agent caught a bullet in his vest. He fell, forcing the CIA to regroup. Yemani formed a shield of water in front of them, catching the bullets.

"Leave, I'll handle this." She said.

"Ma'am, are you..." An agent began.

"Go." She said.

The agents extracted their injured behind Yemani's shield of water and returned topside where an emergency medical helicopter landed. Minutes after they exited the building the entire building collapsed behind them in a deafening crash.

Gasps and muffled chatter overtook the crowd of agents.

"Look," one of them yelled.

Every head in the crowd swung in the direction the agent pointed. Yemani emerged from the rubble, covered in dust and debris. She had a Psychanium knife sticking out of her shoulder and red splotches on her from Psychanium bullets. In her hand, she dragged the target they came after. One of the Circle's

European leaders. She dropped him at the feet of the agent in charge.

"Mission complete." She said as she passed out.

She awoke on a hospital bed in the agency's base in Barcelona. After they'd removed the knife and any other shrapnel they could they let the body heal her. The mission had been eight hours earlier. She exited the room and made her way to the main area where rapturous applause greeted her. She walked down the hall to the interrogation room and entered the secure side where they watched the man through a one-way mirror.

"Mark Palier, head of the Circle in Europe." The agent in charge said.

"He's not saying anything?" Yemani asked.

"Of course not, we'll move him stateside for the full interrogation, here we have limited resources."

Yemani left the secure room and walked to the interrogation side. She sat across from Mark.

"We can do this two ways. You already know what Psychics can do." She said.

"That's why we fight. To rid the world of you."

"What are your plans for Barcelona?"

"Hail the Circle."

He slammed the side of his face on the metal table, breaking a cyanide capsule in his teeth, he foamed at his mouth.

Yemani said something explicit under her breath as medical personnel burst into the room.

She left as they dragged him to the makeshift hospital in the back of the complex.

****

Agents paced around as others turned to extra work as they waited for news regarding Pailer. One doctor came out holding a clear circular capsule.

"He'll live." The doctor said.

The room let out a breath.

"Unfortunately, we also found this. It's a tracking chip embedded in the fake tooth." The doctor said.

"They know where we are?" The agent in charge asked.

"It is still active."

"We can use that," Yemani said as she took the capsule. "It's me they'll want. I can lead them away."

"That's dangerous, I can't sanction that." The agent in charge said.

"Well, I didn't ask," Yemani said.

Her F-type tore down the bridge highway, leading the Circle away from the CIA base. Yemani looked in her rearview mirror. A black SUV swerved in between the traffic, breaking the speed limit. The SUV stayed behind her for a few seconds until the driver floored it, rear-ending Yemani. She jerked forward as the car took the hit. The driver hit her again as a man in thin black tactical gear climbed out the window of the vehicle. He stood on top of the hummer and pulled an SMG from his lower back. He shot at the Psychahium car, tearing through the metal with ease. Yemani sped up as two more SUVs caught up with the first. The man in the SUV jumped onto the roof of her car. He pointed down and shot at the driver's seat, Yemani leaned forward, avoiding the bullets. She jerked her hand upwards, throwing the man off the car with a pulse of psychic energy. He landed in front of her and rolled to a stop on the asphalt. She slammed on the brakes while the SUV rammed her again from behind, pushing her towards the figure. He jumped onto the Hummer, landing on the roof. Her car swerved as the SUV rammed it again. Her car hit the concrete barrier, capsizing. It rolled through the air, slamming on the asphalt and rolling to a stop on its roof.

The SUV drove past, screeching to a stop as they overshot their target. Yemani's ears rang as her brain pounded against her skull. She had a bit of blood running down her face from the shards of Psychanium glass that shot through the cabin. She patted around the vehicle for her seatbelt latch and undid it. She crawled out the window and onto the street where four men had gotten out of the SUV. The man jumped off the hood of the SUV and took a gun from another man. He fired it at the car. Yemani ran and took cover as the bullet drilled itself into the bodywork and exploded. Hot shards of metal and shrapnel rained on the road. The gun read DRRC8934 on the side. She moved behind the remains of her car, peering out at the men walking towards it.

The goggles of the man flashed to life and an X-ray targeting system located Yemani behind the burning car. He raised the weapon and fired again, the car exploded, throwing Yemani off the bridge. She crashed onto the road below, causing a bus to swerve out of the way, throwing itself off balance and onto its side. She stood as the other four men rained fire on her position. She made her way to the bus and tore a hole in the roof, helping the people out. The men from the other SUVs jumped out, attached wire to the back of the trucks, and rappelled down the overpass.

They fired at the bus as Yemani shielded people with a wall of water. The head Circle agent jumped down from the overpass, landing with a crater. He fired at the bus. It exploded, throwing Yemani onto the road. She slipped behind a parked car as the Circle agents canvassed the landscape, looking for their target. People ran across the street searching for cover as empty cars burned on the streets. Yemani peeked her head over the car's hood, surveying the agents. One of them fired at her. She ducked behind the car as the bullets sparked against the silver vehicle.

One agent handed the leader a Gatling gun. He held down the trigger, spraying the landscape with bullets as Yemani ran for better cover. She formed a water shuriken in her hand and threw her hand back, over the hood of the car she hid behind. The shuriken hit one of the Circle agents. The others took cover and returned fire as they confirmed she wasn't defenseless. The agents moved through the urban battlefield, like predators hunting their prey. Yemani moved, careful to avoid the gaze of the Gatling gun. She found two agents moving together. A water tanto formed in her hand and she lashed out, killing both agents with swift strikes to their necks and slipping back into the shadows. She found another agent staring into space. She slid on the hood of a car, kicking him into a truck parked nearby. She grabbed his gun off the floor and shot at the other Circle agents.

The leader with the Gatling gun turned towards her. He held down the trigger, spraying her with Psychanium bullets as she took cover behind a nearby vehicle. She formed another water shuriken in her hand and threw it at the masked figure. It connected, knocking the Gatling gun out of his hands and onto the underpass. He looked down at the gun dozens of feet below and hopped off the roof of the car and onto the street below without saying a word.

Yemani ran out from behind the car and threw another shuriken at him as he reached for the gun. He dodged it with inhuman speed. Yemani raced at him and threw her knee forward attempting to hit him. He dodged, she threw a kick, he blocked it and threw a punch, she dodged it and kicked him back. He staggered as he regained his balance. She kicked the Gatling gun far away from them. He looked in the direction she kicked the gun, and pulled a knife from a pocket, twirling it in his hand. He slashed at her, but she blocked his wrist, he pulled the knife back and struck again. Yemani blocked each strike. He elbowed her in the face as he missed a strike with the knife, throwing her off balance. He slashed the knife down, raking a line from the back of her shoulder to the front, she grunted in pain but didn't back down. She kneed the knife out of his hand and caught it mid-air. She threw it at him, he dodged and pulled a pistol from his back and shot at her. The arm of her suit formed, creating a shield on the forearm and deflecting the bullets.

Yemani rushed at him with the shield out, throwing him back with the force of the Psychanium construct. He turned his head to the Providence incendiary gun on the ground. He picked it up and leaped to his feet before shooting at her. She blocked the bullet with her shield, and it exploded on contact, throwing her back against a nearby vehicle. She stood, rubbing the back of her head. He fired again. She rolled out of the way, shielding herself from the blast with the shield. She jumped behind a car as he fired another. She double-tapped her chest, forming the rest of her suit, a sensual light blue construct with light brown lines running through it. The Yemaya Psychic Suit.

She flew out from behind the car and fired a laser at the man. He dodged it once again with inhuman speed. The suit scanned the man, finding dozens of Psychanium enhancements embedded throughout his body. She flew at him, a Katar blade forming from her wrist. The enhanced dodged the strike and retaliated with two more shots from the prototype. They both missed and exploded in the air. He clicked the trigger, the weapon clicked blank. He threw it to the side and pulled an SMG from his back. He fired at Yemani, and she flew through the air, the bullets grazing her suit. One hit, piercing the suit and lodging itself in her still-healing shoulder. She fell, crashing into the road and dragging a crater as she came to a stop.

She stood and looked at her shoulder, bleeding through the suit. He fired at her again, she formed a rectangular shield from her forearm, shielding herself as the enhanced walked closer. The gun clicked empty. As he reloaded, she struck. She flew at him, body-slamming him with the shield. He flew back and slammed into the door of an abandoned car. He shook his head as he recovered from the hit. Yemani placed her hand on the ground and the water vapor condensed, forming rings of liquid in the air. It flew at the enhanced, slamming him back into a wall of water slamming him to the ground hard. Yemani's suit scanned him, detecting his breathing.

The CIA set up roadblocks and yellow caution tape around the site. Providence's agents had shown up to recover their weapon and Psychanium and administer specialized medical attention to Yemani. Versia landed as one of the doctors finished wrapping Yemani's arm. Her healing would begin soon enough.

"Is this what it looks like when you go on vacation?" Versia asked.

She stifled a laugh.

"How many?" She asked as she stood and walked towards a Providence jet.

"No civilians." Versia said, "We got lucky."

"This time. How many people will die, before we stop blaming only the Circle? How many funerals will we pay for before we say it was on us? How many?" She asked. "When I suggested this could happen three years ago, you all said no, it was impossible, you all shut me down, and now look, the world is as trauma-ridden as the rest of you."

"We're not trauma-ridden," Versia said.

"Yes, you are. All of you. Red, Reese, Caitlyn, all of you are driven by guilt, regret, trauma, something you let happen that hurt others, that's what motivates you. You talk about your childhoods, or lack thereof, where trained for twelve hours a day, I was never like that, I was allowed to grow with my powers, and come into my own. I'm not driven by guilt or regret, I see the world as it is, and understand I have the power to make change. So I do. All of you do it to absolve yourselves." Yemani said.

"Then I guess you're lucky," Versia said.

"No, you need to open up, but you think the world won't accept you," Yemani said.

"Because they won't, how are we supposed to tell the world we can protect them if they think we're mentally unstable children who shoot lasers from our eyes," Versia said as the jet took off.

Yemani took a deep breath. "My grandmother died when I was six. She was the greatest inspiration in my life, the one who raised me to control my powers without locking me in a room for hours on end. She said Psychics are gifts, meant to be beacons for the world, that's the standard I live my life by every day. Did I make the world better? All of you should try it. We make the world better, and the second you understand that, and understand how much not the world, but those who love you, those who matter, care, you'll find peace in everything." Yemani said.

"I'll try it," Versia said.

She held his hand. "I want you to know we care, we all care."

****

Versia took the elevator down to his lab. He spread his hands in the air, opening a holographic display around him.

"Meadow, search records for "The Night of Ten Thousand Terrors", I've never heard of it," he said.

"No such file exists,"

"Do a deep search, full disclosure,"

"You don't have clearance to perform a deep search with this term," she said.

"Do a dark web search, if he knew about it, the files have been dumped onto the internet,"

"I've found it, are you sure you want to dive into this boss?"

"Why, I won't like it?"

"I am unable to open the file even from the dark web. My programming prevents me from accessing it for human eyes."

"Override code Antonio,"

"Access denied,"

"Override code Nolan,"

"Access denied,"

"Override code, Jed."

"Access denied, sorry boss, you'll need to manually hack it."

"Who locked it?"

"Ariyin, the fourth Cyan in your line."

"Who was his wife?"

"Empress Camryn Kennedy-Ikakala the first."

"Override code Camryn."

"Access granted."

Versia smiled a bit.

Meadow opened the file and read it.

"The Night of Ten Thousand Terrors was an event in Psychic history where the Psychics, led by your ancestors, massacred the "Taichono people, a sect that would be located in modern-day Targistan. A late Psychanium meteor landed in their territory, about the size of Rhode Island. Realizing what it was, they sought to connect with the Psychics and convince them the gift should be shared with the world to further progress and humanity. Enraged at this and perceiving a disrespect of their sacred metal, your ancestor Kiris the Second, and Isazisi's ancestor, Ize-Iyamu the Third, demanded they turn over every gram. They refused. Gathering together the other Psychics, and in a unanimous vote, they launched a brutal siege and laid waste to their entire country, killing and destroying nearly everyone and everything." Meadow said.

"Everything?" Versia asked.

"Till today you can still find parts of the land scarred by Psychanium energy weapons,"

"And the people?"

"A near-clean sweep. Till today, the population has still not recovered, and the lack of arable land and potable water was another side effect of the attack,"

Versia put his hand to his mouth."

"The aftermath of this event caused the split between High Watch and the other Psychics."

"High Watch? Do they even still exist?"

"Unknown," Meadow said. "Psychics, including your ancestor, wanted to apologize and make known the crimes they committed and how remorseful they were, but High Watch wanted to revel in what they'd done, show the world their power. This is what the "Unforgivable Crimes" were. For centuries this was a point of contention, before becoming a footnote in Psychic history, hidden from view. That is "The Night of Ten Thousand Terrors."

Versia sat and clasped his hands in front of his mouth.

****

Vashti and Reese sat across from each other in a coffee shop, they both had on hoodies and sunglasses, obscuring their faces. Their drinks arrived.

"How's Isazisi?" Vashti asked as the waitress left.

"He's fine, we think it was another panic attack, his doctors are looking at him now," Reese said.

"Good," Vashti said.

She turned her head from side to side around the coffee shop, packed for a world on full terror alert.

"Should we be getting coffee while the world burns?" Vashti

asked.

"Our satellites are still looking for targets, until then, we have to sit on our hands," Reese replied.

Vashti took a sip while Reese reached over and lifted her sunglasses, seeing her bloodshot eyes with faint bags underneath them.

"You haven't been sleeping?" Reese asked. "Why?"

Vashti took off the sunglasses and placed them on the table. "I feel responsible. Seeing the aftermath of New York, Miami, and the other cities they hit, you're never the same after seeing what you unleashed." Vashti said.

Reese leaned back. "I was first on site after Miami." Reese began. "I watched a kid, trying to pull his dead mother by the arm to safety, from out of the rubble. Another cried for his dad, while he lay under twenty-five feet of steel and concrete, crushed. I've seen war, but none of it prepared me for that, and I-I-I." Tears left her eyes. "I see it every time I close my eyes, I see a child who will never have a father or a mother, and it's our fault. We created weapons of mass destruction and told the world we would keep them safe, now they duck in fear at the slightest sound, wondering if they'll be next. What we've done should be unforgivable. Some people will forever grow up resenting us, and I don't know whether they're right, or they're wrong, and none of us will face a second of consequences. Now I wonder if that's right or wrong." She wiped her eyes with her sweater.

"Then why do you keep going, what stops you from laying there in the morning and rotting?" Vashti asked.

"I have two younger siblings. Twins, a brother, and a sister. When I see the people hurt by our weapons, I see them, I think, what if it were them killed by an attack, what if it was one of them pulling at the lifeless arm of our mother? What if I didn't have these powers to protect them, what if they didn't have their powers, what if I didn't have an army behind me? What then? That's why I get up because if one of them died, my world would shatter. We've already done that to thousands of people, we should never let it happen again." Reese said.

She looked over towards the bar table. A single drop fell from the tap, splashing down in the sink, followed by a loud sound booming from outside. They both turned to the sound and ran outside to the horror of an entire skyscraper collapsing. It fell sideways, crashing into another building as gravity pulled it towards the ground. What could only be dozens of people walking below looked up, their knees buckling and others staggering. A screaming mother grabbed her child and ran as fast as she could. Reese raced towards the zone of the collapsing building. She stretched out her hands, stopping the buildings mid-fall with her **psychokinesis**. She held the buildings until another explosion rocked the landscape, throwing Reese off balance. A father shielded his wife and child in a stroller with his body. The building hit the ground, crushing everyone in the vicinity. The shockwave and dust hit Vashti like a train, throwing her off balance.

Her eyes opened as she pulled herself up, her vision blurry along with a ringing in her ear. She looked at herself, covered from head to toe in dust while Reese had vanished, crushed under the debris. Lifeless limbs stuck out of the rubble, coated in a thin layer of dust, while screams echoed from everywhere as others wailed for help or in pain. On every screen in the area, an audio wave appeared.

"Do you see the beauty of it, the fragility?" A voice said through every speaker in the area. "You Psychics are our vessel. The swift and terrible sword, forged from your metal, turned on a world you swore to protect. They will scream for mercy, they will beg for grace, and this world will shatter, under the weight of your actions. Kill our members, demonize our followers, maim the true believers. But when the flames settle. The only thing left living in this world will be of the Circle."

The audio wave disappeared. Those who survived the attack poked their heads out from behind their hiding places. Vashti's head swiveled from side to side as she took in what happened. Screams, pleading, and begging echoed around her as her vision blurred and she collapsed.

She woke up a few minutes later. Providence's people had already swarmed the site of the attack. Vashti pulled pieces of debris and rock from her dust-coated hair. A Providence Centurion helped her and walked her to one of their medical response vehicles.

The ground rumbled as a red aura coated a portion of the rubble, it rose. Reese pulled herself out of the rubble along with the six people she could save. She had a bit of blood running down her face. Providence's agents helped survivors scale down the rubble and took them along with Reese to seek medical help. She sat beside Vashti as a doctor attended to her cuts, her healing powers worked on the wounds as well. Reese held Vashti's cold, clammy, shaking hands while she stared off into the distance. Reese waved off the medical team and guided Vashti to another mobile tent where Reese sat her down.

"How many people?" Vashti asked.

"Preliminary reports suggest up to two thousand, we're still searching for survivors. We were their initial target, they arrested three Circle members along with the one who told them we were in the area. They were in the building's lobby. They'd made modifications to the weapons which caused it to destabilize, detonating it prematurely." Reese said.

"There you go, two thousand people died, because of us," Vashti said. "Two thousand."

Caitlyn landed at the site of the attack, she entered the tent with Vashti and Reese.

"I'll take care of her," Caitlyn whispered to Reese. "Isazisi wants to see you." She nodded and her suit formed, she took off towards his location.

Caitlyn sat beside Vashti.

"Are you ok?" She asked.

"You know the answer to that," Vashti said.

"What happened?"

"I saw the aftermath of the other attacks, but being here, in the moment. I watched a mother, and her child in a stroller crushed, and I, with all the power in the world, did nothing."

"There's no way you could have stopped the building long enough, and there were thousands of people inside dead the second that bomb exploded.

Tears left Vashti's eyes as she leaned against Caitlyn. "It's ok, It's ok," Caitlyn said as she stroked Vashti's hair. "We'll get through this, stronger than ever."

Reese sat on the couch in their house, and Isazisi walked in.

"Are you feeling ok?" He asked.

"You don't want me to answer that," Reese said.

Isazisi said nothing.

"I've seen with my own eyes sixty-three children killed by weapons we created. I've seen children try to pull their crushed, dead parents from the aftermath of attacks. I've seen mothers shriek in ways that will haunt my nightmares as they attempt to shield their children from a building falling on them. They failed. I saved six people. Six out of the two thousand or more. How many people have to die, and how long will it take before we admit, not to the world, but to ourselves, that this is as much our fault as The Circle? If we are the most powerful beings in the universe that we call ourselves, how could we not keep our weapons under lock? You heard the voice. 'The swift and terrible sword forged from our metal'. We messed it up." Reese said.

Isazisi sat. "No, we didn't, people took our weapons and did horrible things, that was not us," Isazisi said.

"How long are you going to defend this, how long are you going to try to hide behind this shield of deniability? We didn't mess up, it was you. You lead Providence and on your watch, the wall was breached, take it like a man, or keep hiding behind your shield." Reese said.

"My fault? Like everything I do isn't cosigned by the rest of you. I don't care how many people died, because I didn't kill them, all I can do is get justice. When I kill, I let everyone know it was me."

"Then you're exactly like the Circle, congrats. You are the swift and terrible sword."

CHAPTER 19

Alex Zimmer walked out of his company's Japan headquarters and into a waiting convoy of nine SUVs with full bulletproof armoring and reinforced chassis. He stepped into the second to last car.

"Principle is on the move," his security agent said.

"You must have pissed off someone powerful if they had to hire us," one of the agents said.

"Yeah, a shady bank wanted to buy the company in cash, no credit history or records of any kind to speak to. I did a little digging and convinced my bosses to shut down the deal. The bank was furious but remained professional. We hired you guys after someone delivered a handwritten threat to my office after hours."

"You pissed off someone big," the same agent chuckled

"All clear?" Asked the passenger seat agent in the first car into his radio.

"All clear," came the reply from the agents sent to scout ahead.

They drove and came to an empty bridge lit up in a cacophony of colors by the neon Japanese characters on it. A figure stood alone in the center of the road. Wearing white, with black lines flowing through it, a katana on her back, and flowing appendages coming from her head.

"What is it?" A man asked as they approached.

The man in the passenger seat of the lead car snapped a picture and sent it to command, the response came seconds later

"Get out now." The text message read.

"Turn around. Call back-up." The passenger seat agent barked over the radio to the car Zimmer sat in. Additional agents jumped out of their vehicles and primed their weapons.

"You are blocking the road of an authorized motorcade, vacate this area or we will arrest you," An agent yelled to the figure.

She pulled the katana from her back without saying a word.

"Get him out of here." One of the agents whispered into his comm.

The eighth SUV in the line turned around. Behind them stood an all-black Psychic Suit with white lines flowing through it and white appendages coming from its head.

"What's going on?" Alex asked.

"Nothing sir. We're taking care of it." An agent told him.

An agent had taken a rocket launcher from the trunk of one of the SUVs and fired it at the White Psychic Suit. The White Psychic Suit sidestepped the projectile with the swiftness of the wind. She threw her katana, burying it in the rocket launcher, and dashed at the agents, sidestepping bullets as she took them hand to hand. She whipped one of the agents to the side and kicked him in the chest, she ducked and low-swept another. Another shot at her, she blocked it with her palm, ripped the top of the pistol off, and raked him across the face with it. She flipped behind another agent, shot her with her palm laser, and jumped forward, punching another agent in the face. Meanwhile, the black suit rushed forward with his katana, he cut the front of their assault rifles off and kicked both the agents into their vehicle. He blocked more incoming fire with a shield formed from his suit's arm. He threw the shield, and it hit the agent and bounced back.

"We are under attack, send reinforcements." A man yelled into comms.

The two suits finished off the rest of the troops with ease and walked towards Alex's car. His driver stepped out and the white suit shot him in the back. Alex looked around for help before he stumbled out of the car.

"I guess there's no better time to test this now," he said under his breath.

He pulled a syringe from his suit pocket and jammed it into his forearm. He ripped it out and dropped to the ground, convulsing before he stopped, motionless. The two Psychic suits stopped. Zimmer stood, and grabbed a car, throwing it at the white suit, it hit her head on, burying her under a pile of metal. The black suit ran at him. He punched it into another car. The white suit burst out from the crumpled car. Alex picked up another vehicle and threw it at her. This time she punched it, crumpling it like a tin can. He grabbed another car and threw it at her. She sliced it down the middle with her katana. He charged at her and threw a punch. She caught his fist and shoved him into the katana of the black suit. He looked down at the sword pierced through his stomach as the life left his eyes. The black suit pulled his sword from Zimmer and the body dropped. Both suits escaped into the night, completing the mission in total silence.

****

Caitlyn's sports car tore down the streets of Japan, doing one fifty in a sixty-mile-per-hour zone before she came to an abrupt stop on a bridge leading out of the city. Police officers stood guard around yellow crime scene tape. She stepped out as reporters clamored around the scene attempting to take pictures of what had happened. An officer lifted the crime scene tape as she approached where two dozen bodies, each with white sheets covering them lay. She walked up to the lead detective.

"Who was the target?" She asked.

They walked over to a body and the detective pulled off the sheet.

"Alex Zimmer, accountant. Started getting threats so his company put a full security detail on him, got decimated, we think it may be Circle-related, was too perfect, the one signal that made it out said one of his security detail reported seeing Psychic Suits before they kicked the bucket, that's why we called you." The detective said.

She looked at the incision. *A katana. Psychanium. No other metal could do it this cleanly.* She thought.

"It was a katana used, whoever did it wasn't your common hitman." She said.

She closed her eyes and stomped the ground. Psychic waves radiated from her foot, recreating the crime scene.

"Two assailants. Mid-twenties. Wearing armor. He took an experimental strength-enhancing drug derived from Psychanium and lost the fight." She said as she opened her eyes. "Get me a list of private grad schools here, anyone this skilled would be well paid."

May and Kai walked onto their college campus as Caitlyn's car pulled up to the school, she stepped out and felt the presence of the two Psychics.

"They're good," Caitlyn said to Meadow. "They're trying to mask their energy."

"Hey, hey" You can't be here. For the student's safety, only authorized guests are allowed in."

She double-tapped her wrist. Her ID showed up.

"I need to see two of you students. May and Kai." She said.

They showed up at a private office in the administration building.

"Are we in trouble?" May asked, her sharp brown eyes staring into Caitlyn.

"Of course not," Caitlyn said. "You have perfect records. What do you think?"

"Fair enough," May said, brushing her black hair from her face.

"Let's not waste my time," Caitlyn said, switching her tone.

She put a midnight blue cube with intricate carvings on the table. She pressed the top, causing the clear carvings in it to glow blue.

"This is a sonic scatterer, nobody outside this room can hear anything we're going to say." She said.

"Why would that be necessary?" Kai asked, his brown eyes unreadable to Caitlyn.

Caitlyn sighed.

"I know you're the Báisè (White) Ninja Suit, and the Hēisè (Black) Ninja Suit." She said.

Their faces remained unchanged.

"What? What are those?" May asked.

"Spare me the faux innocence please, I know facts you don't even know about yourselves." She said.

Their faces remained stonewalled.

"Your full names are May Hua-Qui Yang and Kai Shi-Zhen Yang, your twins. Your parents are Andrew Yang and Constance Zhao. Your father is the son of a rich industry titan. He was in a type of 'arranged marriage.'" She said with air quotes. "He was meant to marry the daughter of another industry giant, bring the two companies, and their wealth, closer than ever, but fell in love with a girl from a village his father wanted to buy. Yes, cliche." She said, reading their faces. "They ran away together and had two kids, twins. His father found them together on an island off the coast of Japan. He had his son dragged back to China and his wife thrown out onto the streets. That was twenty-five years ago. She put you in a basket and you drifted for eleven hours before a tourist boat found and took you to an orphanage, where you lived up until you discovered your powers at age eighteen, seven years ago. Using those, you took on 'special work' and made plenty of cash." She said. "Your father is still alive, he's over it, but it took a dozen different pills and years of self-blame. As for your mother, she's alive and living in San Francisco. They both have separate lives without each other. Your mother has another two kids, and your father has three. You work for the Circle, who transferred three million to your Swiss account twelve minutes after you killed Zimmer, fourteen hours ago." She paused. "Now. Did I miss anything?" May's eye twitched and Kai rubbed his chin as he looked away. May turned towards Kai.

"母と父はまだ生きていますか?" (Mother and father are still alive?) Asked May.

"彼女はこれをどのようにして知ることができますか?" (How could she know this?) He said.

"私もサイキックです。" (I'm Psychic too.) Caitlyn stated.

Both of their eyes widened.

"We're fruits of the same tree. I can have private jets waiting to take you to your parents or wherever else you'd like to go." She said.

"That still doesn't explain how you know that about us," Kai said.

Caitlyn pointed to the box sitting on the table. "Pure Psychanium." She said. "I have access to resources people only see on movie screens."

"Thank you for everything, but our life is fine working for the Circle," May said.

"Do you know what the Circles endgame is?" Caitlyn asked.

"Not our concern," Mai said. "We kill terrible people and they keep the world safe."

Caitlyn chuckled.

"Keep the world safe? Safe? Have you watched the news in the last few days? Their endgame is world domination and the death of every Psychic." She stated.

"You're lying," Mai snapped. "The Circle gave us a real home when no one else did. The Psychics blaming the Circle for the terror attacks is another way of covering themselves every time anything goes wrong. They misplaced their weapons and people got killed because of it, that is not the Circle's fault. "

"No, they found vulnerable Psychics and a way to accomplish their goal. How much do they tell you about each hit?"

"Enough," Kai said. "Thanks for the offer, but we'll think about it on our own time."

They stood and left the room, closing the door behind them. Caitlyn laid back and ran her hand down her face. She stood, picked up the box, and walked back to her car. She pressed a button on the center console. The car's autopilot took over.

She arrived at her hotel, set up her computer, and tracked her cloaked drones over the city. They tracked May and Kai as they got in their car and drove into the heart of the city to a large office skyscraper before getting out and onto a private elevator. Meadow hacked the cameras and showed the twins getting off on one of the upper floors, a room with no cameras and where phones weren't allowed. The drone identified the glass as soundproof and tinted. Caitlyn took her chest piece in her hotel room and put it on, she double-tapped it, turning it invisible against her chest. She took the elevator to the ground floor and speed-walked out of the building, the car door opened as she approached. The car turned itself on as he slid in. The door closed and the car drove off. She put on her seat belt and took the wheel, driving to the building the twins had entered and walked to the elevator with a passcode on it. She put a finger on the keypad, causing midnight blue lines to extend from her finger onto the keypad. She bypassed the code and stepped on the elevator, arriving on the floor where a platoon of guns greeted her.

"We have cameras." A man said.

"Not a problem," Caitlin said.

She stepped forward, and the fingers of her assailants tensed against triggers as eyes darted from side to side.

"You do know I can sense fear." She said.

"Get the chip out of here." An agent whispered.

A man in the back of the room took off, they leaped out the window from over a hundred stories up with a briefcase in hand. Others followed, crashing through the glass of the skyscraper beside theirs and taking off running, yelps of surprise from the occupants of the other building and anyone on the ground who had seen the events unfold followed. Caitlyn fought past the agents in the room, jumped through the already broken window, and crashed through another one in the building beside it, hitting and rolling into a sprint.

She dashed through the office space of the building, bits of glass falling out of her hair as she darted by. Her smart contact activated, showing an x-ray of the men on the elevator. She burst into the stairwell, the X-ray showed the elevator on the bottom floor, she jumped down the stairwell and rolled into the lobby as the chip sped away in a sedan. She double-tapped her wrist and her car pulled up to her, the door opened and she slid in.

Mid-day car chase she thought as her car revved and she shot off.

She looked in her rearview mirror. Eight motorcycles drove out from a nearby parking garage. She accelerated, and the motorcycles did the same, weaving through traffic as they caught up with her. They raised SMGs to her window and emptied the clips, each bullet bounced off the Psychanium glass.

"It's a Psychanium car, you idiots. How many times will we have to go over this? Bullets won't penetrate it, force it off the road." An agent radioed to the motorcycles over comms.

They shot at the wheels causing the car to swerve. Caitlyn struggled to gain control inside as she wrestled with the steering wheel. She braked hard, and the car stopped, skidding sideways, two motorcycles hit the car throwing their riders off, and the motorcycles hit the ground and exploded. She ripped the car straight, slammed it into reverse, and took off. Everyone watched in shock at the vehicle driving backward. She spun the car and switched it back into drive. She drove forward at the motorcycles and slammed the brakes while drifting, putting the car into a controlled spin and plowing through the motorcycles before drifting the car back straight and shooting off leaving a wake of smoking motorcycle carcasses and unconscious motorcycle riders.

She caught up to the sedan and tapped her wrist setting the car to autopilot. She half stood and twisted herself out the window as she hung on to her McLaren. She pulled herself onto the roof and jumped onto the sedan. She grabbed the side of the roof with her right hand, and her suit's arm formed on her left hand. She jumped down, pulled the whole car onto two wheels with her, and drove her hand into the asphalt. Sparks flew from her gauntlet as it tore through the pitch-black asphalt, the car jostled as it rode on two wheels. She let it go, crashing it into a coffee shop as it came to a rest, lopsided on its roof. Two people stepped out. One pulled a gun on her, she grabbed the gun, twisted his arm down, and kicked him in the side. The other one ran away, but Caitlyn caught up and kicked him in the back of the leg, he fell and she laid him out with one punch to the face. She took the case and walked back to her car. Civilians nearby still recorded on their phones as the girl in the midnight blue car disappeared.

Caitlyn plugged the chip into her computer and cast it to the hotel's flat screen. Insurance would take care of the carnage caused by the chase.

"What did you want us to see?" May asked.

"The Circle's endgame," Caitlyn replied.

"How do we know it's not fake?" She asked.

"I wouldn't tear up a city in broad daylight and put twelve people in the hospital to fake evidence." She replied. "My family is worth trillions, I would never make it that hard."

Caitlyn double-tapped her wrist. On the screen appeared missile schematics along with a rough animation detailing the building of Psychanium missiles. Math detailing a blast radius of double an ICBM, how the Psychanium charge would be loaded into the warhead, and how it would explode. Other pages detailed the construction of Psychanium-powered laser guns and tanks. Spears, which could stop a speeding train in its tracks, battleships and aircraft carriers, fighter jets with unmatched range, satellites with lasers, and rockets. Other files contained details on how they could have the entire world under their control in under a week without Psychics. The last file had the name 'Lava' but was locked.

"No, no, they wouldn't do this, they said they're here to save the world," Kai said. "They said the Circle represented that everyone is equal."

"The Circle represents a small group, controlling everything. The inside, and the outside." Caitlyn said. "But that's not even the worst part."

She clicked on a file folder titled "PSYCHICS" The file showed tabs on everyone from Isazisi to Versia, to Reese, to herself, to the twins, to Vashti, and other suits. Sanjiv in the Ice suit, Jasmine in the Shadow suit, a green suit, a fourth red suit, another person in a pearl-colored suit, another in an all-black suit, and one more in a blue suit. Allen in the Flame suit, Ava in the Magic suit, and even Mia who had gotten her powers a day before. The tabs held their strengths, weaknesses, powers, possible ways to defeat them, and at its core, research on how to kill them in the endgame.

While they had small tabs on the other Psychics, the files on the twins had everything. It detailed their powers, their ability to move without a single sound, their wind-like agility, possible ways to kill them, or even a theory on transmitting their powers through blood transfusions. The twins looked through the file in shock and horror.

"They groomed you for your death. Studying you to gain an edge over us." Caitlyn said.

May and Kai looked at each other.

"Who do we have to kill?" May asked, a frown on her face and her eyes squinting at the screen.

They arrived at the meeting place the Circle had set up, Caitlyn watched from above as the twins walked in, suits built without helmets.

"My favorite twins, we have a new mission for you. A local businessman..."

"No," Kai said.

"What do you mean no?" Their handler asked.

"No," May said.

They pulled out their katanas. Needles shot from the hilts of them, hitting the other agents in the rooms.

"What are you doing?" Their handler asked, his voice breaking. "Did another group offer you more money? We can double anything they've offered you."

The twins didn't answer.

He pressed a panic button on his watch. Around them, rhino suits rose. Their eyes glowed white and their axes and hammers glistened in the light.

Their handler dashed to a car behind the building as a rhino suit hammer smashed where May had stood. She retaliated, slashing at the rhino suit, her sword met the hammer. Kai slashed at the suits in his path. Caitlyn came crashing down from the skylight above, lightning following her, she dashed forward and punched one of the rhino suits in the chest with ten million volts of electricity, the Rhino suit staggered with a fist-sized hole in its chest. She followed with an arrow, leaving a hole through the suit, and it collapsed to the ground. May swung her sword cutting clean through the ax the rhino suit had used to meet the attack. She rushed forward and kneed it in the chin. While it staggered she jumped and drove her sword into its left neck and shoulder, the suit collapsed to the ground and the eyes flickered white, turning off.

Kai swung his sword, shooting a black crescent of energy, it hit the Rhino suit which convulsed, hitting the floor, the eyes flickered, and died. They made quick work of the other suits. Kai sliced two of them clean in half exposing the drivers, who took off running the second they lost the suit. May cut the heads of another two clean off, rendering them inoperable, and Caitlyn jumped on one, swinging around to its back, locking her sword between its head and her chest, and prying it clean off. She threw her sword at another one, Pinning it clean to the wall through its chest. The last one sliced at her with the ax. She stopped it mid-swing, ripped the ax from the Rhino's grasp, broke the blade off, and threw it, cutting clean through the chest and torso of the Rhino suit. The suit collapsed backward. Its eyes flickered twice and turned off, dead.

"What about our handler?"

"I got him," Caitlyn said.

She closed her eyes. A bolt of blue lightning struck on the same bridge they had assassinated Zimmer on less than twenty-four hours before.

"We want to help in the fight against the Circle," May said.

"Yeah," Kai said.

"What about your parents? They'd love to meet you."

"At least we know they're alive," May said.

"We'll meet them," Kai said. "But for now, I think we've made plenty of new family."

CHAPTER 20

The elevator dinged as it reached the top floor of the skyscraper. Versia walked into Isazisi, Caitlyn, Reese, Vashti, Issac, and Sanjiv waiting there. Large windows near them looked out over the morning traffic and the overcast sky.

"So what's this for?" Versia asked as he sat.

"The Circle did three more attacks. One in San Francisco, another in London, and the last one in Shanghai. We've kept them under wraps, but people are getting restless." Isazisi said as holograms of classified footage from the attacks played on holographic displays.

"How do you keep a bomb going off under wraps?" Issac asked.

"We have to plug this, now, I say a full-scale war on the Circle," Sanjiv said.

"We can't start a war, this requires finesse," Caitlyn said as she swished a glass of alcohol in her hand.

"We already are in a war," Issac said.

"How many people died in the attacks?" Reese asked.

"Anywhere from six to seven hundred in each, we're still combing through the sites; the San Francisco bomb was detonated in another skyscraper, the London bomb in a busy market area, and the Shanghai one in an underground train station. We think a minimum of eighteen hundred dead." Isazisi said.

Versia said something explicit as he ran his hand down his face.

"We have to go full offensive," Vashti said.

"How many could die in the crossfire?" Versia asked.

"None, if we do it right, my Renarri are already working across the globe," Isazisi replied.

"You know that's a lie." Versia spat.

"No, if we pull this off right, zero crossfire casualties, most of their bases are remote, and any in large population centers can be handled with finesse, we have dozens of Psychics worldwide already taking down cells," Isazisi said.

"There is no military operation that can be pulled off in a large city, and result in zero civilian casualties," Versia said. "But I guess they're collateral damage to you."

"In every military operation there are unforeseen casualties as a result of actions taken, it's not intentional," Isazisi said.

"You're sick," Versia said.

"I'm realistic, there will be outside casualties in every war and we at Providence live with that, it doesn't mean we enjoy it," Isazisi said. "At Providence, we take the world as presented, not as an ideal of itself."

"If you want me to drop bunker busters on their bases in the deserts and mountains, I'm for it, but we cannot engage in tactical warfare in a city, what are we going to do, destroy the whole city and say we saved it, what, our insurance covers that?" Versia asked.

"We own the insurance company, so yeah," Sanjiv said.

The others stared at him as they understood the question's sarcastic nature.

"We should get rid of some of our weapons," Versia said. "They are a relic of a dark time in Psychic history, and look what we've done."

"You are not going to blame this on us and let the Circle off scot-free are you?" Isazisi asked.

"No, I'm saying, this situation has taught us that we cannot be trusted with our metal. What I'm saying is we can't go around telling the world we can protect them, and not." Versia said.

"I understand what's happened is tragic, but that's radical," Caitlyn said.

"We have those weapons for a reason, and we can't say we're going to disarm ourselves because the Circle caught us by surprise once, every action justifies the end," Isazisi said, "and the end is a peaceful world. The public only knows about attacks in New York and Paris, that's already eleven hundred dead before the three I told you about. Those happened in the last thirty-six hours, there have been nine attacks in total, and the public knows about two, how do you think they'll react when we tell them that we covered up seven? I'd prefer it at the press conference where we tell them we've won."

"Caught us by surprise once? Three attacks in the last twenty-four hours. You can't hold a gun to everyone's head with your weapons, call it protection, and say you got caught by surprise," Versia yelled. "Those are weapons of mass destruction, and they should be far more regulated than they are."

"So because of the Circle, you will throw away ten thousand years of history and tradition?" Isazisi asked.

"Our tradition for millennia has been murder," Versia spat. "All of you know this. Where do you think our wealth came from? What makes us any less complicit in this than the Circle? What? That a paper signed by a bunch of countries says it's ok for us to have these weapons, so when we mess up everyone accepts it?"

"What you are proposing is the throwing away of thousands of years of tradition," Reese said.

"I'm proposing a degree of oversight. Our heritage is murder and weapons? How is that fine? How is our power kept in check, we're a bunch of loose cannons, a bunch of kids sitting on trillions of dollars, with thousands of weapons at our disposal, and the inability to be punished for crimes, how are we kept in check?" Versia asked.

"Providence has a threat assessment list for every Psychic, every government we work with also has a copy," Isazisi said.

"A threat assessment list, why are we on that? The only list you should have is a weapons inventory," Caitlyn said.

"That wasn't funny," Isazisi said.

"It wasn't meant to be, Psychics should not be on threat lists, we are not threats, what do you do, spy on us?" She asked.

"Yes, we do, everything these days has a camera, from phones to cars, to buildings, anything connected to WiFi we can use,"

Isazisi said.

"So you track our movements?" She asked.

"Everything, your purchases, movements, search history, even mine is tracked," Isazisi said.

"It makes sense, we do have copious power, I wouldn't call it too much, but the fact we're not corrupt murders is surprising," Sanjiv said.

"Do you want a reward for that?" Caitlyn retorted.

"That doesn't even make sense," Issac said to Sanjiv.

"Who watches the watchmen?" Sanjiv asked. "What happens when a bunch of superpowered kids can do whatever they want without legal repercussions? We routinely ignore sovereign borders, we kill without oversight, and we have and continue to develop weapons of mass destruction with no supervision. What happens when our mistakes lead to the deaths of thousands via terrorist attacks we enabled? Do we get arrested? Do we face justice?"

"We're not kids, and we didn't enable the attacks. People stole from us and made their own choices, they could've used the technology to solve climate change, create sustainable energy, or end wars, but they decided to start one instead," Reese said.

"If we can end wars, fix the climate, and save the whole world, why haven't we done it?" Caitlyn asked. Everyone stayed quiet. "Yeah, no answer for that." She said.

"Too many civilians would get killed in the crossfire, fixing those problems isn't as easy as saying them," Isazisi said.

"Oh, you care about civilians," Versia said.

"The truth is, every Psychic is a liability, and we have contingency plans for them," Isazisi said.

"Why? Did the new reports asking if Psychics have too much power get to you?" Vashti asked.

"It's no secret we have too much power, our ancestors lobbied hard enough to make it law," Versia said.

"Didn't you massacre one hundred fifteen Circle agents on an island like the Hunger Games?" Sanjiv asked. "You better be on that threat assessment list."

"I am on the threat assessment list, I don't control it, it's run by a separate panel," Isazisi said.

"Of people who work for you?" Caitlyn asked.

"Don't take it personally, we watch everyone," Isazisi said.

"All seven billion?" Vashti asked.

"As best we can," Isazisi said. "But what happened on the island was justified, I still get thank you letters because of what happened there."

"Now that I think about it, I should buy an Island," Sanjiv said.

"What?" Versia asked.

"I don't know, I'm feeling it," Sanjiv said.

"That statement encompasses everything that is wrong with us," Reese said. "The pride that the last names we have is the root cause of this entire tragedy. We got too cocky, we thought that nobody would be stupid enough to touch a Psychic, so when the warning signs flashed right in front of us we did nothing because we thought that our name alone held enough weight."

"Ok, what does any of this have to do with the Circle anymore?" Issac asked.

"I think Versia's point is if we didn't have thousands of would-be illegal advanced weapons lying around, the Circle would never have been able to get them and start blowing up buildings," Vashti said.

"That's unfair, they could have done anything with those weapons, but they chose violence," Issac said.

"Versia does have a point," Sanjiv said.

"You agree with him?" Caitlyn asked. "You would throw away millennia of tradition because The Circle stood up to us? We will crush the Circle and show the world we don't shirk from a challenge. That's the issue, the fast cars and mansions made all of you soft."

"You're one to talk soft, have you taken the easy way out lately?" Sanjiv asked.

"Don't you dare talk about my condition like that, I can show you the scars from my training, I doubt you have many of those."

"You know why we have those weapons, you know what's

coming, the fights that are coming will make the Circle look like pushovers. Aliens, wizards, conquerors. We're kids in metal suits." Isazisi said. He pointed up. "That's the finale, how do you plan on beating them?"

"As a team," Versia said.

"And when we fail, when everyone you care about dies, when you bury your best friend and hand his mother a single rose to say you're sorry, what then?" Isazisi asked.

"Then we'll mourn as a team, and avenge our fallen," Versia said.

"What none of you seem to be thinking about is what this means on a galaxy-wide scale. We got challenged by the Circle, and for a time, they were winning. How do you think that makes us look? How long before a meteorite with an alien monster in it crash lands in Miami because they think we are weak, how long before an alien race decides to test us, before an alien conqueror comes to our earth, to take it, to take our Psychanium, the only Psychanium in the universe. We are a target for every powered individual in this universe who wants an upgrade. A thousand years ago they would've never challenged us. Hell, ten years ago they would've never challenged us, but now, we look vulnerable, and we're sitting here arguing about tradition? There will be no tradition left if we die and the planet is a smoking wasteland." Caitlyn said.

They stayed quiet for a few moments thinking over everything.

"You're still a Tier Zero Agent," Issac said.

"Don't bring up the Tier List, all of us are on it," Isazisi said.

"But you're Tier Zero," Versia said.

"And you aren't?" Isazisi asked. "And Caitlyn isn't? And Reese? And Jasmine and Yemani aren't?"

"It's hypocritical is what it is, it is how the Circle fuels hatred against us, they call attention to the injustice of it. We kill thousands of people, we're heralded as heroes, they do it, and they're terrorists. It's flawed logic, but people who already hate us for what we are don't need much pushing." Issac said.

"You're a Tier One agent, don't wax philosophical," Isazisi said.

"Nobody cares, this isn't a joke, people are dying because of our actions, take it seriously," Reese said.

"I watched a building fall on a mother pushing her child in a stroller," Vashti said. "And we're sitting here arguing about who is scoffing at tradition and who upholds it, while people go to the funerals of their loved ones. How do any of you sleep at night?"

"We don't," Isazisi said.

"Of course you wouldn't," Issac said.

"What's that supposed to mean?" Isazisi replied.

"Whatever you want it to," Issac said.

"Shut up," Caitlyn said. "Nobody..." She began.

"Everybody stop," Vashti snapped. "The point is the Circle is winning, and they are winning not because they have our weapons, but because of what we are. They are winning through fear. What they've done is tell the world that if we can get to a Psychic, we can get to you, and all of you dare to sit here and argue in a tower that cost four billion dollars to build while protests are going on fifteen hundred feet below us, get your acts together."

"The Circle is a product of thousands of years of Psychics prancing around like we own the planet," Versia said.

"What's that supposed to mean?" Isazisi asked.

"The Night of Ten Thousand Terrors," Versia said.

Everyone stayed quiet for a few seconds.

"Do any of you even know what that is?"

"What?" Caitlyn asked.

Versia pulled up images of modern-day Targistan. He zoomed in on an image of the scarred ground.

"What does that look like?" He asked.

"Like a Psychic energy weapon," Caitlyn said.

"Because it is. The Night of Ten Thousand Terrors took place three thousand years ago, where every single one of our ancestors got together and collectively decided to burn a country to the ground."

"Is that Targistan?" Vashti asked. "I volunteer there monthly."

"The reason it's like this is because of us. A piece of the meteor landed in their country and they wanted to share it with the world. The Psychics, so offended by their 'disrespect' for our metal. We demanded it back. They said no, and we destroyed them for it." Versia said.

The other Psychic's jaws dropped and eyes expanded. Only Isazisi sat unfazed.

"No, comment on our heritage?" Versia asked. "Did you know about this?"

"Yes," Isazisi said.

"And you didn't tell anyone?

"It's terrible what happened, but it wasn't us."

"How many more massacres like this have we committed throughout history, and you wonder why the Circle hates us," Caitlyn said.

"I learned about this as a teenager, the rest of you weren't?" Isazisi asked.

"And you didn't feel like sharing it?" Versia asked.

"We are different from our ancestors."

"No, we're not. This is only one of multiple killings and other actions in Psychic history that we would be horrified by today. If you want the full file on our ancestors' misdeeds, Meadow is still compiling it. We still take down governments, we still kill because we can, and we walk around with so much power and influence, that a bomb killing 700 people in New York City didn't even open an investigation into us. Providence operates with no oversight because of actions taken dozens of times in our history with the explicit goal of consolidating our power, thousands are suffering because of it, and it's not the global third world anymore. We got cocky. The Psychics are an institution that some believe are the greatest cause of human suffering in the history of this planet, others think we're saviors sent from above, but we know the truth, blood paid for this building, and we should acknowledge that."

"We do things in the dark, so they can walk calmly in

the light. The Psychics are a foundational institution that has existed for tens of thousands of years, saved millions of lives, helped countless people, and you would destroy those thousands of years of tradition because of your generational guilt?" Isazisi asked Versia.

Versia blasted him through a glass inside the building with a psycho smash.

"Do not ever talk to me about tradition, you scoff at it, which is why your weapons are killing thousands across the globe," Versia yelled.

Isazisi stood, and the arm of his suit flew into his hand. VerIsazisi did the same. They held each other at laser point.

"Don't do it," Versia said.

"Put on the suit, let's go a few rounds, and I'll drop you again," Isazisi said.

"Don't act like I'd let you this time."

They both charged their lasers.

"Don't do it," Isazisi said.

They blasted each other back, both flying through glass panes in the room.

"Put on the suit," Isazisi snapped.

"I'm down," Versia countered.

They both stood from the glass shards. Caitlyn threw two disks from her hands, they latched onto the ground and emitted an electromagnetic lighting bolt, pulling both their suited hands down.

"Everybody calm down." She said. "We're emotional about this, I get it, but we want the same thing, a Circle-free world, but this is exactly what the Circle wants, for us to tear each other apart, so they're free to do what they please. Now, let's focus on this, Isazisi, you make plans for taking out Circle bases as best we can, She held up her finger, showing a midnight blue ring with silver lines running through it on her fingers.

"Every single one of us has one of these, and you know what they mean. Our House Rings signify the oaths we took when we swore to honor the Psychics who came before us. This is not the legacy we will leave."

Everyone else looked at their fingers. They each had rings exactly like hers on them.

"So before we repeat the mistake of our ancestors and tear ourselves apart, everyone think. Are we a family, or are we what the Circle says we are? A bunch of superpowered children who will shatter the world?"

The device turned off and Isazisi and Versia both put down their hands.

"No loose cannons." They both said.

Versia's helicopter took off from the roof of the skyscraper as Isazisi descended in the elevator, he exited the lobby to a swarm of reporters, drowning out the crowd of protestors at the doors outside the tower.

"What do you say to the leaked news that there was a London attack that you covered up?" One reporter asked.

"Did you think you'd be able to keep a skyscraper exploding, that killed seven hundred people under wraps?" Another asked.

He ignored the reporters.

"How do you respond to the allegations of numerous covered-up attacks?" Another reporter asked.

"What do you say to the report of multiple, up to dozens of attacks covered up to protect your reputation and the reputation of Psychics?" Another asked.

"Hey Isazisi, when are you gonna deal with these guys?" A reporter asked.

He stopped and turned. "What do you think we've been doing"

"According to the body count, not enough."

"Is that what you want? A pile of Circle agent bodies?" He asked.

"You've never had a problem with that before." The same reporter said.

"Fine, here's a message I've wanted to send to Circle for a while. I didn't know how to put it gently for the optics, but now, the gloves have come off. We are Psychics. We descend from ten thousand years of history and tradition. That tradition will not die at your hands. I've decided in unison with the other Psychics, that the methods of our ancestors should be brought into the modern era. We will not hold back, we will not show mercy, and we will tear you to pieces. This is what happens when you assault my agents, steal my weapons, and attack my world. If they want a war, they've got one." He pushed past the reporters to his red sports car and sped off.

CHAPTER 21

Versia's lime green sports car pulled up to the gates of a Los Angeles mansion. The computer at the gate scanned his car and it slid open. Four other supercars decorated the driveway, along with a hand-manicured garden full of luscious blue flowers and vibrant green hedges. He looked at his smartwatch, it indicated Caitlyn hadn't checked in since they last argued in the tower. He stepped out and scanned his hand at the door. The lock clicked and he pushed the door open to a dark house. He said something explicit as he found Caitlyn in a chair, unconscious. Both of her arms were laid out facing up, dried blood on them, the same blood had leaked out over the chair and the carpet. Her katana lay on the ground, the top of it caked red with blood. An empty bottle of pills with the word "Sertraline" on it sat on a table beside her body. He took her pulse and let his breath go. Her powers healed the long tracks she'd carved vertically into her skin. His smart contact scanned her body showing her powers counteracting the bottle of pills she'd downed. He tapped his smartwatch.

"Caitlyn had an attempt. No ambulances, keep this under wraps." Versia said.

Versia jolted her awake with his powers.

"What happened?" He asked.

"I tried to kill myself, and failed." She said, slipping in and out of consciousness.

"Why, you know how hard that is for us," Versia said.

"Still worth a shot." She said in the same tone.

"No, it's not," Versia said. "Your depression is getting worse.

"No, it's not."

"Yes it is, Caitlyn, we know your life isn't easy, but we can help you."

"What, tell the world? Tarnish the image of perfection

Psychics have perpetuated for thousands of years? I won't be the one to do that." She said.

"Caitlyn, you're not the perfect golden child, that's ok, you're still human at your core."

"Does it matter," she yelled. "I descend from a long line of legendary Psychic's and my mother never let me forget it. Everything about my life was chosen generations before me, down to my name. Perfection is demanded, is her saying. If you think I'll give her the pleasure of seeing me at my worst you're insane."

"Caitlyn, your mother loves you, she would hate to see you like this," Versia said.

"I have to clear my head. I'm going for Jake." She said as she stood, still shaking.

"You are not in a position to go anywhere," Versia said.

"Prepare the jet, it's not like you can stop me." She said.

"What caused it this time?" Versia asked. She sighed and sat back down.

"I saw it, the carnage our weapons created, the lives that we tore apart, the people that we tore apart. You know, when you can do what we can, the world expects nothing less than perfection. For me to have this, they'll see it, and me as a waste of something they dream of having. They'll look at my childhood and assume I was given everything with a simple ask. I wasn't. They'll see the expensive cars and the silk dresses and think everything is perfect, they wouldn't believe me if I told them I suffered every day. They wouldn't care either, because they see the Psychic in me. They don't see my struggle, they don't see I'm hurting so much I'd rather end my life than live another day of torture, and even if they did, they'd tell me my life's too perfect for me to suffer." Caitlyn said.

"Then why do you keep going, what pulls you out of bed every morning?" Versia asked.

Caitlyn closed her eyes as tears flowed from them.

"I was born with these powers, most people don't know I love art, or music, or reading. They don't know that sometimes I wish

I was like them. Go to school, make friends, make enemies, find love, cry, laugh, grow with my friends, not thinking about how I have to save the world from something I caused. We're different, and that'll always be a part of us, but when you can do what we can, it's not only expectations from the world, it's expectations from yourself. None of us were given these powers to sit on our hands, then bad things start to happen, and you see that you can make a difference, the question becomes why should you not?" She said.

"You know what I think is beautiful? That through everything you've suffered, everything you've faced, that if it came down to it, you would still always give yourself to save others." He tossed her a cube. "Eat that, it'll speed up your recovery," Versia said.

"That's the Versia I know," She said.

"Why do you do what you do?" Caitlyn asked him.

"Because when you have the power to help people, to bring change, who are you to not," Versia said.

He guided her outside where a convoy of Providence SUVs waited. They opened the door for her, and she stepped in.

"We'll take it from here," One of the agents said to Versia.

He nodded. The cars drove off. His watch vibrated. "Great." He said as he looked at it, he double-tapped his chest and flew off.

****

Jake sat in the hospital bed beside the man. The EKG machine beeped every few seconds, but the pale clammy skin of the man told the story. He woke up.

"Jake," he said as he coughed. "What are you doing here, you should be out there, fighting the Circle."

"The hospital called the house, they said I needed to be here," Jake said.

"If the technology of our forefathers hasn't saved me yet, what chance does it have now? Doctors said I should've died years ago, my time is coming."

"Don't say that, when this fight is over we'll divert everything we have to find you a cure," Jake said.

"Jake, if five thousand years of Psychic history couldn't find me a cure, what can we do now? I feel my powers dwindling if only they passed to your father too, but they didn't, only to you."

"The technology will keep you alive for another five years."

His grandfather chuckled.

Jake's wrist buzzed.

"Go, I'm sure whatever it is is far more important, I'm not going anywhere." His grandfather said.

Jake opened the door to his house and stepped in. He walked to his kitchen where Caitlyn stood wearing a midnight blue short sleeve shirt and gray sweatpants, pouring herself a glass of alcohol.

"You know that's an eleven thousand dollar bottle of alcohol," Jake said.

"I know you're good for the money," she responded.

"The better question is why are you drinking again?"

"Must everybody judge my life choices?"

He looked at her arms, they had shallow scarring.

"Caitlyn, did you try to..."

"Yes, and it didn't work, it's not that big of a deal," she said, cutting him off

"It is a big deal, Caitlyn, I hate seeing you like this."

"Well so do I, too bad I can't do anything about it."

"You can get help, we can find you help," Jake said.

Caitlyn took a long swing from her glass and walked towards him while looking around his house, her eyes locked with the bouquet of gray roses on a table.

"I see you kept my gift."

"Why wouldn't I."

"It's a nice house, a really nice house, it's a shame you live alone," she said.

"Well you turned down my offer to move in with me," Jake replied.

She touched his face with her palm, the aroma of alcohol coming off her breath mixed with her flowery perfume. He looked at her eyes, puffy and still a bit red.

"Caitlyn, if you need anything, please, I'm here," Jake said. "So many people go through what you do, so many hide because of what others would think, even we do..."

"But we shouldn't." Caitlyn finished.

"You could help so many people if you told the world," Jake said.

"Then what, every mistake I make someone will bring it up, anytime I do anything wrong it'll be front-page news. The world will always look for someone to destroy because it gains the most clicks, who better than a Psychic." She said.

"Consider it, there's so much you could do." He said.

She pulled him in and pressed her lips to his, she let go after a few seconds.

"I'm hard to love Jake," she said.

"I'm willing to deal with anything and everything," he said.

She put a file on the table.

"All the other Psychics are indisposed at the moment, and they don't think I'm ready for action after the attempt," she said.

"What is it?"

"They'll explain on the plane," She said. "But you might need this." She handed him a gray mouth and nose covering mask.

The Providence jet flew over the Pacific Ocean, the squadron commander, Commander Evans stood and tapped on a screen.

"This is the Providence battleship 'Skyward'. Four hours ago Circle agents hijacked it during a routine trip in the Pacific," Evans said.

"Their demands?" Jake asked.

"Four billion, half in gold ingots, half in Psychanium ingots," Evans said.

"Why so much?"

"Skyward holds 64 Psychanium warheaded long-range attack missiles called Pythons. They can hit any target in this hemisphere, and a single one could level a city. Once launched, there is no way to stop it, recall it, or shoot it down," Evans said. "They also rigged a Psychanium bomb, if it goes off, it's goodnight to everyone on board."

"If it's the Circle they'll get the ransom and fire the missiles anyway. What about hostages?"

"They were changing shifts during the hijacking, only 45 crew on board, that's what made taking it so easy."

"What's the plan of attack?"

"Skyward has one of the most advanced radar systems in the world, it will detect any object moving horizontally, any object with a length of twenty feet or more, and any object from above moving slower than terminal velocity. You'll need to drop in from 30,000 feet to be out of range of the radar." Evans said.

"OK, here's the plan. I'll drop in, disable the bomb and radar, your team will disable the engines, the ship does not move, then you'll come in and help me sweep up, they're zealots, they'll kill themselves before they let us bring them in, and they'll die trying to launch even one of those missiles. Gear up," Jake said.

"You heard the man, let's move," Evans yelled.

The jet climbed to 30,000 feet, the bay doors slid open and Jake looked through clouds at the sparkling ship below. He took a step forward and fell out of the jet. The wind roared around him as he cut through it on his way to the black liquid below, he pointed his toes and flushed his arms with his side, he hit the water and cut through like a knife, the freezing black liquid prickling at his face as he surfaced.

He hopped onto the ship's deck. He tapped his lower jaw and the gray nanotech mask Caitlyn gave him formed over his nose and mouth. He moved across the ship's deck and came to a group of Circle agents chatting and smoking. They had black assault rifles in their hands and black body armor. Jake hopped over an air duct and blasted one of the Circle agents off the side of the ship with a gust of wind, and tanto blade formed in his hand and he rushed another agent and knees him into a wall, he sliced the agents neck, he ducked under the gun of another who swung at him and kicked him off the railing of the ship. He threw the tanto blade at the last agent, burying it in his chest. The agent collapsed and his gun clattered beside him.

Jake grabbed the knife and moved towards the radar room taking down more Circle agents in silence. He kicked open the door to the radar room and pummeled a Circle agent into the wall with a gust of wind. He placed his hand on the console and gray lines extended from it and hacked the radar.

"Radar disabled," Jake relayed.

"Copy," Evan said.

His men parachuted from the jet. Jake left the radar room and spotted a group of Circle agents. He jumped from the ship's railing and landed on a Circle agent, he threw a knife at another and rolled off the man he tackled. He blocked the punch of another agent and kicked him into a wall. A gun cocked behind him.

"On your knees, now," the man said.

Jake put his hands up. Two silenced shots rang out and the man fell. Evans and his team landed.

"Thanks," Jake said.

"You're welcome. My men are disabling the engine, the ship's not moving," Evans said.

"Do we know where the bomb is?"

"Heat signature says below deck, we'll hit the hostages and take out anyone we see," Evans said.

"Copy," Jake said.

He made his way down to the lower level where he encountered the bomb.

"I wouldn't take too many more steps," a voice said.

Jake looked to the side where a man sat.

"The bomb has a proximity sensor, if you get too close this whole ship gets vaporized," Tyler said.

Jake's smart contact scanned the brown-haired man sitting in a chair.

"You're enhanced," Jake said.

"Closest we'll ever get to you," Tyler said.

He pressed a trigger on his hand, starting a five-minute timer on the bomb.

"If you click this again the bomb disarms, if you don't click it in time it's programmed to launch every missile on this ship, then blow it to scrap," he said as he put the remote in one of his tactical vest pockets.

He pulled out a rifle and shot at Jake who dived behind one of the consoles. He raced up the stairs and Tyler followed, shooting at him, the bullets sparked off the metal walls of the ship. Jake formed a knife in his hand and his against the side of the doorway. Tyler came through and Jake kneed the gun out of Tyler's hands. He stabbed downward at Tyler who blocked the strike and kicked Jake back. He pulled a pistol from his back and shot at Jake who rolled behind a console. Jake formed a grenade in his hand and rolled it at Tyler. He looked down at the bomb and jumped through a window as it exploded. Jake rushed out the door and blasted Tyler off a railing with a gust of wind.

He hopped off the same railing, chasing Tyler who rolled to his feet on the ship's deck. He threw two grenades at Jake who caught both of them in a wind construct and threw them off the ship. Jake blasted Tyler into a nearby wall. Tyler reached for a second gun and shot at Jake who ducked behind an object. Tyler dashed to the control center of the ship. Jake boosted up with a puff of wind and caught him. He conjured a blast of wind and slammed Tyler into the wall of the control room, he dropped to the floor. Evans and his men came in and looked at Tyler on the floor.

"The rest of the Circle and hostages are secure," Evans said.

He took the remote from Tyler's pocket and deactivated the bomb. Tyler groaned as he pulled himself onto the console. Jake and Evans looked over. He pressed a button on the console, and one of the silos opened and shot a missile. Jake said something explicit and kicked the man into a wall.

"Where is that missile going?" Jake yelled.

"Doesn't matter," Tyler said, laughing. "You can't stop it."

Jake ran outside and towards the front of the ship and hopped off the railing, nanites spread from the gray housing unit on his chest, forming a gray Psychic Suit with white lines in it. He flew after the missile. His suit's HUD locked on the missiles roaring through the sky.

"Where's it going?" He asked Meadow.

"Seattle," she replied.

"I kind of hate UW, should I let it go?"

"Jake," Meadow said.

"I'm kidding. How much time I got?"

"Three minutes," she said

He fired shoulder rockets at it, and the missile dodged them in the air. He flew closer to it, the middle detected him and sped up.

"Meadow, what's happening?"

"The missile has a proximity sensor, if you get too close it speeds up."

"Can it outrun the suit?"

"In theory, no." She said.

He fired a few more lasers and rockets at it. The missile dodged them. The lights of Seattle flashed in the distance.

"Meadow, I'm trying something crazy."

He boosted forward catching the missile, he lodged himself under it and pushed upwards, and the missile followed. The missile roared into Seattle and flew vertical as Jake pushed it upwards, people on the ground pointed and stared at the white trail it left. Jake fired his suit's thrusters taking the missile into space, he let it go.

"Jake, get out of its range," Meadow yelled in his ear. The missile exploded, and a shockwave washed over the suit knocking out its electronics, Jake free-fell towards the murky black water below. Outside the suit alternated between the stars, then the black as the suit spun in the air.

"Meadow, I need a reboot," Jake yelled, panting in the suit.

The suit's electronics flared back to life and he fired his hand jets stopping his fall. He flew back to the ship where Evans and his men had rounded up the Circle agents. The Providence ship had moved into place to collect the prisoners.

Jake arrived back home. Caitlyn sat on the floor with her back against a sofa in his living room. Red ambient lights reflect off the glass of alcohol in her hand with one poured for Jake resting on the table.

"I don't want to hurt you," she said. "I don't want you to ever come home and see me bled out over the bed we share because I couldn't take it anymore. I don't want you to feel that kind of pain because of me. That's why we can't be together."

Jake sat beside her.

"I want you, I need you more than I need anything else in my life.

Their foreheads touched.

"I don't care about hurting myself. If that's what it takes to love you, I'm willing to love you," Jake said.

CHAPTER 22

Fletcher's SUV clawed its way over the muddy jungle terrain of Ucaudo, Africa.

"How long till we're there," Fletcher asked.

"We've arrived sir, his driver said.

The row of black SUVs stopped in the center of a makeshift camp in the jungle, men with guns slung over their shoulders smoked cigarettes as they leaned up against crates full of armaments. Fletcher's agents jumped out of the vehicles and set up a perimeter. Fletcher stepped out of a middle SUV and looked around at the site. A man stepped forward and stretched out his hand.

"I am Mose, and welcome to paradise," the man said with a crooked smile.

"Thank you for having us."

"Mr. Ugandu will see you now."

Fletcher nodded and followed the man into a large tent surrounded by armed men. A man with a thick gray beard sat on the other side of a table, a cigar lit in his mouth. He wore camouflage with an armband in the red, green, and orange colors of the Ucaudo flag with a red beret hat.

"Mr. Ugandu it is a pleasure to meet you," Fletcher said.

"Of course, any call from our friend Mr. Williams is much appreciated,"

"He's more of my co-boss, but thank you for taking the time to meet with me on his behalf,"

"Indeed, so what is your proposal?"

One of Fletcher's people handed him a piece of paper.

"Here I hold the full file from Providence on you, it fits on one page and reads. 'Jakande Ugandu is an African revolutionary warlord fighting a civil war in his home country of Ucaudo, while his tactics of maiming his enemies and indiscriminately

244

targeting anyone whom he deems a threat to his power are brutal, as he had not dabbled into the world of Psychanium weapons, he is currently to us, no threat at all, and should be monitored, yet ignored. He poses no credible threat at this time."' Fletcher read. "Psychics view you as a warlord to be ignored, which makes you dangerous. The Psychic's file on us reads the same way, and we've put the whole world on notice that we are the most credible threat in history."

"My enemy is not the West unless they become my enemy," Uganda said.

"Our enemy isn't the West either, just the Psychics and everything or, a lack of everything they stand for. Take you for example, most people would think the Psychics, the new gods bestowed upon a fractured world would see you as an evil they have the resources to easily dispel, but until you touch their precious metal, you are simply a problem to your country, and not to their reign. In fact, you've received money from Providence in the past, haven't you?"

"Under their previous regime they did supply me with weapons and finance, they said our goals aligned at the time, but since their heir has taken over, my payments have stopped."

"No matter, we need something from you, and are prepared to reward you handsomely for it."

Ugandu raised an eyebrow.

"So what do you need?"

"The world is on the lookout for us, we've found it hard to continue inserting our agents into cities across the globe. We want to pull off an attack here" Fletcher had one of his agents put a map on the table in front of Ugandu. "And in South Africa."

"So you would like me to insert my people to detonate your weapons, and risk bringing myself to the attention of the Psychic's and the international community."

"We will take full credit and actively distance ourselves from you should any heat fall onto your plate."

"And the payment for this?"

Fletcher snapped his fingers and men brought in three large

silver boxes with handles on the side. They opened the cases revealing four rods of Psychanium on a gray block of foam with cutouts.

"Four rods of Psychanium, with five layers in each box. Twenty rods of Psychanium in each, three boxes, sixty rods total, value, well into the billions, the potential weapons you can make from this, possibilities are endless. If you want to win this civil war, these are the weapons you need, and lucky for us, Psychanium loves to be made into weapons." Fletcher said.

"And of course, once we take over, the entire African continent is yours, nobody will challenge our rule, and you may do what you want with the continent and its resources, which we will, of course, be willing to buy from you and you alone at fair prices, but you'll have a monopoly, therefore your profits will be unlimited."

Ugandu smiled. "I see a fruitful partnership in our future," he said as he stretched out his hand.

Fletcher shook it. "Cheers to our new future"

****

The Providence agent typed away at his keyboard, put on a pair of headphones, and listened to Circle chatter as he watched dozens of different satellite and drone feeds. His computer intercepted an encrypted email. The Psychanium-powered computer system decoded it in less than a second. His eyes expanded before he picked up the phone.

"We know where the Secretary of State is." The agent said.

Minutes later three top generals in Red Cyan's army walked into his office. He stood with his back to the door, watching satellite and drone feeds, while listening to the chatter.

"Sir, we may have located the Secretary." One of the generals said.

He turned away from the hologram screens.

"Where?" He asked.

Hours later Isazisi landed in Africa, in one of the largest cities on the continent. Hundreds of his agents had already moved into place as tourists. He stepped out of the vehicle, and Reese out of another.

"Intel says they have the Secretary of State here, along with a bomb near one of the buildings here," Reese said.

"How'd they get past our surveillance?" An agent asked.

"We don't know, we're looking into it," she responded.

Their drone scanned a house the chatter pointed them toward. Multiple heat signatures lit up on the screen. Providence Centurions in full armor approached the house. Resse pulled out and cocked back a black pistol, she aimed it at the doorway. The armored agents made their way towards the entrance. Multiple box trucks drove out from a wooden warehouse nearby, scattering Providence's troops. The backs on the trucks opened and armor-clad Circle agents jumped out and shot at Providence agents who took cover and fired back as civilians screamed and ran for cover.

"Meadow, scan for the bomb," Isazisi asked.

Meadow scanned the 84-story building.

"That car," she said, as she highlighted it in Red's smart contact. He dashed to it and examined the vehicle parked in the center of the busy market area outside the skyscraper. People cleared out of the way as he looked over it. He reached under the car and found a bomb the size of a laptop.

"It's a disruptor." Meadow said, "It would have toppled the building, killing everyone inside and in the market."

Isazisi turned it over, looking for a timer.

"There's no timer, how long do we have?" Isazisi asked.

She showed him a rising temperature scan in the right corner of his eye.

"Eight seconds," she said.

Isazisi said something explicit and launched the bomb, throwing it as high as he could, his super strength propelling it out of range within the time. The bomb exploded, hurling a red shockwave across the sky. Nearby people took cover as a sound like thunder shattered windows and glass. Someone kicked Isazisi from behind, sending him flying through a nearby vendor's shop.

"Remember me?" The person who kicked him yelled.

Isazisi looked over the man, clad in lighter body armor than the rest of their people.

The person punched him back again as he got up, then grabbed him, throwing him through another vendor's shop. He stood up.

"Fletcher." He said as a katana formed in his hand.

Reese and other agents, still pinned behind a car under relentless gunfire shot back. A group of six Circle members each took one smaller Providence bomb, ditched their armor, and ran into the crowded market area. She slid over the hood of the car and shot two Circle agents, dodged the gunfire of the others, and shot three. An armored truck pulled up at the same time. The back door swung open as more Circle agents jumped down from the vehicle. Reese took a grenade off one of the dead Circle agents and threw it into the truck. It spun on the ground as the Circle agents looked down at it. It stopped and exploded. A Circle agent rushed at her. She dodged a punch and kneed him in the side, spun, elbowed him in the stomach, and grabbed the back of his head before kneeing him in the face; she dropped him and ran into the crowd after the agents.

"Move. Move." She yelled to people as she chased after the Circle agents.

The agents shot back, missing Reese. The agents split off, three on each side. Reese took the left first. One of the agents turned around and ran for her. She jumped forward and kneed him in the chest with her momentum. The other shot at her, but she dodged the bullets and kicked him into a wall. The last one threw a punch, but she blocked it and kneed him in the stomach, she punched him in the face and kneed him again. She slammed his head against the wall, knocking him out cold. She ran and slid through multiple vendors' shops and bounded over parked motorcycles and products as she cut across the shop to the other three agents.

A Providence agent found a yellow vial of liquid sticking out from a dead Circle agent's pocket. They picked it up and said something explicit as they pressed their ear.

"They have Providence bioweapons. Do not let the vials crack or the entire city is in danger." The agent said.

Reese jumped over a vendor, tackling one of the Circle agents. He pulled a gun, she disarmed him and punched him in the abdomen multiple times. Another Circle agent came behind her with a gun, she pushed off the first agent and grabbed a basket off a vendor's table, and threw it at the man, he blocked it, she used it to sweep him off his feet and did a complex takedown on both of them, wrapping herself around their necks as she brought both of them down. She rolled over one of the agents, still holding his wrist as she kicked the other in the face. She punched the one she held in the face before rolling back, grabbing his gun, and aiming it at him. He pulled another gun at the same time. The first agent also had a gun while the third held up one of the vials.

"You know what it is. Drop your gun." The Circle agent said.

She took her left hand off the gun and turned it towards herself as she closed it.

"Don't try anything," The Circle member yelled.

A red knife formed in her closed hand. She glanced at a large shard of glass on the ground, half buried in the sand. She slid her foot over it. She pulled the trigger, threw the knife, and kicked the shard into one of the agent's chests in the space of a second. The third agent dropped the vial, and she reacted, grabbing it before it hit the ground and springing back up in one motion.

"Vial secure." She radioed as she let out a pained breath.

Fletcher stomped on Isazisi's head, but he rolled out of the way and swiped at Fletcher's head with his sword, Isazisi blocked a kick with his forearms and dodged a few other strikes, getting back into position. Isazisi spun the sword in his hands. He sliced at Fletcher who dodged each swipe with inhuman speeds.

"The second-generation of Psychanium enhancements, they make us humans like you," Fletcher said.

He threw a punch, and Isazisi dodged it. Fletcher threw a

kick, and Isazisi blocked it with the flat side of his sword and retaliated by swiping at Fletcher's neck. He dodged it and reeled backward off balance before feeling his neck for any marks, he looked up.

"I thought you were more than your metal," Fletcher said.

Isazisi stood straight and tossed his sword, it landed in the sand with its trademark ring.

"Let's see," Isazisi said.

People hidden around the fight pulled out their phones and recorded. Fletcher cracked a smile.

Fletcher swung first. He threw a punch, Isazisi blocked it and retaliated with a knee to Fletcher's side, Fletcher threw a high kick, Isazisi blocked it, and threw a punch, Fletcher blocked it, Fletcher threw a roundhouse, but Isazisi dodged it and hit him with a series of aerial kicks, sending Fletcher rolling. The phones followed him. He stood and wiped the blood off his mouth. Fletcher threw a mid-level kick at Isazisi, he blocked it and answered with a series of front kicks. Fletcher blocked each of them. The men came face to face. Fletcher rammed his head into Isazisi's, and he staggered. Fletcher punched him back with inhuman strength and kicked him into a wall. Fletcher pulled a knife. He stabbed it at Isazisi, who blocked it, driving the knife into the wall behind him. Fletcher ran the knife horizontally through the wall as he cut, the knife flew out as it ran out of wall. Isazisi punched the unbalanced Fletcher in the side before kicking him back, Fletcher staggered and Isazisi hit him with a reverse kick, sending him through a wall. Fletcher moved around on the floor as he struggled. He pulled himself up, resting on his knees.

"You were never ready for me," Isazisi said.

"Maybe, but what about one of your weapons?" Fletcher asked.

He let his hand go and a cylindrical Providence bomb rolled forward and exploded. Time slowed around Isazisi as he put his hands forward, containing the blast in a red bubble of energy. The heat still radiated onto both of them through the bubble, burning at their skin. Isazisi's hands shook as he contained the explosion. He threw the bubble upwards. It exploded in the sky, painting it red once again. People around him screamed and ducked as the red dissipated into the blue expanse. Isazisi sat, laid back with a labored breath, and said something explicit.

****

His agents came by and set up a mobile headquarters as they administered medical support to civilians and arrested Circle agents. Fletcher sat handcuffed to a chair, he had cuts and bruises scattered around his body.

"Where is the Secretary?" Isazisi asked.

"Lawyer," Fletcher said.

"We're Providence, we don't have to do that," Reese said from the corner.

"I still have my rights," Fletcher said.

"Those rules don't apply to us," Isazisi said.

"What separates you, from me?" Fletcher asked.

"I have a piece of paper that says it's ok," Isazisi said.

"Is that why you were going to torture Andrew?" Fletcher asked.

"The gladiator suit I killed?"

"Was his life simply another you could take without need or remorse?"

"He's a terrorist, he killed himself before giving me the pleasure of doing it myself."

"I guess we're all just the killers then," Fletcher said.

"Just you," Isazisi said.

"You don't remember? Oh, what you and your family have done. What the institution you prance around in the name of has done for you to stand here today. You spit in the face of all that is righteous on this earth."

"I saw the file, I know what my ancestors did to yours. I am not my forefathers. "

"It's either fate or cruel destiny that you would personally wrong me again and again."

"I know about the research project. Using our funds to move

Psychanium weapons was your decision."

"I'm not even talking about that. You really don't remember? Mexico City? Oh, I suppose a decade is a long time ago. Sixteen-year-old Isazisi, the new head of Providence, and eager to show the world how cruel you could be. Your mission in Mexico. Cartel was helping move weapons for my group. I'd cut myself off from the Circle for a while at that point, my rebellious early twenties, and of course, I'd been fired from Providence at this point and you. You came crashing down from the sky, the Red God, and you killed without hesitation. Do you remember the one woman present? My whole team. Who you killed for no reason. She posed no threat to you, they'd already surrendered, and you still took her life, all of their lives, and I came back from a meeting and found them slaughtered. I watched the security footage, they surrendered, you didn't need to do that. You just wanted to prove a point. We were engaged, the wedding already planned, and you took her from me. You took my first love from me, you took my second from me. At that point, I truly understood where the Circle's hatred for you came from. I would suggest you kill me where I stand, or I will never stop hunting you until I've burnt your whole world to the ground, the way you did mine."

"That was your fiance," Isazisi said, trailing off.

"What's your justification now, where is your signed paper from the universe saying you have the right to give and take life?"

"Do you know what the Circle has taken from me? What your group has put me through? The loss, the pain, everything?"

"Don't compare your suffering in a palace, to me burying my wife," Fletcher screamed.

"Do you know who I buried because of you?" Isazisi whispered.

"Like I said, I guess we're all just the killers."

"Maybe we are."

Isazisi stretched out his hand, putting it in front of Fletcher's face. He used his psychokinesis to comb through Fletcher's mind. Fletcher scrunched his forehead as he resisted. Isazisi moved his hand closer to Fletcher's face as he exerted more of his power, Fletcher screamed.

Isazisi walked out of the interrogation room.

"How are we looking on civilian casualties?" Isazisi asked one of his agents.

"Thirty-six killed in the crossfire, another seventy-nine injured,"

Isazisi said something explicit.

"Is there something we can do for their families?" He asked,

"Our lawyers are already on their way to the victims' families, we'll negotiate to take care of them for the rest of their lives."

"Thank you," Isazisi said.

Fletcher while left alone in the room flicked a small metal disk from his fingers onto a nearby computer. The disk stuck and spread out slightly.

Back at a Circle hideout, a computer came to life.

"He got us in," the Circle agent said. "When Providence is done with a weapons factory they take the Psychanium and leave everything else behind, these factories can manufacture hundreds of exosuits and robots for us. I just need to take over them."

He clicked on a few keys and his screen flashed green. Across the world, dozens of abandoned Providence bases flared to life, robot arms moved and welded, sparks flying.

Isazisi walked into the control room of the mobile command center.

"He has a strong mind, but I'm stronger. The Secretary of State isn't here, he's on an oil tanker two hundred miles off the coast owned by Norcorp Oil," Isazisi said to the CIA and FBI agents with him on the ground.

"Can we get a visual?" One of the agents asked.

Isazisi double-tapped his wrist. From space, a drone capsule launched from one of his satellites. The capsule broke as it entered the atmosphere above the Atlantic Ocean. The drone activated and surveyed the oil tanker from a distance, relaying video of a few dozen shipping containers present on the ship's deck. The drone scanned for heat signatures, finding more than a dozen in a shipping container along with an additional fifty or so walking through the rows of containers. The drone also picked up the weapon signatures of stolen Providence tech.

"Can we breach, send an assault team?" One CIA agent asked.

"No, the demands they made when we captured Fletcher were for our surrender, if they don't get that, they'll kill the hostages, but as long as they think they can negotiate, they'll stay alive. This has to be done with stealth, an assault team would alert them in seconds." Isazisi said.

"What do you propose?" The agent asked.

"Four of us. We go in, kill the engines, and take out as many Circle agents as we can. Your teams will be standing by in speed boats for the rescue. Then, we blow up the ship and set the Circle back two hundred million." Isazisi said.

The agent nodded and signaled to his people.

"You heard the man, gear up." The agent said.

****

Caitlyn surfaced without a sound from the depths at the back of the ship. Versia surfaced from the right side, Reese from the left, and Isazisi from the front. Caitlyn jumped on board and slinked into the shadows as a lone agent walked by on patrol. She came from behind and put him in a headlock, taking him down. She threw the body overboard and moved further into the ship, coming to three agents leaning against the containers making small talk. She dropped from above and elbowed one in the neck, she punched the other in the face before throwing her elbow back, hitting the third in the face. She reverse-kicked the first agent and kneed the second in the stomach. She grabbed his head and slammed it into the container, leaving a dark red mark. She threw a throwing knife into the first agent's neck, killing him where he stood, and punched the last one in the face, causing him to slam his head on the container, leaving another dark red splotch. A midnight blue katana formed in her hand as she approached another group of six agents also talking. She dropped from on top of a container, stabbing one of them from behind, through the neck, and into his chest. She ripped out the sword and rolled over to another agent who fumbled with his gun, she cut him down. Another agent threw a punch, she dodged it and cut him down. She elbowed one of the agents running at her from behind and kicked him into one of the containers. She cut down the fifth agent and threw her sword, killing the last agent who reached for the alarm. She pulled the sword from his body and the wall, made her way to the ship's cockpit, and killed the agents inside. She disabled the ship's engines and main controls, the vessel wasn't going anywhere anymore. She made her way to the top of the cockpit, shrouded in darkness as a bow and arrow formed in her hand.

"I'm in overwatch position." She said as she knocked an arrow.

Versia made his way around the ship, coming to a group of agents standing around talking, one pulled out a deck of cards as another dragged an empty barrel over. Versia threw a taser dart, burying it in one of the agents, he kneed one of the agents with a running start, knocking them out. He elbowed an agent behind him and punched one in front of him. He swept one beside him off his feet and dodged the punch of another. He kicked one into the shipping container, he hit hard and remained motionless. Versia dodged a few more attacks and retaliated, knocking out the rest of the agents. He made his way towards the shipping container the drone had identified.

Isazisi jumped on board. He threw a knife from the shadows, hitting one of the Circle agents from behind. They fired at him, alerting the other agents to intruders on board. Reese fought her way through a dozen Circle agents and to the shipping container.

Isazisi cut down two Circle agents with his katana, and he threw it at another, impaling him through the chest. He blocked the punch of another agent and threw them into one of the containers, banging their head and leaving a red mark. He dodged the punch of another and kicked them overboard.

From her perch on the ship's cockpit, Caitlyn fired off an arrow, hitting a Circle agent in the back. She knocked another one and fired, hitting another agent. She took what cover she could as gunfire raked her position. She pressed a button on her bow, causing her quiver to arm one of the arrows with a lighting explosive. She knocked the arrow and shot it towards the gunfire. It exploded with a loud humming sound as it took out multiple Circle agents.

"That's our cue," the lead agent said.

From a ship a few miles out dispatched the CIA agents.

Resse grabbed the lock on the container and crushed it with ease, opening the shipping container. Everyone inside recognized her. She led them to the side of the boat to the waiting CIA agents. Reese lowered each of them onto the boats with her **psychokinesis**. A Psychianium bullet hit her shoulder as she lowered the last one. She fell forward, clutching the back of her shoulder. She turned around to a Circle agent with a Providence weapon in his hand. He raised the gun to take another shot. Reese's eyes glowed red. Lasers shot from them, cutting the man down. She swung her head, cutting through the handful of shipping containers. Her eyes returned to normal. She laid back, still holding her shoulder.

Providence ships had arrived and agents arrested any Circle agents alive. A doctor had removed the bullet from Reese's back and the wound healed itself. Isazisi and the other two checked on her.

"The bullet missed everything vital, didn't even touch the bone," Reese said.

Each of their wrists vibrated at the same time, Caitlyn glanced at her wrist and looked up, her eyes grief-stricken and her eyebrows clenched.

"What?" Isazisi asked.

"Another attack. Bioweapon. Cape Town." She said.

CHAPTER 23

Allen held the clippers up to the plant's stem and cut. The large reddish-orange fruit dropped into his hand. He placed it in a basket slung over his shoulder. He moved to the next fruit in the column and did the same. Birds chirped in the sky and landed on nearby trees as they surveyed the island. Ava walked out of the stilted wooden house overlooking the rows and rows of green fields growing the fruit. She had purple flowers in her hair with bracelets made from seeds around her wrist.

"What's the Firefruit for?" She asked.

"The meteor piece that landed here changed the genetics of the plant life, meaning Psychic Firefruit only grows here, and the volcanic solid is the most fertile in the world, meaning it's the perfect apology gift," Allen said.

"Apology to who?" Ava asked.

"Everyone, the families of every single person killed in a Circle attack," Allen said.

She looked out over the fields. "That's going to be a lot of fruit." She said.

"Nothing compared to a human life," Allen said.

Ava took him by the hand and sat him on the stairs of the house.

"It's not your fault." She said.

"How. We were both consulted when creating these weapons was put on the table. We were both told the potential risks of something like this happening, and we still said yes." Allen said as tears came to his eyes.

"We did this to people. As much as we shifted the blame onto the Circle, in the end, it's our weapons, and we hide out on islands and in mansions while the people we swore to protect bury their loved ones."

"You're not wrong," Ava said.

"No matter how we shift the blame, we are the root."

"How do you cope with it, knowing it's our fault?" Allen asked.

Ava kissed him, with passion. She pulled her lips away.

"I cope knowing that we can stop future attacks," Ava said.

Both their wrists buzzed. Ava swiped at hers.

She whispered something explicit. "Another attack."

Allen buried his head in his hands and rubbed his face.

"We have to go. We're ending this." She said,

****

Isazisi, Versia, Reese, and Sanjiv walked into the meeting room. At a long table sat leaders from every major intelligence agency on the planet.

"There was a biological attack in Cape Town five hours ago, nine hundred dead." One of the agents said as video footage of the attack played on a large screen. "We have confirmation it was a Providence weapon used, that's attack number ten."

"Two undercover Providence agents posing as weapons buyers were injured in the blast, we've airlifted them to one of our bases, they'll live, my full resources are also deployed helping give medical attention and to assist in finding missing persons," Isazisi said. "We believe that another actor, Jakande Ugandu may have been involved in helping facilitate the attack."

"The warlord?"

"Yes, he hasn't been a threat to us now, so we're approaching that angle with caution."

"Noted. We also received these videos." Another agent said as he swiped on a tablet.

"Violence will make the world listen." The man yelled. He had no mask on. The video continued in the background.

"This is the first video they've sent claiming responsibility, the others were via hacked texts," Versia asked.

"Damn, what are these guys trying to do, start a new caliphate?" One of the agents joked.

"Why Cape Town?" Reese asked.

"Africa was the last continent to not have an attack, and most other cities are under surveillance. You can't walk through Los Angeles or Amsterdam anymore without seeing dozens of cops at every corner." One agent said.

"This is escalating, we need it plugged now." Another agent said.

"We're taking care of that as we speak," Versia said.

"The second video?" Isazisi asked.

People around the room looked at each other and shifted in their seats as others whispered to those beside them.

"What?" Isazisi asked.

"It's addressed to you specifically." One of the agents said.

"Play it, everyone should see," Isazisi said.

"There's also a line of code embedded in it. When we play it the second time, it'll be sent across the internet, and the entire world will see it." One agent said.

"Go ahead, I have nothing to hide," Isazisi said.

One of the agents nodded to the one manning the computer. He pressed a few buttons. The video played and a maskless man spoke.

"Isazisi Irving, the red God of the sky. We want to see the world burn till it comes crawling to us for salvation, the attacks will not stop till we have what we want, but for you. I revel in the thought of you going to sleep every night with the blood of thousands on your hands, do you even think about it, or is it easier to ignore the news reports? Five people close to you we took, and it's taken this long for your crusade to begin, is there blood on your hands? Is there? How much was necessary? Do you still have nightmares? Violence will make the world listen. Hail the Circle." The man said. The video ended.

"What five people did they take?" One agent asked.

"I don't want to talk about it," Isazisi said.

"Are they dead, kidnapped, what?" Another asked.

"We are not talking about it," Isazisi yelled.

Everyone stayed quiet. Isazisi turned his head from side to

side and composed himself.

"This is a new low," Isazisi said.

"We need this taken care of before any more people die, these attacks aren't good for people or the economy." The agent said.

"We'll take care of it," Reese said as she stood.

The other Psychics stood as well. Reese and Isazisi left the room.

"Do you want to talk about what happened in there?" She asked.

"No, I'm not ready to share that yet," Isazisi said.

Reese respected his response and didn't pry anymore.

....

Fletchers sat in hand and leg cuffs in prison transport, chained to the ground. The truck made a right turn and a loud explosion rocked the outside, followed by gunfire. Bullets cut down the two Providence Centurions in the truck who stood. Fletcher peered through the holes but saw nothing. Outside a loud machine cut through the metal door, and they swung open revealing masked Circle agents with advanced weapons.

"Let's go, sir," one of the agents said.

Fletcher couldn't help but crack a smile.

****

Fay sat in her cell, her all-white jumpsuit clean as the day she'd put it on. A single Providence agent walked up to her cell and tapped the glass.

"Have one of the Psychic's sent you to end my suffering?"

"Hail the Circle," the agent said.

Faye stood up. From the floor, sparks flew and a chunk of rock dropped into the hole. Fletcher came through.

"Your sacrifice is never not rewarded," he said.

An alarm sounded.

"Go, I'll hold them off," the agent said.

The door leading to the cell room opened, and the agent fired at the Providence Centurions. Fay jumped in the hole as gunfire from the Centurions cut down the Circle agent. Fletcher threw a

Providence grenade through the hole.

"Take cover," one of the Centurions yelled.

The grenade exploded in a red energy wave as Fletcher, Fay and his agents made their way to a waiting Providence vehicle. They drove out the front gates and onto the next target.

****

Two Providence Centurions loaded The Chairman onto the prisoner transport vehicle.

"Where am I going," he asked.

"Quiet, you'll know when we get there."

A few minutes into the drive gunshots rang from outside. The back of the transport opened to Fletcher and Fay standing there.

"Well Mike, always saving you aren't I," Fletcher said.

Mike hopped out of the transport.

"I won't even complain,"

Fletcher laughed and embraced Mike.

****

Versia stared at the picture in his hand. His breath intensified as he stared into the photo. His hand shook as beads of sweat rolled over him as he held back a torrent of emotion. Vashti sat beside him.

"Everything ok?" She asked.

"The nightmare is expensive, but the memories, those are free," Versia said.

Vashti looked at the image in his hands.

"What is it?" She asked.

"It's a reminder to protect what you love, and avenge what you couldn't," Versia said. "Like you."

Vashti blushed.

"Protecting what I love at all costs. That's something I couldn't do before, protecting you, that's all I think about. I stay awake at night because the nightmares of losing you are too real. I don't sleep anymore because I could never live knowing I let something happen to you as I did to others. We don't have all the time in the world, so I cherish what I have. You're my anchor, my north star, losing you would crush me, I'd never be the same, always trying to reach you, knowing I never can, knowing you're in a world where we can't be together for so long. All the power in the world, and I will use it to protect you." Versia said.

She kissed him with no warning.

"I love you more than you could ever know," Vashti said.

"I know," Versia said.

....

Lily sat on the docks of her family beach house, the humidity sticking to her light brown skin as her feet hung over the edge and dipped into the cool water, one could get a faint whiff of salt coming off the ocean as in the distance yachts and fishing boats sped through the water. She looked over where humongous cargo ships made their way out to sea. She walked back inside the house. The doorbell rang, and she opened it. Outside stood Versia, carrying a bouquet of blue roses.

"The last time you brought me flowers your mother thought she should start planning our wedding," Lily said.

"Yeah, she gets excited about stuff like that."

"Yeah." She said as walked back into the house. "What do you need?" She asked.

"Your help," Versia said.

He gave her a box.

"What is it?" She asked.

"Open it," Versia said.

She lifted the cover of the box. Inside sat a silver pendant designed in the traditional Maori style with an ocean blue gem at its center. Diamonds and deep blue sapphires garnished the piece, with intricate designs cut into the silver.

"It's beautiful." She said, "It's too nice. I can't accept this."

"You have nicer."

"If this is an attempt to ask me out again. It won't work." She said.

"No," he said, chuckling. "You already know about Vashti ."

"Then why?"

"It's your core crystal."

"I thought the core crystals were destroyed." She said.

"We thought so too, a Providence expedition found them at one of the old cities and took years to extract all of them."

He handed her the roses.

"Lillies would've been too ironic for my taste," he said.

"You'd be the first one to not try and make that joke."

"I don't want to push, but we need you back in the field, I know you haven't been cleared, but after South Africa, we can't have this continue," Versia said.

"Then I'm ready," Lily said.

"Are you sure, you're a last resort," Versia said.

"I have to. I visited the kid in the hospital yesterday. I have to do it for him." Lily said.

"You never did say what happened," Versia said.

She sighed. "I guess it'd be good to get it off my chest."

Versia sat.

"I chased the Circle-enhanced agent, she'd already planted the bomb, and by the time I found it, the timer reached ten seconds, and I could do nothing. One kid in the building had hidden when the commotion started, seven years old. I took the kid and shielded him with my body as the bomb exploded. It tore through everything, bringing the whole building down. Shrapnel from the bomb hit my arms, so my powers worked overtime to make sure I didn't bleed out. I think I went into shock at least four times." She said, chuckling as she reminisced. "The building collapsed with us on a middle floor, so I was also protecting the kid from a thousand pounds of debris that would have crushed us. I'm pinned sideways and he's in front of me. So my torn to-shreds, bleeding arm, and Psychic shielding are sustaining half a building of weight. Don't even get me started on the secondary bomb that landed four feet from our faces. The Circle tampered with Providence's technology, rendering the second bomb useless, but we didn't know that." She chuckled again. "For twelve hours, I waited for the Circle to kill me. They dug us out as I went into shock for the fourth time, I would've died if they found me twenty minutes later. That's why I have to fight; for the kid, who watched me almost die four times protecting him. For the people we're sworn to protect. That's why."

Versia took her hand. "There's a war coming. The Circle versus Psychics. Psychics versus Psychics, alliances are shifting. Beings are coming, that even we may not be able to stop. But this, this we can stop. That's why I fight." He said.

"What do we need to do?" She asked. He gave her another, larger box.

"Are you sure you're ready," He asked.

"Ready as I'll ever be."

She opened the box. Inside rested a Psychanium tanto blade, with a cyan handwoven grip on the handle.

CHAPTER 24

Sanjiv sat on the stairs to his mansion, a downpour of rain pattered his body, but the cold didn't affect him. Jasmine walked out of the house and sat by him in the rain.

"Are you cold?" She asked.

"I don't get cold." He said.

She looked forward. "What's on your mind?" She asked.

"The South Africa attack, I feel, it's my fault." He said.

"How, you didn't detonate it?" She asked.

"No, but I designed it. Isazisi asked me for a cryo-based weapon, and I made one. I didn't watch the autopsy of the victims, but I saw the pictures. It works by freezing your lungs and heart, and shattering them when inhaled. I saw hundreds of people cut open, revealing the carnage of my weapon." Sanjiv said. He used rain running down his face to hide the tears.

"I feel the same," Jasmine said. " I already told you about my brother, but the Shanghai attack. I designed the bomb that detonated. I infused Psychic technology, along with toxic plants from the Shadow Realm meant as an aerosol weapon that could be dispersed throughout a terrorist cave. Now I watched as it killed hundreds of people. I watched the autopsies. Their insides were horrific, eaten away, pitch black, even some of the doctors threw up after seeing it. I don't sleep anymore. Every time I close my eyes and lie down I see the lifeless eyes of that twelve-year-old whose insides were incinerated by something I made to protect him. We made every one of those weapons to protect them, now they look up in horror as black smoke pours from the tops of residential buildings."

They both sat in silence for a few seconds, neither wanting to be the one to speak first.

"Tomorrow, we take them down," Sanjiv said.

"We won't fail," Jasmine said as she shifted closer to Sanjiv.

She touched his hand as she looked him in the eye. She kissed him, with passion. She pulled her lips away.

"Does this mean we're a thing again?" Sanjiv asked.

"If you're asking me to dinner, my answer is yes."

CHAPTER 25

The Psychics gathered at Isazisi's home where he hid in another room, he sat back in his chair, staring into the bottom of his empty glass, motionless and staring into space. Resse took his hand.

"Are you feeling ok?" She asked.

He snapped out of it and sighed. "If this is what both of us want it to be, I think I should be honest with you." He said. He took a deep breath. "I'm bipolar." He said.

Reese looked surprised but did an adequate job masking it.

"Can I help?" She asked.

"No, even my powers can't fix it, but they can keep it at bay. I have to mask it, you know, running an organization like Providence, leading armies, being a Psychic, you have to be perfect, your people have to trust you, especially with this much power resting at my fingertips." He said. "There isn't room for failure when you're bulletproof when your team isn't." He took a labored breath. " There's a stigma, especially against men. The world doesn't care about people like me, like Caitlyn, they'd rather shove us in the closet and pretend we don't exist than confront the problem, they'd rather misdiagnose us than accept we have a problem that's out of our hands, and I'm lucky. I have the resources, support, and love that so many people like me never get. I can get secret therapists, I can use the newest, most expensive experimental treatments, and I'm surrounded by people who understand and have empathy for what I'm going through. I'm lucky, so many like me aren't. The most powerful beings in the universe, and I still have a real-world problem." He looked down. "But it's a part of me, like Providence, like my powers, like anything, like you."

"You should tell the world, people need to know it's not something to hide away," Reese said.

"I should, but what's next, how can they trust me if they think I'm not one hundred percent all the time," Isazisi said.

"It does not matter," Reese said. "If you can help even one person who suffers from the same thing as you, be more accepting of themselves, you've done more than your weapons ever could."

Resse moved to her knees on the bed behind him. She put her hands beside both sides of his head, a red energy glowed between them as wisps of energy floated around his head.

"You've locked this away deep, I can't get to it," she said.

"Yeah, I'm working on that."

She stopped and sat beside him. She kissed him, with passion. She swung her legs over, sitting on him. She pulled her lips away.

"I hope that makes you feel better." She said, She hugged him. "If you need anything, to talk, reduce stress, anything. I'm here," Reese said and left the room. Isazisi smiled and left after her.

****

"We believe the Circle has one last end game, something planned in Austin, Texas. If they are going to hurt people, we have to step in, this isn't another isolated attack, this is the finale." Isazisi said. "The Circle will do anything and everything to ensure their endgame. Some of us might die on this mission, if anyone wants to back out, now would be the time."

"We're with you to the end," Jake said.

"Is everyone in agreement?" Versia asked as he looked around.

"Let's get them," Caitlyn said.

****

Isazisi flew into the airspace of Austin, Texas.

"He's in the High Psychic's Cathedral," Megan said.

Isazisi landed outside the cathedral with a metal *thud,* and walked inside where Fletcher sat on the stairs.

"Come to pay for the sins of your forefathers? Fletcher asked.

"Based on what I learned we'd be here a while."

A Spire of Psychanium rose from the ground behind Fletcher. Four clamps spread from it and smashed into the ground. Megan did a scan of it and showed it going deep into the earth.

"What's the Psychanium for?" Isazisi asked.

"We realized that terror attacks in cities across the globe created fear and death, while part of our goal, to advance our true purpose, we needed something definitive. The attacks kept you and authorities running around chasing leaders and bases while we designed and built this. It's a Psychanium shock wave oscillator. Using Psychic energy waves it'll disrupt lava flows around the globe triggering select volcanoes to erupt simultaneously. Our estimates suggest a quarter of the world's population will die. The survivors will inherit a world of fire and ash, where you will be dead, and where we, who possess a monopoly on Psychanium and its technology will be the only ones who can offer refuge in growing food, energy production, and cleaning up from the eruptions. The world will bow before us. Seems like something your ancestors would do, right?" Fletcher said.

"My generation isn't like that," Isazisi said.

Around the city other Psychics landed, while an emergency alarm sounded.

"Everyone needs to seek shelter and get off the streets," Jake yelled, his wind powers carrying his voice throughout the city.

"It doesn't matter where they run, billions will die in the carnage and even more in the ensuing chaos."

"And what about you, how will you survive?"

"Texas was picked as it is far from any volcanic activity. Our resources here can sustain us for decades if needed. After the eruptions the device will project a shield around the city, allowing us to coordinate with our Circle bases in other countries. Of course, after we've killed all of you here, we'll use Providence's technology to repair the world in areas they have agreed to give up any form of resistance. They'll have no choice."

"We'll stop you."

"You can't." A gray suit with black lines built around Fletcher and formed a mask on his face looking like a Psychic suit.

"I see you copied us," Isazisi said.

"Now it's even."

"It's you versus all of us."

"Well, I have some friends on the way," Fletcher said.

Fletcher shot a gray blast of energy from his fingertips into Isazisi's chest, blasting him through the doors and out of the cathedral. Fletcher flew out and slammed into Isazisi, pummeling him into the asphalt. Outside a white Psychic suit with pink lines dropped out of the sky, flanked by dozens of Rhino and Gladiator suits. Another all-black Psychic suit dropped into the city. Their masks retracted revealing Fay and Mike, while Circle agents with jetpacks and tanks came as well. Other circle robots also flew into the Austin airspace.

"Protect the people first," Versia related to everyone. "We heard what the weapon can do, find a way to stop it."

Versia lasered down a group of Circle robots. Caitlyn knocked an arrow and shot it into a crowd of Circle agents, electrocuting them. Versia flew to the cathedral and had Meadow analyze the device. She highlighted eight holes in its side.

"It has an eight-key failsafe. If the keys are inserted and turned at the same time it will shut down the device," She said.

"Everyone hear that?" Versia asked.

"Yeah," Sanjiv said as he froze a group of Circle agents. A white Rhino suit smashed a hammer into Sanjiv's back, throwing him into a building. He turned around and looked at the suit's neck.

"Some of the Rhino and Gladiator suits have keys around their necks; those are the failsafe keys."

Sanjiv flew at the white Rhino suit, it swung its hammer at him, he dodged it, and slid on the ground shooting two lasers into the suit's back, it staggered and regained its balance. It swung its hammer at Sanjiv who blocked it with a nanotech shield. Shots from numerous Circle robots pelted him while the white Rhino suit took advantage and uppercutted Sanjiv with its hammer. He slammed into the asphalt and came to a stop. He stood and made a fist, freezing the robot solid. A sword formed in his hand and he flew at the white Rhino suit, he sliced at it and it blocked with its hammer. The white Rhino suit threw a punch at him, he dodged and punched it back. He flew at the staggering suit and placed two hands on its chest, freezing the suit. Sanjiv ripped the key off the suit's chest.

"I have the first key," Sanjiv said. He flew towards the cathedral to put it in.

Away from Sanjiv, Resse directed people into a building.

"Go, go, get off the streets." She yelled. An explosion rocked the ground behind her as a gladiator suit flanked by dozens of Circle agents and robots landed. They shot at Reese who shielded the people as they ran into the building.

She flew up, her feathers spreading, they barbecued the gladiator suit and the agents and robots flanking it. A ball and chain thrown by a Rhino suit behind her slammed her back down to earth. She stood as the sky above her darkened, and red lightning flashed across the sky, A red bolt of lightning crashed down, spreading like a spider, incinerating the Circle's troops.

"Caitlyn, you wanna bring a light show to Austin?" Reese asked.

"Why not," she replied.

Caitlyn flew into the air, and bolts of lighting formed around her. They raced forward like the fault line of an earthquake, tearing through everything in their path. She hit the ground and rolled. She grabbed arrow after arrow from her quiver at lightning speed and knocked it on her bow. Her arrows tore down the Circles troops like they weren't even there. Her suit AI identified a towering building in the city. Caitlyn flew to it and grabbed its spire. Dark clouds formed in the sky and a bolt of blue lightning crashed down on the buildings and spread, cutting through the Circle's troops.

Nearby Allen burned through the Gladiator suits and robots. He jumped and slammed back down, hitting the ground. Cracks formed in the earth and flames exploded from the ground, racing towards the circle. It cracked as if an earthquake had begun and Lava seeped up through the cracks. The Circles robots sank and drowned in the orange sea. Ava threw her Sphinxes left and right, they banked in the air flying back and cutting through the Circle assailants. She formed two more Sphinxes. They spun like buzzsaws and she threw them, sawing through the Circle's robots.

"Send in phase two." Fletcher barked into his comms before Isazisi punched him into the ground. He retaliated with lasers from his fingers.

Flames appeared in the sky as something crashed through the atmosphere. Robot satellites hit the city creating tidal waves of dirt as they came to a stop. The Psychics formed energy wall shields to minimize the damage. The robot's capsules opened up, near copies of Providence's Jaeger robots. They brought their fist down on the Psychics who avoided it. Blades came out of their wrists. One of the robots raked its blade across the ground, knocking away Psychic's and Circle troops alike while carving through buildings. The robot stepped forward, attempting to crush whatever it could in its path. Multiple robots throughout the city looked to the sky.

"Horizon Level Threat detected." They said in unison.

A beam of red light shot down from the sky. Out of the beam shot a red sword, it smashed through two of the robots, decimating them. A solar flare shot out from the beam, it sliced straight through another of the copycat robots causing it to fall over with a loud crashing sound. The light dissipated leaving behind a deep engraving in the street. Inside stood Project Red.

"It's over now," Allen called out.

Some of the Circle agents and suits staggered slightly.

"Your desecration will not go unpunished," Issac said as he ran at them, he floated and smashed his sword down in the street, tearing through a group of Circle agents with red energy.

Lily ran forward, she pulled from a nearby lake, forming a ring of water around her. Using them as tentacles she shoved the Circle out of the way and rode the water like a wave to one of the copycat bots. The water shot up like daggers, impaling the Circles robots in multiple places. A Rhino suit sliced at her and she ducked under the blade. A katar formed on her wrist, she sliced through the neck of the Rhino suit, and it sparked and fell over. Another Rhino suit swung at Lily. A column of water rose, shielding her from the strike. The water column shot forward, impaling the suit. Lily turned around where Yemani tore through the Circle and their troops. She flew over towards Lily, knocking another suit back. They both took cover. One of the Rhino suits swung at Yemani. She blocked the strike with a shield on her arm. The suit kicked her back into a nearby rock. She stood as it brought the ax down on her again. It kicked her farther into the ground. She rolled out of the way as it brought the ax down on the place she'd been lying. Inside her suit, her eyes glowed a blue color. She boosted toward the Rhino suit and formed a water sword around her hand. She sliced at the suit, cleaving it in half. The suit dropped to its knees before the top half slid off the bottom. She flew in the direction of more of the Circle's agents and cleaved through them as she fought her way toward their main leader.

Jasmine and Sanjiv took cover as the Circle rained fire on them.

"So are we ever going to talk about it?" He asked her.

"Really? Now? When people are shooting at us?" She replied. Sanjiv stood and made a fist, the suits shooting at them froze solid.

"So how about now?"

"Didn't we already schedule dinner?"

She lipped her gun over their cover. She rained fire, each shot a direct hit. She sat back down as they returned fire.

"Yeah, we'll talk then."

She hopped over their cover and rolled to her feet. Time slowed around Jasmine as bullets and artillery from the Circle whizzed by her. She found her targets and pulled the trigger six times, hitting six targets in the head. She slid under the hammer swing of a Circle suit and shot upwards shooting it through the neck. She dodged the stomp of another and stabbed the suit in the side of the head with a tanto blade. She ripped the blade out and threw it at another Gladiator suit. Jasmine watched a group of civilians run for cover as jetpack Circle agents flew towards them. Jasmine turned into a wisp of shadows, she impaled the

Circle agent from behind. She reformed into her human body and directed the people into a nearby concrete building. A beam of pink energy lasered Jasmine into the ground. Fay landed as Jasmine stood.

"How do you like the suit, beautiful isn't it?"

Jasmine looked up and down the suit, a sneer on her face. "That is not yours to steal," she yelled.

Fay staggered as Jasmine flew at her and punched her into a building. Shattered glass and metal rained onto the street below as Fay bounced through a building. Jasmine flew at her on the other side, her suit's targeting system locked onto Fay. Missiles and rockets rose from the suit's wrists, shoulders, and back and fired at Fay enveloping her in a sea of flames.

"You should've stayed in your cell," Jasmine said.

Wisps of black smoke extended from Jasmine's body and swarmed Fay, she dropped to her knees, clutching her neck, her helmet retracted as she gasped for air. Jasmine walked up to her as she struggled to raise her hand. It glowed pink and shot a laser at Jasmine blasting her back. Fay coughed as she regained her composure. Jasmine stood as her suit did a diagnostic.

"You are not worthy of this power," Fay yelled. "You are a murderer who masquerades as a hero,"

"I didn't know that would happen to you, that was never our intent," Jasmine said.

"I don't care," Fay said.

A sword formed in Jasmine's hand, Faye pulled out a white handle, she flicked it, extending a pink energy whip with white metal cylinders every few inches. Fay cracked the whip at Jasmine who dodged it, she sliced at Fay, and it grazed her armor. Fay cracked the whip again, it wrapped itself around Jasmine's sword, she pulled Faye towards her and punched her in the face mask. Fay stood, but Jasmine blasted her into the ground with a shockwave from the wrist of her suit.

"Stay down," Jasmine said.

Faye pulled herself up on some nearby rubble and her helmet retraced, revealing cuts on her face.

"No more warnings," Jasmine said.

Fay obliged, resting against the concrete stones.

Mia threw her blades and cleaved through the Circle's troops. They came back to her hands. She threw another blade, it cut through a Circle robot and banked in the sky, flying back towards her. She threw the other blade at it. They collided, and the blades shot in opposite directions, cutting down more Circle troops.

Isazisi fought his way through a horde of circle robots, they hopped on him, while Fletcher flew away. The robots clawed at Isazisi's armor like wild dogs, trapping under them. The light faded as they continued clawing at his face mask, leaving him unable to see. Seconds later they exploded off of him. Through the smoke, his eyes glowed a deep red as his cape fluttered in the wind. Lasers pierced through the smoke. Cutting down the Circles troops as a steady beam raked the battlefield. He flew and lasers shot from his eyes. The field burned as he cut through the Circle. His katana formed in his hand and he cut through the Circle's troops like a hurricane through a city. Isazisi flew up as red lighting formed on and around him. He stabbed his sword into the ground creating a shockwave of lightning, tearing through the Circle's troops and robots.

A black laser came from the sky, carving the land in front of Versia. He looked up at Mike in his all-black Psychic suit. He dropped from the sky landing with a metallic *thud*. Mike pulled out a Psychanium sword on his back. Hexagons formed in Versia's hand creating a silver katana with cyan lines in it. Mike rushed at Versia who blocked the strike. Mike fired a series of wrist and arm-mounted missiles at Versia, they exploded enveloping him in flames. Versia pulled the flames in and blasted Mike into a building. Versia chased him, punching him into the ground. Mike flew up, and Versia chased him into the stratosphere where they exchanged and dodged laser blasts. Versia flew above him and shot a dual laser into the chest of his suit, the suit fell and Versia flew at him, pummeling the suit into the streets of Austin.

Mike groaned as he didn't even try to get up. Meadow

identified Fletcher in the area.

Versia body-slammed Fletcher in the sky, slamming him into a nearby building.

"You disrespect our culture with that caricature," Versia said.

"You like the suit? I made sure they did it exactly like your ancestors, everything we're doing is exactly like your ancestors. Killing everything we see." Fletcher said.

"That isn't us," Versia said.

"It doesn't matter, you're killers, no better than us."

A dual-sided blade formed from Versia's hand, he sliced at Fletcher who dodged it and shot a palm laser at Versia, knocking him out of the sky. Versia shot up and they flew around shooting at each other as the fighting took place on the ground below.

Jake blasted a gust of wind at a Circle robot, cutting it down, he dodged the laser fire of another and retaliated with a wrist-fired missile. Jake's entire left side shuddered as a gray sword swung at his head, he leaned backward dodging the sword as it ground against the top of his face plate. He rolled forward and out of the reach of the gray and black gladiator suit in front of him. He caught a glimpse of a gray key around the suit's neck. The gladiator suit peered behind Jake to a group of people running for cover. It pointed its wrist upward and fired a missile at a building causing a large chunk to dislodge and fall towards the people. Jake flew at the piece and caught it with his psychic powers.

"Go, go, go," Jake yelled as he held the chunk up. The gladiator suit threw its sword at Jake causing him to fly forward and lose his connection to the debris. It fell and Jake blasted it to bits with a palm laser as he slammed into another building.

"That is your weakness, you're here to protect the people, not stop us." The gladiator suit said.

"We're trying to multitask," Jake said.

A katar blade formed from Jake's wrist and he flew at the gladiator suit, slamming it into the ground. The gladiator tossed

Jake off itself and threw its sword at him, he dodged with the swiftness of the wind and slid behind the gladiator. He caused a burst of wind to shoot the gladiator upwards and slam it down onto a mountain of debris, impaling the suit. Its eyes flickered and turned off. He ripped the key from its neck and flew to the cathedral. He placed it in its designated location.

"Second key in place," he relayed.

Vashti's daggers cut through the Circle's troops, she used her webs to blind them as she jumped to each and cut through their vital parts. She rushed one, slicing the robot's head clean off. She flew up. Her hand turned into a dual-sided blade. She jumped onto one of the copycat bots. She raked the sword down the robot, and explosions followed as she carved through the metal.

Isazisi cut down a group of Circle agents.

"Megan, send the Lifejets, we'll need to start evacuating people in case we can't stop the device, what's its power at?"

"47% sir, you'll need to stop it soon, once it gets to 75% it'll be ready to activate. It's still billions dead at that power level. There will be no minimum safe distance."

A mace took him out of the sky. A gladiator suit on the ground approached him but a bolt of red lightning shot from the sky, burning it to a crisp.

"We need to move faster," Isazisi said. "Once the device is armed there's no safe place."

"Everyone hear that? Find the other six keys." Reese relayed.

Caitlyn made her way over cars and pieces of fallen buildings as she tracked down trapped civilians. She lifted a large chunk of a fallen building freeing dozens of people. Nearby a Providence Lifejet landed. A black, boxy, four-thruster-powered jet with strap-in seats. People made their way to them as they landed and they flew towards landing pads away from the city and defended by Providence Centurions.

Caitlyn looked at a black Rhino suit with a dark blue key around its neck. She knocked an arrow and shot it at the suit, it hit and exploded into blue lightning bolts, and the Rhino staggered. Caitlyn knocked another arrow and shot it, it buried itself in the suit and shot another electric shock through it. Caitlyn knocked two arrows and shot them, they banked in the air and buried themselves in the back of the Rhino. She folded her bow into a staff and raked the Rhino across the face. It swung at her with its battle ax, she dodged it and placed an electric bomb on its thigh. The bomb exploded bringing the suit down to one knee. It swung its ax and caught her in the face, throwing her to the ground. The Rhino stood and slammed its ax into her chest, inside her suit the structural integrity counter dropped from 100 to 92, and the Rhino slammed the ax again, dropping it from 92 to 84.

"Caitlyn, wake up," Meadow said.

"Caitlyn, Caitlyn," Meadow yelled. "Sorry, but this is going to hurt."

Meadow shocked Caitlyn in the suit, she woke up and rolled out of the way of the ax, she unfolded her bow and knocked an arrow. She shot it straight through the side of the Rhino suit's head. The suit dropped to both knees and the floor face first, she rolled the suit over and took the key. She flew to the device and inserted the key.

"Third key in position," She said.

In the city, Mai's fans cut through the circle, as her wind sent them flying into each other. Jake sliced through them with his sword.   Resse looked over at a gladiator suit with a blood-red key around its neck. She shot a blast from one of her palm lasers at it, and the suit staggered. She flew it, her hand turning into a rocket-powered mallet and punched it across the face. The gladiator suit swung its sword at her, but she blocked it with a circular nanotech shield. She shot a burst of lightning at the suit, it used the sword as a lightning rod and slammed the ground shooting the red lightning bolts at Reese, she dodged them and the gladiator threw the sword at her, knocking her out of the sky. Her suit's peacock feathers spread from her back, she raised both her hands and charged a laser blast and along with the feathers shot a hole through the gladiator suit. She took the key from its neck and placed it in the device.

"Fourth key in place," Reese said.

Versia blasted Fletcher into the ground, a nanotech sword formed from his hand and he stabbed it into the ground where Fletcher rolled out of the way a second before.

"I thought you were the Psychic who didn't kill," Fletcher said.

"I'll make exceptions where necessary," Versia said.

Isazisi tore through a Rhino suit and ripped the key off its neck. Vashti did the same to another and so did Jasmine.

"Key's in place," they relayed.

"Where's the last key?" Versia asked.

"You'll have to take it off my cold dead body," Fletcher said.

Caitlyn blasted him into the ground with a bolt of lightning.

Jake leaped through the carnage of the battlefield, cutting down whatever Circle troops she saw. He watched Fletcher standing up from Caitlyn's lightning and a gray javelin formed in his hand. He threw it at Fletcher at full speed. The helmet of his full Psychanium suit took the force of the impact seconds before it would've gone through his head. He stood from the near-miss javelin strike, his head ringing from the impact. He turned his head from side to side, watching his troops be cut down. He charged his palm laser and shot them at Versia who countered with his own. Isazisi flew above Versia and shot his lasers, combining them with Versia's, Reese joined in with a surge of red lightning, and Caitlyn supplemented it with her lightning. The other Psychics joined in overpowering Fletcher, his suit melted as the combined blasts of the Psychics shot through his. The Psychics let up. Fletcher dropped to his knees and fell backward. Versia flew over to him and placed his hand on the partially melted chest of Fletcher's Psychic suit, he hacked the suit and the nanites parted. Versia took the cyan-colored key from his chest, he and the other seven Psychics ran to the machine, and Versia inserted his key.

"You'll have to turn them at the same time," Meadow said.

"Same time everybody," Versia said.

The eight Psychics turned their keys at the same time and nothing happened.

"What the...?" Versia began.

"Energy signature is still rising, I don't know what happened," Meadow said.

Versia ran to Fletcher.

"How do we shut it down?"

"Like I would tell you," Fletcher said. "If the failsafe didn't work there's nothing to be done. This world will crack under the weight of your actions."

"Do you want to die with your machine?" Versia yelled.

"It's Psychic energy, seems to be more your forte than mine, figure it out," Fletcher said.

Versia ran to the group.

"I have an idea," he said. "But it's dangerous."

"What is it?" Sanjiv asked.

"The device is oscillating Psychic energy between the top of the device and where it reaches in the earth to charge itself, as it bounces around the Psychanium tube it gains energy. If we can generate enough energy by striking the top of the device at the right time when the energy wave is on its way up, we could cause the tube to break and stop the oscillation." Versia said.

"That kind of energy wave striking the top of the device could kill us and would level the city, there's still millions of people stranded," Caitlyn said.

"Meadow ran the calculations, only Isazisi and I would need to generate the energy meaning the others could form a shield around the others,"

"That kind of energy bouncing off the shield would kill both of you," Caitlyn said.

"It's my idea, Isazisi, are you down?"

"It was my weapons, I'm with you to the end."

Reese walked up to him. "This could kill you,"

"If the device goes off it kills billions, us too, I have to do this," Isazisi said.

Reese sighed. "Come back to me, I don't care if you have to pull yourself up from the depths of wherever, come back to me."

"I will."

Vashti walked up to Versia. "I won't try to talk you out of it, just don't leave me alone, you always come back, I need you to do it at least one more time."

"We got this," Versia said.

Versia and Isazisi stood on opposite sides of the device while the other Psychics stood in a circle outside the damaged cathedral. Caitlyn rose into the air, her eyes glowed midnight blue, and metallic-looking midnight blue lines formed and extended in front of her body. Jake's body rose, his eyes glowed gray, and metallic-looking lines formed and extended in front of his body, the other Psychics did the same and their eyes glowed in their respective colors while metallic-looking lines formed and extended in front of their bodies and connected with the other Psychics lines. A dome energy shield formed around the cathedral.

"See you on the other side," Versia said, they both had their helmets off.

"Likewise," Isazisi said. "Megan, what's the timeline?"

"The wave is on its way up, thirty seconds till it reaches the middle," she said.

"Thirty seconds," Isazisi said.

Isazisi's suit fist glowed red, and Versia's fist glowed cyan.

"Have you ever held this much energy?" Versia asked.

"No, let's smash this thing."

Both their helmets formed.

"Now," Megan and Meadow yelled.

They both smashed their fists into the top of the device sending a ripple of Psychic energy down the device, the two waves met and sent a shockwave up the shaft, it exploded in a horizontal shockwave, leveling the cathedral and creating a blinding light. The other Psychics closed their eyes before the light subsided.

Versia and Isazisi lay on opposite sides of the blackened device, their suits half-black. Reese and Vashti ran to them. Vashti pressed on Versia's neck, opening up his face plate, he lay unconscious with his nose bleeding. Reese opened up Isazisi's faceplate, she touched the top of his forehead, jolting him awake. He sat up breathing heavily. Versia sat up as well.

"Did we do it?" Isazisi asked.

"No energy signature detected," Megan said.

Fletcher stood up. "We'll still find another way," he said.

Jake blasted him with a gust of wind, he remained on the floor motionless.

"I guess that's that," Jake said.

"Guess it is," Versia said. "We won."

The Psychics remained there, taking it in.

CHAPTER 26

Versia and Isazisi walked by the original meteor. Isazisi ran his hand across the meteor.

"Preliminary reports suggest up to a thousand people may have been killed in Austin," Isazisi said.

"That's unfortunate, we'll do everything for their families," Versia said.

"Insurance estimates put the damage caused in the tens of billions, we'll cover it," Isazisi said.

He bent over and touched a crystalline flower near it. The meteor's properties had caused it to affect the environment. Plants around it became more resilient to disease and pests.

"Maybe tradition does need to change, maybe we got too cocky," Isazisi said.

"The legacy of each Psychic is complicated," Versia said. "We can only navigate these waters together."

"I made a two hundred million dollar donation to children's hospitals around the country." Isazisi continued.

"Is that out of generosity or guilt?" Versia asked.

"I heard they say there's a correlation, but I don't know, it felt right," Isazisi said.

"Seventy-five million to the New York Victims Fund," Versia said. "That's my guilt and generosity. Pain, fear, flaws, they think we don't have them, that we're perfect one-dimensional people." Versia said.

"All we do is hide our feeling better, how many of us are messed up right now?" Isazisi asked.

"Too many," Versia said. Isazisi nodded.

"You've seen the vision too?" Versia asked.

"Yes," Isazisi said. "He's coming. The meteor is nearing the star. He'll break free."

"So what are we going to do?" Versia asked.

"Fight, like we always have, but I think the world would be

better in our hands," Isazisi said.

"We're not conquerors. We were given this power to protect," Versia said.

"But you see what's happening. The entire planet is crumbling around us." Isazisi said.

"Then use your influence to make change without violence," Versia said.

"It won't work. They've made up their minds. They're more loyal to their short political terms than the future of seven billion people." Isazisi said as he looked up. A meteor shower had begun.

"It's begun," Isazisi said.

"Well, I guess this means he's coming," VerIsazisi said.

They both looked upwards, the shower of white meteors had already begun.

CHAPTER 27

Dozens of reporters whispered to each other, awaiting the announcement about to be given, cameras flashed every second at the row of ten Psychics sitting in front of them, dressed to the nines. Dozens of world leaders including the Secretary of State sat on stage as well. Versia stood and walked to the microphone. He leaned in

"It's been a painful time for thousands of families across the world. Thousands of people were killed by the weapons we said would protect you, it is, and always will be our fault." He said. Sniffles could be heard among the crowd. "Today though, I have good news. I can confirm. We have defeated the Circle." He said.

Every reporter's hand shot up as everyone clamored to ask a question.

CHAPTER 28

The priest spoke to the large crowd clad in black. People cried and dabbed their faces with white cloths as they held back tears. The priest continued, telling stories of the woman's life, what a great child she was, and what an amazing woman she would have become. The priest spoke of a better place, of a higher calling, everything to console a grieving family. Off to the side in an all-black tuxedo, surrounded by his security dressed in black and white tuxes stood Isazisi. The sun shone, beating down on the funeral goers dressed in black while birds chirped in the distance.

The priest ended his speech and allowed the audience to toss flowers onto the coffin. They had no idea who offered to pay for the funeral but accepted anyway. First, her family members went, next her friends, and soon everyone had thrown a white rose onto the white and gold coffin. Isazisi walked forward and to the proceeding. He walked up to the grave flanked by his security to the surprise of most of the audience. He wasn't sure if they recognized him as he had on black sunglasses. Some stared at him with squinted eyes while others whispered to those beside them. He said something in an ancient Psychic language and tossed a single black rose onto the coffin.

"I'm sorry." He whispered. He turned and left.

He stepped into the backseat of a red SUV. Reese sat in it as well.

"It's not your fault, you know." She said.

"Of course, it's not. It's a bullet I made that passed two millimeters by my face, and I'm supposedly one of the fastest beings in the universe." Isazisi said.

"Her death is on whoever pulled the trigger, you cannot..."

"Don't worry," Isazisi said, interrupting her. "I'm already well acquainted with loss."

Reese said nothing as the fleet of SUVs drove away.

****

Dozens of bodies laid strew in the hallways, covered in blood. Blood coated the walls as well from where Isazisi had slammed their heads. The ones clinging to life by a thread groaned in pain at even the slightest shift as they succumbed to their wounds. Isazisi hit one man over the head with a fire extinguisher, killing him. He swung it around, hitting another man's face, slamming his head against the wall as he recoiled from the hit, leaving yet another bloodstain on the walls. He dodged a punch thrown by another man and hit him in the face with the bottom of the extinguisher, killing him too. He dropped the extinguisher as a tanto blade formed in his hand. He blocked a punch from one man and stabbed him in the side of the neck, he ripped the blade out as he dodged another punch. He kicked the man backward as another threw a kick. He blocked the strike and stabbed the man half a dozen times. The one he had kicked came for him again. He dodged the strike and bashed the man's head against the wall. Isazisi dodged another punch and stabbed the man. He dodged another strike and buried the knife in yet another assailant. The last one came on him. Isazisi dodged the punches and slammed the man's head into the wall, he kicked him as he bounced off it. The man rolled around in pain, gathering himself before he stood again. Isazisi took the fire extinguisher again and beat the man until he remained motionless. He stood and looked around at the seas of bodies left in his wake. He looked at himself in his knife, covered in even more blood than before. He walked over to a solid steel vault door. He grabbed it by the handle and ripped the five-thousand-pound door off its hinges. One man cowered inside, every single guard had been sent out to try and stop The Red Cyan. He grabbed the man and dragged him out of the building.

The man awoke in an all-glass box where a faint blue and white ambient lighting cast around the room. The man looked forward. Isazisi stood there, flanked by two Praetorians and two

Centurions. He stepped up to the glass. The man stood and came forward as well.

"Hansen was a dead end, Fletcher was a dead end, Jessica was a dead end, Fay was a dead end, and the rest of the Circle's leadership were glorified puppets, including you," Isazisi said.

"So, I guess that makes everything, not my fault." The man said.

Isazisi ignored him. "I'm gonna need you to tell me where your real boss is. Where is Keynote? Where is Mr. Williams?" Isazisi asked.

****

Jake and Caitlyn's horses raced across the dusty green and brown countryside.

"Where are we going," Caitlyn yelled.

"Just wait, you'll see," he responded.

The horses continued for a few miles before stopping overlooking a flat plateau of land.

"You brought me out here to see dirt," She asked as Jake helped her off the horse.

"Well not quite," he said as he led her towards the edge.

"Me and edges don't have a great history," she said.

"I promise I'll never let you go."

He swiped his hand over the landscape, clearing away a layer of dust and revealing thousands of blue roses with bolts of lightning flowing up and down them.

"How-how did you plant these here?"

"Well after you showed me the picture of the cave back home, I made a few phone calls, and planted them here."

"Thank you," she said as she brushed a strand of her jet-black hair out of her face.

She reached over and wrapped Jake in a hug as the duo looked out over the thousands of flowers.

****

Kai and Mai stepped off the plane and into two waiting SUVs on the tarmac. The car drove each of them into a different suburb and stopped in front of two modest houses. Each of the twins stepped out and looked over the house, they walked to the front door, and Mai rang the doorbell, and Kai miles away did the same. A middle-aged Asian woman opened the door to Mai and an Asian man to Kai.

"Hi, but we're not interested in purchasing anything," Mai's house said.

"Oh, I'm not selling anything. I've imagined this moment in my head a thousand times, but I don't know how to put it. I'm your daughter." Mai said.

The woman stared at her with a blank expression plastered on her face.

"Hey man," Kai's door said. "Are you doing a fundraiser for the football team or something? You know I love to support school spirit, let me go grab my wallet."

"Uh, no, it's just, it's, I'm your son," Kai said.

The man stared at his face, and his eyes expanded with surprise.

****

Ava levitated above the floor, her legs crossed, meditating. Around her floated wisps of purple energy and books written in an ancient Psychic language.

"He will come, bearing power unmatched, seeking crystals of power, and revenge on his kind for imprisoning him. Blinded by his own goals, he will destroy everything, unless pierced by a shard, which shall render his reign to its end. He is the fallen prince of the Psychics." A voice said.

Her eyes jolted open as she fell with her books.

"He's coming," she said.

****

Isazisi stood in the wind, quiet and solemn. High in the mountains, a gray overcast sky, and tall yellow grass with a single orange-leaved tree to top it off. The trunk of the tree has words carved into it in an old Psychic language. Isazisi stared at the base of the tree, his lips contorted into a frown as he played with his fingers. Versia walked up behind him.

"We won," Versia said.

"That doesn't bring back what they took," Isazisi said.

"Did you find him?" Versia asked.

"We have some solid leads," Isazisi replied.

"We're family. If you need anything, we're here." Versia said.

Isazisi nodded. He placed down three red flowers at the site of the graves.

"Do the nightmares ever end?" Isazisi asked.

"No, but we learn to live with them," Versia said.

Versia placed his arm around his friend and led him down the mountain. The time for reminiscence would have to be later.

CHAPTER 29

The meteor floated untethered in space, unconfined by the constraints of gravity, it passed by a large white star as it fell towards it. The person inside awoke and took his first breath in millennia. He flexed his fingers as he relearned how to use his body. He took a deep breath and envisioned the crystals. He was back.

THE END

About The Author

Osawese Agbonkonkon is a writer from Frisco, Texas. A Track and Field athlete at the University of Oregon, and a huge fan of the Golden State Warriors. He is majoring in Economics while also on the Pre-Law track. He hopes to attend law school after his undergraduate education. When not writing he spends his time training for the Olympics, watching movies, and daydreaming for new ideas. Some of his favorite restaurants include Wingstop and Golden Corral, much to the dismay of one of his four sisters. Psychic Suit is the first in what he hopes to one day make a universe of superheroes. Join him on this journey as he builds a world to be explored.

Made in the USA
Middletown, DE
24 October 2024

63200619R00166